A LONELY
PLACE TO DIE

A LONELY
PLACE TO DIE

A Hellfire Pass Western

William W.
Johnstone

AND J.A. JOHNSTONE

PINNACLE BOOKS
Kensington Publishing Corp.

www.kensingtonbooks.com

PINNACLE BOOKS are published by

Kensington Publishing Corp.
900 Third Avenue
New York, NY 10022

All Kensington titles, imprints, and distributed lines are available at special quantity discounts for bulk purchases for sales promotion, premiums, and educational or institutional use.

Special book excerpts or customized printings can also be created to fit specific needs. For details, write or phone the office of the Kensington Sales Manager: Kensington Publishing Corp., 900 Third Avenue, New York, NY 10022. Attn. Sales Department. Phone: 1-800-221-2647.

PINNACLE BOOKS, the Pinnacle logo, and the WWJ steer head logo Reg. U.S. Pat. & TM Off.

First Printing: October 2024
ISBN-13: 978-0-7860-5056-7

10 9 8 7 6 5 4 3 2 1

Printed in the United States of America

CHAPTER ONE

It was too late in the day for gunshots. Marshal Shadrach Nelson wanted nothing more than to wearily make his way home to a good supper fixed by his wife, Ruth. He considered ignoring the shots, then knew where his duty lay. The good people of Utopia, Colorado, didn't pay him to turn his back on such things.

He cut down the crazy main street. Most towns had straight-as-an-arrow streets, at least the ones traveled most. Whoever had laid out this town had followed a drunk cow. Two sharp bends in the street took him toward the Gold Dust City Saloon. It was one of thirteen—or was it fourteen now?—gin mills in town and usually one of the more sedate watering holes. Ralph Rockwell and his lady friend, faro dealer Missy, liked to keep it quiet.

"A saloon fit for a family," Missy often joked. If the family was a bunch of crazy lead miners from the northern side of Hellfire Pass or soot-covered coal miners from the southern wall of the canyon, that was.

To his surprise, the ruckus didn't come from inside the saloon. He walked faster when two more shots rang out farther down the street. The final one was followed by a pitiful whimpering that died slowly. He'd rather have heard angry shouts and venomous curses. That meant someone had to be alive. But when a sound like that died . . .

. . . somebody died.

He slid the leather thong off the hammer of the .44 Peacemaker resting on his right hip, slung low and tied down if he needed to make a fast draw. He looked like a gunfighter for a reason. It kept trouble at bay and few dared challenge him. He towered above most cowboys at a cloud-scraping six-foot-two. In spite of the way his wife fed him, he was whipcord thin and moved like a coiled snake ready to strike. The small paunch starting to hang over his gun belt was the only sign age touched him. He looked like death-come-a'walking and used that to cow the less-determined troublemakers.

The cutthroats without a trace of conscience got a taste of how fast and accurate he was with the Peacemaker.

He sucked in his breath when he heard an argument rising. That meant the two wrangling over God knew what were still alive. As much as he wanted to break into a run, he kept his pace steady. Running headlong into trouble was a sure way to get killed. Worse, there were still outlaws lurking around Utopia who'd ambush him just for fun. Rounding another dogleg in the street brought him to the edge of town. Two men faced each other. One held a still-smoking pistol.

"Clint Larson, you put that hogleg back into your

holster or there'll be hell to pay." Shad rested his hand on the hickory wood handle of his own pistol.

"He killed my dog! Marshal Nelson, he killed my dog!" The unarmed man clenched his hands into fists. Charlie was ready to lash out.

"That miserable fleabag's been killin' my chickens. He tore up my rooster! He's still got feathers all over his muzzle!" Clint Larson lifted his pistol when Charlie advanced on him, fists raised.

"Back off, both of you." Shad stepped between them. His presence caused them to halt. Shad was taller than either of the scrawny old men. His long dirty blond hair swirled around his shoulders as he spun from one man to the other. His eyes were colder than emeralds. He shoved Charlie back with his right hand and grabbed a handful of Larson's filthy denim overall. A quick tug downward caused the man to bend forward. Shad snatched the six-gun from his hand and tucked it into his gun belt for safekeeping.

"He never done such a thing. Spinner wasn't like that at all, a chicken killin' monster? He'd never!"

"Mongrel," Larson growled. "Like its owner!"

The two went for each other again. Shad shoved back. Both men staggered away.

"I can't believe you two brought this argument into town." Shad heaved a sigh. This wasn't the first time he'd separated the two neighbors. They had small plots of land high up on the south wall of Hellfire Pass, down on the Denver side just beyond where the Gallagher family claimed their coal mines.

"I want him arrested." Charlie took a deep breath and

yelled, "I want him strung up by his skinny neck. He killed my dog. Old Spinner was mindin' his own business and—"

"I'm throwing you both in jail until you cool off."

Charlie looked furious at the idea of spending even one minute in a cell. Clint Larson turned belligerent.

"Doin' to us won't keep that black train from comin', Marshal. Then you'll be real sorry."

Shad had no idea what he was talking about and didn't care. He herded both men to the jailhouse. Leroy Early looked up from where he sat behind the marshal's desk.

"Not them again?" the deputy asked.

"Different cells," Shad ordered.

"How about I put one in the first cell and the other in the back? That'll give 'em an entire cell to act as no-man's-land." He kicked open the door leading into the back room with the cells, then pushed the two combatants in.

Shad dropped Clint Larson's gun on the desk and waited for Early to return.

"You might as well let them kill each other, Shad. They're fightin' worse than the Gallaghers and Morriseys."

"Nothing's worse than them and their blood feud." Shad shook his head sadly. "I've given up asking what started that feud. At least I know what's behind Clint and Charlie's hatred of each other."

Early coughed and tried not to smile too much.

"Both of them bein' rejected by Lady Sarah ought to have made them blood brothers, not mortal enemies."

"Leroy, you know how she is. A madam's not supposed

to send her customers away hating each other and the world."

"That's how Sarah gets her jollies. More 'n one man's gotten into a fight to defend her honor."

"Honor? Her? That'd be the world's shortest fight." Shad laughed ruefully. "She'd steal pennies off a dead man's eyes."

"And ask for change," his deputy added. "You about ready to turn over the keys to me for the night? Ian's already gone home, such as it is."

Shad's other deputy, Ian Shannon, shared the day shift with him. Leroy Early kept the town honest overnight. Shad took a good look at his deputy. Early was ten years younger than his forty-four and had yet to show the strain of the job. Ruth had mentioned more than once how she'd found stray gray hairs among Shad's blond on the pillow in the morning. He had accused Ruth of finding her own hairs, but her dark hair was still untouched by the winter's snow of aging.

It was hard to admit, but he wasn't getting any younger.

He even had a grandchild on the way. Letting Early take over duty as marshal and finding a job not as demanding kept nudging Shad's thinking these days. Ruth had left him. So had Miriam, but they'd come back when he'd made peace with Miriam's new husband, Richard Williamson. After he'd lost his own son, Shad had let his wild nature run free until he was unbearable. The idea that Williamson would ever replace his natural son was out of the question.

But a grandchild?

Being a marshal put him in danger all the time. Clint

Larson hadn't meant to kill anyone with that six-gun. Shad wasn't even sure that the man had shot Charlie's dog. Clint would starve to death if he didn't raise chickens. He thought it was the man's eyesight that was bad, which made his aim stray from dead center. Without proof, Shad thought Larson could have shot his own rooster by accident. But waving a gun around the way he did, even Clint Larson could have plugged Shad by accident.

Dead was dead, whether from an intended bullet or an unlucky shot.

He stopped in the doorway and looked back. Early had closed the door into the cellblock to cut down on noise from the two yammering insults at one another. The deputy looked up from his week-old copy of the *Rocky Mountain News*.

"You hear anything about a black train?" Shad asked.

Early shook his head. "Is it something in the paper?"

"Clint mentioned it. I just wondered."

"Maybe it has something to do with the Gallaghers supplying coal to the railroad. Black train. Coal. They load up a freight train every week to supply the Denver yards in addition to the two daily trains."

"I've never heard of either of the daily trains being called that, either," Shad allowed. At noon a train from Denver came through. At midnight one from Central City and Georgetown arrived. If it wasn't for those cars carrying prospectors and freight back and forth, Utopia wouldn't exist.

"Do you think I ought to wire the railroad office in Denver?" Shad asked. "They might be planning a special with gold or something more valuable than their ordinary freight."

"Sussman would charge you for the telegram. He's like that." Early snapped the newspaper and turned his attention back to the latest goings-on along the Front Range.

Shad walked slowly uphill to his house looking out over the pass. Utopia curled around in the canyon, so he only had a good view of part. The railroad depot was out of sight, as he had been told repeatedly by his daughter as she sat on the porch and looked for a hint that her husband was coming through town from Denver and could visit.

"You've got the nose of a bloodhound," Ruth said as he came in. With practiced ease, he looped his gun belt over a hook and put his bowler on a peg beside it. Only when the iron was no longer weighing him down did he feel that he was home.

"Smells good. You haven't cooked up stew in a couple weeks."

"It takes too long to cook. Besides, I haven't been able to get carrots." Ruth bustled about telling him how she had to dicker with a neighbor to get the vegetables.

Shad settled in his chair, half listening. He had no interest in such domestic things, but having his wife back after she left him a few months back was a relief.

"Where's Miriam?" he asked.

Ruth pushed her dark hair back and wiped sweat from her forehead with the edge of her apron. It was getting on to spring but heat from the stove filled the room. Shad opened the door. That let in flies, but the early evening breeze made up for swatting the buzzing pests. He'd see to getting a sheet or two of flypaper from Sampson at the general store. After all, it was the time of year when the annoying insects swarmed after hibernating for the entire winter.

"She'll be here soon enough. She went to the store to see if Rich sent a new letter."

"It's got to be galling, separated like that but only a few hours apart on the train."

"It is, Pa, it is." A pregnant Miriam came in. He saw that she had a letter tucked under some herbs she'd gathered.

She kissed him, then went to help her mother. Shad looked hard at the letter, trying to see enough of the envelope to decide if she had opened it or kept it pristine to savor for later.

"What do you hear from Denver?" he finally asked when it became obvious his daughter wasn't going to share.

"Nothing much. Rich is hunting down a gang holding up trains. The home office has offered a nice reward to anyone catching them."

"To anyone stopping them, more likely," Shad said. He knew how those rewards were doled out. Dead or alive meant dead.

"Get the biscuits, dear, will you?" Ruth asked her daughter. "Then you sit yourself down. I'll finish."

"I'm not an invalid, Ma." But Miriam settled down beside her father and fussed with rearranging the plates and spoons.

"Has your husband mentioned anything about the

black train?" Shad helped himself to the stew, then fielded a hot biscuit. His mouth watered at the aroma. All he'd eaten since breakfast was a pigs knuckle at one of the saloons. It had been such a dreary day he didn't even remember which one.

"You can call him by his name. Richard. Rich. Or Mister Williamson, if you want to be formal."

"He's not that formal."

"Neither are you, Shad. You're both saddle bums, but we're the women who love you in spite of that." Ruth settled down after giving them each a glass of water. She presided over the amounts on her husband's and daughter's plates, then tended to her own.

"Well? Has he mentioned hearing anything like that?" He watched her closely.

"Rich hasn't written about any black train. Does that have something to do with coal?"

He shook his head. If a railroad detective hadn't mentioned it to his wife, it wasn't anything for a small-town marshal to worry himself over.

At least, Shadrach Nelson hoped that were true.

CHAPTER TWO

"You're up at the crack of dawn, Shad. Any reason?" Leroy Early dropped his feet to the floor from the desk and scooted forward, ready to leave the desk chair and go home to sleep in a real bed.

"Too much thinking," he admitted.

"That'll keep a man up all night," Early said. "There're better ways to be kept up."

"Go fetch Charlie and bring him out here."

"Not Clint?"

"In a minute. Charlie first." Shad dropped into the chair his deputy vacated. He chewed on his lower lip as he thought. Definitely too much thinking going on.

"You fixin' on lettin' me go, Marshal?"

"I am, Charlie. Tell me straight. Did Spinner go after Clint's chickens?" He saw a play of emotions that finally ended with the man fessing up.

"He might have. Old Spinner's been gettin' out, roamin' about the hills, more and more lately. He ain't never done such a thing before, but I wasn't there to see."

"Fair enough. It's a hurtful thing to lose your dog."

He waited for Charlie to agree, then said, "You know the Reverend Jakes?"

"Well, not more 'n on 'howdy and how are you' terms. I don't always make it to church regular-like."

"Rumor has it his dog's had a litter of puppies. You might find one to train."

"Train?"

"Not to eat Clint's chickens. But a puppy's a barrel of fun. That ought to keep you occupied for a few weeks. Tell the reverend I sent you over."

"I don't have to go to church to get the dog, do I?"

Shad tried not to laugh.

"That's between you and the reverend. If you convince him you'll give one of the litter a good home, he might overlook it that you're not in the front pew every Sunday. Now get on out of here."

"Thanks, Marshal." Charlie touched the brim of his hat and disappeared into the chilly morning.

"You took care of that real nice, Shad," Early said.

"The reverend ought to like getting rid of another of those mongrels. Have you seen them? Ugly. How can a puppy be ugly?" Shad laughed, then settled down. A quick gesture told Early to bring out their other prisoner.

Early led Clint Larson out. The man looked at the floor and was reluctant to speak.

"You shot his dog," Shad said. "Even if his dog killed your chickens, you don't kill a man's dog."

"Got to get another rooster. And more 'n a few hens."

"Do it. I'll see that Charlie keeps his dog away from your poultry."

"Kin I go?"

"Get out of here," Shad said. As Larson shuffled out, he stopped him. "I've got one more question. What did you mean about the black train?"

Clint Larson jumped a foot and shook his shaggy head, denying anything he'd said. Shad waited. Silence got more out of some men than outright threats. It worked on Clint Larson.

"Just something I heard. A drunk, maybe, over at the Gold Dust City shootin' off his mouth."

"Go on. Don't give me reason to come after you."

"My smoke wagon. You givin' it back to me?"

With obvious reluctance, Shad shoved it across the desk. Larson took it as if it were some religious relic, smiled just a little, then lit out.

"What's this all about, Shad?"

"Danged if I know. It sounds dangerous. If it is, I need to head it off before it gets to be a menace to everyone in Utopia."

"I see Shannon coming down the street. See you at sundown."

Shad waited for his other deputy before heading over to the saloon. The doors were open in spite of the early hour. Ralph Rockwell worked his broom back and forth on the boardwalk, kicking up a small dust storm. In spite of the cool morning, sweat already made his bald pate gleam in the sunlight. He looked up when the marshal approached.

"Ain't got any fights to break up, Marshal. Leastways, not yet. You're welcome to find a chair inside. Missy can get you coffee. Not much else done yet."

"I'll take you up on the coffee later. I wondered if you'd heard anyone talking about a black train?"

Shad saw how the saloon owner caught his breath. He had out-waited Clint Larson, and it had worked. The silence weighed heavily and finally got too much for Rockwell.

"It's like this, Marshal." He swallowed hard as he leaned on his broom. "I don't know for certain sure but I think he's back."

"Who's that?"

"Mind you, I'm not sayin' it was him. I didn't see him but the voice. It sounded the world like him." Rockwell began pushing the broom around, rearranging the dirt on the boards. "I'd say it was Billy Dixon."

"I ran him out of town."

"I remember you doin' that very thing a year back. Like I said, I didn't set eyes on the polecat. Only heard him shootin' off his mouth the way Dixon used to do."

"What'd you overhear him say?" Shad rushed on, "It doesn't matter if you're sure about him being Dixon."

"He was talkin' with one of them Gallagher boys like they was old trail hands ridin' the same range."

"And they mentioned a black train?"

Ralph Rockwell nodded once, then lowered his head and began sweeping in earnest. Shad took his leave. Once Utopia had been a devil's den of outlaws. The name Hellfire Pass had been deserved, with the entire area serving as a hideout for more than fifty owlhoots. When he had taken the marshal's job he had chipped away at the cutthroats. Ones and twos, then more were either arrested and sent to trial over in Denver or run off. Shad cared little how he got rid of them, as long as they left his town.

His fingers brushed over the worn butt of his Peacemaker. The ones that weren't arrested or scared off ended up in the cemetery above town. At one time he had tried to keep count but gave up when he and both his deputies had shot it out with the Blackmun gang. The bloodshed had been something not seen since the Indian wars. Shad closed his eyes as he remembered. His two deputies. Leroy Early and his son, Abednego. Abe had been a hothead and about the best shot with his six-gun that Shad had ever seen.

His son had been murdered by the former owner of the rail yard. Shad still wished Arthur Brushwell had lived to stand trial. Putting a noose around his filthy neck would have been satisfying. Knowing that Brushwell had met his maker was almost as good.

If Beatrice Gallagher's relative was palavering with Billy Dixon that meant trouble was brewing. She had a hatred built up for Shad that knew no bounds. Beatrice had put two slugs into Abe but it had been Brushwell who had finished him off with a bullet to the head. Beatrice and Dixon formed a powerful explosive that promised nothing but an explosion in Utopia.

He spent the rest of the day walking around town, talking with business owners and occasionally chasing youngsters playing hooky back to school. But nowhere did he catch sight of Dixon.

While the outlaw might be camped out up at the Gallagher's Calcutta coal mine, he suspected Dixon of staying closer to town. The most likely place was the freight yard. The new owner, Gadsden Renfro, had made a point of avoiding Shad and his deputies the past few months. In a small town like Utopia, that was suspect, but folks respected everyone's privacy. Too many had dark things in their past they wanted to forget.

A quick look at wanted posters hadn't turned up Renfro's picture, but that meant nothing. Utopia wasn't a place the US Federal Marshal considered worth even a sheet of ink-smudged paper.

The day went by slowly, but finally sundown turned the sky over the Rockies a violent red with fingers of purple and gray groping for the tallest peaks. He waited after Shannon left and Early reported for another night's work.

"You aren't gonna find a thing, Shad," Early told him after he heard what the marshal intended to do. "Nothing, that is, but a cold reception from your missus for bein' late again."

"I won't take long. If anything's going to happen, it'll be soon."

"The rats come out at sundown, is that it?" Early unfolded a newspaper and began reading without another glance in the marshal's direction.

Shad hurried across town, found the railroad tracks, and followed them to the depot. Several windows were lit up with the flickering light from coal oil lamps. The station master, Sussman, worked as telegrapher as well as about everything else at the station. He had a cot in a back room and often slept at the station rather than hire an assistant.

Shad had caught him stealing from the railroad but

hadn't turned him in because he'd helped bring down Arthur Brushwell. Ever since then, Sussman had avoided the law as if fearing Shad would change his mind and charge him for embezzlement and theft.

If the railroad hadn't arrested Sussman, the bosses back in Denver weren't likely to do so now. Shad thought that was their problem. He had told his son-in-law and was sure Williamson had talked it over with his superior. The only reason Shad could think of that Sussman still put in the long hours was that finding another man willing to work such long hours—and who knew Morse code—was impossible.

He went up the station house steps carefully. Every other step creaked. He avoided them and reached the platform. The steel tracks disappeared quickly into the dark. This stretch was at the summit. Walking as quietly as he could, he went to the ticket window and peered in.

Sussman wasn't stretched out on his cot. Listening hard for the telegraph key chattering out dits and dahs convinced Shad the depot master wasn't even in the building.

A quick look at the Regulator clock slowly ticking off the seconds in the passenger lobby made him sigh. It was hours until the midnight train pulled in for water and a full tender of coal.

That coal all came from the Gallagher mine. Without it being delivered regularly, the railroad wasn't likely to keep a twice-daily schedule—or maybe even keep this line running. There were other routes from Denver to

Central City, though they were longer and used far more coal for the trip.

Shad stayed in the shadows and listened hard for any sounds. The usual night cries filled the air. A coyote lamenting its lack of a mate. Bugs buzzing and chirping and causing nocturnal predators to go crazy chasing them. The steel rails even creaked like an old man getting out of bed in the morning. Heated during the day, they contracted when the sun went down.

But through it all he heard what he'd expected. Voices.

Moving quickly, he dropped down to the tracks and followed them to the spot where a water tower dropped its spout to fill the engine's boiler. He veered away and made his way into the freight yard. Mountains of coal waiting for shipment to Denver turned the area into a miniature Garden of the Gods.

He rounded one twenty-foot-high mound and stopped dead. Near crates of cargo waiting to be shipped was the source of the increasingly heated argument. Four men crowded together. Sussman stood in the middle, surrounded by Renfro and one of the Gallagher clan. Shad had seen him around town but couldn't remember his name.

The fourth man caused him to draw his six-shooter. Billy Dixon provoked the others, poking Sussman repeatedly and then shoving the Gallagher back when he tried to step up. The only one he didn't badger was Gadsden Renfro.

"We'll be ready, Billy. Honest," Gallagher said plaintively. "Bea's promised you, hasn't she? She don't go back on her word. Ever."

"She might be honest, but I've never seen any of the rest of her relatives with that particular trait," Dixon said. "I wouldn't trust you as far as I could kick you."

"You got no call sayin' that. You know you can count on me when the cards are down."

"Shut up, Jeremy. Get on back up the hill and tell Beatrice everything's got to be ready." Renfro gave orders like he was in charge, but Dixon couldn't let it lie.

"And be sure she ponies up the money she promised. I need it. I got expenses down in Blackhawk."

"Everything's still on schedule?" Jeremy Gallagher sounded eager.

"Get the money. Specie is better than greenbacks. The men I deal with don't trust paper money."

"I don't know why," Renfro said. "Most of 'em don't have teeth to bite down on a coin to see if it's gold or base metal."

This set off an argument between Dixon and Renfro. As Shad moved closer, Sussman faded into the dark. By the time Shad came within a few yards, Gallagher had also disappeared like smoke.

"You're keeping mighty sorry company, Mister Renfro. This is Billy Dixon, wanted criminal." Shad had his six-gun out, cocked and pointed. Having the bead on the outlaw stopped Dixon from drawing his own pistol.

"I ain't got any poster on me, Nelson. You got no call arrestin' me."

"Has he been working a swindle with you Mister Renfro? Billy Dixon's never done an honest deed in his life."

"I never saw him before tonight. Sussman wanted

me to hire him to work in the yard. You got a beef with him?"

Shad snorted. Such a clumsy lie made him all the more suspicious of the freight yard owner. And he knew everything he needed to know about Dixon.

"You might not have a poster out, but you've got the law after you somewhere. Maybe over in Denver. How about I check with the federal marshal?"

"I've taken a liking to Utopia, Nelson. I don't think I'm gonna leave."

"Mister Renfro, why don't you go to the jailhouse and tell Deputy Early to come on over? I want him to escort a prisoner to the federal marshal in Denver."

Renfro and Dixon exchanged a quick look. Then the freight yard owner left without a word.

"If nothing else, I'll see you run out of town again. You're like a bad penny. You keep turning up."

"Your life's not gonna be worth a plugged nickel, Nelson. Let me be."

"What do you need Gallagher money for?"

"I don't know what you're asking, Marshal."

"Reach for that six-shooter, and I'll drill you clean through, Dixon." Shad pointed his Peacemaker at the outlaw's face.

"You wouldn't shoot me down in cold blood."

"Nobody'd ever find your body. There're played out mines all through these hills. The ones not abandoned by the Gallaghers have been quit by the Morriseys. It'd be right fitting if you ended up at the bottom of a shaft in some lead mine."

The crunch of boots on cinders made Shad swing about. He turned back to Dixon.

"Why're you here, Shannon? I sent Renfro to find Leroy."

"He ran into me and decided he wanted a drink, so he gave me your message. What can I do?" Ian Shannon walked around and got a better look at their prisoner. "As I live and breathe. Billy Dixon. You keep comin' back, don't you?"

"I'd wanted Leroy to escort him to Denver and turn him over to the federal marshal."

"I'll do it. I can use a change of scenery. 'Less you want to take the trip downhill yourself."

Shad considered the trip just for a moment. The only reason, other than turning Dixon over to the law, was to see his son-in-law. He wasn't sure Richard Williamson wanted to see him any more than he wanted to share a drink with his daughter's husband.

"If you're willing, you go."

"I won't get my pay docked?"

Shannon always looked at the world as if it was out to steal him blind.

"Full pay. I'll even see if I can't convince the mayor to pony up a few extra dollars for your trouble."

"Suits me. What do we do until the train comes? It's more 'n four hours 'til midnight."

"Assuming the train's on schedule," Shad said.

"Sussman must have a deck of cards in the depot, but I ain't gamblin' away my bonus," Shannon warned.

They returned to the station with Dixon between

them, arguing over what to do if Sussman had cards. And if he didn't.

By the time the train arrived, loaded coal and water, and pulled out with Shannon watching over Billy Dixon, Shad was exhausted. He had gotten rid of the outlaw once more, but he knew the real challenge for him lay ahead.

He had to explain to Ruth why he'd missed dinner.

CHAPTER THREE

"You're like a dog with a bone, Shad," Leroy Early said. "Why's it botherin' you so much?"

"I can't rightly say. It's just that the people muttering it under their breath think it's something." Shad pursed his lips. Something he ought to know. As marshal it was his job, and the people talking about the "black train" weren't sharing with him. The very words carried menace, and for some reason he took it personally.

Maybe worse was that no one shared with him what sounded like a common rumor running around town.

"One thing that makes you a good law dog is how fierce you get trackin' down a scallywag." Early walked to the jailhouse door and looked into the rising sun. "That's also your worst trait."

"I found out who killed my son," Shad said, his ire rising. "Brushwell's dead and buried. That's all past. History. Nothing more to lose sleep over."

"While you were gnawin' on that bone, your wife left you and so did your daughter. While it doesn't much look like it, your daughter mighta upped and married Williamson to get away from your obsession."

"Who's being obsessed now?"

"You, Shad. You've replaced finding Abe's killer with findin' out about this here black train. It doesn't sound healthy to me for you to go sniffin' 'round town huntin' for something that might not even exist."

"There's nothing wrong with keeping my finger on the public pulse. As I see it, being marshal is more than tracking down lawbreakers. I need to head off trouble. This sounds serious."

"It sounds dumb, if you ask me, but then you aren't askin', are you? You're too busy worryin' yourself sick over it to do your real job." Early hitched up his drawers. "Time for me to get on home. Maybe I'll get some breakfast on the way. That new waitress, the one with the bright red hair, was kinda flirty with me the other day. I can't say I was disinclined, either."

Shad watched his deputy walk away. Early was slightly bowlegged from the days he'd spent riding herd up in Wyoming. He cut a decent figure for any woman interested in going courting. Close to six feet tall, he had piercing gray eyes but a quick, easy smile that made his mustache bob all around. Most of all, he had a good head on his shoulders, seldom panicked, and knew how to do his job without much fuss.

Settling into his chair, Shad scowled as he pondered what Early had said about tracking down gossip. He shook it off. He was marshal and decided what was important. What Clint Larson had said sounded like he meant something that was of concern to not only Shad but the entire town. Utopia depended on the railroad for its very existence. Coal coming from the Gallaghers'

Calcutta Mine was the only reason the train stopped here or that any commerce with either side of the Rockies existed.

Miners going west. Gold going east. And coming out of the ground around Utopia was a steady stream of the hard, black gold. And without the depot, the Morriseys would have to ship their lead ingots by wagon. While it was better going downslope than coming up with a heavily laden freighter, it took longer and cost more getting the lead to Denver.

He smiled just a little. Leadbottom Morrisey owed much of his family's prosperity to Beatrice Gallagher's coal mine. And the two feuded endlessly. The nights both families left their holes in the ground and came to town always caused trouble as serious as firing a bullet into a bundle of dynamite.

With a sudden heave, he shot out of his chair and started the long walk across town to the railroad depot. As expected, Sussman was hunched over his telegraph key, sending messages with a single-minded fury that blocked out everything around him. Another telegraph line came into Utopia and ended at the stagecoach office. Shad doubted Egan, the stage manager, bothered with his telegraph line any longer. Maintaining a separate line was expensive, and the railroad had reduced stagecoach traffic to once or twice a week. No passengers, no revenue to keep the business running effectively. For all he knew, the railroad line sent and received messages cheaper than offered by the stage company.

Sussman finished his keying and leaned back, sweating

from the effort. He jumped a foot when he saw the marshal.

"How long have you been spying on me?"

"I wasn't spying. I was waiting. I didn't want to interrupt you."

"You can't listen in. These are personal telegrams. Or business. A lot of them are railroad business."

"I wouldn't know that if you hadn't told me," Shad said. He hid a smile, thinking that his son-in-law could have read those messages. Richard Williamson had told him he knew Morse code because of one of a chain of jobs he'd held before landing his current employment as a railroad bull.

"Buying a ticket out of town, Marshal?"

"So I can avoid the black train?"

Sussman jumped again, then looked around like a cornered rat.

"What makes you say that?"

"Tell me about the black train."

"I don't know what you're going on about. You got business or are you just wasting my time? I've got a job to do." He stared at the telegraph key, as if willing it to begin chattering so he could return to it and ignore the lawman. It stayed quiet. Sussman began sweating even more.

"Why didn't you tell me that Billy Dixon was in town?"

"He ain't now. You sent him to Denver."

Shad nodded. He began prowling around, poking into corners to see Sussman's reaction. The station agent betrayed nothing now. While this wasn't much of a poker face, it presented better than his look of outright fear. He stared long and hard at the depot agent, but Sussman had ginned up his courage.

Shad left without another word, but he heard Sussman let out a gust of pent-up breath. More than not cottoning much to him, Shad wondered what deviltry the railroad agent was up to. He had been part of Brushwell's scheme to cheat the railroad on the coal they bought. Rather than think of Shad as his enemy, Sussman ought to have welcomed him as an ally since he wasn't arrested and locked up for his part in the swindle.

A slow walk through Renfro's freight yard turned up nothing of interest. Shad picked his way up and down Utopia's deserted streets. This was another quiet day. Too quiet. The calm before a storm. The calm before the black train came. Whatever that was.

He knocked some mud off his boots before going into the Gold Dust City Saloon. It was mid-morning but customers already came in for a beer and lunch.

Ralph Rockwell pointed to a sign.

"Glass of beer and a beef sandwich for a dime. For you I'll throw in a pickle, Marshal." The bald-headed barkeep polished a small glass, ready to draw the beer. The lunch special's beer was half the size if he asked for a draft without the food.

"Still not worked up an appetite, Ralph," he said.

Missy came over.

The three of them swapped pleasantries and finally Shad got around to asking—again—about the black train. Faro dealer and bartender exchanged a quick look, then both denied knowing anything. Both of them had always been honest citizens, or as honest as any could be in Hellfire Pass. They never caused trouble and even took care of some that boiled up in the saloon so he or his deputies weren't bothered.

That didn't let them off the hook for keeping what they knew from him.

He looked around the saloon and saw nothing to alert him to trouble. And why should it? It was not even lunchtime. He touched the brim of his bowler in Missy's direction, then stepped into the street to look around.

Early began to seem more and more like a newfound prophet. Shad reluctantly admitted that he was conjuring up a boogie man where none existed. As he wandered the streets, he considered spending more time with Ruth. And seeing after Miriam. She would deliver him a grandson in a month or so. That made him smile even broader. It would be a boy. It was a matter of faith with him that was true.

He jerked around as movement out of the corner of his eye caught his attention. A man vanished around the corner of the hotel after slipping out the front door. Shad drew his six-shooter and ran for all he was worth after the man. He rounded the building and instantly regretted his haste.

A bullet sang just above his head and took off his brown bowler. He ducked instinctively and lifted his Peacemaker to return fire.

The man who'd ambushed him was gone.

Heads poked out from doorways all around.

"Who got shot, Marshal?" called one shopkeeper. "Anybody need Doc Paisley?"

"Get on back to your work," Shad said, slipping his

six-gun back into its holster. He picked up his bowler. It had been close to new. Richard Williamson had given it to him, at Ruth's insistence he was sure, when his old one had one too many bullet holes drilled through it.

He wiggled his finger in the hole. This one was on its way to becoming the twin to his old hat. With exaggerated precision, he put it on and pulled it down so the brim touched the tops of his ears. Stetsons were good for a working cowboy. He had worn them in his day, but around town he preferred the bowler. Shad stopped by a windowpane and used the reflection to tip it to a jauntier angle.

"That's better," he said to his image. He tried to resist the temptation but failed. He stuck his finger into the hole and wiggled it about.

"You shooting up my patrons, Marshal?"

He turned to see a smallish woman dressed far too old for her true age. Netty Michaelson managed the hotel.

"Looks to be the other way around, Miss Michaelson. I saw a man run out the front of your establishment and followed. Being suspicious was the right thing to do. He took a shot at me."

"Who was it?" She moved closer and looked up at him. He towered a full foot over her five-foot-two.

"You have to tell me. You said he was one of your customers."

"I was in the back room doing my accounting. I came out the back door when I heard the gunshot. I never went through the lobby."

"Who's tending the front desk?"

He knew the answer before she answered.

"Mind if I have a word with Mary Beth?" he asked.

"She's supposed to be cleaning when she's not checking in guests. Don't keep her too long." She spoke as if every word hurt her tongue. Shad wondered if some bad blood was developing between his son's former lady friend and the hotel manager. He looked down at Netty and started to ask who owned the hotel. Netty had never claimed to own the property. Rumors swirled around town that some silver magnate in Denver kept the hotel for his mistresses, but Shad had never seen any evidence of that.

Mysteries all around him.

He stepped around her and went inside. Mary Beth Yarrow looked up from a stack of envelopes. She sorted through them to place in boxes behind the desk.

"Good afternoon, Miss Yarrow," he said, pinching the brim of his bowler. "You putting up the mail?"

"You are so observant, Marshal." She mocked him.

Shad wondered what his son had seen in her. She was of average height, had well-enough kept brown hair and muddy brown eyes that made her appear a little on the dull side. From what Abe had said, she got very little sleep, so he excused that. When she wasn't working in the hotel in exchange for a cot in the back room, she worked long hours at the general store. Mary Beth had turned down a job as a schoolteacher because married women weren't accepted for the post.

That told Shad she'd set her sights on Abe as marriage material the day she came to town.

"Who was it that ran out just before the gunshot?"

Her lips thinned and her muddy eyes turned cold.

"I don't know who you mean. Nobody's left the lobby in the past half hour."

"Netty's outside," he pointed out.

"She's been at the store buying yard goods. We need sheets for the upstairs rooms."

He considered her attitude and what had to be an outright lie. Whoever had rushed around the side of the hotel had come from the lobby. It hadn't been someone sitting on a chair along the boardwalk who'd gotten flushed when he spotted a lawman walking down the street.

"Might be you went upstairs? Or into the back room?"

He scratched his head. Netty Michaelson had said she was in the back room working on the ledger books. Mary Beth claimed her employer had been at Sampson's General Store looking over fabric to sew sheets. If he had to choose who told the truth, Netty Michaelson won.

"I never budged. Miss Michaelson wouldn't like me wandering around like that."

"How've you been? After Abe's death?"

She shrugged and then said in a flat tone, "I've been getting by."

"Any chance of getting the teaching job?"

A flash of anger crossed her face, then vanished behind an emotionless mask.

"The job's filled. I had my chance."

"Is there anything holding you in Utopia?"

"I put flowers on Abe's grave every Sunday. There's nothing other than that."

Shad hadn't known she did that. He had gone to his son's grave once since the funeral. That had been on Abe's birthday. If any flowers had been left the Sunday before, they'd blown off by that Wednesday afternoon.

"You should find yourself a new beau," he said. Not realizing he spoke until the words slipped from his lips, he added, "Billy Dixon's in Denver by now."

"No, he's—" Mary Beth looked daggers at him. "I need to get back to work. Miss Michaelson might dock my pay for lollygagging." She lowered her eyes to the envelopes on the counter, pointedly ignoring him.

He bid her a good afternoon and stepped out. Main Street zigged and zagged away. Whoever had tried to ventilate him was somewhere out there. Shadrach Nelson walked slowly down the middle of the street, keeping a sharp eye out.

The rest of the day was as boring at most of those before it. He wasn't sure that was a good thing anymore.

CHAPTER FOUR

"You got company a'comin', Bea."

Beatrice Gallagher looked up from a map spread across a table. She had marked a dozen points with tiny red dots, but nothing looked right. She wished her Aunt Winifred was here to help her figure out everything.

She *almost* wished Winifred Gallagher was here.

"Who are you talking about, Bobby?" Her young cousin was hardly old enough to shave, but he strutted around like a banty rooster. He was her Aunt Martha's boy and had big ambitions. She'd have to watch him when he got a little bigger. Or maybe not that much bigger.

"Him. You know the one. He was here before makin' cow eyes at you. And you looked like you was sweet on him, too."

She tensed, thinking he meant Patrick Morrisey. But Bobby didn't sound the alarm that a Morrisey tried to sneak up on them. For all she knew, Bobby had no idea she and Patrick had been lovers. He probably did know she'd tried to kill him. Beatrice touched the derringer in the folds of her skirt. That gun had done well by her, but she had missed Patrick's heart.

"You mean Billy Dixon?"

"He's the one!"

She heaved a sigh. Dealing with the outlaw was enough to wear her out when she had so much else to do, but he was necessary. Beatrice carefully folded the map and tucked it between two books on a shelf behind her, then picked up the lantern from the table.

A dozen rooms had been formed in the vast cavern by hanging canvas from poles. Hers was the finest of the lot, but she longed for a decent room with a feather bed and furniture that didn't give her splinters when she sat down.

After she'd killed her aunt, she looted the hillside behind a rundown shack for all the money Winifred had squirreled away. Beatrice had found more than five thousand dollars her aunt had swindled from the railroad and, she suspected, from the rest of the family. They were Gallaghers and they were share and share alike in the profits from the coal mine. Winifred had been responsible for counting the money from the sale of the coal, and she had divvied it up among the family members.

Beatrice was still trying to find what amount to take so that the rest of the family wouldn't get suspicious. She'd do that soon enough and then she could leave this miserable hole in the ground and find a real house aboveground.

"High up on Hellfire Pass," she said softly. "That's

where I'll put the house. And another in Denver. A fine one."

"What are you goin' on about, Cousin Bea?"

"Nothing, Bobby. You take a rifle from the rack before we go up top. You watch Billy Dixon real close, and if he tries anything or I give you the signal, you put a bullet in him."

"Really? You'd let me shoot him? Kill him?" The youth almost skipped to the slope leading up out of the ground. At the mouth of the mine, he grabbed a Winchester from a rack of a dozen rifles and began sliding cartridges into the magazine.

"You're not going into a fight with the Morriseys," she chided. "Don't waste those bullets now."

"I want to be ready," he said eagerly. He looked around to see if anyone was eavesdropping on them. "Bea?"

"What?" She climbed the steep slope, and it winded her. When the incline leveled off, she put down the lantern and blew it out. She pushed aside a plank door with brush nailed on the outside to hide the entrance.

"What's the signal? How'll I know when to plug that varmint?"

"You'll know. Just don't get an itchy trigger finger. Right now he's worth more to us alive than dead."

"But not for much longer, right?"

She squinted at the sun. From here every inch of the last quarter mile of the trail leading to a line shack was visible.

"Only when I say so, Bobby. Not an instant before."

"I'll get up there in the rocks," Bobby said.

She nodded absently. All the family knew that was

the spot commanding most of the approach to the cabin. He only mentioned it to show how mature he was and how ready he was to defend the family honor.

Walking down a trail to the back of the shack took her past a portion of the hillside that looked as if prairie dogs had dug a town. This was where her aunt had hidden most of the swindled money. Beatrice had found more than two dozen Ball jars stuffed with paper money buried and stashed under rocks. It had taken her the better part of a week after gathering the greenbacks to move it all to a new hiding place.

The hardest part had been making sure none of her family saw her either finding Aunt Winifred's money or caching it farther up the mountain in one of those fancy hollow rocks. She had broken open the plain rock and found a hollow interior with purple crystals studding the wall. That struck her as a fitting place for all the money. When put back down on the ground, it looked like any other rock.

She pulled back a plank in the wall and slipped into the line shack. Beatrice barely had time to drop into a chair when Billy Dixon breezed in, all smiles and acting like he was cock of the walk.

"Ain't you a sight for sore eyes." He pulled up a chair and moved it around the table to sit beside her.

She moved her chair away so the corner of the table separated them.

"What are you doing here?"

"Not even a howdy for your best guy?"

Beatrice glanced past Dixon to a broken window. Bobby popped up and watched. The rifle barrel rested on the windowsill. She turned her attention back to the outlaw. If Bobby did get an itchy trigger finger, it wouldn't be much of a loss. The boy was a good shot and wasn't likely to hit her by accident.

"If you aren't going to answer my question, I need to go. Unlike some of us, I have work to do."

"You don't belong in that coal mine. You're way too purty, Beatrice my girl."

She said nothing. He finally heaved a deep sigh of resignation.

"I need a place to hide out for a while."

"What have you done?"

"Well, I just took a shot at the marshal. I was in a hurry and missed, but I did send his silly hat a'flyin' like a bird." Dixon chuckled as he remembered the sight.

"Why'd you do that? I warned you to avoid Shadrach Nelson. For the moment."

"Well, little darlin', it's like this. He put me on a train to Denver with a deputy to make sure I got there. I couldn't stand the thought of bein' so far from you, so I took care of the deputy. Jumped the train and came back. Getting away from that deputy wasn't easy.'"

"He ran you out of town?"

"I came runnin' back right away. But if that law dog sets eyes on me, he'll gun me down. He's had it in for me ever since me and the boys ran with a couple other gangs that made Utopia our hideout."

"Don't bother telling me how he cleaned out the lot of you and sent you running like scalded dogs. I've heard the stories ever since I was knee-high to a grasshopper." She chewed her lower lip as she thought.

Dixon tensed and started to protest. She needed him, so she had to pour some oil on the increasingly storm-tossed water.

"You can stay here in this cabin but you can't go back to town whenever you want. I don't want you tipping my hand on what's going to happen."

"It won't matter one whit. There ain't nuthin' Marshal Shadrach Nelson can do to stop it."

"I don't want you shooting him."

"Now that's the first real passion I've heard in your voice, darlin'. It's touchin' you think that much of me."

"If he fills you full of lead, that's all right with me. *I* want to be the one to shoot him."

"There's that passion again. What about you sharin' some of that fire with me to help pass the time?" He reached for her. He froze when he heard the hammer come back on her .45 derringer. The sight of her fist filled with the small gun braced against the table, the muzzle inches from his heart, took the leer off his lips.

"The marshal is mine. You can have any of the Morrisey family you want. All of them. They're fair game to you and your gang."

"I need some more money to recruit. I heard tell that Lariat Wallace is over in Central City. Him and his boys'd be real helpful cleanin' up Utopia. But they're big time. They've got rewards on their heads. It'll take a heap of money to get them to take the train into town."

"I've heard of him," Beatrice said. She nodded slowly. "He's a good choice, but the time's not right yet."

"I'd hate to have a good man like that move on."

"Good man," she snorted. "He'll stick around Central

City for a spell. That's where the gold is being mined. Unless he gets greedy, he won't have the law after him for a couple weeks."

"You got this all planned out, don't you?"

"You said you jumped the train to Denver. How'd you get back to Utopia so fast?"

"My, my, smart as well as purty. I found myself a horse since I'd left mine back in town. The marshal didn't see fit to put it into a boxcar for me to ride around Denver."

"He sent you there for trial. What were the charges?"

"Bein' such a fine specimen of a man," Dixon said, puffing out his chest. He glanced down. The twin-barreled pistol still pointed at his chest. This deflated him. A little.

"I'll send one of my cousins by with food for you. Don't stray too far from the cabin."

"Will you come tuck me in when the sun goes down?"

Beatrice stood. The derringer disappeared into the folds of her skirt. She smiled and said, "You'd better hope not."

Billy Dixon didn't have any comeback for that.

CHAPTER FIVE

"Something big's happening at the depot," Billy Dixon said. He leaned back in the rickety chair with his feet hiked onto the table. With a splinter taken from the table leg he picked his teeth.

Beatrice Gallagher glared at him. The way he stared at her made her want to remove him permanently. If he was tossed down an old mine shaft, the rats would eat his putrid flesh and he'd never be found.

"Who'd look for you?" she asked herself softly.

"What's that, lil darlin'? Don't matter. You've got your ear to the ground. The train's been at the depot too long. They took on water and loaded your coal, but they're not leavin' for Denver."

She opened the cabin door and yelled for her cousin. Bobby dutifully ran over. She had posted him above the shack with his rifle. If Dixon had tried to leave, he'd have to ride out with a couple ounces of lead in him.

"What's going on at the station?" she asked.

"There's a big shipment gonna be made." Bobby looked past her at Dixon, who leaned against the door frame, still picking his teeth.

"It's not us," she said. "That means Leadbottom is shipping a ton or two of lead ingots."

"That must be it. I saw the two city slickers, the ones what always bring a sack of money with them when they come from Georgetown."

"Money?" Dixon pushed past Beatrice. "How much?"

The youth smiled crookedly and said, "Heard tell it might be as much as a thousand dollars. It might be more since this shipment's bigger than most. Leadbottom's been hoardin' them lead bricks."

"The Morrisey lead's none of your concern," Beatrice snapped. "And Mister Dixon, you'll mind your own business, too."

"I wouldn't mind mindin' your business, Sweet Bea." He laughed. "You ain't my sweet pea. You're my Sweet Bea. Get it?"

Beatrice pulled her hand from the folds of her dress. Over and over she told herself she needed him. As insulting as he was, he wasn't anywhere near as bad as Shad Nelson. The marshal knew she had killed her aunt, even if he never arrested her for it. He was saving up to get her for something where he had ironclad evidence, and all because she had tried to cut down his son.

Brushwell had finished off Abednego Nelson, not her. She needed to be more careful with her aim and practice more. She had shot Abednego twice in the chest but hadn't come close to killing him. Not like Brushwell did.

Staring at Dixon's broad back made the itch almost unbearable. But she needed him.

For a while longer.

"Bobby, saddle up our horses. I'll see firsthand what's happening."

"Saddle my nag, too, Bobby," called Dixon as the youth turned to go.

"If you show your face, the marshal will arrest you." She stared hard at him. He ignored her, and that caused her to fume. She had to repeat to herself over and over that she needed him.

"Nelson is an ignorant cuss. He won't be lookin' for me. He thinks I'm in Denver."

She stared at him in wonder.

"If his deputy rode the train all the way to Denver without you, all he needs to do is send a telegram back to Utopia."

"Deputy Shannon'd never do that. It'd be too embarrasin'. He'd want to come back and tell the marshal to his face he lost his prisoner." Dixon pursed his lips. With a quick move, he tossed aside the toothpick. "Knowing Shannon as I do, he maybe won't even return. He'll get to Denver and drift on."

"How do you know the deputy?"

Dixon laughed and slapped his thigh.

"Me and him got to talkin'. I distracted him with my charm and wit and then conked him on the head. I left him tied up back in the mail car 'fore I jumped off."

"Cousin Bea, lookee there." Bobby pointed across the freight yard.

"Must be a dozen men loading the ingots," she said. Her quick calculation made her perk up. "Two thousand dollars for that much. Leadbottom's been hiding it out for this one shipment."

"There's a different engine," Bobby said. "Bigger, more powerful. That's what'd be used for a long freight train."

"Or one with a few very heavy cars."

She caught her breath when Patrick Morrisey shook hands with one of the well-dressed men. The other handed over a metal box. The shiny brass lock reflected sunlight in all directions as Patrick took hold. Leadbottom waddled on over and shook hands with the businessmen, then gave Patrick an earful. Although she wasn't able to overhear what the Morrisey patriarch said, she knew he warned Patrick to be careful and not lose the money.

"I've seen enough," she said. "Bobby, you and Mister Dixon get on back to the mine."

"What? The ride down here's parched me something fierce. Let's go have a drink, you and me, lil darlin'. There's more 'n one gin mill in town. There's a dozen we can choose from to find a nice, dark corner where we can—"

Her hazel eyes turned to steel. She tossed her head to indicate the road back up onto the mountainside.

Dixon went for his six-gun, then froze. Bobby had the rifle trained on him.

Without a word, she urged her horse onto a back street and made her way across town. This time of day, the hotel offered a decent afternoon tea. She was tired of the meals cooked up by the rest of her family. Out of a dozen Gallagher women, not a one could fix a meal that didn't taste like cow flop and then sit in her belly until it rumbled in pain. The one man who could cook after working on a chuck wagon during a trail drive,

Bobby's older brother Jeremiah, had been shot up when Shadrach Nelson and the railroad bull went after Brushwell last fall. A bullet had busted up his elbow, so he was close to useless.

Beatrice rode around back and dismounted. Netty Michaelson needed a stable hand to tend customers' horses, but she was a tightwad. Beatrice walked around to the front and halted. Patrick Morrisey stared at her. He clutched the money box under his arm.

"Bea?" His voice came out weak and pathetic. It figured. He wasn't much of a man.

"Excuse me. I'm going inside."

Patrick hurried around and opened the door for her. She gave him a cold look, lifted her skirts, and slipped inside where Netty Michaelson greeted her.

There was a long pause, then Netty asked, "You and Mister Morrisey for tea?"

"One," Beatrice said pointedly. "Just one today."

She followed the hotel manager into the dining room. Patrick scurried around and pulled out her chair. Beatrice walked to the other side of the table and seated herself.

"Don't be like this, Bea. I don't care that you shot me. I forgive you. You were all het up over the marshal killing your aunt."

"Are you going to kill your father?"

"What? No! I can't do a thing like that. Not even for you. I know we discussed it, but, dang it, he's my pa."

"There's no way we can ever be together again as long as Leadbottom is telling you every little move to make."

Patrick started to sit.

She strained just a little. She hooked her ankle around

the chair leg and pulled it into the table to prevent Patrick from settling down.

"Look, look here." Patrick fumbled out a key and turned it in the padlock. He opened the lid. It was stuffed with greenbacks and a considerable number of twenty-dollar gold pieces. "We just sold the biggest load of lead this year."

She sniffed.

"Hardly what I receive for a weekly load of coal. I sent five cars to Denver last week and plan to send that much more this week. And there's the twice daily tender load from the scheduled trains."

"Me and you, Bea, me and you can take the money and be out of Colorado 'fore anybody knows we took the cash." He held out the box. The expectation on his face was pathetic.

"Mister Morrisey, do you remember what they called my aunt before her unfortunate death?"

"Bea . . ."

"They called her the Coal Queen of the Rockies. With her death, I have assumed that title. The Calcutta Mine supplies the railroad with enough coal to run fourteen daily one-way trips and take quite a few car-loads to Denver."

"I can get a couple more horses. We can swap riding them and outrun any pursuit. I don't think my pa'd realize I was gone until tomorrow."

"Or never," she said nastily. "That seems like a fortune to you. It's nothing to me. Now, Miss Michaelson is bringing the cart around. I must select my sandwiches and desserts. And," she said louder, "Netty, what types of tea do you have today?"

"Only one, Miss Gallagher. An herb tea from dandelion greens I picked myself."

"That will be fine." She leaned out to look around Patrick. "You are leaving, aren't you, sir?"

"Bea!"

Netty Michaelson pushed the wheeled cart forward between Patrick and the table. He stepped away. Beatrice thought she saw the sparkle of tears in his eyes.

"That one, Netty. And two of those. What do you call them? Petit Fours?"

As the hotel manager served the tasty tidbits, Beatrice leaned back and stared out the bay window. Patrick walked to the bank as if he were climbing gallows steps. If he refused to do as she wished, she had to find another way of getting rid of Leadbottom. None of the other Morrisey family had the wit of a marmot. The longer they worked in their own mines, the worse they became.

Patrick might still serve her purpose, but it looked increasingly as if she had to find a different way to take over the lead mine. That had to be better, she decided. Being married to Patrick was hardly the way she wanted to spend her days—or nights.

She sampled one of the pastries.

"Excellent, Netty. Did you bake these yourself?"

"I did, special for afternoon tea."

"I'll have to come more often. Or," she said, smiling winningly, "hire you to be my personal cook."

"You're too kind, Miss Gallagher. But as attractive

as the offer you might make me to throw meals together for you, there's no way I can leave the hotel."

"I understand." But Beatrice didn't. She wondered if she should find out which of the rumors about a silver magnate in Denver owning the hotel was right. The mines along the western slopes of the Rockies were peppered with claims that turned many men into millionaires overnight.

She patted her lips of crumbs and picked up the china teacup. Down the street, Patrick stood outside the bank talking with Wilson Reese. The bank president tried to pry the box from Patrick's grip. When he failed, they exchanged a few words. Reese pointed into the lobby, then held the door open for Patrick.

Parting with the money, even to put it into the bank, was hard. And he had offered her all of it. She took another sip of the bitter tea. As she returned the cup to the saucer, she froze.

Across the street from the bank someone moved in shadows.

Billy Dixon had watched Patrick hand over the money from the lead shipment to the banker. She'd have words with Bobby Jones about how he had not properly escorted Dixon back to the mine when she had ordered him to do so.

Until then, she sampled another of the scrumptious dessert pastries—as was befitting the Coal Queen of the Rockies.

CHAPTER SIX

"Did you get him delivered?" Shad Nelson asked when his deputy strolled into the jailhouse.

Ian Shannon grunted and looked around, casting a quick look into the cells in the back room.

"No prisoners," he said.

"Dixon," Shad persisted. "What did the US Marshal say when you turned him over?"

"Not much. What did you want him to say?"

Shad saw his deputy was in another of his dark depressions. Sometimes the black cloud fluttered around the man's head for a week or two, and then it disappeared, and there wasn't anyone in Utopia who was brighter and more cheerful.

"I figured you would like a break." He opened his desk drawer and pulled out two crumpled dollar bills. Using his finger he pushed them across the desk in Shannon's direction.

"What's that?"

"I said I'd ask the mayor for a bonus since you had

to go to Denver on business. That ought to cover your meals."

"Yeah, guess so." Shannon scooped up the greenbacks and tucked them into his vest pocket. "Anything happen worth mentioning while I was gone?"

Shad started to tell him about the big shipment Lead-bottom had sent down to Denver, but that hardly seemed like the gossip Shannon wanted. A quick shake of his head satisfied the deputy that his boss didn't have anything worth sharing.

"I'll get out on patrol."

Shad watched him go. Most men would have boasted of going to Larimer Square and getting drunk or laid or in a fight. Shannon played his cards closer than that to his vest. In a way Shad was surprised his deputy had come back. Shannon was a drifter at heart and had been in town almost two years. This might be the longest he'd stayed in one place in his life. And he didn't have an anchor holding him.

As far as Shad knew, Shannon didn't have a lady friend to keep him here. That meant he liked the job enough to forget his wanderlust, at least for the time being. That suited Shad. Ever since his son had been gunned down, he had relied heavily on Shannon and Early. Two deputies and not three made keeping the peace harder, but Utopia had been quiet.

Even the Gallagher-Morrisey feud had cooled down to a simmer.

He yawned and wondered if he should let Shannon deal with the lawbreakers by himself. Shad wanted to see if Miriam needed anything her ma wasn't able to provide her. Without her man around, Miriam got moody.

Pregnant women were like that.

Stretching, he stood and went to the door and looked out as far as he could along the zigzagging main street. He caught his breath when he saw two men trotting along. They went around a bend in the street before he got a good look at them.

"I know you varmints," he said aloud. But he couldn't identify them. His brain itched trying, then he quit. Whenever he had crossed paths with them, it had been a long time ago.

He started south to get on the trail leading upslope to his house, then found himself heading eastward toward the hotel. If the two strangers stayed anywhere, Netty Michaelson had put them up. It wouldn't hurt to ask after them.

Stride long, he passed Sampson's General Store. He waved to Mary Beth Yarrow as she put up merchandise in the display window. She saw him but made no move to wave back. Shad felt a little hurt. If Abe had lived, she would have been one of the family. By now she would have been delivering him a grandchild. Abe's death had soured her on even being polite. Shad wasn't sure why, and it hurt him a little, but he had learned to be content with what he did have.

Miriam's baby would be his first grandson.

"Definitely a son," he said. He hadn't asked his daughter if she had picked out names yet. His busy mind turned over his choices of names. Steps automatic, he rounded a corner and went to the hotel.

No horses were tethered at the side. The stable in the dilapidated shed stable around back looked mighty empty, too. He tried to remember the horses the two men rode. Sometimes he identified horses quicker than he did their riders. The brief glimpse hadn't been enough to get more than an impression.

It wouldn't hurt to ask Netty about her guests.

As he climbed the steps to the boardwalk, a shot echoed down the street. Shad turned, hand going to the butt of his six-shooter. He swiveled about, trying to locate the source of the report.

When another one sounded, he lit out at a dead run. The gunfire came from the direction of the bank. The doors were wide open, but inside was too dark for him to make out any figures.

Then three masked men burst from inside. They waved their six-shooters around and carried gunnysacks that weighed them down.

"Drop your guns!" he shouted. "You're under arrest!" Shad raised his six-gun and got off a shot when all three turned on him.

The air filled with lead. He ducked when one bullet sang past his ear. This made him miss his next couple shots. The masked men ran around the side of the bank.

More men came boiling from the lobby. Wilson Reese frantically swung a sawed-off shotgun in every which direction. His eyes were wide and wild, and spittle flecked his lips.

"Holdup! Robbers! Bank robbers!" He discharged

the shotgun in Shad's direction, forcing the marshal to flop belly down in the street.

"Stop shooting, you fool. It's me. Shadrach Nelson!"

"Marshal Nelson?" Reese looked around. His panic grew when three riders galloped around the side of the bank. The outlaws had tethered their horses behind the bank while they robbed it.

Reese jumped back to keep from being run down. He discharged the second barrel at the fleeing robbers. One of the owlhoot's horses stumbled and fell. The bank president had hit the horse in the rear leg.

Shad scrambled to his feet and ran toward the fallen horse. The outlaw's leg was pinned under the horse's struggling weight.

"Give up. I'll shoot!" Shad got off another round and missed the robber by inches.

In response, the other two robbers galloped back, guns blazing. Distracted, Shad got off another shot, and then the hammer hit a spent chamber. The leaden hail coming his way forced him to take cover behind a rain barrel at the side of a building.

He frantically reloaded, but this gave the bank robbers the chance to pull their partner free. He staggered a step, then was pulled up behind the leader.

Shad stood and took aim. The bucking horse, weighed down by two men now, spoiled his shot. But as the horse wheeled about, Shad recognized one rider.

"Dixon! Billy Dixon!" He stepped out and emptied his Peacemaker again at the retreating thieves. Seeing he had no chance to hit any of them now, he turned to the bank president.

Wilson Reese sat with his back against the front wall of the bank. He clutched the shotgun to his chest as if it was a baby. Shad knelt by him. The man was covered in blood. When he touched him, Reese jumped a foot. He came out of his shock and cursed a blue streak.

"Get them, Marshal. Stop them. They took everything. Every penny in the bank. I'm ruined! Ruined!"

"Where are you hit?"

"I . . . I'm not wounded. Stop them!"

Shad pulled away Reese's coat, expecting to see bullet holes in the banker's chest. His vest was drenched, but there wasn't any damage.

"Where'd all the blood come from?"

"Newman. They gunned down my head teller. I held him. I held him and grabbed the shotgun kept under the counter and I chased them out and—"

By now a crowd gathered and listened as the banker rambled on incoherently.

"Somebody fetch Doc Paisley. Mister Reese isn't hurt, but at least one of his tellers is." Shad tried to imagine a man losing so much blood and not being dead. Stranger things had happened, but he wasn't going to bet a plugged nickel on it this time.

Billy Dixon had not only robbed the bank but he'd killed a man doing so.

"They hightailed it toward Denver," someone in the crowd said. He pointed to the road leading east out of Utopia.

Shad turned to ask for more details. He stopped and stared in shock. Ian Shannon stood across the street, saying nothing, as immobile as a statue. Shad pushed his way through the crowd and went to his deputy.

"Where were you?"

Shannon gestured vaguely and mumbled, "Down the street. Not here."

"Round up men for a posse. Reese is rattled but at least one of his tellers got shot up pretty bad." He took a deep breath. "And they cleaned out the vault."

"Leadbottom's not gonna like that," Shannon said.

"If they got everything, a powerful lot of people aren't going to like it. Morrisey wasn't the only one with money on deposit." He tried to figure out his deputy's reaction and couldn't. "Get a move on. And bring my horse around. The bigger the head start those cutthroats get, the harder it'll to catch them."

Shannon walked away, showing no real hurry to obey. Shad almost shouted at him to get a move on, then spun and stalked back to find out what he could from Reese about what was stolen.

It was worse than he reckoned.

CHAPTER SEVEN

"A dollar a day and a shot of whiskey when we get back," Shadrach Nelson called to the gathered men.

"Is there a reward if we catch them varmints?"

"If any wanted posters are out on their heads, you get that." Shad heard some murmuring. Nobody liked that. It was too much like drawing to an inside straight. It had a chance of paying off but not a good one. He added what they all wanted to hear. "And a hundred-dollar reward for each of them put up by the bank."

He glanced toward Wilson Reese. The banker might have swallowed a bitter pill if his expression was any indication. Declaring any reward grated on his banker's fiduciary sensibilities, but getting back everything looted from his vault justified such a huge reward.

"How's Garrison doing?" another voice in the crowd piped up.

"The teller's doing all right. Doc Paisley said he's weak but nothing a shot of whiskey and a week's rest won't cure."

A few chuckled. "That's Garrison for you. He'll do anything to drink on the job."

Another called out, "And a week in bed! What a layabout!"

This joshing at the expense of the injured teller broke the reluctance of the newly formed posse to take part.

"Saddle up! Let's ride. We have to catch them before the sun goes down." Shad looked westward. That meant hardly more than three hours. This deep in Hellfire Pass sunset came fast. Tall mountains were sure to send shadows across any trail before they even spotted the bank robbers. He had to do the best he could with the recruits. Most all of them in his posse acted as if they were going on a Sunday picnic rather than after dangerous criminals.

At least he had convinced them to ride with him. Shad thanked his lucky stars for that.

Not a one of them looked like a frontiersman able to follow a trail or even shoot his six-shooter straight. They were mostly the bored customers in any of the thirteen saloons in town. One or two moved like they were used to hard work. After the railroad finished laying track, a good number of men who'd driven steel spikes and moved railroad ties had found themselves out of jobs.

"You want me to ride along, Shad?"

"You get to keep the peace in town, Leroy," he told his deputy. "Shannon'll ride with me this time."

"That a smart thing on your part?" Early rubbed his stubbled chin in thought. "I asked around. More 'n one saw Shannon standing and watching the robbery. He didn't do a blamed thing to stop them. He never even drew his pistol."

"Not until later," Shad said. His other deputy stood

by himself across the street from the bank. Shannon had acted funny after taking Dixon to Denver.

Since he was nigh on sure that Dixon had been one of the robbers, Shad wondered how diligent Shannon had been about delivering Dixon to the Federal Marshal. He'd sent a telegram but Sussman claimed there hadn't been an answer. The railroad depot agent and telegrapher had been known to slack off on his wire duties when it came to the marshal's messages. Without any proof that Sussman was lying about even sending his telegram to Denver, Shad had to believe him.

"You'd better get on their trail," Early said. He glanced west toward the mountain peaks, just as Shad had done. They shared a concern that the robbers would escape if night fell and the posse lost the trail.

Shad motioned for Shannon to mount up. The deputy looked surprised, then obeyed without a word. He was always a taciturn galoot, but now he was even less likely to mutter even a curse under his breath. Something had taken all the wind from his lungs.

"You think they'll head straight for Denver, Marshal?" One of the posse rode so close Shad smelled the liquor on the man's clothing. If the rider came any closer, the marshal was afraid he'd be overwhelmed by the whiskey on the gusty breath.

"Hard to say. Denver or Colorado Springs. They made off with so much money, they might keep on going east and avoid any town until they get somewhere they can spend the money safely."

"Or them three might ride different directions."

Shad hoped that wasn't the case, but Shannon had a

good chance of being right. If they stayed together as a gang, they left distinct hoofprints. He couldn't remember the last time he had seen three riders come into Utopia together. The road was so steep, most folks would take the train, even if they had to pay extra to put their horse in a freight car.

But this was all downhill. Riding would be easier and the robbers had lit a shuck when they left the bank.

"Two!" he said suddenly. "We're looking for only two sets of tracks. Reese shot one of their horses from under him."

"I got a trail over here, Marshal," called the town blacksmith's assistant. "But there's three of them."

"Musta stole another horse," Shannon said. He slumped back in the saddle, staring down at the pommel rather than engage his boss.

Shad dismounted and examined the hoofprints. He ran his fingers around the muddy rim of one print, as if he had a chance to see the horse and its rider this way. Three horses had come this way recently—within the last hour. Pacing off the stride, he knew the horses had been galloping.

"This is the trail," he said, swinging back into the saddle.

Aware of the warm sun on his back, he pushed the posse as hard as he could. When the shadows length-ened and he had to zigzag to keep the robber's trail in sight, he knew night was going to do him dirty. Track-ing in the dark on this rocky ground was hard, even with the full light of day.

"I lost 'em, Marshal." The smithy's assistant rode in

a wide circle. "If they keep on heading downslope, we might have a chance of spotting them. There's a big meadow a couple miles ahead."

"Crossing it'd take close to a half hour," Shannon said. "If we catch sight of 'em, they won't get away."

Twilight turned the landscape into a bleak wilderness. As Shad rode along more slowly, worried about his horse stepping into a varmint's burrow, he realized the futility of pursuit.

"Got another trail over here."

Shad trotted to where another of the posse had dismounted to relieve himself. By sheer luck he had found a game trail cut recently by steel horseshoes. The tracks led into a heavily forested area.

"We'll never spot 'em in the woods," Shannon said. "If that's their trail."

"They know the area as good as we do," Shad said. "Going straight downhill to that meadow would have done them in. That's why they cut away from that path and went there." He stared into the dense forest.

"Maybe," Shannon said. "Maybe not."

He walked back to the rest of the posse. They milled about uneasily.

"Marshal Nelson, them robbers can shoot us like crows on a fence out here in the dark."

"Get on back to town. It's too dark to stay on the trail." He heard a collective sigh of relief.

"What about that drink you promised? Are we gonna get it?"

"Find Deputy Early and have him take you all to the Gold Dust City. Ralph will set you up with a drink." Shad shuddered thinking what the posse would tell Early. "Don't go drinkin' more than a bottle of rotgut now."

"Each?"

"You all get on back to town," Shad said, smiling in spite of himself. He watched them hit the trail to Utopia, riding single file. When Shannon walked past, he reached out and grabbed the reins on the deputy's horse. "Don't be in such a hurry."

"We aren't headin' back, too?"

"We're going after them. Dixon made off with a powerful lot of money."

Shannon didn't utter a word. In the dark, Shad wasn't able to see his expression, but Shannon's entire body was tense.

"I've been thinking on it. I thought I saw two men riding into town before the robbery that looked mighty familiar."

Shannon held his tongue.

"Before, when I ran Dixon out of town, he had two sidekicks with him. Herk and Squinty."

"I remember," Shannon finally said. "I helped hog-tie them in the freight car so they couldn't escape."

"You see them before the robbery?"

"What are you gettin' at, Marshal?"

"I only saw their backs as they rode past, but you were around the bank. Did you catch sight of them— and Dixon—before they robbed the bank?"

"In the freight car a year back is the last time I laid eyes on them."

Shad started to press Shannon about delivering Dixon to the Denver law dog but froze when he heard something moving in the woods. A twig snapped. The sound of a foot crushing debris on the floor. Sounds no animal, either predator or prey, would make.

He went for his gun as a report rang through the forest. A bullet whined past his ear. Moving so fast, he lost his balance on his rearing horse and fell to the ground. Momentarily stunned by the impact, he heard footsteps approaching over the thunder of his pulse in his ears.

Gunshots deafened him. It took Shad a second to realize the fire came from behind him, higher up, from Ian Shannon.

"Get up." His deputy grabbed his arm and pulled him to his knees. All the while, Shannon fired steadily into the trees. When one pistol came up empty, he did a border shift and grabbed for the six-shooter in his left holster.

By the time his second six-gun hammer landed on a spent cartridge, Shannon was crowding Shad to take cover. Still dazed, the marshal flopped onto his side and began rolling. The motion cleared his head. He came to a halt when he slid down into a narrow gully. Resting his pistol on the lip of the ravine, he waited until he saw movement in the woods.

Shadows moved. Shad fired. He was immediately fired on by three separate gunmen. He picked the one in the middle and tried to figure out where the body behind the gun was. He emptied his Peacemaker and was rewarded with a grunt. Hurried whispers told him the other two went to the aid of the man he'd winged.

Shad began to fire with deadly rhythm. As his deputy

kept the outlaws moving around in fear of their lives, he reloaded. His hand steadied and his vision adapted to the darkness. A dark figure moving across a darker tree caused him to fire three quick shots. Again he was rewarded with a howl of pain.

"They're turning tail and running," Shannon said.

Shad's ears rang from the gunshots, but he felt the thunder of hooves through the forest floor. He scrambled to his feet, reloading as he went.

"Don't be a fool, Marshal."

Shad ignored Shannon. He plunged into the woods, hunting for a target, any target. While he wanted to bring down Billy Dixon, either of his henchmen would do right now. He was furious that they had ambushed him. Moving from tree to tree, he reached the spot next to the game trail where they had dismounted and fired at him.

He ran his fingers around a boot print in soft ground. Fresh. He felt something wet and lifted his fingers up high to get a better look.

"Blood!" He motioned for Shannon to join him. Together they had a chance of running down the fleeing outlaws.

Shad realized after a few seconds that Ian Shannon wasn't coming to support him. Torn by indecision, he stared into the pitch black forest and then back where his deputy had mounted once more and sat waiting.

He retreated. Shannon silently held out the reins to his horse. Shad stepped up. For several heartbeats he stared at his deputy, then said, "We can't catch them. Let's go back to town."

He tugged on the reins. His grateful horse trotted away from where the gunsmoke and blood had filled the air. Shad's only victory came in knowing he had wounded at least one of the robbers. If his luck held, he'd winged another.

He rode back to Utopia with Shannon alongside. Neither said a word.

CHAPTER EIGHT

"We got a visitor on the road," Bobby Jones whispered. "You want me to shoot him, Bea?"

She looked up from a stack of notes she'd made and scattered across a map of Hellfire Pass.

"How do I know if I want you to shoot him if you don't tell me who it is?"

Bobby looked sheepish and grinned shyly.

"It's the one who calls you his 'lil darling' all the time."

Beatrice considered telling her cousin to go ahead and remove this thorn from her side. Billy Dixon presumed too much. He acted like he was running things. She was the Coal Queen of the Rockies now and deserved some respect.

She deserved a lot of respect, and she got none of it from him.

If only she didn't need the contacts he had across the entire stretch of the Rockies' western slopes. She heaved a sigh of resignation.

"You'd probably miss with your elbow like that."

Bobby flexed his right arm and winced. He shifted

the rifle to his left hand and stretched his right arm out straight. He grimaced just enough to warn her that any marksmanship on her cousin's part was suspect.

"I only banged it up a little on the coal cart. It don't hardly hurt me anymore."

"You watch him real close now, you hear?" She gathered all her notes and folded the map. Her eyes momentarily took in the terrain on the other side of the pass. That was all Morrisey land. Getting control of it required more maneuvering than she'd anticipated, but she'd end up owning it all. Controlling the high ground on either side of the canyon meant she controlled the railroad, as if she didn't hold the reins of power there already.

The train needed Gallagher coal—coal she controlled with an iron hand.

The Gallagher clan would own every rock in what was now Leadbottom's domain. She already considered which of her relatives to put in charge of digging the lead out of the far mountainside. Too bad some of the most dependable of her kin had been killed. Bobby was a mite too young to be given such responsibility, but there were others. His experience mining coal was good enough to believe he had a feel for grubbing out lead from hard rock. She might season him by having him run the lead smelter. That was the most profitable part of the Morrisey empire. Who wanted lead ore? Everyone wanted the refined lead bricks to melt into bullets and dozens of useful products.

But that was all future worry. Right now she needed Dixon and the army of cutthroats with which he promised to swoop into Utopia and remove the marshal and his deputies and anyone else keeping her from becoming the mover and shaker all along the railroad tracks from Denver to Georgetown.

She grew impatient enough that she cared less now whether she or Dixon removed the marshal. As long as Shad Nelson ended up in the town's cemetery, she'd be happy.

Tucking away the papers in a small safe, she spun the dial to be sure it was securely locked. She pushed through the canvas hangings and crossed the large, high-vaulted cavern where most of the coal had been dug out. This was the first vein struck by Winifred's pa. It had petered out quick, but the frantic effort had left a huge underground room where they were safe from about any attack.

Four different tunnels led out so she'd never be trapped here. Beatrice trudged up the slope and came out behind the line shack. Bobby pushed through after her and slammed the camouflaged trapdoor.

"I'll get into the rocks above the cabin," he said. "From the way he was ridin', he won't be here for another ten minutes."

She didn't bother asking why her cousin thought that. From the bottom of the hill along the road with all its switchbacks took only a few minutes on horseback. Less if the rider was in a powerful hurry. Getting fully loaded wagons brimming with coal required much more skill since the driver had to ride the brake all the way down to keep the mule team from getting run over. But ten minutes?

But even the empty wagon returning to the current active mine mouth wasn't much of a pull.

She worried that something had gone wrong and that Dixon brought her the bad news. He knew better than to rush, if that were true.

Bobby ducked out of the cabin by pushing aside a board on the back wall. She sank into a chair and waited longer than she expected. When Dixon kicked open the door, she came out of her chair and took a step toward him.

"You're all shot up!" Beatrice cared less that he looked bad enough to die than she'd have to find a new ramrod for her scheme to remove Shadrach Nelson and the rest of his law dogs.

"Now, now, lil darlin', it's good you care so much about my condition." He stepped over and grabbed the chair across the table from her. He moved it so he sat beside her.

"That's not your blood," she accused. "Are you wounded?"

He flexed his arm. A tear in his sleeve showed where he had bled and caused the cloth to mat to his skin. She had scratched herself worse than this. From what she saw, Bobby's cracked elbow was worse.

"Herk got himself all bloodied. We was ridin' through the forest and tangled with low-hanging limbs." Dixon tugged the shirt free where it had stuck. "The same thing happened to me. The trees around these parts can be dangerous if you don't pay them the proper respect."

"Respect," she said bitterly. "You don't know the meaning of the word." She moved her chair around the table to get away from him. A cold stare kept him from moving his chair again to follow her.

"Now, my lovely dove, that's a cruel thing to say to a man who is head over heels in love with you."

"You robbed the bank. I told you to stay clear of town. Is that how your crony got shot up?"

"No, no, I meant it when I said Herk got injured in the forest."

"Nelson led a posse. Did you shoot it out with them? After you went and robbed the bank when I told you not to."

"They won't miss a few dollars." Dixon grinned broadly. "You ought to thank whoever stole that money. It was mostly Morrisey money."

She mulled that over. Having Leadbottom hurt like this was a good thing, but Dixon wasn't offering her any of the money. He didn't even fess up to robbing the bank. If she hadn't already known because one of her kin had been in town and reported straightaway, she knew Dixon wouldn't have mentioned the robbery at all.

"Herk and Squinty," she said. Seeing his surprise made her feel better. "They rode with you?"

"You surely do know a lot about my friends, don't you?" He stared at her coldly.

"Only because I'm so interested in you," she said in a sweet-as-sugar voice. She batted her eyes in his direction, then gave him a look as cold as the one he cast on her. "If you don't start doing as you're told, I'll find someone else to recruit the gang."

"Lil darlin'," he said, "there ain't nobody else who

can find enough killers to run that marshal out of town. He's a one-man army."

She saw how he touched his arm where the shirt sleeve had been torn. That told her more than Dixon intended. He had been in a shootout with Shadrach Nelson. He would have bragged on it if the marshal had been winged.

"When they arrive, it's got to be fast. I don't want the marshal having enough time to get lawmen in from Denver." She snorted in disgust. "I certainly don't want him bringing in 'Glory Be' Parsons. That man's a stone killer."

"And Nelson ain't? Sheriff Parsons will be occupied somewhere else when the time comes to bring in my 'friends.'"

"What are you planning?"

"You worry about keeping the Morrisey family up on the north side of the pass. I'll take care of everything else. There'll be all kinds of desperate crimes committed to keep the sheriff at home in Georgetown."

"Once the marshal is gone, it'll be necessary to root out Leadbottom and his family. Will you have enough gunmen to do that?"

"Of course I will. I've got plenty of money to recruit."

"I meant, will you have enough *left* after taking care of the marshal and his deputies."

"And his deputies?" Dixon laughed outright at that. "He's not got as many men at his back as he thinks."

"His son's dead." Beatrice closed her hand unconsciously, as if clutching her derringer and pulling the trigger again.

"I don't mean him."

"You want more money? Is that why you came up here?"

"No, no, I got enough for the time being. I wanted to see my lovely little mountain flower again." He reached out and grabbed her hand before she could pull back. "Even if you got coal dust under your fingernails, you're the purtiest filly I ever set eyes on."

"There'll be time for that afterward." Beatrice jerked hard. It took a second tug to pull free of Dixon's grasp.

"There'll be a rich kingdom up here to run," he said. "I hope you've got a place for me all picked out."

"Oh, Mister Dixon, I do," Beatrice said. She smiled.

He looked disconcerted for a moment, then laughed. They understood each other. He thought she would be easily removed once the town was freed from the rule of law. It had been run by outlaws before. It would be again.

And she knew Billy Dixon wasn't going to be in any position of power when the dust settled. She had that all worked out. The Coal Queen of the Rockies wasn't fooled by a man who thought he was as slick as butter. Not in the least.

CHAPTER NINE

Shadrach Nelson let his deputy walk away slowly. He watched until Shannon disappeared around a bend in the street. Only then did he feel the tensed muscles throughout his body relax. He almost collapsed with relief. There wasn't any way in hell now that he'd turn his back on Ian Shannon. The deputy had destroyed two years' worth of trust they'd built up with each other.

"You need a drink Shad."

He nodded. Leroy Early had been at his side for a long time. The two of them had rooted out the outlaw gangs that had plagued Utopia years back. He wished he trusted Shannon the way he did his other deputy.

He wished he *still* trusted Shannon.

"I finished off the pint bottle in the desk drawer."

"You don't have to tell me," Shad said. "I found the empty bottle a day or two back. Dammit, Leroy, you might have replaced it with a full one."

"Like this?" Early pulled open the bottom drawer with a screech. A quick move pulled out a full pint bottle of bourbon—or what passed for it in Utopia. Most of the swill sold in the saloons had never been within five hundred miles of Kentucky. That didn't stop him from appreciating the smooth flow of the whiskey down his gullet, even if it was most likely grain alcohol cut with rusty nails for color and a touch of something potent to give it the kick of a mule.

The deputy silently handed it to him. He pulled the cork out with his teeth and spat it out.

"Not planning on needing that again? Whatever's eatin' you must be terrible fierce."

Shad took a long pull and waited for it to slither down his gullet. When it reached his belly he almost doubled over. The liquor carried quite a wallop. He took another swig, smaller this time, but no less needed. The puddle of warmth in his belly spread and relaxed him. Not only were all the aches and pains erased, but it was easier for him to think about Ian Shannon without getting het up.

Early took the bottle and upended it.

"Not so much. Leave some for me."

"It's my bottle. I paid for it," the deputy said, but he lowered it and passed it back.

Shad sloshed the now half-full bottle around, watching the waves inside as they caught light and turned it into a small rainbow.

"I never asked but I think Ralph cuts it with nitric acid to give it more body."

"No need to find out. This is perfect the way it is." Shad took another hefty pull and set the bottle on the desk. He stared at it, catching his own reflection in the glass. He wasn't sure he liked what he saw.

"You're gettin' all suspicious in your old age. Is that it, Shad?"

He wanted to reach for the bottle again, but the quick drinks were already taking their toll. His knees turned wobbly. Vice required practice, and it had been some time since he'd had anything more than a beer to drink. And that had been with lunch. Ruth frowned on drinking in the house, and he respected that.

And drinking on the job was a good way to end up dead.

"What happened out there? When you caught up with the robbers?"

Shad spilled his concerns, then ended, "But he saved my life. He stood by me and gave me a chance to take cover and reload. I don't understand what's going on in Shannon's head."

"He's a complicated fellow. He don't talk much of his past, but he's been drifting for years. All his life, maybe. Utopia is the one place where he's stayed the longest."

"Because he's a deputy? Or does he like us? Me?"

"Now, Shad, that's something I am at a loss to say. I'd need to be one of them fancy mind readers in the circus. If I had that ability, I'd play poker more often 'n I do." Early shook his head sadly. "That tinhorn gambler fellow that was here in town 'fore you chased him away cleaned me out. Every last penny. That'll teach me to bluff when all I've got is a pair of deuces."

"I need to see if Sussman got a reply to my telegram down to Denver. If I was a betting man, I'd lay everything on Shannon never delivering Dixon to the lockup there."

"If I were a betting man with more than the price of a bottle of whiskey in my pocket, I'd bet with you."

Shad looked up. Early shared his suspicions about the other deputy. He wasn't sure if that surprised him.

"The bank robbery," Early supplied. "He stood across the street and watched it. He's not the sort to freeze up."

"I've seen him clear leather with both six-shooters. He's a crack shot with a gun in either hand. When he opens up with that pair of guns at the same time, he could back down an entire cavalry patrol."

"He let Dixon go—both times."

"Why'd he do a thing like that?"

Early took a small sip from the almost empty bottle. He stared at the finger left in the bottom. With just a hint of reluctance, he handed it to Shad.

The marshal wasn't too proud to finish the whiskey with a single gulp. By now the tarantula juice worked its magic on every muscle in his body. He felt almost normal.

"If Dixon had bought him off, why stay in town?" Shad's well-lubricated mind raced. A dozen "whys" came to haunt him. He didn't much like what any of them meant.

"Dixon doesn't seem to be in a hurry to leave Utopia," Early said. "Shannon might be waitin' to help him out when he tries something more than robbing the bank."

"He got away with a lot of money. Even split three ways amongst greedy cutthroats like Dixon and his two partners, that should have been enough for them to go on one hell of a bender. Not here. In Denver or Colorado Springs. If they caught a train south, they could be whooping it up in Santa Fe with purty señoritas on their arms."

"Dixon wasn't too happy when you ran him and the other two out of town. They were the last of the outlaw gangs who considered Utopia their very own hideout."

"That might be it," Shad said, "but I have the gut feeling that there's more to it."

"More than robbing the bank?"

"The train's carrying more gold from Georgetown and Blackhawk now. They might be eyeing a shipment."

Even as he spoke, Shad felt he was wrong. Or maybe he wasn't entirely right. He got to his feet, took a second to steady himself, and said, "I'm going to find out why Sussman hasn't heard back from Denver."

"Do you want to know, Shad? What if Shannon let Dixon go?"

"That's something I have to know. There're other ways of looking at it. Dixon might have escaped, and he's too embarrassed to tell me."

"If Shannon was ever embarrassed about anything in his life, he wouldn't start with that. He'd either track Dixon down with his last breath or he'd go to Denver and disappear. We'd never see him again."

Shad braced himself, then took a tentative step. He was steady enough to walk.

"Hold the fort. I'll be back when I find out if Sussman even sent my telegram."

"Don't get into any footraces." Early chuckled as

Shad bounced off one side of the door and rebounded from the other.

Shad started walking across town to the railroad depot. He sucked in the cold, thin air and felt the alcoholic fog blowing away from his mind. He felt a little queasy, but he'd put more than a half bottle into an empty stomach.

As he walked, he consciously touched his Peacemaker and tried to draw it a few times to get into the rhythm. By the time he climbed the steps to the railroad depot, he was sure he had burned off all the whiskey befuddling him and making his movements just a little clumsy.

"Sussman!" He saw the station agent in his cubbyhole, hunched over the telegraph key. The man looked up, saw Shad, and almost jumped out of his skin.

"What can I do for you, Marshal?"

"My telegram. The one I sent to the Federal Marshal in Denver. Has there been an answer?"

Shad wished he was in a poker game with the telegrapher. Sussman's mouth worked like a fish's as it flopped around on a riverbank. Whatever he said was going to be a lie.

"Too soon. You know how them lawmen in the big city are. Answering a 'gram from a Podunk town like Utopia isn't high on the—"

Shad looked past Sussman out into the freight yard.

"Send the same telegram." He glared at Sussman, then shifted his gaze back to the freight yard and the two people he saw between two large mounds of coal waiting to be loaded into the noon engine when it arrived from Denver.

"I, uh, well, you'll have to pay for it again."

Shad tossed the man a silver dollar. Sussman fumbled it but didn't drop it. Before he could say anything, Shad went out onto the platform and rubbed his eyes to be sure he wasn't seeing a booze-blurred vision of what he wanted to see.

He wasn't.

With a smooth motion, he drew his six-gun and went after Billy Dixon.

CHAPTER TEN

Shad Nelson tried to move quietly, but walking on the cinders covering the freight yard made that impossible. When he was within a dozen yards of Billy Dixon, he betrayed himself with a loud crunching sound.

Dixon spun. He pushed the woman with him away and went for his six-gun.

"Don't!" Shad's warning went unheeded. Dixon got off a quick shot at him.

The marshal returned fire, fanning off three quick rounds that sent Dixon scurrying away like a rat in a grain elevator. Shad ran forward, took another shot at Dixon as he worked around a mound of coal, and headed for a warehouse at the edge of the railroad tracks.

"Are you all right?" he asked. He wasn't surprised to see that the woman was Mary Beth Yarrow.

"Why are you shooting at me?" she asked, outraged.

"Dixon robbed the bank. I'm going to arrest him. Why were you talking to him?"

"I don't know a thing about that. He . . . he's been courting me."

"That's a bad choice, Miss Yarrow."

"You said that about your son and me. That's the difference, though. I wanted Abe. He loved me, and I loved him. Billy? He only wants one thing." She brushed her skirts to clean off soot gathered by simply walking through the rail yard. The mountains of coal provided a never-ending source of coal dust when the wind blew, as it did constantly through Hellfire Pass.

"Get on home." When she hesitated, he put a steel edge to his words. "Go back to the hotel, if that's where you're staying. You don't want to get arrested along with an owlhoot like Dixon."

"You wouldn't arrest me!" She saw his expression. "Oh" was all she said as she backed away, then dashed off.

Shad reloaded the spent rounds, took a deep breath and stalked off after Dixon. If the outlaw had a lick of sense, he'd run and keep running. From Dixon's brazen actions in the past week or so, Shad knew that wasn't going to happen. In a way he was glad, as much as he wanted to be rid of the man. Questions needed answers.

At the top of his mind was getting Dixon to tell him what happened when Shannon was escorting him to Denver. Never before had he wished for a deputy to be hoodwinked. Better that Shannon was careless and lost his prisoner than letting him go free.

Ahead loomed the water tower with its swinging spout. The engine pulled up and the water poured into its boiler. Immediately behind was a hill reached by a ramp. The bin atop the hill was filled with coal, then dumped down into the tender car for the rest of the trip downhill to Denver or Georgetown. He carefully looked at the dark recesses where Dixon might hide.

The scrabbling about inside the warehouse warned him that the outlaw had chosen to get lost inside the building, thinking he'd never be found amid all the crates and supplies shipped to and from Utopia.

Shad pushed the door open using his foot. Although darkness hid him if he stood in the doorway, any vagrant spark of light from the depot was all it'd take to outline him. The sounds from the warehouse told him Dixon plunged straight through, possibly hunting for a door on the far side.

He'd be disappointed. The only doors faced the railroad tracks. Loading and unloading was easier that way. The road in front of the warehouse was plenty good enough for wagons to cart supplies to the local merchants.

Moving slowly, he slithered around the doorjamb and pressed his back against the wall. The warehouse was as still as a graveyard. Dixon either had discovered there wasn't any escape and waited for a chance to ambush him, or he had found a way out. Digging a hole under the warehouse wall was one way to get free. If a dog or coyote already had burrowed in, Dixon wouldn't have much of a chore enlarging it.

The way the hair stood up on Shad's neck warned him that the outlaw was still inside and waited for him. Dixon had ambushed him once already when he and Shannon had skirted the forest. What didn't work then was better done now.

He advanced one step at a time, moving as silently

as any Ute warrior on the warpath. The rough wooden crates were stacked higher than his head. Shad craned his neck to see if any clue as to Dixon's whereabouts showed. A small movement. The thrust of a pistol barrel. Something dislodged and fell to the floor.

Nothing. He saw nothing. He edged along, using the rough wood crates to guide him deeper into the warehouse.

He found a stack of crates where several had been moved, forming a stair step to the top of the heap. The wood creaked under his weight as he worked his way up. He slowly rose to chance a quick peek at the tops of the other crates.

The bullet came close to taking his head off. Sudden pain along his forehead made him jerk away. The slug had torn through the brim of his brown bowler. He thrust his finger through and wiggled it around, then cursed. This had been a new hat only a few months before. Now it had a hole in the crown and this new one in the small brim.

He had come close to wearing the bowler to his grave. Another couple inches over and the slug would have plowed through his head. As it was, the shallow crease across his forehead bled freely. If he didn't stop the bleeding he'd be blind in another minute. Taking time he couldn't waste, he took off his bandanna and tied it around his head as tight as a cinch around a bucking bronc's belly.

"You still there, Marshal? I saw that hat of yours. Did I put a bullet through it, or did I put it through the hat *and* your head?"

Shad shifted around to face the direction of the voice. Dixon moved cautiously now. From the soft padding of feet coming toward him, Shad knew his chance to catch the robber was at hand.

He had one chance. He took it.

Popping up, he braced his pistol butt against the top of the crate. He swiveled back and forth, hunting for his target. Small movement, then a shadow that stopped moving. He fired. Shad was rewarded with a muzzle flash from Dixon's gun. The outlaw had fired into the crate and not at him.

In the brilliant flare, Shad saw Dixon double over and clutch his side. This was the perfect time for him to capture the outlaw. For all he had done, Shad felt exhilaration as he emptied his Peacemaker into the shadows.

"Dang, Marshal, you're a cold one. You wounded me something awful, and here you go tryin' to kill me."

Shad didn't believe that for an instant. Dixon's voice was too strong for him to be seriously wounded. He jumped down and circled the stack of crates where Dixon had been shot. A dark splotch on the top crate came away wet on his fingers when he touched it. Blood. He hadn't been wrong thinking Dixon was carrying an ounce of lead in his gut.

But it wasn't enough. The outlaw was still alive and kicking.

Moving faster, Shad found another stair step of crates to the top. He threw caution to the wind and crashed up. With a lunge he fell belly down and looked around for any trace of the outlaw. A dark shape moved near where he had initially shot at Dixon. The robber tried to overrun his position and use the elevation to fire downward. Shad had outfoxed him. Three more quick shots in Dixon's direction brought a new shriek of pain.

The shadowy figure threw up its hands and tumbled off the crates. Shad heard the thud as Dixon hit the floor. He got his feet under him and rushed forward until he towered over the moaning, struggling man on the floor. Shad cocked his six-shooter and pointed it at Dixon.

"You're under arrest. Or you can die here on the spot. What's your pleasure?"

"Don't shoot, Marshal. I dropped my gun."

Shad dropped down to sit on the edge of the crate. He kept his six-shooter pointed at his prisoner. Then everything changed in a flash.

Dixon had been lying on top of his gun. He rolled to the left and grabbed his pistol. Shad squeezed the trigger. His heart sank when he heard the hammer fall on an empty chamber. At the instant he heard the metallic click, he threw himself backward. Dixon's shot sailed past him.

"You're gonna die, Marshal. Here and now. You're out of ammo."

Shad somersaulted back and grabbed at his gun belt for more rounds. Only three were left. He knocked out the spent brass and reloaded, eyes on the edge of the crate. He expected Dixon to come after him right away.

With his Peacemaker only half loaded he took aim and waited. And waited. His heart hammered and he heard nothing but his own pulse in his ears.

"Dixon? Come on. You're not turning chicken, are you?" Goading the outlaw didn't work. Shad rolled to the side, reached the edge of the crates, and dropped to the floor.

All too aware he had only three rounds left, he began stalking his foe.

Shad spun around the edge of the crates where Dixon had fallen. Only a dark puddle on the floor remained. He dipped a finger into it and sniffed.

"You're hurt worse than you think, Dixon. You're bleeding like a stuck pig. Give up and I'll get you to the doctor. He can patch you up."

Nothing moved in the warehouse. Then a loud noise echoed through the warehouse. Cursing, he ran toward the door where he'd entered. The door banged open and shut in the rising wind. He kicked it open, raced through, and swung his gun from one side of the freight yard to the other.

Dixon had disappeared.

A bright flash of lightning over the distant mountain lit the mounds of coal. For a brief instant, a man standing atop one mocked him. He got off a shot. Another lightning bolt showed only an empty heap of coal. He'd either missed or shot at a ghost.

Knowing the danger of carrying a pistol with only two rounds, he prowled the freight yard for twenty minutes. Billy Dixon was gone. The only satisfaction Shad took in the extended fight was the amount of blood from the outlaw's wound. He was in serious shape.

"Maybe you'll die," he grumbled. But he knew his luck wasn't running that well tonight. With fitful rain spattering down on him, he tromped back to the jailhouse.

CHAPTER ELEVEN

"My cousin'd want me to shoot you," Bobby Jones said. He ran his fingers up and down the front grip on his rifle, as if thinking how good it'd feel to draw a bead and end this miserable galoot's life.

"Now, you got that wrong, boy. Plumb wrong," Billy Dixon said. He bent over a little more and vented a loud moan. "She's sweet on me. You can see that. Killin' me would put you in dutch with her."

"Bea told me to stop anybody on this road. This ain't the one you came up before."

"Came from the freight yard this time. I got shot there." Dixon moved his hand away from his side to show the bloody wound. "Bea'd surely want to hear all about it since it was her favorite marshal what almost done me in."

"Marshal Nelson done that?" Bobby scratched his chin, then gripped the rifle with both hands again. "I heard folks 'round town talkin' 'bout him. He don't wound men. He kills 'em."

"I'm too cussed to die."

"You do look like you're fixin' to kick the bucket.

That's more blood 'n I ever seen, 'cept maybe when Uncle Harry got his hand cut off by one of the ore carts. He was on hands and knees and reached out just as Kenny pushed a loaded cart out. I swear that hand of his went flyin' and he gushed blood for close to a minute before dyin'. That was in the third mine we opened up. We closed it right after, but it weren't on account of Uncle Harry. The vein played out fast."

"How nice. Get me to Bea so she can patch me up." Dixon rested his bloodied hand on the butt of his six-gun. The world spun around him. For the first time since he had found the trail up the Gallaghers' mountain to their coal mine he felt downright puny. The pain was so bad he couldn't tell if the bullet had passed through him or was still inside. Either way, he had to have someone tend to him before he passed out.

He sat on a rock beside the road and waited. Bobby shuffled his feet.

Dixon wobbled and caught himself at the last instant. He had been strong getting this far. Now all energy left him. He had to make one final appeal or cash in his chips for good.

"Tell my lil darlin' I'll miss her."

"You mean Bea?"

Dixon tried to answer, but the wave of black swept over him.

"It wasn't worth the effort," Beatrice Gallagher said.

"I thought you wanted him, Cousin Bea. I did. I'm sorry if you didn't. I can dump him down a mine shaft."

"You did right, Bobby. He's still useful."

"Danged right I am." Dixon tried to sit up, but the pain in his side prevented it.

"I've taped you up. If you move around too much you'll pop open the stitches."

"Wouldn't want to bleed on your fancy sheets." He ran his fingers over the sleek cloth under him.

"I'd have to take it out of your hide," Beatrice said. "Or you can just tell me where you stashed the loot from the bank robbery."

"I'm woozy, not stupid." Dixon laughed at that. It hurt.

"If you let Shadrach Nelson put a slug in you, that's downright stupid. I told you not to show your face in town."

"Where am I? Everything's so dark. You got a dozen kerosene lamps that I can see and it's still dark."

"You're underground, Mister Dixon," Bobby said. "This here's our main livin' quarters."

"In an old mine?"

"It played out," Beatrice said, "and it was too big, too good, to walk away from. I brought the whole family down here so we can be together."

"Aunt Winifred's the one what made us all come."

"Bobby," Beatrice said sharply. "Get back to the trail. You did good intercepting this one."

"I couldn't let a wounded man get past me. That'd be awful."

Beatrice spoke softly to him for a moment, then he left whistling a jaunty tune.

"All he needs is some encouragement. He's still young." She turned and dropped onto the bed beside

Dixon. The bounce made him wince. "What's wrong?" she asked. "This pain's the price you get for not following my orders."

"We're partners. I don't work for you."

"You might want to think some on that if you want to leave this mine shaft any other way than in a coffin."

Dixon looked at her sharply. "You're not fooling me, lil darlin'. You wouldn't carry me out in a coffin. You'd just find an abandoned stope and leave me there to rot."

"Folks don't rot underground. They mummify like the Egyptians." Beatrice saw he had no idea what she meant. Her eyes darted to a wood plank along the back wall where she stacked a dozen books. Some of them had been shipped in from as far off as St. Louis.

"Why don't you stretch out on this fine bed alongside me? I can do with some company while I recuperate."

Beatrice pushed his hand aside when he reached for her.

"You can't stay here. It makes the rest of the family edgy having an outsider here."

"You're breakin' my heart, lil darlin'. But I need to get into town to find my partners."

"Squinty and Herk?"

"There's not a whole lot you don't know, is there?"

"Be out of here before sunrise. I'll send Bobby to show you which tunnel to use."

"I'll need help figurin' out when sunrise is all cooped up underground."

Beatrice swirled about in her skirts and flounced off. She'd had about all she could stand of his lip. The sooner the black train arrived, the better.

* * *

"You didn't give him a horse, did you?" Beatrice fixed her coldest stare on Bobby Jones.

"You said not to. He lit out on foot."

"Describe how he left."

"I don't follow you, Cousin Bea. Oh, how was he gettin' on? He wasn't limpin' or anything like that. He walked real careful-like, but you'd never know he'd been shot. You fixed him up real good."

"I should be a doctor," she said dryly. "He'd lost a fair amount of blood, but the gunshot wound wasn't too serious. It went through his side and didn't even break a rib."

"Can I go with you? I can fetch my horse and—"

"I'm riding alone today, Bobby. Get on back to your post and keep an eye peeled for trouble."

"You expectin' the marshal and his deputies to come chargin' up here?"

"Something like that," she said, not expecting Shadrach Nelson to knock on her door at all. Keeping her cousin occupied with what he thought was an important job kept him alert for the time being. When the fighting started, she wanted him close by. She didn't have eyes in the back of her head. Dixon and the rest of his gang wouldn't stop at killing until all the Gallaghers were gone. Her plans had to come together before that assault started.

She rode slowly down the slope and reached the main road into Utopia. Dixon had come this way a couple hours ahead of her. On foot and walking gingerly, he'd be about to the edge of town. He said he wanted to palaver with his two partners. Beatrice wanted to find them, too. The trio had plenty of money stolen from the bank.

Some of it, a very small amount, belonged to the Gallagher family. Mostly she had kept the money from the coal sales safe by burying it all over the mountainside, just as her Aunt Winnie had. Trusting banks was foolish. It surprised her that Leadbottom thought it was a good idea to put all the money from the recent sale of the lead ingots into the bank.

Dixon skirted the rail yard and took a more devious route through town. She was glad he hadn't tried to go down the main street. Following him through the zigzags would have been tedious. To her surprise he seemed to be heading for the bank.

She had to laugh at the notion that Dixon had robbed the bank and then turned around and deposited the loot in that same bank for safekeeping. Not even the cocky outlaw would be that arrogant—or stupid.

She drew rein and watched as Dixon kept to the far side of the street and moved through shadows to hide his face. He walked faster once past the bank and headed directly for the hotel. Beatrice cursed under her breath. She had hoped he would make a beeline for Herk and Squinty. If he had, stealing the money they'd taken from the bank would have been child's play. They'd never have suspected her of coming after them and their loot.

But this?

Beatrice circled the block and came up on the hotel

from the eastern side. She slid from the saddle and walked to the back door. It was locked, but she rattled it enough to make the latch come loose. Beatrice slipped into the hallway leading to the lobby.

She stopped at the first partly closed door when she heard Dixon. Her temper rose when she made out the words.

" . . . but lil darlin', you know you're the only one. You're the gold in my mine. You're the biggest, grandest nugget I ever did find!"

Beatrice pushed the door open a few more inches. Dixon stood with his back to her. Looking away at the far side of the room, Mary Beth Yarrow shook her head vigorously.

"I don't want anything to do with you, Billy. I've been warned!"

"Warned! What low-down, no-account snake in the grass'd ever warn you away from me? You just spit out the name!"

"The marshal. He said you're an outlaw. You robbed the bank."

"Shad Nelson. I might have known. He's had it in for me since our paths crossed. I showed him up, and he hates me for it."

"Is there a reward on your head?"

Dixon snorted in contempt. He stepped up and grabbed Mary Beth's arms. She struggled to get away, but he was too strong. With a quick spin he whirled her around and took her in his arms. Their faces were inches apart.

"Look into my eyes. I'm tellin' the Gospel truth.

There ain't a reward on my head. I'm a law abidin' gent. It's Shad Nelson that's the liar. He ought to be locked up in that jail instead of puttin' honest men behind bars."

"It . . . it's not true? Any of it?"

"Lil darlin', you can trust me when I say I'd give my life for you. You're the only thing I think about lyin' out under the stars, starin' up at the sky. It's so lonely out on the trail, but your beauty keeps me from gettin' too down in the mouth. Thinkin' of your beauty keeps me warm all night long."

"Really?"

He kissed her. She struggled in the circle of his arms, then melted slowly. They broke off the kiss.

"That's what I need. The memory of those lips'll keep me warm all night long, and the nights are gettin' cold now. What say you do a mite more to warm these bones and—"

"Billy, no." Mary Beth pushed him away. "I've got to get to work at Mister Sampson's. He'll raise Cain if I don't show up on time. You know how he is."

"I've heard rumors," Dixon said. "Just one little peck on the cheek to keep me goin'?"

Mary Beth bobbed forward like a chicken going after grain and disengaged from him.

"You're my lil darlin', lil darlin'. Don't you forget it."

"Billy, meet me tonight? Six o'clock out by Standing Rock?"

"I'll count the seconds." He tried to kiss her again, but she dodged away.

Beatrice opened the door to a storage closet across

the hall and ducked into it. Through a crack she saw Mary Beth head for the lobby. Billy Dixon whistled a jaunty tune as he left through the back door.

When they were both gone, Beatrice stepped out. She looked toward the lobby, then followed Dixon out the back door. By the time she went into the alley, he had vanished. Hurrying now, she took her horse's reins and stepped up. A quick snap of the reins got the horse trotting down the zigzagging main street.

Two turns brought Mary Beth Yarrow into view. The woman hurried along, looking distraught. It quickly became apparent where Dixon went. The jailhouse was around the corner. She had arranged to meet Dixon later that evening.

"Tell the marshal, get a reward, and get rid of Dixon." Beatrice's lips thinned into a razor's slash as her ire built. The other woman must think of herself as a Nelson because she and Abe Nelson had been sparking.

Beatrice put her heels to the horse's flanks and cantered around the corner. Mary Beth was a dozen yards from the jailhouse.

"Wait!" Beatrice called out. "Mary Beth, I need to talk to you."

"You're Beatrice Gallagher. Whatever do you have to say to me?"

"Goodbye, lil darlin'," Beatrice said. Her derringer spat out both barrels. The first bullet struck Mary Beth in the chest. The second tore through her head.

CHAPTER TWELVE

"This won't look too good when word gets around," Leroy Early said, staring at the woman's body.

Shad had to agree. Mary Beth Yarrow was gunned down less than ten yards from the marshal's office. He and Shannon had been elsewhere in town, leaving the office empty. Early had discovered the body when he came in for the night patrol duty. People shot anywhere in town was a tragedy. Having a young woman murdered on the marshal's doorstep was something gossip would feast on for weeks. It'd be even worse if he never found the killer of the woman his son had been sweet on.

"From the look of it, someone on a horse shot her." Shad tried to figure out how tall the killer was. The question is why. "This wasn't an accidental shooting."

"Not with two rounds in her."

"She doesn't look to have been robbed. That necklace is one Abe gave her. It's not worth much, but it's gold and glittery." Shad saw reason to believe Mary Beth Yarrow hadn't worn any other jewelry. That would have gotten in the way of her cleaning chores.

Early gently tugged back Mary Beth's shawl. "The

first shot probably hit her in the chest and knocked her to the ground. The second shot to her head was meant to be sure she was dead."

Shad looked at the angles of the entry wounds. Again his deputy had come to a conclusion that fit the facts.

"Why was she killed? She wasn't robbed." He kept returning to that. Utopia wasn't the kind of town for such cold-blooded crimes. Killings here were done in the heat of passion or because too much liquor had been consumed.

Shad picked up a small clutch purse and opened it. "There's no money inside, but she wasn't rolling in the greenbacks."

"What aren't you telling me, Shad?"

"Why do you think I know more 'n you about this?" He felt a twinge of guilt that he had been responsible for the woman's death.

"Don't play poker with me, Shad. No, let me say that you *should* play poker with me. I need the money. You look downright shamefaced about something. You didn't shoot her."

"Thanks for that."

"It's not your style. But you caused her death in some way."

"I told her to tell me if Billy Dixon met with her. He must have. She was on her way to the office, and he figured out she was going to turn him in." Shad made a gun out of his thumb and trigger finger and mouthed "bang!"

"It's time to ask around if anyone saw him. On horseback. Riders don't get much attention, even a bank-robbing, murderous crook like Billy Dixon."

"I'll see that Martin Donovan's notified." Shad sucked in a deep breath and let it out in a gust. "Reckon I'll see to the funeral. I owe it to her. Abe owes it to her."

Leroy Early left to begin asking shopkeepers along the street if they'd seen anything. Gunshots during the day weren't unusual. A couple quick rounds fired hardly drew attention unless the bullets were aimed at them or their stores.

After Shad talked with the undertaker and made arrangements for the woman to be buried near his son, he went directly to the hotel. Netty Michaelson looked up from her ledger behind the clerk's desk. From her scowl she wasn't having a good day.

"What can I do for you, Marshal?"

"When was the last time you saw Miss Yarrow?"

"A couple hours back. If you see her before I do, tell her she's fired. She was supposed to be at this very desk. I won't tolerate anyone not being at work when she's supposed to, especially not even giving me a whisper of warning."

"You don't have to fire her," Shad said. "Somebody beat you to it."

"What's that mean?"

Shad gave the hotel manager the news.

"That doubles the time I have to spend here until I hire another desk clerk." The hotel manager made an ugly face and looked as if she wanted to spit.

"Yeah, too bad," Shad said dryly. "Did you ever see her with Billy Dixon?"

"That snake?" Netty Michaelson shook her head. "I never saw her with any man other 'n your boy. I had to chase him off too many times. He was affecting her work. Even after he was gone, she'd moon around here and slack off on her chores."

"If you see Dixon, let me know. There's a reward on his head."

"How much?"

Considering how his advice had turned on Mary Beth Yarrow, Shad hoped the same might be true with the hotel manager. He left before he said something he'd regret. Netty was the center of most gossip in town, or so it seemed. To find out more, he'd have to check with his wife and daughter since no one else was going to tell him flop.

Shad checked the places where Dixon might have been seen and came up empty-handed. He returned to the jailhouse as Early came in.

"I got nothing, Shad. Nobody noticed a rider—"

"That's a surprise," he said with more than a little resignation.

"More 'n that, nobody heard a gunshot. You want to ask around again? The saloons are filling up for the night's drinking."

"Keep your ear to the ground. Otherwise, don't go out of your way. I think we've hit a dead end on this."

"Did she have any family to tell?"

Shad shook his head. He and Abe had never seen eye to eye about the woman. He was sorry now they hadn't been able to talk more. As much as he felt guilty about scaring her into coming to him if she talked with Dixon, he was getting a gut feeling the outlaw wasn't responsible. Throughout his queries, he had asked about Dixon.

No one had spotted him. Considering the rows the cutthroat had been involved in before he got run out of town, he was known to most everyone.

After pursuing down the gang that had robbed the bank, townsfolk knew Dixon was worth more for the reward than he was as a drinking chum.

When he'd come back and Shad had sent him and Shannon to Denver, it had been the talk of the town. Everyone knew Dixon. And no one had seen him.

"Get on home, Shad. You weren't responsible, so don't blame yourself."

Shad left Early in charge of watching over Utopia. He walked slowly to his house. His daughter sat on the porch.

"Ma didn't hold supper for you. There might be something left over," Miriam said.

"It's all right. I'm not hungry."

"I heard about Mary Beth."

Shad stared at her. "You are a wonder. You must have the ears of a jackrabbit to hear all you do up here about things happening in town."

He settled into a chair next to his daughter. He stared down at Utopia. The town was lit up with kerosene lamps in about every window. If the town continued to grow, there'd be gas lamps along the streets eventually. That was something only big cities did. Or it used to be only big towns. He wasn't sure he wanted to see Utopia grow that much, but with the railroad coming through to the gold and silver mines on the western slopes and the coal mine feeding that travel, there wasn't much chance of local growth slowing down.

Boomtowns came and went. They grew like weeds when a strike was announced and blew away like a thistle in a wind when the precious metal played out. But coal? The railroad would need that to power its engines forever.

"I reckon the whole danged mountain is filled with coal," he said.

"Pa, at times I think you're losing your mind. What's that got to do with Mary Beth being shot?"

He thought for a moment, then said, "I'm not sure. It's just the way my mind works."

"Wanders," Miriam corrected.

"You heard that I told the undertaker to bury her near Abe?"

"My brother'd approve. He was going to marry her."

"Like you married Williamson," he said. "Have you heard from him lately?"

"I get a letter every time the mail comes. The stage is only showing up once a week now. It costs more to send the letter on the train, but I've been telling Rich he needs to pay the extra. That way I can get his letter within a day or two and not a week." She patted her belly. "I'm keeping him up-to-date about our daughter."

"Son," Shad corrected automatically.

"We've been arguing over what to call her—him."

"Don't tell me. Wait for the first squall before saddling the boy—child—with a moniker."

Shad found himself relaxing as he talked with his daughter. It had been too long since he had found such peace and even hope for the future. He finally went into the house, oblivious to anything happening in town.

The relief felt good, but he knew it would go away soon.

Beatrice Gallagher sank down between the two rocks as she waited. The distant sounds she had grown up with in the mountains comforted her. Then, slowly, the sounds of nocturnal animals hunting and being hunted died down until an eerie silence settled on the land. She gripped her derringer a little tighter, then forced herself to relax.

"You there, lil darlin'? You come on out. I saw your horse. I know you're hidin' here somewhere." Billy Dixon walked past her. She had an easy shot, if she wanted to take it. But caution dictated otherwise. She hadn't thought he would scout the area first, yet he had if he found her horse.

He was cautious but also eager for his assignation with Mary Beth Yarrow.

Beatrice stood. The sound of her skirts rubbing against rock alerted Dixon. He spun around and held out his arms, ready for a passionate embrace. The expression on his face when he realized the wrong woman had come to meet him was precious. Beatrice wished she'd had a photograph of it to hang up in the coal mine to remind her never to trust anyone ever.

"What are you doin' here?"

"Why, you were asking after your lil darlin'. Here

I am. Or were you expecting someone else? Another 'lil darlin'?"

"No, no, there's only you, Bea, my love. You've got no call questionin' my love for you."

"You are such a liar." She moved away from the rocks and made sure the derringer was ready. Behind Dixon rose the Standing Rock that gave the place its name. She saw not the rock but a giant finger pointing to him as her target. The urge to cut him down surged in her again.

"That's not what I want to hear from those lovely lips."

"She's dead, Billy."

This expression topped even the one before.

"What do you mean?"

"Someone put a couple slugs in her as she made her way to the marshal's office. That kept her from telling Shadrach Nelson about this meeting place, right about now."

"She sold me out!"

"She would have. It's all taken care of now. She's not going to collect a reward for betraying you."

"You shot her?"

Beatrice twisted from side to side, acting coy.

"Lil ole me? Would your real lil darlin' do such a thing?" Before he had a chance to answer, she added, "Cross me again and I'll give my family the all clear to drop you down a really deep petered-out shaft in the mines. I've heard that a man with broke legs might last for a week if he licks water off the walls. After a day or two you don't even mind having a black tongue."

She sauntered closer, moved a step past, and swished her skirts around his feet. Beatrice looked over her shoulder in a come-hither fashion. She batted her eyes at him. Seeing him turn pale was worth the effort.

"But the pain might cause an earlier death. If it doesn't, starvation sets in after a week. Even eating raw rats can't give enough food for a big, strapping man." She brushed her left hand over his chest. "A big, strapping man like you."

He grabbed her wrist and twisted. Their faces were inches apart.

"You will do as I say from now on," she said, ignoring his action. "It was stupid to rob the bank, but you'd better use that money to recruit your gang."

"You're in no position to tell me what to do." He tightened the grip on her slender wrist and lifted. Then he gasped.

"I've got two shots. I can blow both of them off, one at a time." She shoved her derringer hard into his crotch. "Then you wouldn't be good for anybody."

Beatrice pulled free and stepped back. She held the double-barreled pistol away from where Dixon had any chance to bat it from her hand.

"Fifty men," she said. "That should be plenty."

"I'll need a lot more money to recruit that many cutthroats."

"You've got the money I already gave you. And the bank money."

"Lil darlin', you drive a hard bargain."

"Yes, 'lil darlin' does." She motioned for him to clear out. He started to say something about being dismissed like this, then reconsidered. The derringer still pointed between his legs. He grinned wickedly, but failed to pull off any menace.

Beatrice watched him go. Being a cad in love wasn't the only way Billy Dixon would try to cheat her. She had to be ready for him when he double-crossed her.

When he *tried* to double-cross her. She'd show him what it meant to get crosswise with the Gallaghers.

CHAPTER THIRTEEN

"Do you feel it, Leroy? It's like an hour before a storm." Shad stared down the empty street.

"Cat walkin' on your grave again? You'll find all the trouble you can handle if you go lookin' for it." Leroy Early wiped the last of the excess gun oil from the trigger mechanism of his Smith & Wesson, then reassembled the gun. He balanced it in his hand. "This is all you need to handle any problem you'll find in Utopia."

A quick move returned the well-tended six-gun to his holster.

"I can't say what it is I'm feeling. Things look all right, but they aren't."

"We've hunted high and low for Billy Dixon. He's nowhere to be found."

"That's got me worried more 'n I care to admit. What are the odds of him hightailing it from town? He won't stray far until he's finished with whatever he's planning, and it's not robbing the bank again." Shad clenched his fist and lightly banged it against the doorframe. Frustration welled up. Dixon was out there. So was trouble.

"All we can do is keep askin' folks if they've seen him. He'd be a danged fool stickin' around town after robbin' the bank. Banker Reese has hired a few lay-abouts to annoy his customers, pretendin' to be guards. They won't do squat keepin' a real *ladron* at bay." Early got to his feet and pushed past the marshal. "Time for me to do some prowlin'. Why don't you get on home?"

"I have been keeping Ruth happy showing up for dinner three nights in a row."

"Maybe that's why you're all jumpy. You're worried about disappointin' her if you break that string."

"Things are better," Shad said. "In fact—"

Gunfire interrupted his thought. He touched the butt of his Peacemaker and said, "I'll come along, just to be sure."

"There's only one shot. I can handle that."

A second shot made Early out to be a liar. He shrugged and waited for the marshal to step out of the jailhouse door so he could follow. The pair of lawmen hurried down the main street, looking left and right as they made their way toward a saloon where the fight inside had already spilled into the street.

"Looks like we got Morrisey problems tonight," Early said. "That's one of the newcomers. Leadbottom put out the call all through Colorado for kith and kin to come work in his mine. They're comin' in like rats to cheese."

"They don't show any better sense than the ones who've been working the mines for years," Shad said. He grabbed one man by the collar and yanked him around. Early took care of the man flat on his back.

"You got a snootful of booze?" Shad asked, shaking the man hard. The man didn't have to answer. What beer he hadn't spilled down his shirt had ended up as foam in his beard.

Shad spun him around and shoved him to a chair on the boardwalk.

"You set yourself down there and don't move."

"You got some nerve, Marshal High 'n Mighty," the man slurred. "Who gives you the right to tell a Morrisey what to do?"

He tried to stand. Shad kicked the chair out from under him. The man crashed to the boardwalk and sprawled on his back, staring up with glassy eyes.

"Neither of 'em has a gun, Shad."

He looked into the saloon. That meant that corralling the shooter still had to be done. He made sure his six-shooter rode easy and pushed through the swinging doors. A quick look around told the story. Most of the customers pressed against the walls. Two men in the middle of the saloon faced each other, six-shooters drawn. They waved their irons around wildly but weren't shooting.

Again.

"Shad, be careful," Early warned.

"You, Morrisey," Shad called at the top of his lungs. "You put down that gun right now."

Both men obeyed, then looked at each other in drunken confusion. They turned back to face the marshal. By then he had come within reach of the first one. Shad drew his gun and swung hard. The barrel landed on the first man's forehead. The loud crack of steel against bone sounded like a gunshot.

The second man stared dumbfounded at his relative. A quick move landed the Peacemaker across the back of the man's neck. He went down, too.

"Any other Morriseys in here wanting to cause trouble?" Shad looked around, expecting to see others step forward. A glance over his shoulder showed why. If there were any lead miners here, they stood stock-still. Leroy Early had his well-oiled S&W out and cocked. The way he looked, he was ready to cut down any man foolishly taking up the marshal's challenge.

"Barkeep," he called. "Have these miscreants done any damage?"

"Naw, Marshal, they only put a couple holes in the ceiling. Don't amount to a hill of beans." The bartender cleared his throat and said in a lower voice, "If anything, the rest of my customers have been enjoyin' the show. Saves on me needin' a piano player to keep 'em dancin' around."

"I'll stack them on your doorstep. It's up to you if you let them back inside."

Shad and Early dragged the two unconscious men outside and piled them atop the other two.

"You fixing on throwing my boys in jail?"

"Good evening, Leadbottom. I haven't seen you in town recently. Where've you been keeping yourself?"

"You know the answer to that, Marshal. I been sending my boys out hunting for the skunks that robbed the bank."

"Do tell." Shad motioned for Early to holster his pistol. Leadbottom Morrisey filled up half the street, or so it seemed. Five more of his family were spread out around him as guards. They were armed with axe handles and shotguns.

"You aren't doing anything to catch the robbers. Most all of my money was in that bank. Whoever robbed the bank robbed the Morrisey family. They robbed *me*."

"I've only got two deputies, Leadbottom. And I rustled up a posse and went after the crooks right after they stole the money."

"My money, Marshal, that was my money."

"I didn't think you trusted banks."

"I came to you before when somebody broke into my cabin and stole my money. You didn't catch that thief, either."

Shad had his suspicions about that. Leadbottom's son Patrick had been the likely thief. He'd stolen the money to pay off a blackmailer.

"I haven't seen hide nor hair of Patrick, either. Are you keeping him hard at work in the mines?"

"He's out with the others tracking down the bank robbers. He's the only one I trust."

"It's good to have family, Leadbottom. But I don't cotton to vigilantes. You rein in your boy. Tend to mining lead up on the mountainside, and we'll all be happier."

"Why should I sell my lead when the money I get from it'll be stole?"

"Those your kin?" Shad jerked his thumb over his shoulder at the four lying unconscious on the boardwalk. "They're going to wake up soon enough with powerful headaches. Get 'em on home or they might have more serious problems." He rested his hand on his six-gun to emphasize the point.

"It was the Gallaghers."

"What's that?" The sudden change of subject took Shad by surprise.

"They stole my money. They're responsible for robbing the bank. Ever since Winifred upped and got herself shot, they've been downright sneaky in everything they do. Don't trust that Beatrice Gallagher. I don't for one teeny second."

"I haven't got an ounce of proof any Gallagher robbed the bank." He started to say that he did know but couldn't find Dixon, Herk, and Squinty, then held back. Naming the robbers only set Leadbottom on a path to vengeance.

"They was peace-loving, neighborly folks until Winifred died. Trouble's brewing with that witch Beatrice leadin' them."

Shad blinked in disbelief. The feud between the two families went back to when Utopia was hardly more than a widening in the trail through Hellfire Pass pioneered by Zeb Pike himself back in the day. Leadbottom and Winifred had never spoken in a civil tongue about each other that he remembered. The head of the Gallagher family being gunned down had softened Leadbottom's memory of her.

Or maybe it was closer to say that Leadbottom's brain was softening.

He wondered if stirring the pot would set off a bloody war. Beatrice Gallagher had been free and easy with the use of her derringer. Shad suspected, although he couldn't prove it, that she had killed her aunt to take control of the family and the lucrative coal mine. Beatrice insisted to any who would listen that Shad had pulled the trigger, but her loud denunciations only made him all the more certain she had killed her own relative.

"You're welcome in town as long as you and your boys don't get too rowdy," he said. "And keep the guns holstered. I don't want to get the mayor to declare an ordinance about checking guns at the city limits."

Such a law would increase his headaches enforcing the peace tenfold. More. Even normally peaceable cowboys would rail against it and create a ruckus.

"We ain't ever that way. We're law-abiding folks."

Shad cleared his throat to keep from laughing. Only this was never a laughing matter. The Morrisey clan were as bad a shot as they were drunks. Over the years, more than one citizen of the town had been injured by wayward flying bullets. Luckily the only ones who had died were either Gallaghers or Morriseys during these drunken rampages.

"Get them out of here," Shad said, looking at the stirring pile of drunks behind him. It reminded him of turning over a rock and watching rattlers unfold.

Leadbottom growled. The ones with him who were sober enough to obey went to help their relatives. After they'd staggered away down the street, Shad said to Early, "How long do you think this is going to last? This standoff between me and Leadbottom?"

"You should have sent the lot of them back up the hill to their homes."

"I can't believe Leadbottom said all the things he did.

It sounded as if he and Winifred Gallagher were the best of buddies."

"Shad? Listen!"

"They didn't get far, did they?"

"Only down the street to the next gin mill." Early checked his pistol as he walked in the direction of the gunfire. It was going to be one of those nights.

Shad trailed Early, wary of ambushes. Ever since Dixon and his partners tried to shoot him out along the road to Denver, he had been wary of dark spaces and strange sounds.

As he rounded a corner in the road, he saw a half dozen of Leadbottom's family across the street from the Hard Times Saloon. They fired steadily into the building. Part of the wall already turned into dust. No woodpecker ever had such luck ruining a piece of wood.

Light shined through dozens of holes. Shad doubted all of the holes were newly drilled, but the Morriseys added a fair number even as he came up.

"Leadbottom, stop them right now!" He fired his Peacemaker into the air to get their attention.

That was a mistake. They turned their six-shooters on him. The momentary pause in the fusillade gave him warning enough to dive for cover. He wiggled like a snake to get behind a watering trough. For a few seconds the water shielded him from the gunfire. Then too many holes were blasted through the wood and it drained. Lead drilled right on through both sides, forcing him to burrow down in the muck.

"Leadbottom! I warned you!" He poked his head

around. Only one of the miners showed himself. A quick shot brought a yelp of pain.

"I been hit, Pa! I been hit! I'm dyin'!"

Shad doubted that. The man's voice was too strong. At best he had been grazed. Waiting while bullets bored through the empty trough proved hard. Shad wanted to drive them back, but to expose himself now meant his life.

"Got one, Shad," came Early's call from across the street. His deputy had taken refuge in an alleyway.

"There, get him!" Shad cried. He hated directing the deadly attention toward his deputy, but the tactic worked. Those that had pinned him down shifted their aim toward Early.

Shad was glad to see his deputy had the good sense to retreat down the alley. Having the entire building between him and the deadly gunfire was barely enough.

Digging his toes into the mud, Shad launched himself forward. Before the Morriseys caught sight of him attacking, he vaulted over one of them and pointed his six-gun at Leadbottom's head.

"I warned you to get out of town. Call them off or I swear I'll blow your pea-sized brain out."

"You got a half dozen guns pointed at you, Marshal. You sure you want to make threats like that?"

"My dying gasp will be to curse you, Leadbottom. And with my finger on the trigger, any jerk back will send you to the Promised Land." He paused. "More likely, you'll be going the other way."

"You won't catch them bank robbers what took my money but you will stop my boys from havin' fun."

"Three," Shad said. Leadbottom stared up at him. "Two . . ."

"Men, clear out."

"But Pa," complained one across the street near the saloon doors, "Harry said them robbers was in there spendin' our money!"

"One," Shad said.

"I told them to leave," Leadbottom said peevishly. "What more do you want me to do?"

Shad fired.

Leadbottom jumped a foot. For a man of his girth it was a respectable distance. He threw up his hands and turned pale under the layers of dirt caking his face.

"Get outta town, *now!*"

This produced the result Shad wanted. The miners all began creeping away like whipped dogs.

"You might be the Gallaghers' hired gun, Nelson, but you're not gonna make me cower in fear."

Shad saw that Leadbottom had pissed his pants. He motioned with his gun. This time Leadbottom rounded up his family and herded them down the main street.

"Anybody hurt inside, Leroy?" he called when he saw his deputy looking around inside the saloon.

"Some of them never noticed anything goin' on 'round them."

"I never knew the Hard Times served such potent hoochinoo."

"These boys have just been at it most of the day."

"The excitement's over, Leroy. I'm going home to take a bath."

"It's not Saturday night, Shad."

"I need to get the gunsmoke smell off before Ruth'll let me in the house."

"Smart woman. I can hold the fort till morning. You just be here on time to relieve me. You and Shannon."

Shadrach Nelson could make that promise for himself. He wasn't sure about his other deputy.

CHAPTER FOURTEEN

"There's no need to be so jumpy, Miss Gallagher. The coal doesn't bruise one little bit when we dump it."

Beatrice Gallagher glared at the station master. Sussman had such a condescending air about him she wanted to push him into the bin and let him be loaded under the ton of coal going into the steam engine's tender. It'd serve him right.

"I've got six carloads of coal going to Denver," she said. "Have you cleared the right of way? I don't want to have my train collide head-on with one coming uphill."

"That's never happened in all the years I've been runnin' this here depot," Sussman said primly. He looked as if he had bitten into a bitter persimmon.

"It has," she said and began reciting the day and outcome for each of the collisions. "All were caused by the depot master's error."

"Not me. Not a one of them was my doin'. Those wrecks are scattered all over Colorado, some as far south as Durango. I know my business. If you'll excuse me, so you'll stop distracting me, I'll get on with it." He turned and walked away. She expected him to spit since he was so mad.

Beatrice had no interest in the man's state of mind as long as he did his job. She knew he had been engaged with the previous freight yard owner to defraud not only the railroad but her Aunt Winifred. For whatever reason, the marshal had put a couple slugs through the freight yard owner and left Sussman in his job.

She thought it had something to do with Shadrach Nelson's son-in-law working as a railroad detective. Some underhanded deal had let Sussman off scot-free. Since all the money he had swindled was long gone, all she cared about now that her aunt was moldering in a grave was Sussman not cheating the Gallagher clan anymore.

If he stole a nickel now, he stole it from *her*.

"He's the one, Cousin Bea." Bobby Jones crowded close. He clutched his rifle tightly and made a few tentative moves to pull it to his shoulder and fire.

"The engineer?"

"His name's Davey. Highballin' Davey Fulbright. Him and Sussman got paid off to steal our coal. That's what ever'body in town says."

She nodded slowly. The engineer wore a tall black-and-white-striped hat that made him an easy target, even for a poor marksman like her cousin. Not only Fulbright but all the other engineers on the Denver to Georgetown route had to have accepted bribes. Since she had posted her own family members to oversee loading the coal, the engineers' bribes had dried up. That had to make her an enemy in their eyes. The new freight yard manager wasn't skimming money off her profits, either. She saw nothing but fury in Gadsden Renfro's eyes whenever they talked.

Beatrice didn't care. Soon enough she would control more than the Calcutta Mine. From her vantage atop the ramp above the tracks, she looked across the pass to the other side. Like pox, black tailings spilled downward from played-out mines. Leadbottom Morrisey burrowed like a marmot into the hillside to claw out lead. On the far side of the mountain, he operated a smelter to reduce the ore and pour lead ingots.

All that would be hers one day. Soon. Just as control of Utopia would be within her grasp. Being elected mayor was out of the question since she was a woman, but with one of her family installed she'd have plenty of clout.

She chuckled, wondering what people would say if she installed Bobby as mayor. He did whatever she told him, and he was still wet behind the ears.

Coal mine. Lead mine. Taxes from the town. Lease holding for the railroad's right of way. It all added up to a fortune as great as any of the silver magnates in Blackhawk or the other boomtowns along the western slopes of these mountains.

"Has a careful inventory been taken of our coal, Bobby?"

"My sister Belle's done tallied it all. She has the page she writ it all down on over by the tracks. You want I should fetch her?"

"You stay up here and keep a close watch on them." She pointed toward the depot. "Especially Sussman. I'll make certain Lulubelle's added up the weights properly. Even a few pounds off means a great deal when we ship as much coal to the railroad as we do."

"You gonna teach me all that, Cousin Bea?"

"What grade did you finish?"

"Third," he said proudly.

"We'll see after this shipment. I suspect I'll have my hands full and will need someone like you—and Belle— to keep up with the daily chores."

"I don't like doin' little chores. I want to do important things."

Beatrice laughed. "It's all important, Bobby. And it'll become even more important when we Gallaghers take over." She swept her arm around, encompassing not only Utopia but all of Hellfire Pass.

"I heard you and that Billy Dixon fellow talkin'," he said. "The black train?"

"Don't go mentioning it. It's got to be kept a secret." Beatrice put her finger up against her lips to caution him to silence. He nodded eagerly, pleased as punch to know a secret she entrusted to him.

She made her way down the steep ramp and doubled back to stand directly under the chute loading the coal into the tender. A shower of soot cascaded over her. She hurried to get out of the way. A young woman stood just behind the tender, clutching a sheaf of papers. She looked up as Beatrice approached.

Lulubelle Jones was the spitting image of her cousin. She was five years younger than Beatrice but otherwise Bea thought she was looking into a mirror. Belle even dressed like she did—copied the way she dressed.

Seeing the way the girl's skirt weighed down on the right side warned Beatrice that her cousin was probably armed with a derringer, too.

There was hero worship and there was striving to be like someone to replace them. Beatrice worried about how much she'd have to watch her back around Belle. She was her Aunt Martha's daughter, and Winifred and Martha had been at each other's throats for as long as Bea remembered.

Too many Gallaghers showed soaring ambition. It was up to Beatrice to keep them all in line by giving them just enough money or power or acknowledgment to satisfy them rather than letting their dreams turn into nightmares for her.

"Belle, dear, you're doing such a fine job. Let me look." She took the papers from the girl's hands and glanced over them. Belle had her own system for tracking the weights and how the railroad paid for it, but Beatrice knew from experience what the numbers should be. She handed the papers back.

"Thank you, Cousin Bea. You're doing a fine job running the Gallagher family."

The whistle startled her.

"There's nothing to be scared of, Cousin Bea. That means the train's about ready to pull out."

"They'll pull out only when I give them the signal," Beatrice said sharply. Then she smiled and said, "Would you like to give Mister Sussman the signal? You deserve a little reward for such good work."

"That's mighty nice of you to say so. I would." She started to wave but Beatrice stopped her.

"Let me get aboard."

"You're going to Denver? Nobody said a thing about that." Belle looked concerned. She was the sort who needed to know every detail to be happy. Beatrice doubted the girl would ever be happy with the way the world changed so fast.

"It's time to renegotiate the price we're selling the coal for, dear. And there're other things I need to look into in the city."

"Who're you leaving in charge? Of the mine and . . . things?"

"All will run smoothly without me for a few days. Everyone working in the mine knows what to do for the next month. The new vein will be expanded, and there's no need to blast. Just keep the boys from taking any of the dynamite stored in the cavern."

"I can do that," Belle said, smiling. She enjoyed having important duties as much as Bobby.

"Watch things closely, now. It won't be hard keeping to the quotas I have posted. I'll tend to the blasting when I get back."

"You know how to do that? You can figure how much dynamite to use to blast?" Belle's hazel eyes went wide.

"I'll teach you how, one day. Right now, you get on up and let Mister Sussman know I'm ready for the train to leave. Give the signal." She kissed Belle on the cheek, grabbed an iron handrail, and pulled herself up onto the metal platform in front of the lone passenger car on this train.

With six heavily loaded coal cars, the engine, tender, and caboose presented a considerable weight to pull. Luckily most of the trip was downhill from the ten-thousand-foot pass to Denver's five-thousand-foot altitude. Here and there along the track were inclines that required considerable engine power, but if Highballin' Davey Fulbright timed the descents properly, momentum carried the train up most of those minor slopes so he saved on steam.

Belle scampered away and waved her white hanky. The depot agent worked the metal flags on a tower by the passenger loading platform. The engineer let out a long blast from the steam whistle and the narrow-gauge engine began moving slowly.

Beatrice went into the Pullman car to avoid hot cinders fluttering down from the smokestack. She passed through the colored section with its two bench seats and Franklin stove, empty this trip, and into the main car. Only a half dozen passengers rode through to Denver. She eyed them as she made her way down the aisle. Two miners, two women looking distraught at the rigors of the impending trip, and two men in business attire. She recognized one as a hardware vendor from Central City. He probably made more in a month than the Calcutta Mine made in a year. Prospectors needed picks and shovels, blasting powder, and chisels and sledgehammers. He sold them all at exorbitant prices to the starry-eyed gold hunters.

This freight train carried her coal to Denver markets. Those same empty cars would be loaded with the various tools used by prospectors for the return trip over the mountains.

She settled down toward the back of the car, scooted

over, and stared through the smudged, dirty window as
the train pulled out. A quick wave to Belle and then another to Bobby high on the loading ramp, and then the
train steamed away from the station. She sat on the wrong
side to get much of a view of Utopia, but she saw all she
wanted of the town every single day from up on her
mountain.

Gallagher's Mountain.

She half closed her eyes and fell into the rocking
rhythm of the train making its way out of Utopia and
down a steep incline before hitting a series of up
and down slopes. Once past those, the trip was almost
entirely downhill. She let her mind drift to what lay ahead
for her. Taking over the entire town was less of a goal
than ruining Leadbottom Morrisey. Her uncle had named
the Calcutta Mine after the Black Hole of Calcutta. When
she was owner of the Morrisey mine, she needed to
rename it. Erasing all memory that the Morrisey family
had ever owned it was important.

But what name was best?

"Wipe them out. Every last one of them."

She blinked when she saw that speaking aloud at-
tracted the attention of one of the women. The look she
got for such a public display like a common drunk made
her laugh. Beatrice was above such petty criticism. Let
the woman think whatever she wanted. The next time
she rode the train through Hellfire Pass every single
inch of the track would belong to the Gallaghers.

She wiped away at the window and stared into the
countryside. Occasional clouds moved across the pure
blue sky, casting oddly shifting shadows. She played

games with the images. A cow and a dog and a man astride a horse.

That brought her up. She dropped the window to get a better look without the greasy glass. Not one man but a half dozen. All masked.

"We're being robbed!" she cried. All four men turned and stared at her as if she was daft. "There! Out there. Look! An entire gang of robbers."

The men moved to see what caused her to be so distraught.

"Out there. Close to—"

Her words were smothered by a loud screech of tearing metal. The car tilted, throwing her against the window. Then a new cry of tortured metal deafened her. Beatrice clung to whatever she could find. The bottom of the seat. The window.

In horror she looked out and saw the ground rushing up. The car crashed with a bone-jarring shudder. Then it began sliding on its side. Dirt and rock and shredded vegetation blasted through the window into her face.

She screamed. Her voice was drowned out by louder noises of the Pullman car sliding downhill. Rocks tore at the sides. Glass shattered. The sound of escaping steam was deafening.

When the car finally came to a halt, other voices echoed in her ears. Men moaned. Women shrieked in panic. The stench of burned metal made her nostrils flare.

Beatrice pushed herself away from the window and began picking shards of glass from her arm where she had crashed into the window. Twisting around she looked up—across the car. The other side showed nothing but blue sky dotted with the puffy white clouds she had found so engrossing only a minute before.

Moving painfully, she got her feet under her and climbed across the seats to the far windows. All of them had broken or popped out of their frames as the car twisted and bent in its downhill descent. Beatrice got one foot against the seat and stretched. She caught the open window and pulled herself half through it.

Behind on the tracks stood the six coal-laden cars and caboose, all intact and upright on their wheels. Turning slowly, she saw a different image of hell. The engine and tender were on their sides. The derailment had taken out the front of the train but preserved her precious shipment.

And then she heard Davey Fulbright screaming for his fireman to run for his life.

The boiler cracked open and spewed steaming water an instant before the explosion.

CHAPTER FIFTEEN

"Well now, here comes trouble on the run." Leroy Early pushed his hat up on his forehead, spat, and then hitched up his gun belt.

Shadrach Nelson widened his stance just a little, as if bracing for a high wind. The way the railroad station master came running meant nothing but trouble. Sussman waved his arms about like a windmill that'd lost its governor. He shouted incoherently and looked around wild-eyed as he stumbled toward the lawmen.

He crashed into Shad and hardly knew it.

"Whoa, there, hold your horses. What's got you so riled up?" Shad shook the depot agent to break him out of the panic.

"There. It . . . it's awful. You gotta do something. The telegraph's out. I can't . . . I can't."

"You can't put together a thought that means a thing, Sussman," Early said. He spat again, barely missing the agent's shoes. For some reason this indignity calmed Sussman. He pushed away from the marshal and glared at the deputy.

"You don't know how terrible it is."

"We don't know what you're talkin' about." Early turned to the marshal. "I've got business to tend to, Shad. Let me know if he starts makin' sense. I suspect that'll be on a cold day in July." Early gave Sussman a dirty look and started to leave.

"Wait, wait, Deputy, it'll take both of you. And Shannon, too. All three of you. A rider just told me the terrible news. The train to Denver derailed! Not five miles outside town, he said." His voice rose to a shrill whine rivaling a steam engine's whistle.

"The one what just left?" Early looked at the marshal. "That's serious. There were five coal cars goin' down to Denver."

"Six. There were six. But the engine done blew up. It went boom!" Sussman threw his hands high into the air. His face flushed again, and his panic returned. He started to run off, but Shad restrained him.

"Leroy, go round up as many men as you can find. Make sure there isn't a fire burning toward town."

"The train!" Sussman screeched as if in physical pain. "Marshal, do something!"

He turned to the depot agent and said sternly, "I'll see what can be done. The town burning down because of all the coal being spilled and the boiler blowing up worries me a mite more than damage to railroad property." He tipped his head toward his deputy in silent command.

Early lit out. The depot agent started to follow. Shad grabbed Sussman by the shoulder and spun him around so they stood face-to-face six inches apart.

"The railroad's had this happen before. What are you supposed to do?"

"Telegraph for help. I only got a half dozen men working in the yard. Renfro's supposed to put together a crew, but I can't find him. It . . . it's his job. Duty. He's the one with the men to handle a disaster like this. Oh, what are they gonna say down in Denver? I'm gonna get fired for certain sure."

"There's no reason to believe you can't rustle up help, I suppose. Gadsden Renfro has a habit of being in the wrong place at the wrong time," Shad said, remembering how the freight yard owner palavered with Billy Dixon. "Listen real close, Sussman. Go round up as many of the freight yard crew as you can. You've got a couple mechanics. Get them and whatever tools they'll need on a handcar."

"I can do that," Sussman said skeptically. "But they might not listen to me."

"Now. Do it now!" Shad spoke sharply. Sussman jumped a foot and then ran back to the railroad depot. He'd found someone to tell him what to do and had a mission. At least Shad hoped the man obeyed. The railroad was the town's lifeline. Cut it and Utopia would be in a world of trouble.

Shad shook his head. This wasn't anything a lawman should do. This was railroad business. It was railroad business and he'd handle the problem because people listened to him.

He went to the stables and saddled his horse. By then Early had a dozen men ready to cut a fire line if the fallen engine had started a blaze that threatened to spread upslope toward Utopia. It was all he could do for the town. If the southern side of the mountain turned into a conflagration, there was little anyone could do to stop it from working its way up to the pass. Forest fires burned upward until they reached a summit. Anything in the way wasn't likely to survive a fierce blaze.

Shad heeled his horse and galloped from town, taking the bends in the road at a breakneck speed. The farther downhill he rode, the stronger the stench of burned metal became. Shad cut across a meadow and down a short slope to the railroad tracks. He reached the bed. It looked right but everything else felt wrong.

He took a deep whiff of the air. The smell of hot metal and burning coal made his nostrils flare. But wood smoke wasn't mixed with it. Riding along the tracks, he turned a bend and came to the top of a long slope downward. The first thing he saw was the caboose and coal cars standing on the tracks just as pretty as you please.

But the good news ended there. He caught his breath at the sight of the engine turned on its side. The rivets on the boiler had popped, and large sheets of iron were scattered about the countryside. Somehow the boiling water had gushed out, cooled, and put out tiny fires caused by scattered coals from the ruptured firebox. The tender car had scattered coal as far as the edge of the woods fifty yards away. It looked as if some giant had fired at the ground with a shotgun loaded with black pellets.

He rode slowly, letting his horse pick its way down the hill. Only when he reached a point level with the caboose did he see that a passenger car had also derailed and lay on its side. Over the hissing of steam and the sizzle of glowing coals he heard piteous cries. Humans in pain.

Shad hoped that Early sent the fire crew he recruited on down the line when no threat to Utopia was uncovered. He had no hope that Sussman's rail crew would get here any time soon, though the handcar would provide a quick way to get the injured back to town where Doc Paisley could tend them.

He dismounted and went to the side of the passenger car. A head popped up from a broken window.

"You bringin' help?"

"You one of the crew?"

"Me and Gus were in the caboose. We got four passengers in bad shape." The crewman paused, looked confused, then added, "And one of 'em went runnin' off into the woods like her hair was on fire. It wasn't, though. She looked real healthy, but maybe she was scared."

"What can I do?"

"Stomp out any fire and go see to Davey."

"The engineer?"

"He finally rode his last highball." The crewman dropped back into the passenger car with a tinkle of breaking glass.

Shad walked around, carefully avoiding sharp-edged metal where the cars had been ripped apart by the derailment. Not seeing rampant fires allowed him to turn to other disagreeable matters. Bodies of the engineer and stoker lay sprawled some distance away.

He knelt by the engineer. The man was horribly burned

from a steam blast. Shad hoped he had died fast. The fireman lay a half dozen paces away, face down—or Shad corrected himself—the parts of the stoker that had survived the explosion. An arm was missing and nothing below the knees showed.

The man had been dismembered by an explosion but there wasn't much blood. The fire had charred parts, and the steam had cooked what was left.

He wasn't sure what to do. Shock held him. Shad stared for what seemed an eternity. When his horse nudged him, the hypnotic spell broke and his mind raced.

Burying the men was out of the question right now. Someone had to claim the bodies. Sussman should have his crew here with a handcar soon enough, though he saw no sign of men arriving along the tracks higher on the hill. He stared at the spot where the engine had left the tracks.

There wasn't a rail where the front wheels had rolled. The only way for the track to disappear like that was for someone to have removed it. He scratched his chin, considering what that meant. Shad started back to the overturned passenger car to see if he could lend a hand when a sharp pistol report echoed through the woods.

He spun, hand going to the butt of his Peacemaker. Movement at the very edge of the pine forest warned him. A smooth move whipped out his six-gun, but the target proved fleeting. The person ducked into the woods, out of sight.

With a deep breath to settle his nerves, he started walking. Everything warned him to wait for help, whether it came from Sussman's crew or Early and any of the men recruited to stomp out a fire hardly mattered. He needed someone to watch his back.

Only he didn't have it.

A second shot hastened him along. At a loss to know what to do at the derailed train, he felt a curious relief to be tracking down a gunman. He understood what to do if he faced a man holding a six-shooter. He slid into the cool, dark woods. The pistol clutched in his fist roved back and forth, hunting for a target. More barely seen movement drew him deeper into the woods. Using one tree after another for cover, he advanced. What he discovered perplexed him.

A man and a woman fought.

He recognized them both immediately when Beatrice Gallagher began cursing at Patrick Morrisey.

"You beast! I'll rip your eyes out!"

"You tried to shoot me again," the man said, holding the woman's wrists to keep her from fulfilling her threat. He was forced to turn sideways to keep her from kneeing him in the groin. She fought like a wildcat.

They continued the fight until Patrick caught a heel on a rock. The two toppled to the ground with a loud thud.

Beatrice came out on top, wiggling and kicking to do the most damage to him as possible.

"Bea, darlin', stop."

"You derailed the train. You tried to kill me!" She fought even harder.

Patrick rolled from side to side trying to dislodge the furious woman. He failed.

As she whaled away at the man, her tattered blouse fell away, leaving her bare to the waist. Her skin was pockmarked where burning cinders had landed on her. Cuts and scratches showed she had been near a window when it broke. Large black-and-blue bruises began to show, and none of it slowed down her furious attack.

"I've got him, Bea," Shad said, grabbing her wrist and yanking her off-balance. She kept trying to hit Patrick, but Shad never relented. He had no good feelings for Patrick or any of the Morrisey clan. They had kidnapped two other men and put him and them to work as slave miners in their lead mine. It rankled Shad that he had no proof since the other two were dead.

His word against the entire Morrisey clan amounted to cow flop in a court of law. He had no love for Patrick or Leadbottom or any of the Morriseys, but he had even less for Beatrice Gallagher.

With a jerk and heave, he cast Beatrice away. She landed hard, sitting on the ground. He had to admit, even cut and burned the way she was, she presented a beguiling picture. It was easy to see why Patrick had been drawn into her arms.

Her nakedness became obvious as she struggled to get to her feet. Shad felt a tad embarrassed at her unclothed state and looked away.

"You, stay down," Shad ordered her. A quick turn away let him face Patrick. He shoved his six-gun toward the man to enforce his command on him, too.

As he did so, he lost his balance. Patrick kicked out and knocked the gun flying.

Things got confused then. Shad instinctively grabbed for the gun and fell to his knees. The weapon landed a few feet from Beatrice. She rolled over and picked it up with both hands.

"I've got more 'n two shots now," she cried in triumph. "You're gonna pay for what you did to me. You derailed the train to kill me. And you tried to spill my coal!"

The gunshot went wide of its target.

Shad scrambled forward and dived to knock the gun from her grasp. She held on, but he ruined her aim for a second shot. The two of them mixed it up. The gun went off a third time. Shad winced as the hot barrel pressed into his arm. He grabbed again. This time he tackled her and drove the woman to the ground. She tried to knee him in the groin but caught him in the breadbasket. He grunted, closed his eyes to the pain, and fought on. It wasn't as bad as some bar fights he'd been in, but her blow still slowed him down.

"He's getting away! You're letting him go!"

Shad glanced over his shoulder. Beatrice was right. Patrick Morrisey was smart enough to avoid the fight over the six-shooter and hightailed it to find refuge deeper in the woods.

"Let go of the gun," he grated out. "I'll catch him."

"I'm gonna kill that skunk!"

Beatrice caught him on the side of the head with an elbow. For an instant he saw stars. Then he went deaf in his left ear as she fired his own gun just inches away. Shad reared up and drove forward. His weight was enough to knock her back flat on the ground. He snatched up his Peacemaker when the impact knocked it free.

"Stop him, Marshal. He's getting away!" She pointed.

Shad backed off, as cautious of the woman as he'd be

of a stepped-on timber rattler. He got his feet under him and stared at her.

"Cover up. You're downright lewd, nekkid like that."

For the first time Beatrice understood how her clothing had been burned and torn and ripped from her. She crossed her arms over her breasts.

Shad took one final look, shook his head, and then ran after Patrick Morrisey. The woods swallowed him up fast. Tracking on the pine-needle-covered ground was impossible. Even checking limbs and bushes for broken twigs failed to give him a hint where Morrisey had run. Slowing, he let the blood hammering in his ears settle down. His left ear still buzzed from the pistol's discharge so close, but he cupped his right ear and listened hard.

All he heard were the usual forest sounds. Wind high up. The small scurries of animals as they foraged. When he heard a louder sound than rabbits or marmots, he turned in that direction.

His gun came up. He cocked, aimed, and prayed. Shad tried to remember how many rounds he had left. However many shots he had would never be enough against a black bear, even a half-grown one.

Running was useless. Unless he had a buffalo rifle, a gun wasn't much use. The only thing he could do was face certain death if it noticed him intruding on its forest.

The bear reared up and used six-inch claws to strip away bark on a tree. It drove its snout down, eating bugs or moss or whatever it sought.

Shad felt sweat pop out from every pore. And then the

bear dropped to all fours and ambled off. All muscles turned to water, the marshal leaned forward and braced himself against a tree. If he had any luck after this brief encounter, he hoped the bear found Patrick Morrisey and ate him for dinner.

He backtracked to where he had left Beatrice Gallagher. The woman glared at him when it was obvious he hadn't captured her one-time lover and would-be killer.

"He did it, Marshal. I know he did. Why else would he be out here if not to pull that rail from the tracks?"

"I'm not disputing that, Bea."

"You will address me as Miss Gallagher," she said hotly.

"As befitting the new Coal Queen of the Rockies?" His tone mocked her. He enjoyed the way she dropped her modest pose for a moment, drew back a fist, and threatened to punch him. She sputtered and once more crossed her arms over her chest.

"I heard two shots. Like those from a derringer."

"So what?"

"Nothing I can prove, but your aunt was shot with two rounds. So was my son."

"You caught his killer. The real killer *confessed*."

"I got a new murder in town. Abe's lady friend, Mary Beth. She was shot twice. Like she ran afoul of someone with a derringer."

"You'll do anything to avoid your duty, won't you, Marshal? Patrick Morrisey derailed the train and tried to kill me. From the look of it he did kill at least a couple others."

"I saw him and you fighting, but I don't have any evidence he was responsible for removing that section of track."

"He ran!"

"Who wouldn't with a wildcat like you trying to kill him?"

"So who's responsible, Marshal Nelson? You got big ideas."

"Train robbery, bank robbery. We seem to have a rash of crimes we never saw before in Utopia, at least not for a good, long time. It might be the same gang that did both."

Her expression froze. Beatrice Gallagher jerked around and stalked toward the train.

"I have no idea what you mean."

He stared at her bare back as she stormed off. Somehow, he thought she knew exactly what he meant—and knew who had robbed the bank and caused the train derailment.

CHAPTER SIXTEEN

Shad and Beatrice sat on the forward edge of the handcar. The two men from the caboose pumped hard to get the vehicle up the steep hill. He dangled his legs down, toes occasionally kicking at a rock along the bed of the tracks.

"Stop that," Beatrice said testily. "You'll catch your foot and be dragged under the car."

"I didn't know you cared, Beatrice . . . Miss Gallagher."

"I don't other than you're the one most likely to run Patrick Morrisey to ground and see him hanged. That's what they do with train robbers, isn't it?" She looked back over her shoulder at the engineer, Gus.

Gus and his partner exchanged quick, knowing looks. The woman's movement caused the coat they'd given her to flop open more than a little, giving a delightful view.

"That's what I'd do if 'n I caught him, Miss Gallagher," the railroad man agreed. "It's something awful causin' us to derail like that. It's about the worst fear a railroader has, being caught in a derailment."

"That's our fear," his partner said. "There's nothing worse than bein' tossed around when a car goes off the rails."

"It was awful. We seen the bodies." Gus shivered and pumped a little harder, as if putting more distance between them and the train wreck made the memory fade.

"Yeah, Davey and whoever he had stokin' the fire-box today died right away. It's a wonderment none of the passengers died." Gus' partner was more than willing to keep the conversation going so Beatrice half turned to look over her shoulder.

Shad wanted to warn the woman that this exposed more of her bare skin to the railroad crewmen, then decided she had to look after herself. Let Gus and his partner get a small reward for their work pumping uphill to get back to Utopia.

"It's a good thing that fellow was out in the woods and came to rescue you," Gus said.

Shad jerked around and almost lost his balance. He caught himself on the edge of the handcar.

"What are you talking about?"

"Don't you go saying things you don't know for certain, Gus darling." Beatrice let the coat flap open a little more. Shad reached over and jerked it shut to keep the man working the handles focused on the question.

"We heard screechin' 'n all," Gus said. "I was up in the dome of the caboose and saw the engine flip over. Davey hit the brakes and slowed up enough so the cars behind the Pullman didn't derail."

"That's so. When the engine went over, it snapped

the coupling. If we'd been goin' faster, the whole danged train might have been flipped onto its side."

"He saved my coal," Beatrice said. "He's a hero. I want a statue built to him in the town plaza."

"We don't have a plaza," Shad said, "and what did you mean some guy rescued her?"

"I saw him at the edge of the forest. There was screechin' 'n screamin', and he ran right toward it all because he saw Miss Gallagher there crawlin' through the window. He pulled her out and held her real close."

"He tried to kill me. He's a Morrisey pig."

"What'd he do? The two of them?" Shad wanted to quiet her to find out what the railroaders had seen. It sounded as if they saw something entirely different from Beatrice.

"He dragged her away from the worst of the fire. The firebox had done split open and spewed out flamin' hunks of coal. He saved her from that." Gus sounded confident, even envious that someone got his arms around Beatrice Gallagher.

"I saw him, too," the other man spoke up. "He carried her to the tree line. Then everything got all mixed up and me 'n Gus bailed out of the caboose to go do what we could."

"You might say we was heroes, too, goin' after the passengers the way we did with all that fire and smoke and all."

"The man in the forest saved her? Miss Gallagher?"

"We'd a' done it but we was too busy with the other passengers. They was hurt bad," Gus said.

"And Miss Gallagher was in safe hands," the other crewman added.

"Did you hear two gunshots?"

The two men looked at each other and shook their heads.

"The noise was fierce, Marshal. The boiler blowed, and things were slidin' downhill, makin' quite a racket," Gus said.

"You two ought to get a bonus," Shad said. "I'll see that Mister Sussman hears of all you did."

"That, well, him," Gus said almost under his breath. "He'd get us rewards and keep it for himself. He's like that."

"I'll make sure that doesn't happen."

"You got our votes when you're up for election, Marshal."

"They're not citizens of Utopia," Beatrice said sourly. "You just bought votes from men who can't vote for you."

Shad turned to the woman.

"They're saying Patrick saved you. Is that the way it happened?"

"He derailed the train. If he didn't do it, Leadbottom did. Or ordered it. They want to get back at me for—"

"For what? Leadbottom was all het up over the bank robbery since most of the money taken was his."

"I don't know anything about that." She crossed her arms and bent forward to keep from looking at him.

"Leadbottom tried to derail your coal train to get even with you for robbing the bank?" It sounded incredible to him, but it made a loco kind of sense. The two families had spent years blaming each other for every slight. The robbery was about the biggest crime to hit Utopia in years, and Leadbottom had suffered the most from it.

Leadbottom thought in simple terms. He'd blame the Gallaghers for stealing all his hard-earned money and try to retaliate in kind.

"I wouldn't doubt that Leadbottom or one of his slimy kin killed that woman you're going on about," Beatrice said.

"Why would he do that, not that he's not able and willing should the need arise?" Shad knew of other cases where the Morriseys had murdered men in cold blood. The problem was always proving it. They managed to hide the bodies well on their land. The petered-out lead mines were as hard to search as those coal mines on Gallagher property.

He shivered at the thought of the bodies dropped into those bottomless pits and buried deep in the mountainsides. Between the two families, they could have hidden more bodies than were buried in the town cemetery.

"For him killing is a pleasure. Why'd he need a reason?"

"Mary Beth knew something and was on her way to tell me." Shad saw this caused Beatrice to tense up again.

"We're gettin' close, Marshal," Gus called. "I see Sussman up there on the platform wavin' us down."

"As if we'd want to keep on goin'," his partner said. They chuckled.

"Remember what you said 'bout gettin' us rewards for all our brave actions," Gus reminded Shad. The two men stopped pumping on the handle, and the wheeled cart came to a halt a few feet away from the depot.

Beatrice hopped down and pulled the coat even tighter around herself.

"I've got to get back to the Calcutta and let everyone know I'm fine. First I need to find when the tracks will be repaired and my coal can be delivered to Denver."

"Now, Miss Gallagher, ma'am, that's gonna take a while," Gus said. "There's a lot of heavy liftin' that needs doin' to get the wreckage off the tracks."

"And the owner'll want to retrieve as much of that ruined engine and Pullman as he can. Piecing it back together's not likely but they can use what's left as spare parts," his partner explained.

She ignored both men and made her way up the steps to where Sussman looked like a frightened bird being hunted by a hawk. She backed him up a pace before he stood his ground. Arms waving around, he tried to placate Beatrice. Shad saw he failed.

"Glad it's Mister Sussman what's on the receivin' end of that bile," Gus said. "She's got one nasty temper, don't she?"

"You boys rest up. Don't let Sussman send you back down to the wreck, unless you want to go."

"Now, Marshal, anybody down there's in for a couple days' backbreakin' labor. Me and Gus need to conserve our strength and get our health back. Don't we, Gus?"

The two climbed down from the handcar and slipped off while Sussman listened to Beatrice's diatribe. For his part, Shad knew what the woman was saying. He'd heard most of it on the trip back into town. Keeping the peace was never easy. He needed to be sure Shannon had taken care of things while he and Early were gone.

"I do need to hire another deputy," he said to himself as he began the slog across town to the jailhouse.

Muttering that sentiment caused a dark cloud to engulf him. The feeling of impending doom grew daily, and he didn't know why. Billy Dixon was part of it, but the feud between the two families from either side of the pass built, too.

There was something more. The black train.

He smiled ruefully at that. Until the tracks leading to Denver were patched up, no train was coming from that direction.

But the telegraph lines were out. Still. Getting Sussman to do anything about the railroad telegraph was not likely. The other line going to the stagecoach office needed repair, too, but badgering that depot agent into sending someone out to fix it was more likely. Egan was afraid of his own shadow. Convincing him of dire things happening if he didn't get a telegram through to the federal marshal in Denver would be easy enough.

If it came to that, Shad could send a letter on the next stage heading downhill. That'd take longer, but the Denver marshal wasn't as likely to ignore an official letter.

He reached the jail and intended to stretch out on one of the cots in a cell to catch up on his sleep. Shad took a step in and froze. A man wearing a colorful serape draped over his shoulders rode past in the street. The rider wore a large-brimmed sombrero with golden tassels dangling all around the brim. The fancy stitching on the crown had been done in silver thread. The sunlight glinted off those strands as the man rode, never looking left or right.

Shad stepped back out, drew his six-shooter, and reloaded.

He hurried after the man. Shad saw the horse tethered outside Gold Dust City. He went to the horse and ran his fingers over the silver conchas decorating the saddle. The stirrups had been waxed to protect the intricate tooling. Shad made out the design of a saguaro on one and a prickly pear on the other.

If he hadn't been certain about the rider's identity before, he was now. He made sure his gun slid easily from his holster, paused at the double swinging doors, and then went in.

Ralph argued with the sombrero-wearing man.

"Don't have any of that mescal. I got some tequila. Will that suit your fancy?"

The man pushed back the serape to show a sawed-off shotgun slung from a tooled leather strap over his shoulder.

"No, amigo, it won't do to take the taste of trail dust from my tongue. Mescal. Mescal or there'll be trouble."

"That trail dust's got into yours ears, mister. I have tequila. If I hunt for it, there might even be a half bottle of pulque, but I ain't got mescal."

"The Mexican Kid knows that, Ralph," Shad said loudly. "He's just itching for a fight. Isn't that right, Kid?"

The man turned slowly. The tassels on his sombrero twisted this way and that. Another man might have been distracted. Shad knew better. He lifted his six-shooter and pointed it at the man.

"He calls himself the Mexico Kid but he's from Detroit. I never did hear your real name. Now why is that, Kid? Might there be a wanted poster out in your given name?"

"You have the advantage on me, Marshal. You know my name."

"Keep that shotgun under your arm. Lift it an inch and I'll blow you away."

"That's not very neighborly, amigo."

"You've got a short memory, Kid. I ran you out of Utopia a few years back. You rode with the Wheeler boys then."

"They rode with me."

"Not my recollection. The short one, Gimpy Wheeler, was the leader. As nasty a sidewinder as you'd ever step on."

"Do you intend to gun me down, Marshal?" The sunburned face cracked with a smile that showed two gold teeth in front. "I've not committed any crime in your fair town."

"Ralph, give him a shot of whatever's close at hand. None of the good stuff since I'll pay for it. To show how neighborly we are in Utopia."

The barkeep poured a shot glass to overflowing. The Mexico Kid ran his fingers up and down the sides, dipped his trigger finger, tasted the liquor on it, and nodded. With a quick move, he knocked back the liquor.

"It's not mescal. Get a bottle of mescal for me before I return."

"Don't bother, Ralph. The Kid is leaving town. Now."

Shad stepped back and let the Mexico Kid pass through the doors. He waited for him to mount.

"Ride east, ride west, I don't care. Just ride."

"You can chase me out of town, Marshal Nelson, but soon there will be too many of us." The Mexico Kid laughed raucously, let his horse rear and paw at the air, then hit the ground in a full gallop heading east toward Denver.

Shad sagged and then sat heavily in a chair. His knees had turned watery. He was afraid the outlaw was right about there soon being too many owlhoots to run out of town. He felt like he was in a pot of water just now coming to a boil.

And the Mexico Kid had remembered his name.

CHAPTER SEVENTEEN

The stagecoach hit another chuckhole and sent Richard Williamson careening about the compartment. He braced himself against the side to keep from crowding the passenger beside him.

"Sorry," Williamson mumbled.

"Dusty, too," the man said. He folded his arms across his chest and stared out.

Williamson studied the man and cemented his appraisal formed over the past fifty miles from Denver. There had been a slight chemical smell when the man started the trip. That had vanished, replaced with sweat and dust. Williamson suspected the man was a notions peddler. He might even mix up a batch of his own snake oil to sell. Some men billed themselves with fancy titles like Professor and Doctor but this one lacked the aspect necessary to draw a crowd, much less entertain and intrigue them.

Definitely a man who sold his potions to doctors. Some of them might even work, for all Williamson knew.

"You going to see Doc Paisley?" he asked.

The man jerked around, eyes wide in surprise. Then they narrowed.

"How'd you know that?"

"I know the doc. My wife knows him even better by now. She's expecting any time now."

The peddler looked Williamson over for the first time. Until now he had been more interested in staring out the coach window at nondescript rocks and endless vegetation.

"Do tell. You have any idea what he might be in the market for. I sell . . ."

"Drugs," Williamson said. He touched his nose to hint at how he had come to that conclusion.

"You're a real smart gent. Pharmaceuticals, they call 'em back east. I get supplies from St. Louis. But Doctor Paisley is the only sawbones between Denver and Georgetown, if I heard rightly."

"I think you did. How'd you happen to come along right about now?" Williamson wondered at the man's reaction. He became less sociable and more guarded.

"Heard there'll be a need real soon for what I sell."

Williamson stared at him. The man turned away and once more memorized rocks and clumps of buffalo grass and blue grama. Seeing his brief conversation was over in a puzzling way, he pushed aside the leather curtain on his side of the compartment and looked out. A smile came to his lips when he saw the eastern edge of Utopia.

"Almost there?" asked the man seated across from him.

Williamson nodded once. He had not spoken to the

only other passenger during the entire trip because of the way he knocked back whiskey. The man had gurgled when he boarded the stage, and had emptied three flasks so far. By Williamson's estimate, he still had at least two flasks hidden away in his coat pockets.

He also saw the shoulder rig weighed down by a small-caliber pistol. Booze and guns were a dangerous combination in the confines of a stagecoach compartment. Added to the man's wild eyes and pulsing vein in his temple made a temperament no sane man crossed.

There'd been a time when Williamson would have goaded the man to see how far he could go before he exploded. He'd been younger and stupider then. And he hadn't been married with his first child expected any time now. Those considerations filled his thoughts every day. He hoped they didn't make him hesitate when he had to use the six-shooter slung at his hip.

"I'm meetin' up with old friends," the drunk said. In spite of putting away so much whiskey the man didn't slur his words. "You got the look. Might be you know them."

"What look's that?"

"Gunslinger."

The potions salesman jerked around and stared at the man across the compartment, then his eyes darted to Williamson. He had to have noticed the fancy tooled leather holster and maybe the well-oiled, well-used six-gun in it. He just hadn't made the guess that the other man did.

"Not me," Williamson said. "Who're you meeting up with in Utopia?"

"You wouldn't know them if you're not in the business," the drunk said. He squeezed his eyes shut and then opened them slowly. The two bloodshot eyes fixed on Williamson with deadly intent.

If the man took it into his head to draw, Williamson would be at a disadvantage. Seated, it was hard to pull his iron at his right hip. The other man had only to reach under his left arm to clear leather and get smoking.

A dozen ideas flashed through Williamson's head. Grab the other man's wrist and keep him from drawing. Then he saw the drunk carried a knife sheathed in the top of his boot. If he wrestled too much, using both hands, he'd expose himself to a knife thrust from the man's free hand.

"How many men have you killed?" Williamson asked.

"Now that's not a question I hear too often. What makes you think I keep count?"

Williamson shifted slightly on the hard bench seat. This put him in position not to grab the man's wrist but to deliver a punch to his nose or throat. Either would stop both gun and knife attack.

"You seem like the kind who knows how to cipher."

This produced a chuckle. "I like you, mister. It'd be a real treat to face off with you." He cleared his throat and added, "You're a damned law dog, aren't you?"

"Was," Williamson allowed. "That's not where my paycheck comes from now."

"So you 'was,'" the man said. "That's good enough

for me, but some of the snakes I wiggle along with would consider it a pleasure to put you in a grave."

"We're here. There's the stagecoach office," the peddler said, too loud.

The stage rattled to a halt. The peddler shot from the compartment like he had springs in his butt. Williamson didn't move a muscle.

"Go on, former law dog. You first."

Williamson moved slowly as he followed the peddler to the dusty street outside the stage office. Hair on the back of his neck rose as he anticipated getting shot. He walked steadily to the office door.

"Howdy, Mister Egan," he called.

"You're back, Williamson. I was wonderin' if you'd avoid town 'til after the big event."

"I'm back here on business, but it'll be good seeing the missus." He watched the gunman collect his saddlebags, sling them over his shoulder, and walk away. His gait was a tad unsteady, but that might have been caused by riding in the stage rather than downing so much liquor.

"Not many passengers these days, thanks to your employer," Egan said. "Business hasn't picked up much, even with the derailment."

"That's why I came by stage," Williamson said. "Do you know that gent?"

Egan leaned outside, as if the sunlight would burn him to a crisp. He shook his head.

"Can't say that I do. But he's got the look."

"What look's that?" Williamson saw Egan go pale and move back into his office.

"We're gettin' more men through that look like they're here to kill something—someone."

"The other passenger said he was here to sell Doc Paisley drugs, like he knew some epidemic was on the way."

"Epidemic? Lead poisoning," mumbled Egan. "The rumors are getting louder. When that happens, you can bet your bottom dollar on them bein' true."

"I never heard that," Williamson said. "So the louder someone talks, the truer his words are?" He had to laugh at that. Egan vanished into the stage depot's dark interior.

"You got any more luggage, Deputy?" The driver dropped Williamson's saddlebags to the ground and poked around in the boot.

"Traveling light," he said, "and I'm not a deputy anymore."

"Well, whatever you call yourself workin' for the railroad."

"Rich is good. And that's my name, not how I got because of what the railroad pays me."

This gave them both a laugh.

The peddler had listened to the byplay and smiled. He came over and asked, "Your wife need any drugs? A pregnancy out here away from Denver hospitals can be hard."

"What're you selling?" Williamson asked.

"I've got an elixir or two that might fix her up if she gets morning sickness. Settles the stomach right away."

"She's due any time now. Or within a month, maybe. I don't know much about womanly things like that."

"Well, then, there are some fine potions in my bag that'll soothe a fussy infant. Cries all night? A drop or two of this quiets 'em right down." He fished out a tiny bottle with an eyedropper. "One or two drops and the tyke goes right to sleep."

Williamson hesitated. The man forced the bottle into his hand.

"Take this as a sample. When you need more, I'll be around. Just ask the doctor—Paisley, you said? That's the name. Yes. He'll know where to find me because he'll be buying 'bout everything I have to offer." The peddler opened his bag and showed dozens of brown bottles.

"We won't need this for a while. As I said, the baby's due in weeks, not days." He fingered the bottle. "What is this?"

"A fine tincture with a drop or two of laudanum. It's the latest concoction from the Continent." He hesitated than asked, "Do you need an asafetida bag? I've got special herbs that'll keep you healthy. Just wear the bag around your neck."

"This'll do me, thanks," Williamson said. He put the bottle into his coat pocket.

The peddler tipped his hat and asked for directions to the doctor's surgery. Williamson pointed him down the street. The peddler set off, whistling tunelessly.

Williamson hefted his saddlebags and started walking toward the marshal's office. He preferred to see his wife first, but talking with his father-in-law was needful. Williamson thought more highly of Shadrach Nelson than the marshal did of his son-in-law. That didn't bother Williamson any. He and Miriam loved each other. What the rest of the Nelson family thought of that didn't matter.

He poked his head into the office. The deputy seated behind the desk looked up. Leroy Early grinned.

"Figured you'd be back before the big event," Early said.

"Where's Shad?"

"You need your time card punched by him, do you? He's over at the train station." Early perked up. "You come in on the train? They finally replace that missing rail?"

"You give me too much credit to control what goes on with the railroad. I was sent to find out what happened, not to fix the tracks. There's some delay in that." Williamson shook his head sadly. "More than some. They have to bring in a crew from down south around Pueblo."

"You got here. That's all that'll matter to Miriam."

"I'll leave my saddlebags. Don't let anybody steal them."

"You trust me not to go through them and see if you got something from the big city I might take a cotton to?"

"Take what you want. Just leave the presents for Miriam and the baby."

Early laughed and shooed Williamson from the office.

Crossing town took longer than Williamson wanted, in spite of hurrying. All the talk about his wife and the baby to be had whetted his appetite for seeing them.

He'd do the bidding of the railroad officials, but he was a family man now. He had added responsibilities.

He followed the tracks toward the depot. When he came within fifty yards he saw Shad on the platform arguing with Sussman. Whatever the matter under discussion, Sussman was not happy. More than once Shad poked him in the chest with a stiff index finger, and the depot agent backed away.

He reached the steps leading up to the platform, expecting Shad to be waiting for him. Instead Sussman stood there, arms crossed and looking daggers at him.

"You, too? I should have known they'd send you."

"If you mean your boss—and mine—you're right." Williamson looked around. "Where'd the marshal get off to?"

"He thought he saw a Morrisey boy down the tracks and took out after him. They've been causin' all kinds of mischief ever since the bank got robbed."

Williamson hunted for his father-in-law and didn't see him.

"You need to get the telegraph line fixed," he told Sussman. "The boss is angry that he can't talk to you."

"I can't say it's been botherin' me none." Sussman shuffled around and glanced into the telegrapher's office with rows of lead-acid batteries. The black telegraph key sat forlornly on a desk, silent. "Not havin' two trains a day come through has given me a chance to catch up on my sleep."

"Not that you had much catching up to do." Williamson thought he caught sight of a youngster duck behind a pile of crates at the far side of the freight yard.

"If you want to spread your bedroll in the storage room downstairs, you'll need to fill out all the forms."

"I've got a bed to sleep in," Williamson said, distracted now. "Get a crew out to repair the telegraph wires."

He didn't wait for Sussman's feeble excuses. The drop to the tracks from the passenger platform was about six feet. The impact sent a shock through his hips. Sitting in the stagecoach for close to eight hours had stiffened his joints.

Stretching his legs felt good as he went to find Shad. The urchin darting around the cargo had to be what lured his father-in-law away from chastising Sussman for whatever had annoyed him. He reached the far side of the freight yard and looked around for Shad.

The soft scrape of shoe leather against the top of the crate behind him was all the warning he had before a rock crashed down on top of his head. Rich Williamson pitched forward, hands outstretched in an attempt to keep his face from grinding down into the cinders.

Another whack sent a sharp pain into his skull. Through blurred eyes he saw feet moving in front of him an instant before a kick landed hard on his shoulder.

CHAPTER EIGHTEEN

His vision was blurred, but Rich Williamson saw the foot drawing back for another kick. With a convulsive jerk, he lifted up from the ground enough to trap the foot between his body and the ground. Before his attacker pulled back for another try, he shoved down hard and grabbed. His hands found a scrawny leg. One hand yanked on a denim-clad trouser leg and the other circled an ankle.

Heaving upward again, he slammed his full weight into the trapped leg. A squeal gave him his reward. The body attached to the punishing foot and skinny leg crashed hard to the ground. He heard the breath gust from the lungs. Wiggling like a snake, he worked up the surprisingly short distance so he could drive his knee into an exposed belly.

Blinking hard, he recovered his vision. His shoulder ached and his head felt as if it would split in two. If his Stetson hadn't cushioned the two blows, he would have been out like a light. As it was, he'd have a hangover like he'd been on a bender for a week.

"Lemme go. You're hurtin' me."

He bent forward and drove his knee harder into the captive boy's belly. This cut off all the protests. The boy's dirty face turned bright red. His eyes bulged and threatened to pop out. Williamson kept up the punishment until he recovered his senses. The spot on his head where he'd been beaned by the rock would grow a goose-egg-sized lump, but for now he was thinking better.

"Is there any reason I shouldn't keep doing this?" Williamson bounced a little, letting up with the pressure only to apply even more as he sank back down. The boy's lips rippled like a big-mouth bass out of water.

He moved to one side and grabbed the boy's collar to keep him from running. From the grunts and gurgles coming from his captive's mouth, he wasn't in any condition to escape. That suited Williamson just fine.

"Why'd you clobber me with a rock?"

"Wasn't no rock. It was a lead brick. One of my uncle's bricks."

"So you belong to the Morrisey clan?"

He got a hate-filled glare in return. The boy's rancor flooded back as the pain subsided.

"You assaulted a lawman," he said.

"You ain't no lawman. You're one of them railroad dicks. My pa lost a toe when one of you shot it off. All he was tryin' to do was hitch a ride on one of your danged freight cars."

"I'd say my fellow railroad bulls showed terrible aim. They should have drilled him right through the gullet." Williamson shoved his palm down on the boy's chest and knocked the wind from his lungs again.

"But that doesn't explain why you hit me. I never shot your pa."

"He's three years dead. He got crushed in a mine explosion."

"That explains it all, then. Your pa dies so you bean whoever you want with a hunk of lead." Williamson got a firmer hold on the boy's collar and lifted. It hurt a mite to support the boy's weight when his shoulder had been kicked so hard, but he made a point of not showing any pain.

He shook the boy until his teeth rattled, then he shoved him away.

"Explain why you go around attacking people."

"Railroad dicks ain't people. No more 'n Marshal Nelson's people."

"You have a low opinion of the law. That's going to land you in the clink."

"You fixin' to arrest me? Go on," the boy said defiantly. "My Uncle Leadbottom'll have me out quick as a wink."

Williamson saw it would be a badge of honor if he tossed the boy into a jail cell. The boy would have proven himself capable of defying the law. It was like a Sioux warrior counting coup.

"You see Marshal Nelson around here?"

"You think if I had I wouldn't of decked him, too?" The boy tried to spit. Williamson grabbed him by the collar again and tried to shake some sense into him. It was a losing battle.

"Run along. Don't be lurking around the freight yard. The next one who sees you might take a shot at you.

Don't count on them being as bad a shot that you'd only lose a toe."

The boy cursed a blue streak as he turned and ran off in the direction of the Morrisey side of the pass.

"Shad, you're growing your enemies younger by the day." He brushed himself off and looked around for his father-in-law. If Shad had come after the boy who had smashed a hunk of lead down on his head, he had missed him completely.

Williamson rubbed the two lumps forming on his scalp and exercised his shoulder the best he could. He peeled back his coat, vest, and shirt and saw an ugly bruise forming. A black-and-purple splotch the size of his hand stretched from the top of his shoulder down halfway to his biceps. Hiding that from Miriam would be hard.

He looked around. Telling Shad he had arrived was less agreeable now than it had been. If he went up to the Nelson house, he could greet his mother-in-law and his wife. Let Shad find out he was here to investigate the derailment later.

As he hiked back toward the depot, the buzzing in his head increased. He wobbled as he walked and then realized he almost toppled over. Reluctantly, he went to a crate and sat on it until he cleared his head. Too many men he'd known had taken whacks to the head and passed out. He wasn't close to doing that but his vision was a trifle blurred. Worse, it sounded like an entire beehive buzzed around inside his head.

Williamson leaned back and rested his head against another crate. Closing his eyes relieved some of the sensation of the world spinning around him. The buzzing refused to go away.

He sat upright when harsh voices drowned out the buzz.

". . . you didn't do what I told you."

"You coulda killed more 'n the engineer and stoker. That's no way to hold up a train."

"It wasn't me. It was those crazy Morrisey owlhoots."

"Dixon, you're makin' things too hot around here for me. Stop it. Go on up to that fine lady's mine and enjoy yourself."

"Until the train comes."

"It won't come up from Denver."

A cruel laugh sounded that made Williamson pop open his eyes. For a moment he thought he had drifted to sleep and was dreaming the voices. Something about the way the man laughed convinced him he wasn't asleep—or passed out.

"That's not what you said before, Dixon. You fixin' to double-cross me?"

"Renfro, old partner, I'd never do that." Again rang out the laughter that chilled the soul. "We're in this together."

"Yeah, together," Renfro said uneasily. "Don't you forget it." There was a long pause, then, "The train's comin' from Georgetown? Does Sussman know?"

"That fool doesn't know a thing. He'd spill his guts to Nelson if he caught a whiff of what's on the way."

Williamson stood, braced himself for a moment to keep his balance, then slid his six-shooter from its holster.

With his thumb on the hammer, he edged around the crate and looked around for the two men.

A dozen feet away, the freight yard owner and Billy Dixon stood almost nose to nose, as if they were readying for a prizefight.

"You can both grab a handful of cloud. If you so much as twitch, I'll fill you full of lead."

In spite of his warning, both men bolted. Williamson got off a shot at Billy Dixon. The outlaw cut to his right and found a crate to use as a shield. Gadsden Renfro darted in the other direction and found a hidey-hole before Williamson took a shot at him.

The single shot was all he got before Dixon opened fire. Williamson let his giddiness work for him. He weaved about as his head spun in crazy circles. The way he fell forward was totally out of his control. It duped Dixon into firing a couple more times and missing by a country mile.

On his belly, Williamson braced his gun hand on the ground and fired at Dixon. A couple splinters from the side of the crate drove his foe back.

"I'm arresting you for trespassing on railroad land," Williamson called.

"I own the yard. I ain't trespassin' on my own land. Stop shootin', you danged fool." Renfro popped up to look around. Williamson saved his ammo. If Renfro didn't shoot at him, there was no call to waste an ounce of lead on him. Dixon was the real threat.

"You operate the freight yard because the railroad lets you."

"I bought it fair and square! It's mine!"

Williamson rolled over and came up with a stack of crates between him and Dixon. From here, he was hidden from Renfro, too. He had no doubt Renfro would betray him to the outlaw. Whatever they planned, they were in it together up to their ears.

Getting his bearings, Williamson clambered up to the top of the crates. Dixon might think he'd circle around to get at him from the far side.

It took only an instant to realize he and Dixon had the same idea. He faced the outlaw atop the crates. For an instant they both froze. Then Dixon started firing wildly. Williamson fanned off the remainder of the ammo in his gun. One round caused Dixon to drop to his knee, moaning in pain.

"Drop the iron, Dixon." Williamson pointed his empty six-shooter at the outlaw.

"He's outta bullets, Billy!" The warning came from Renfro down on the ground. Barely had those words been uttered than Dixon grinned. He lifted his six-gun and pulled the trigger.

The dull click as the hammer struck a spent cartridge was the sweetest sound Williamson had ever heard.

With a curse, Dixon flung himself off the stack of crates. From the dull thud that followed, he hit the ground hard. Making way across the crates, Williamson reloaded a couple rounds. He cocked and aimed when he got to the edge where Dixon had dropped away.

Nothing.

The outlaw hadn't been dazed by the fall. He had lit a shuck and was nowhere to be seen. Williamson whirled around and pointed his six-gun at Renfro. The freight yard owner had finally found enough gumption to leave his hiding place.

"I'm mighty angry right now, Renfro. You take one more step and I'll make you wish you were never born."

"You're out of bullets." Renfro took a step. Williamson fired. The round nicked Renfro's arm. It was hardly a scratch, but the report and sudden pain jerked him around in surprise.

"You shot me!"

"I've got more rounds with your name on them. Don't move." Williamson slid off the crates and landed heavily. He walked to where Renfro stood quaking, his hands in the air.

"You don't have any reason to shoot at me."

"That was Billy Dixon. You know he's a wanted man."

"I don't know any such thing. What the marshal says isn't the Gospel. And you've got no authority over me. I'm not even armed!"

Williamson swung his pistol hard enough to stagger his prisoner when he reached to pull open his coat. Renfro fell to the ground. With a few quick pats Williamson saw that the man told the truth. He wasn't packing.

"You're wrong about me having no authority over you. This is all railroad land. You may have leased the land, but the railroad owns it, and there's a clause that says you can't conduct illegal activities."

"What've I done that's against the law? I was talkin' to a man who wanted to ship freight. He was gonna be a customer."

"It sounded like you were taking orders from him."

"He's a possible client. You got to butter up men who're gonna pay you money to ship freight." Renfro made the claim as if he wanted to see if Williamson bought anything he said.

"Get to your feet. I'm going to put you on ice until I find out what's happening. From the looks of it, I won't like a danged bit of it. That means nobody at the railroad's home office will, either."

"You're arresting me? But you work for the railroad. You can't arrest anybody. You're not a lawman."

"No," Williamson said, shoving Renfro ahead of him, "but my father-in-law is. And that's good enough."

CHAPTER NINETEEN

"If you've got a spare cell, I've got an occupant for you." Richard Williamson shoved Renfro into the marshal's office.

Leroy Early looked up from the newspaper spread on the desk. His bushy eyebrows wiggled like caterpillars.

"You don't waste time, do you, boy?"

"Keys?" Williamson caught them when Early tossed them over. It took him a few seconds to be sure Renfro was secure before returning to the office. He dropped the keys onto the middle of the desk and perched on an edge.

"What's the charge? Other than being a jackass?"

"He and Billy Dixon were discussing some mischief. I was too far away to hear what, but the two of them being in cahoots ought to be enough to hang Renfro."

"Maybe not hang him but certainly tar and feathers," Early said.

"That's a waste of good feathers. Hold him until I get a chance to talk to Shad. Have you seen him?"

Early shrugged. "He was over to the freight yard last

I heard. If you didn't see him, he musta lit out after somebody."

Williamson rubbed the lumps on his head. Shadrach Nelson wasn't likely to have fallen prey to a kid with a brick the way he had. He still hadn't seen hide nor hair of the marshal, and throughout the fight with Renfro and Dixon, Shad hadn't put in an appearance.

"He's not the kind to waste time in a saloon," Williamson said.

"How good of you to say that about me." Shad stepped into the office. He looked past the two men into the cellblock. "You caught him doing something illegal?"

Williamson related everything he'd seen and heard.

"I hit Dixon a couple times. If he's bleeding badly enough, he'll go to the doctor to get patched up. I can go and see." Williamson stood. He forced himself not to wobble around. His vision doubled for a second, then the world snapped back into focus. The whacks to the head had affected him more than he wanted to admit. Nothing a little rest wouldn't cure. Miriam's hand on his forehead, soothing him, would go a ways toward a complete recovery.

"He knows I'm hunting for him. The more I look, the more trouble I find brewing."

"What else is there, Shad?" Early scooted to the edge of the chair and folded the newspaper. "You didn't tangle with either of the feudin' families, did you?"

Williamson didn't like the sound of that. The feud between opposite sides of Hellfire Pass caught the town in a deadly crossfire. And when the town was in both Gallagher and Morrisey sights, that put the railroad in a precarious position.

"I chased the Mexico Kid out of town, but he won't go far."

"Him?" Williamson laughed. "What a fake. He tells everyone he's from Mexico when he's really from—"

"Detroit," Early and Shad finished together.

"That doesn't make him any less dangerous. The bulls down south said he robbed a D&RG train out of Durango. There wasn't proof, and by the time they decided to nab him anyway, he'd gone." Williamson thrust out a hand to lean against the wall. This steadied him.

"Came north to bedevil me from the looks of it," said Shad. "He's not the only one. Dixon and his gang keep coming back like bad pennies. There's only one reason for that. They're thinking on taking over Utopia, like they did in the old days."

"Do you think the derailment has something to do with that?" Williamson chewed on his lower lip as he thought on the matter.

"That was Morrisey's doing. I'd bet good money on that. Maybe I'd even give you odds." Shad turned glum. "And I mean Leadbottom, not Patrick. He actually risked his life to save Beatrice Gallagher."

"That don't mean nuthin', Shad. Patrick coulda pulled out the rail and then repented the act when he saw Beatrice was aboard."

"It feels wrong to me," Shad said.

"They have been causin' more of a ruckus in town," Early said. "Not all our trouble comes on the train."

"That makes Utopia look like a battlefield," Williamson said. "The two families feuding and all the outlaws coming into town."

"It makes me wonder how much rot there is already here," Shad said. He looked over his shoulder in Renfro's direction.

"That's my concern, Pa."

Shad looked at the railroad detective with daggers in his eyes.

"Don't go calling me that, not in public."

"Is this office public?" Early looked around and grinned from ear to ear. "All family."

"Family," grumbled Shad. He reached out and slammed the door between the office and the cells. Renfro might still catch a word or two through the closed door, but that'd be all.

"Finding Dixon is up to you, Marshal, sir." Williamson took a bit of fun out of poking his father-in-law.

"I should lock you up with Renfro," Shad said. "You railroad people do nothing but cause trouble."

Williamson's cheeriness faded.

"I'm replacing him as manager of the yard. If I could find somebody to replace Sussman, he'd be gone in the wink of an eye, too."

"You could do the job, Rich," Early said. "That'd be reason for you to stay around Utopia."

"Keep that to yourself, Deputy Early. The wrong people might overhear you and take it into their heads you're right." Williamson hesitated, then added, "You know how they are in the home office. They're always hunting for ways to save money. Being a detective, master, and and telegrapher and running the freight yard all at the same time's not what I want to do every minute of the day."

"I was joshin' you. Just a little. Go on, you two. Clear out. I can handle things."

"Thanks, Leroy. I'll see the boy up the hill to the house. He might get lost in a big town like Utopia after rattling around little old Denver."

Williamson threw his saddlebags over his shoulder and followed Shad from the office. He looked around and heaved a sigh.

"Are you thinking about what Leroy said? There're worse jobs than being train agent."

"I can send at a decent rate to be telegrapher, too. The trouble is, Shad, that I enjoy being a detective."

Shad didn't answer. He had the same problem. He enjoyed being marshal. For all the headaches, now and then the rewards made him glow with civic pride. Keeping the peace in a town where entire families had it out for each other was always a chore. When he succeeded, it was something others weren't able to achieve.

"There's one of Leadbottom's boys, unless I miss my guess," Williamson said.

"They're all touched in the head. That makes them doubly dangerous when they get a snootful of whiskey."

"He's had more than his share." Williamson dropped the saddlebags and made sure his gun rode easy on his hip.

"My job, not yours," Shad said. He went to where the youngster spun around and around like a dust devil in the middle of the street.

With every spin, the Morrisey kin let out a loud howl like a lovelorn coyote.

"Does Leadbottom know you're raising such a fuss?" Shad stepped closer. Wide bloodshot eyes narrowed when the lead miner saw him.

"Uncle Leadbottom warned me 'bout you. Said you was conspirin' with the Gallaghers to do us dirty." He stopped turning and fought to keep upright. "Conspirin'. That's the right word, ain't it?"

"Those are recent cuts on your hands," Shad said. The miner's hands were heavily callused but bright pink streaks showed where something sharp had slashed his tough skin.

Leadbottom's nephew raised his hands, took another turn around on unsteady feet, and then cried, "You cain't prove I pulled out that rail just 'cuz I got cuts from iron on my hands. No way to prove it was them spikes holdin' the track that cut me when they popped out."

"Are you saying you had something to do with the engine derailing?" Shad blinked. Drunk and crazy. The entire Morrisey family was drunk, crazy, and dangerous.

"They had it comin'. Them Gallaghers, 'specially the slut what tells 'em all when to jump. Like little fleas on a hot griddle, the whole bunch of 'em. 'Jump, little flea,' Beatrice Gallagher says and they do."

Shad held Williamson back. He had overhead the confession.

"He might be too drunk to know what he's saying, son."

"That's exactly the way to get to the truth. He's too drunk to lie."

"He might be making it all up, too, just to hear himself talk big." Shad stepped to the side so he and Williamson bracketed the soused miner.

"Tell us some more. How'd you do it? How'd you remove the rail so the train would leave the tracks and blow up?"

"Showed them Gallaghers, I did, I did." The young miner blinked hard. He realized he was caught between two men, and neither of them looked agreeable. The realization built up steam and then rushed full speed into his besotted brain.

He went for his piece tucked into the waistband of his trousers.

Shad drew and swung his Peacemaker like a club. Williamson dived forward and tackled the man around the knees. Shad missed his blow. Williamson wrestled the writhing, fighting man to the ground.

"Kill you. All you law dogs!"

Before the miner got off a shot, Shad stomped down on the hand clutching the six-shooter.

"Let me pull your fang," Shad said, picking up the pistol. "You're off to jail."

"My uncle'll get me out! I ain't done nuthin'!"

Williamson held him securely as Shad quickly searched him for other weapons. A knife tucked into a sheath at the small of his back was added to the six-gun. Together Williamson and Shad got the kicking, biting man to his feet.

"Calm down or I'll let him buffalo you like he intended." Williamson shook the drunk until his teeth rattled. This made the prisoner settle down.

They half dragged him back to the jailhouse. Early looked up.

"I wondered if I should have gone to see if anyone got shot. I should have known you two'd be in the middle of it."

Shad dropped the knife and pistol onto the desk.

"When he sobers up, ask what he knows about the train derailment."

"And if he does have something to say on the matter," cut in Williamson, "he's my prisoner."

"Railroad business," Early said, nodding. He grabbed Morrisey by the collar and dragged him to an empty cell. When he returned he said, "We're gonna need more lockups if you keep addin' to the prison population."

Shad looked at his son-in-law.

"It may come to that. Dixon deserves to be put in there. And the Mexico Kid."

"Dixon never goes too far without his partners," added Williamson. "You're right again, Leroy. We need to plan for more customers in the Utopia Iron Bar Hotel."

"Get on out of here. Don't go through town or you'll come back with a dozen more of these yahoos." Early kicked the door to the cellblock shut and pointed outside. "Go. Git. I already regret you shifting me to day after you sent Shannon off to Denver. Night was more peaceful."

As they hiked up the hill toward the Nelson house, Williamson added, "Leroy has a point about needing more facilities."

"Facilities? Is that a fancy name you got down for the calaboose in Denver?"

"Cages. Cells. Call 'em what you will, if more outlaws pour into town, you'll need a place to store 'em til you can ship them down to Denver."

"Leastways, they won't be coming from Denver as long as the railroad is busted."

"They can ride in. Or come by stage like I did."

Shad didn't say anything about the "black train" rumor darting about Utopia. Any train bringing trouble to town had to come from the western slopes. The population of Denver provided an army of cutthroats, should they all decide to take a ride on the train. Coming from the west reduced the number.

At least he hoped that was so.

"We're cut off from getting help with the telegraph wires down," Williamson said. "I'll make sure that Sussman repairs the railroad 'graph."

"Watch yourself. We're being spied on." Shad grinned. "We've been discovered!"

Miriam let out a loud squeal of pleasure and made her way clumsily down the steps, then ran to her husband. Shad kept walking, climbing the steps to the porch. Ruth stood framed in the doorway.

"You should have told me you were bringing a guest for dinner."

"No guest, family," he said. He kissed her and, arm around her waist, herded her inside. Miriam and her husband would come inside when they got good and ready.

He hoped it didn't delay getting food put on the table too long. He was hungry, and it had been a long day.

CHAPTER TWENTY

"He'll burn yer whole danged town to the ground. Just you wait and see!"

"Shut up, will you? I'm trying to sleep." Gadsden Renfro rattled the bars in the cell separating him from the other prisoner. "Marshal! Make him stop yammerin' like that."

Shadrach Nelson closed the door between the cells and his office. He sat in his chair, then moved it a few inches farther away as his two prisoners continued to shout at each other.

"He's right, you know," Rich Williamson said. "Leadbottom will burn Utopia to the ground if he takes it into his head."

"The boy's got a point, Shad," Leroy Early said, looking at Williamson. "Them lead minin' fools don't have good sense. Whatever stray thought flutters through their heads is what they do."

"No accounting for their actions. Just react, not plan," Williamson added.

"I've got four men yawping at me. Two I've already

locked up. I can fire one of the others." He scowled at Early, who ignored him.

"But you can't get rid of family, Marshal." Williamson grinned broadly. "Mix in that I don't work for you and the best you can do is run me out of town."

"Miriam'd go with you. She did before," Shad grumbled. "This time she'd take my only grandson with her."

"It could be a girl," Early pointed out. "You know you'd like a granddaughter what looked like Ruth."

"I'd be happy with one that looked like Miriam," Williamson said. "But he's right. It's going to be a boy. I feel it in my bones."

"We agree about that much," Shad said. He heaved a deep sigh. The stewpot of family and law enforcement was coming to a boil. It got harder all the time keeping things separate and not giving him a headache.

"Let's move on with that as a starting line," Williamson said. "There's nothing much we can do about the outlaws coming into town."

"I can arrest Billy Dixon and his henchmen if I find them."

"The Mexico Kid didn't mosey too far off, less I miss my guess," Early said.

"If he and Dixon are in cahoots, they're hiding out somewhere close," Williamson said. "Where'd that be?"

Shad felt as if his head was going to explode. He had thought on this and every conclusion wasn't pretty.

"So?" asked Williamson. "Are they hiding out on Gallagher land or Morrisey?"

Shad looked sharply at his son-in-law. The boy came to the same conclusion he had.

"Either way makes the feud between the families all the worse."

"I've seen the railroad topographical maps of Hellfire Pass from when the engineers laid out the route. Spying on the Gallaghers is harder than poking around the Morrisey mines. The land where the Calcutta Mine is located now is almost impossible to watch without being seen. The slopes . . ." Williamson shrugged.

"They live like moles, too. A few cabins are above-ground, but they live in played-out mines. Watching all the entrances to those mines would take an army company."

"So, Marshal, we start with Leadbottom and his thieving family?" Williamson touched the six-shooter at his hip.

"That's an easier place to start," Early agreed, "but what're you gonna do if you find that Leadbottom's hidin' them outlaws?"

"Scout first, plan the attack, then take 'em out," Williamson said. "The train tracks have to be repaired eventually. You can ship anyone you arrest down to Denver. The Federal Marshal's got a whole lot more room in his jail than you do here."

Shad felt his headache turn into an avalanche. A growing cold knot in his belly added to his discomfort. Miriam had insisted on fixing breakfast and had left out important ingredients in the biscuits. Saying a word about it would have started a flood of crying and alienated Williamson. Better to scarf up biscuits more like a Morrisey lead ingot than start a civil war in the family.

He motioned Early to silence. Shannon had lost a

great deal more in the marshal's eyes. He had lost his trust. If he didn't need at least two deputies, he would have fired Shannon. Keeping him on was a risk, but as long as Shannon did nothing more than bust up fights in the saloons and patrol the streets keeping down petty crime, the gamble was worth it.

He had tried to hire another deputy, and no one in Utopia wanted the job. More than one had mumbled about "the black train" and backed off.

Shad doubted he could run far enough to avoid feeling he had let down the town if he hightailed it.

"I can find a spot to spy on them if I get close enough by sundown." Shad heaved himself out of his chair. "Keep the home fires burning, Leroy."

"Till Shannon relieves me. What do you want me to tell him about where you got off to?"

"Nothing," Shad and Williamson said in unison. Shad stared at his son-in-law. They thought too much alike for him to be comfortable.

"Let's go," Williamson said. "I remember a spot or two from that topo map where we can—"

"'We can' nothing. I'm going alone. You toddle on back to the house."

"Sorry, Shad, you're not my boss. I work for the railroad."

"You keep telling me that. However, as marshal of Utopia, I can order you around all I want."

"Leroy, is that third cell open?" Williamson asked. "I think my father-in-law's fixing to toss me in it."

Early shook his head and looked at the marshal.

"Well now, Shad, that cell's got a broke lock. Anybody put in it could waltz out the minute I turned my back."

"Remind me to fire you for not keeping up with maintenance." Shad motioned to Williamson. "Let's ride. I've got a spot or two in mind."

"That'll be right for two men?"

"What do you think?" Shad went to the livery, saddled, and hit the trail. It didn't surprise him that Williamson waited for him. Where the railroad bull had found a horse and tack was something of a mystery, but Williamson was a resourceful fellow.

"How likely are they to spot our horses?" Williamson asked. He dug around in his saddlebags and pulled out field glasses.

"This is away from the roads they use to get the lead to the freight yard," Shad said. He put back his own field glasses. Let Williamson carry his own. Shad wanted to keep his hands free to go for his six-gun should the need arise.

"A good place to watch," Williamson said. "If I recollect the map, the main lead mine's right above us. Two smaller ones are farther around the mountainside. But I have no idea where their cabins are."

"Leadbottom's scattered them all over this mountain and the one due west of here. That's where they smelt the lead. It takes a passel of men to dig out the ore but even more to reduce it to bricks."

"I can smell it from here, and it must be a couple miles away," Williamson said. He secured his horse and wiggled between two boulders to stretch out on a flat rock. After scraping his elbows back and forth a few times to get rid of sharp gravel, he settled down on his belly. Field glasses pressed to his eyes, he began scanning the area around the Morriseys' mines.

Shad found a smooth rock and sat. His view of the mine mouths was limited, but he had a better look at the road leading uphill. That came from the small cluster of shacks where Leadbottom and his closest kin lived.

"It'll be too dark to see pretty soon."

"The moon was full a few days ago. That'll give plenty of light," Shad said.

"They're more likely to come out when it's dark and nobody can see them," Williamson said. He paused, then added, "If there's anyone to find."

Again, Williamson's thoughts echoed his own. While Leadbottom was a burr under his saddle, Shad thought Beatrice Gallagher was more likely to give Dixon asylum. All he hoped to do spying on the Morrisey mines was to prove Dixon and his gang weren't here.

That didn't mean they hid out at the Calcutta Mine, but it made more sense than them finding a camp anywhere around the pass that Beatrice didn't know about. He had found the threads of gossip all around Utopia led to the new Coal Queen of the Rockies.

"The day shift's leaving," Williamson reported. He fiddled with the focus on the field glasses, then returned to watching as the miners made their way downhill.

"They won't come past us. Their cabins are in the other direction," Shad said. He didn't expect to find Dixon or his partners among the miners. Wherever they hid out, if Leadbottom Morrisey sheltered them, they'd keep as far from the mines as possible. Doing real work or even being around men who did real work was anathema to men like Dixon.

"You know them like the back of your hand," Williamson said in admiration. "A dozen of them looked like they marched straight for us, then cut back and disappeared."

"Any sign of activity at the mine?"

"I don't see anything at the main mine, but the smaller one . . ."

"What? What is it?"

"Two men ducked into the mine just above us on the hillside. They moved in shadows, and I couldn't identify them."

"Dixon?"

Williamson shrugged.

"Only two men going into a mine shaft's not enough to do serious mining. It might be Dixon and one of his henchmen."

"Or something else." Williamson laid aside the field glasses. "There's one way to find out." He stood, brushed himself off, and started to climb up the hill above them.

"Whoa, you're not going anywhere. Not without me. If that is Dixon, you can't arrest him. I can."

"Can you keep up?"

"Can you move without creating a commotion?" Shad pushed past Williamson and picked out his path up the mountain like a sure-footed mountain goat. He heard Williamson following. The two of them together made less noise as they climbed than a coyote trotting along. They were both skilled enough to mimic natural sounds.

Shad kept a sharp eye out for sentries, but there wasn't any good reason for Leadbottom to watch for snoops. Unless he hid the outlaws and wanted to avoid the law sneaking up to arrest them.

They reached the mine where the two men had entered. Shad kept his breathing shallow to keep from panting. He hated to admit that Williamson was able to make the climb and not seem out of breath. Or was he? Looking closely in the dark, Shad thought he saw Williamson doing the same as him. The younger man was used to Denver and its mile-high altitude. And he was used to walking around Hellfire Pass with twice the altitude.

At least Shad told himself that.

"What do we do? There's no point hanging around outside the mine waiting for them to come out." Williamson chanced a quick peek into the pitch black mine.

"I don't think anyone's on guard duty outside," Shad said. He still felt a twinge entering a Morrisey mine where he had such a bad experience a year earlier.

"What'll it be? Stay outside and wait for them to come back or go find what they're doing inside after all the others have left?"

Shad decided fast. He slipped around the rugged timbers supporting the mine ceiling and was plunged into darkness. He reached for a lucifer, then changed his mind. Pressing his hand against the cold stone wall, he advanced slowly. There wouldn't be a pit this close to the mouth for him to blunder into.

"Here. Found it," he said. He ran his fingers along a rocky ledge just above eye level. He picked up a few half-burned candles and passed them to Williamson. Working his way deeper into the mine let him grab a couple more. Turning his back to the depths of the mine, he flicked his thumb across the match. It flared with sulfurous fury, then settled down to a fitful sputter.

"Hold out your candle," he said. Williamson silently obeyed.

They had two flickering candles. He held up his to get a better look at the rock ledge.

"Here's a candle holder." He passed the tin pan with a raised shield on it to his son-in-law, then put his own candle into another.

They made their way deeper into the mine. The tin shield hid the flame—a little—from the pair who were already deep in the mine.

"This looks all played out," Williamson said. He dug his thumbnail into the wall. "No lead oxide to be found here."

"None's left. I'll give this to Leadbottom. He's efficient when it comes to picking out every last scrap of metal from the mountain."

They shuffled along carefully. They overturned a few rocks and created some noise but nothing that worried Shad. The two men already in the mine wouldn't just sit around waiting for someone to come after them. Whatever business they had in the mine occupied their attention.

He hoped.

"What do we do?" Williamson held up his candle.

Shad looked back at him and cursed under his breath. He had been so intent on following the main shaft, he had missed a drift angling away to the right. Williamson had been alert enough to see it.

Shad listened hard. Sounds came from deeper in the mine, but he couldn't tell from which tunnel.

"We can split up." Williamson took a step down the side drift.

"No, don't. We stick together. It's safer that way if we run into a den of those vipers."

Williamson nodded. The grim expression on his face showed his frustration.

"We both check this way," Shad decided. Continuing along the main tunnel was reasonable, but Williamson had discovered what might be a hidden passage, as much as any cut shaft underground could be hidden.

"We're close, whichever way it is. Let's go a few paces. If we don't find anything, we can come back here," suggested Williamson.

Shad pushed past the railroad detective and walked gingerly down the tunnel. After a dozen yards he stopped and knelt low. His candle cast its flickering yellow light on the ground. Shad looked up.

"The tracks for the ore cart have been yanked up." Williamson snorted in disgust.

"They abandoned this tunnel and used the rails somewhere else."

"We haven't lost much time," Williamson said.

"Who's in a hurry? All we're doing is scouting," Shad said.

They started back to the main tunnel, then Shad froze. He placed his free hand against the tunnel wall.

"It's shaking," he said.

"It's not an earthquake, Shad. This feels like they're drilling."

"More like they've just finished drilling. The vibration's stopped."

They looked at one another in shock. Both men lit out running. The explosion knocked them off their feet and the roof caved in on top of them.

CHAPTER TWENTY-ONE

Shad threw up his arms to protect his head as rock and timber crashed down on him. He deflected some. A rock the size of his head glanced off his arm. As he reflexively turned to push it away, a timber supporting the roof smashed him in the shoulder. His knees buckled, and he fell heavily.

Choking from the dust, eyes stinging, he tried to see what was happening. His candle had gone out, but somehow Williamson's still flickered. The tin holder had been placed on a tiny shelf above the cave-in.

"Williamson? Rich!" He gagged on the dust filling the tunnel. "Are you still alive?"

"Hard to say" came the hoarse reply. "I must not be in Heaven since you're here."

"Why you . . ." Shad surged to his feet and began yanking away the rocks and wood pinning Williamson to the floor. His temper died down when he realized his son-in-law only mocked him to get a response. He wanted to know how badly injured his son-in-law was. The answer surprised even Shad, who bled from cuts all over his upper body but was able to move fast and lift heavy beams that threatened them both.

Slowing when he exposed the railroad detective's prone length, Shad said, "Dig yourself out. I've carried you as far as I can."

"You're some help, old man." Rich Williamson shook himself and pushed to his hands and knees. He shed gravel and dust like a dog shaking himself free of water. He rose and braced himself against the mine wall. He grinned, his dirty face in contrast to his white teeth. "It looks like we're both still alive and kicking."

"What happened? Did they try to kill us?"

"A blast, but I don't think it was supposed to catch us. They're dynamiting somewhere else in the mine. This section's been scavenged for ore cart rail and even wood supports."

"Used 'em to go after a richer vein," Shad said. He wondered how lucky they were, if that was so. Weakening the roof here meant they were at risk of a new collapse.

Shad fumbled around and found his dropped candle and the tin carrier. It took a few seconds to get the wick blazing away. But the sudden flare that died down warned him that the air was going to get close soon.

"We've got to burn up all the air from here to the end of the tunnel before it gets dangerous for us." Williamson held up his candle and peered down the shaft past the point where the ore cart tracks had been pulled up.

Shad wiped his nose. The dirt caked on his face began breaking free. He helped it along. It came off in bloody chunks.

"How're we going to get out of here?" He moved the candle around the rock fall plugging up the shaft. "We don't even have a pick and shovel."

Williamson looked at his hands and made a face.

"These hands are good for a lot of chores. Scratching away the rock's not one of them."

"I want to wrap mine around Leadbottom's neck." Shad turned from the blocked tunnel and peered deeper into the tunnel. "There's got to be an air shaft down that way." He held up his candle. The flame burned hotter when he held it higher.

"Air shafts aren't usually too big, but we don't have much choice."

"If we have to wait very long, we'll be skinny enough to make it up a chimney." Shad started walking.

"Don't remind me that I've missed a meal or two recently."

"That was your fault. If you and Miriam hadn't gone off you'd have had plenty of Ruth's good cooking." He wiped his lips. "Breakfast this morning left something to be desired. I swear your wife made those biscuits out of concrete."

"She's your daughter." Williamson was silent for a moment and then said, "I make better biscuits out on the trail."

"Don't we all?"

The two continued to banter. It took their minds off their potential fate, trapped underground until they starved to death. Both stopped dead in their tracks when the ground shook again.

"What's going on?" Williamson asked.

"The Morriseys are blasting again. That's the only explanation. They must not have blown away enough rock with their first charge." He touched the wall and felt vibrations. "We may be in for more trouble. They're drilling now. When they get a few more holes bored into the rock, they'll set off new explosions."

"Get moving," Williamson said, crowding Shad ahead of him. "This mine's not built to take more of their antics."

Shad felt the walls. Heavier tremors started. Old, weakened supports creaked and more dust cascaded down on them. Legs pumping, he raced into the darkness. The candle flame struggled to keep up with him when he ran flat out.

"Wait, stop, Shad!" Williamson grabbed his shoulder and pulled him around.

"We've got to get away from the cave-in. It's . . ."

He looked up and saw wan moonlight. The night sky was the most beautiful sight he'd ever seen. Even better, fresh air gusted down. The wind was kicking up.

"That's big enough even for an old man with a paunch," Williamson said. "Get going. I'll boost you up."

"Old man? Paunch?" Shad spun on Williamson. Then he saw the broad grin. Again his son-in-law joshed him.

Williamson put his candle down on the floor and cupped his hands, waiting silently. Shad added his so they had a little better light to work by. The best place to begin the climb was at the far side. The air shaft was more than adequate to squeeze through.

"If you're up for it, give me a boost." Shad put his

boot in Williamson's cupped hands. He let out a yelp when he shot upward like a Fourth of July rocket.

He grabbed, caught a rock, and pulled. Kicking and pulling, he scaled the shaft with only a few cuts and bruises along the way. He drove his toes into the chimney's side and heaved hard, bending over the lip. The cool breeze in his face gave him fresh energy. With a final effort, he flopped onto the ground.

He looked up at the crescent moon, then lowered his sight to an astonished miner holding a pick.

"Where'd you come from?" The man's face was hidden in shadow but his question showed no fear, only surprise at finding anyone flat on his back staring at the moon.

"I'm rising up from the depths of hell," Shad said. He recognized the man as one of Leadbottom's cousins.

"You ain't no demon!" Recognition finally came. The man half turned, readied himself, and swung the pick around. Shad rolled over and over. The sharp edge of the pickaxe missed him by inches and sank into the hard ground.

He swung to his feet, hand going to his six-gun. He reacted instinctively. Both hands rose to block the pick crashing down in a wild overhead blow. The impact knocked him off-balance. He slipped and slid downhill. The miner followed him. Only another wild swing that missed saved Shad. The miner tumbled to the ground when he failed to connect with his target.

"Stop right there," Shad said, finally dragging his smoke wagon from his holster.

"Leadbottom tole us to stop any of you law dogs

pokin' 'round. Go on, shoot me. You'll have ever' last one of us here in a thrice." The miner lifted the pick for a new assault.

Shad recognized that the man was right. A gunshot in the dead of night would bring the Morriseys howling down on his neck like a pack of wild dogs. But he had no choice. He cocked the Peacemaker.

He stepped aside as the man crashed to the ground and slid along the slope on his face.

"You do like to live dangerously," Williamson said.

"You wanted me to shoot him?"

"I wanted you to help me out of the mine." Williamson brushed off dirt and then kicked the pick away from the now-stirring man's hand. "What are we going to do with him?"

"For two cents I'd cut his throat. For another penny I'd toss him in the cell with his kin."

"On what charge?"

Shad spat dirt from his mouth, then wiped his lips with his sleeve. That only added a new layer of filth.

"What's it matter?" He stepped over and swung his six-gun in a short arc that ended on the top of the man's head. With a grunt, the miner collapsed to the ground. "We'd better hightail it."

"We can drag him back to the air shaft and dump him into the mine," Williamson suggested.

Shad paused to consider that. He finally decided against it.

"We need to skedaddle."

"It's getting too hot for my liking, too," Williamson said.

"They were blasting down that mine shaft. Dixon and his gang weren't hiding out there. Not a one of them's done an honest day's work in their lives."

"We should check the other mines to see if they're holed up there."

Shad laughed. Williamson had a sense of humor.

"Horses. They'll hide their horses somewhere nearby so they can make a quick escape."

"Let's start looking, then. And don't forget that works both ways. They might find our horses. I'd hate to lose that nag I'm riding."

"Where'd you steal it? You came into town on the stage."

They began making their way around the mountainside, passing directly under the Morriseys' main mine. The black tailings carried a stench that caused Shad's nose to drip again.

"I borrowed it. The railroad keeps a few ponies for use if crews have to ride out to repair the tracks or string new telegraph wires. Sussman wasn't using any of them, so I took the strongest-looking one."

Shad hardly listened. He kept an eye peeled for other Morrisey boys out prowling, though it was too early in the morning hours now for many to be about. They either snored in their cabins or were passed out drunk.

"My feet are getting mighty sore, Shad. I'm used to riding, not walking."

Shad shared that, only he was more used to sitting.

He silently turned and hunted downslope until he found a road that ran close to where they'd left their horses.

"This has been a bust," Williamson said as they reached the hiding spot. "All we accomplished was nearly getting blown up."

"We learned something, other than to be careful poking around in an old mine." He looked across the valley at the other side of Hellfire Pass. "We know where Billy Dixon and his gang aren't."

Williamson stepped up and sat astride his horse, following Shad's gaze.

"Do we scout the Gallagher claim?"

Shad shook his head. If it had been dangerous searching Leadbottom's mines, it'd be downright deadly getting caught in Beatrice's coal mine. He turned his horse toward town and trotted off, Williamson eating his dust.

CHAPTER TWENTY-TWO

"Don't be too long. Ruth won't like it." Williamson touched the brim of his hat and rode off in the direction of the Nelson house.

Shad watched him go. It took all his willpower not to ride with him, but that wouldn't do. He had a job. Being marshal in Utopia was a boring chore most of the time. Lately, it had been anything except dull. A quick heartfelt prayer for the old peace that had lulled him into lethargy was likely to go unheeded.

He squinted and pulled the short brim of his bowler low enough to shield his eyes from the rising sun. He and Williamson had been out longer than he thought. It was another day breaking over his town.

He dismounted at the side of the jailhouse. Every muscle in his body ached. He needed a shot of whiskey to ease some of the pain. Early kept a bottle in the bottom desk drawer. A sip or two would never be missed.

He stepped into the office. Ian Shannon snored away, head down on crossed arms behind the desk.

"Wake up. It's time for you to go home to . . . sleep."

The deputy snapped to attention, alert now. He rubbed one eye, then stretched and yawned.

"Where's Early? He usually gets here before you," Shannon asked.

"Leroy's probably on his way. I got here ahead of him. It was a long night."

Shannon looked him over. Shad knew he was a fright. His clothing was ripped and filthy. A few minor cuts oozed blood and matted his blond hair to the side of his head.

"Did you win?"

"You should see the other guy," Shad said. "How're the prisoners?"

He stared at Shannon because of the man's reaction.

"There's no call for gettin' all upset, Marshal."

Shad went to the door into the cellblock and looked in. Only Gadsden Renfro sprawled out on his bed. The other two cells stood empty, their doors swung wide open.

"Where's the Morrisey boy?" His hand moved unconsciously to his pistol.

"I let him go. He was causin' a ruckus. It was quieter when I booted him out."

"You don't have the authority." Shad felt a curious hollowness now. Shannon had released a prisoner with no good reason. "He was in jail for disturbing the peace—and whatever else I could think up."

"Those aren't much in the way of charges. Keepin' him locked up was a sure way to rile Leadbottom and bring his kin to town. We're better off gettin' rid of him."

"That's not for you to say. You're only a deputy."

Shad faced Shannon squarely. "Ever since I sent you to Denver with Billy Dixon, you've been acting odd. What happened? Did you let Dixon go scot-free, too?"

"What if I did? This isn't any kind of way to run a marshal's office. You make up the laws as you please."

"That's how I keep the peace. Dixon likely robbed the bank, him and his gang. He shot at me and has been hanging around the railroad depot. He's scouting there like he intends to hold up a train. That's private property, so he's guilty of trespassin', at the very least. If anything's gone missing, my money's on him to be the thief."

"That's a while lot of supposings. And what's your interest? Not our worry. That's all railroad property."

"What happened between you and Dixon?"

"I don't have to be treated like I'm some kind of criminal." Ian Shannon grabbed at his vest and plucked off his badge. He tossed it on the desk with a loud clatter. "Find some other yahoo to come when you call and dance to your tune. I quit."

"That's fine," Shad said, his dander up now. "You saved me the need to fire you. If you're not out of here in ten seconds, I'll arrest you for letting Morrisey go free."

"As if he's any kind of criminal." Shannon made an obscene gesture and stormed from the office.

Shad started to go after him, then stopped. Leroy Early came around the jail. He took a quick look at Shannon's back and then at the marshal.

"It looks like I got here in the nick of time. Otherwise, I'd've missed all the excitement." Early paused. "Maybe

I should have lived up to my name and come a few minutes earlier to catch all the commotion and not just the end."

"We need to figure out how to keep the peace with just the two of us."

"Shad, you do have a way of ruinin' a man's day. So you chased him off? That's not much of a surprise. Shannon's been itchin' to get fired for a while now. What pushed you over the edge?"

"He quit." Shad went on to tell his remaining deputy what had occurred.

"Now that's mighty peculiar. Do you think Shannon was bought off? Leadbottom's got a powerful lot of money, or he did before the bank was robbed. Bribin' a deputy is certainly somethin' he'd consider."

"I don't think so. He'd bust his family out of the jail. Leadbottom's a man of action, not something sneaky like bribery. Something more's at the bottom of Shannon letting our prisoner go."

"Get on home and catch some sleep, Shad. You need it. And get a bath. I bet Ruth won't let you into her clean house until you knock off the dirt first. We can cuss and discuss this when you get back."

"When I get back for the night patrol," Shad said tiredly. He slapped Early on the back, walked to his horse and mounted. It was good having a dependable deputy and a horse willing to carry him just a mile farther.

"It was real quiet, but it's only Tuesday. The rootin' 'n tootin' won't start until Friday night," Early said.

"You think you can rustle up a new deputy by then? The weekend needs at least two of us and there's no way you can work a full day without a break." Early rubbed his eyes. "There's no way I can, either. Neither of us is gettin' any younger."

"I've asked around town. I stand a better chance of hiring *him* than I do of getting someone to pin on the badge." Shad pointed toward the cell where Renfro sat muttering to himself.

"Make that new family member of yours an offer. He worked as a Deputy Federal Marshal over in Denver, or so he says."

"He's not inclined," Shad said. "The railroad pays him more 'n Utopia ever could. I don't know for a fact but Rich makes more 'n I do."

"Don't you go quittin' to take a job as a railroad bull." Early put up his hand to shade his eyes from the rising sun. "It's time for me to grab some sleep. Don't forget to feed that varmint."

Shad didn't have to ask who his deputy meant. Renfro stirred now, rattling the bars like a caged animal. He understood Shannon's intent letting Morrisey go. If Shad didn't believe so much in the law, he'd shoo Renfro out of town just to see the last of him. But even if he didn't believe in enforcing the law, Renfro was more Williamson's prisoner than his. The freight manager had been conspiring against the railroad.

After fetching breakfast for both his prisoner and himself, Shad settled down and read through yesterday's newspaper left on his desk after Early finished it. The gossip was stale, and national news was lacking because the telegraph was still down. Whatever news there was came from a week-old copy of *The Rocky Mountain News*.

"Don't go anywhere," he called to Renfro. The muffled reply was probably obscene, and he paid no attention.

Out in the fresh morning sunlight, he stretched his aching joints. Being trapped in a mine affected him more than he cared to admit. If the vet didn't have some horse liniment, he'd have to endure the stiffness until it wore off. As he started walking down the crooked main street toward the railroad depot, he wondered how much the town had to offer to get Williamson to accept as deputy.

As marshal.

Shad was willing to hand the badge over, especially to his son-in-law. Rich Williamson wasn't the same as his own now deceased son, Abednego, but he had worked closely with his own flesh and blood. Abe had been a good deputy. He would have been a better marshal than his old man. He wasn't sure Richard Williamson would be better but he'd certainly be different.

He stopped at the foot of the steps leading to the train depot passenger platform. A deep breath and he rushed up the steps. Slowly or stopping would have doomed him to embarrassment. Sussman watched as he planted his foot firmly on the platform.

"What brings you here this fine morning, Marshal?"

"You have to know, Mister Sussman. The telegraph. When are you sending a crew out to repair the line?"

"Well, there's good news and bad. The good news is

that the line to Georgetown's been fixed. The bad news is that it's down again."

"Don't care what's happening in the gold fields. Have you any notion how long before the wires to Denver are ready again?"

Sussman jerked as if someone stuck him with a pin when a familiar clattering sounded from the telegraph room.

"I should have mentioned it earlier, I suppose," Shad said. He pointed at the key. "Get on over there. I have a telegram I want to send to Denver."

"Th-that's coming from Georgetown, not Denver. I sent a crew out to repair the eastern line, but they haven't come back yet." Sussman swallowed hard, looked around like a cornered rat, and added, "I'll let you know when the line's fixed."

Shad had to rely on Sussman. All he heard were buzzes when the key began chattering furiously.

"Don't you go running off, Marshal."

Shad looked over his shoulder to see who spoke. Rich Williamson strode up, fingers hooked into his gun belt.

"Mister Sussman here wasn't listening close enough. That's the sign for a Denver operator. Is that Underwood, by any chance?"

"H-how'd I know? I missed the start of the message."

"Now, now, Mister Sussman, that's not exactly true, is it? The speed, rhythm, and style are like a signature. That 'gram's coming through from Denver."

"It might be Underwood."

"Why don't you just go on over and send a message?

I think the marshal's got one ready to go, don't you, Marshal Nelson?"

Shad went to the ledge on the ticket window and scribbled out a quick message to the Federal Marshal in Denver. He silently pushed it across to Sussman. The agent took it. His hands shook as he looked at it.

"Legible enough to read? I can dictate it, if you want." Shad watched the agent's reaction. The man had gone pale. His head bobbed up and down. He went to the telegraph key and sat by it. A quick look in Shad's direction and how determined the marshal was lit a fire under him. He began tapping out the telegram.

"He's at the heart of trouble in Utopia," Shad said. "Thanks for letting me know the telegraph wires are back where they belong."

"I'm going to ask the home office to replace him. I don't have the authority unless I catch him stealing from the railroad."

"Early wants to ask if you're interested in changing jobs. Utopia needs another—"

Williamson shoved Shad to the side and flung open the door leading back to the telegraph. Sussman looked up in panic.

"You're not sending to Denver. That telegram's going to Georgetown."

"I . . . I have to clear the line. This is—"

"Get out of the chair," Williamson said, shoving Sussman aside. His hand rested on the table, finger on the polished wood telegraph button.

"What was he doing?"

"He ignored your telegram and sent a message to

Georgetown. I didn't catch its content but did that the code alerted the operator there and not Denver."

"You're wrong, Williamson. You didn't hear right. You're not a real telegrapher. You can't know. You—"

"Shut up," Shad said. "Let the man send my telegram."

Williamson bent over the key, moved Shad's script around, and began tapping out the Morse code.

"He's not expert. He misspelled a lot of the words."

"Then it's good the message is simple enough to understand." Shad started to gloat when he felt something go wrong.

Williamson still tapped out the message, but the sound was different. He stopped and leaned back. He almost snarled, "The line went dead. I don't know how much of your message got through."

"Dead?" Shad turned to Sussman. "What happened?"

He fought to keep from strangling the man. Where Sussman had been panicked before, a broad grin lit his face now.

"The crew must be working on the line. There's no telling how long it'll take 'em to get it all repaired."

"What was the message you sent to Georgetown?"

"Why, I just answered that the line was clear. That's all."

"There was more, but I didn't catch it," Williamson said. He tapped the key a few more times. The electric spark was gone. The telegraph line was dead.

Shad had the feeling Utopia was, too.

CHAPTER TWENTY-THREE

Richard Williamson tapped the key a few more times. Dead. He wondered at Sussman's pleased expression, as if he wanted the telegraph line to be down. The man might be a lazy lout, but this went beyond sloth. He wanted the line down for some other reason.

"Who's out fixing the wire?" Williamson asked.

"One of the men who worked in the freight yard. I don't know his name, but he said he'd done work like that before for the Army."

"I'll ride out and see if I can help him," Williamson said. "I've had some experience with stringing wire."

"Of course you have," Shad said. "There's not a whole lot you don't have experience doing, is there?"

"A few things." Williamson smiled. "I've never been a pa before." He pursed his lips. "I've never been a husband, either, but that's working out just fine."

"What are you two going to do?" Sussman looked from one to the other. "I've got work to do."

"What's that?" Shad asked. "Until the repairs are made on the rail that got pulled loose, the Denver route's closed. And there's no reason for the Georgetown train to come up, unless it's bringing passengers to Utopia."

"What few folks that do come up, go right on back down," Sussman said. "Gettin' the train on the turn-around downhill is a chore and not one I do often. It takes a good engineer and me giving precise directions."

"That's not something that happens too often, is it, Sussman?" Williamson looked over the train schedule. "All the passenger traffic is in from Denver."

"Most of the freight, too." Shad pushed Sussman out of the way as he returned to the passenger area of the depot.

"You keep an eye on him," Williamson said softly when they'd left Sussman behind in the telegraph office. "He's up to something."

"Fire him. Put somebody else in his place."

"I've got no call. With the tracks being repaired he's not doing anything so he can't be doing anything wrong. At least as far as the railroad is concerned. But he's up to something."

"When the telegraph line's fixed, send a message to your Denver bosses to replace Sussman."

"I will," promised Williamson, "but for the time being, it's to our advantage to see what he does. He must be in cahoots with Dixon. He certainly plotted something with Renfro."

Shad walked with Williamson to the outer passenger platform.

"What do you expect to find?" Shad asked.

"It's mighty curious that the telegraph went dead just

as I started to send your message to Denver. Coincidences happen, but there've been a few too many of late."

"The derailment? The telegraph out?"

"Other things," Williamson said. "Look after Miriam and the baby for me."

They walked in silence back to the jailhouse where Williamson took his leave. He slowed when he passed the Gold Dust City Saloon. It was too early in the day for customers to crowd in for lunch. His belly growled, reminding him that he hadn't eaten breakfast. Time pressed in on him like some wild ore crusher. Williamson kept walking and went straight to the stagecoach office.

The morning wind caused the telegraph wires to hum. He looked around. There wasn't any business here. In another few months the stagecoach would be out of business. Passengers would come on the train, mail was already being sent that way, and once the only telegraph into Utopia, the railroad again stole away the stage company's business.

"Mister Egan," he called when he saw the depot agent timidly watching him from just inside the doorway. For a moment he thought Egan would slam the door and lock it. If ever a man acted like a fearful rabbit peering from its burrow as a coyote sauntered past, Egan was it.

"What can I do for you?"

"I need to send a telegram."

"Use the railroad's. You work for 'em. You prob'ly get to send it for free."

"The line's down."

"Just like the train." Egan sounded frightened rather than happy that his biggest competitor was out of business for the time being.

"I'll pay the going rate. The 'gram's meant for—"

"Save your money. Can't do it."

"Why won't you?"

"I didn't say I wouldn't. I said can't. The line's down somewhere between here and Denver. I suppose the home office knows, but I can't even let them know until a stage comes through. Won't happen for another couple days."

"I'd offer to ride out and fix it for you, but I have to see to repairing the railroad's property first."

Egan stared off into the distance. He made a vague gesture.

"The line goes over the low range and from there down into Denver. It's as close to straight as a crow flies. Not like your telegraph."

"The railroad followed the easiest route to lay track. It was natural to string wire along the road."

"If you want, I can give you tools and some spare wire. I don't have much. Just a few yards." He eyed Williamson. "Do you know how to splice wire? That much wire might be all you need." Egan held up a small spool of telegraph wire.

Williamson considered the matter for a moment and then silently held out his hand. Egan passed over what he had before rummaging about for a leather pouch bulging with lineman's tools. Williamson took those, too.

"I'll see about fixing your line. If the signal comes through, send this message right away." He scribbled a few lines on a scrap of paper and passed it to the stage agent.

"You fix the line, that's the least I can do." Egan licked his lips. "I don't suppose you'd consider having me send it at a discounted rate?" When he saw Williamson's sour expression, he grinned weakly. "I'll send it right away for free. Just send along three dits and a dah."

"V?"

"That'll let me know you were victorious in mendin' the wire."

Williamson shook his head as he left. In all his born days, he could never figure what went on in other people's heads. He mounted, caught the sun reflecting off the telegraph line, and started riding. Giving the horse its head kept a steady pace without him thinking much about anything other than staring up at the wire.

He'd ridden about an hour, heading up into the hilly part of the terrain just east of Utopia, when he saw the problem. Williamson trotted to the pole and stared at it. Someone had used an axe to chop the telegraph pole plumb down. A few minutes riding took him to the next and the next. All three had been deliberately chopped down.

He dismounted and tugged at the wire. The poles were down, but the reason they strung the line on poles was to keep it off the ground where critters might gnaw on it. For a quick-and-dirty fix, he saw no reason patching the wire and leaving it on the ground wouldn't work.

And then he began patching the wire.

Long sections of the wire had been cut into foot-long lengths. Slicing this much back together would take days, if it was possible at all. He had a couple yards of repair wire. If more than a few segments of the downed wire had been tossed aside or carried away by animals, this line would never be repaired. The stagecoach company's line needed more extensive work than he could give.

Dejected, he mounted, got his bearings, and rode northeast. This path would cross the railroad tracks eventually. He was already miles from town, and the break in that telegraph line might be back toward Utopia, but he doubted it. Whoever had chopped down the other telegraph poles had done it where it was most inconvenient to restring the line.

Before he knew it, he found the tracks. He glanced back toward Utopia and considered returning to town. He wasn't any kind of repairman. Then Williamson decided to ride a few more miles along the tracks before reversing his path. It wouldn't hurt for him to find the spot where the train had derailed. Going to Utopia by stagecoach had bypassed the wreck.

As a railroad detective, he felt the need to investigate the scene of the crime closely. Hearing his father-in-law's taradiddle did nothing to give a full picture of what happened. If anything, Shad had dwelled overlong on taking Beatrice Gallagher back to town rather than investigating the deaths of the engineer and fireman.

Williamson drew rein when he saw the caboose poking up at the top of a rise. He approached slowly. Six cars weighed down with coal stretched in front of the caboose. Then he saw nothing but a scene out of hell. The single rail that had been removed lay downhill, partly hidden by pieces of the steam engine's boiler. When the engine tipped over, the boiler burst. It had sent shrapnel blasting a hundred yards. That large sections of the engine hid the removed rail told him the track had been sabotaged.

A sour taste came to his mouth. He already knew the train had been sabotaged. Finding who'd done it mattered less than keeping them from doing it again. Let Shad arrest the vandal. It was Williamson's duty to bring to justice whoever murdered the engineer and fireman.

He rode around the tipped-over coal tender. Lumps of coal had been spread over a hundred yards going downhill. He took off his hat and held it over his heart for a moment when he saw the two graves higher on the hill. They were fresh. These had to be the final resting places for Davey Fulbright and his stoker. Williamson felt a moment's anger at himself. He didn't even know the man's name who had died along with Highballin' Davey.

Williamson dismounted and walked closer. Both men's names had been crudely carved into wood crosses.

"Rest in peace, Davey. You, too, Enoch White."

Davey Fulbright had been cheating the railroad but stayed with his job because finding a replacement for such an experienced engineer was almost impossible. A dozen different railroads competed for personnel. Rather than abandon the Denver to Georgetown route going through Hellfire Pass or even reduce the travel by half, the railroad brass decided to overlook the man's thievery. He had accepted less than a full load of coal every time he stopped at the Utopia depot, paid full price, and pocketed a few dollars for looking the other way. The complicitous freight yard manager had been gunned down, paying for his theft with his life.

And Sussman's role had been ignored, too. Williamson sighed. It was easier to ignore wrongdoing than to punish it. For all he knew, that was the attitude behind someone derailing the train.

"Maybe you paid, too, Davey Fulbright. Maybe you paid. It just took a bit longer." Williamson settled his Stetson back on his head, mounted, and continued riding along the tracks, a sharp eye on the telegraph wire.

When the track repair crew came, they could fix any break in the telegraph. But would they? Williamson had worked with some of those men. They thought of themselves as railroad royalty. He had seen more than one track man shout down a company officer and get by with such insolence. All workers were in short supply. It was easier to replace a station manager or even a director than it was a man who swung a sledgehammer and drove spikes to keep the road open.

Williamson shifted from one side of the track to the other so the sunlight shined off the wire. He had heard how the Apaches cut a line and then tied the ends together with rawhide. A causal examination showed a complete line, but the electricity wouldn't flow through the rawhide strips. The gleam told him these wires were intact.

Another hour riding brought him to a shallow U-shaped valley. As he entered a stand of trees near the tracks, he felt something eating at him. He moved to the tracks to get a better look. The boring routine of riding and looking had dulled his senses. An entire section of wire was missing between two poles.

He rode closer, slung the end of his lariat around the pole, and worked his way up slowly. At the top, he stared at the bare-naked glass insulator. A wire should have run through it. From the stub of copper poking out, he figured it had been cut through using a sharp knife. Retreating, he got back into the saddle and rode to the next pole. He didn't need to climb this pole. There was no way of proving it, but he guessed the same sharp knife that had severed the wire at the other pole had done the same dirty work here.

Circling around for a few minutes failed to turn up the downed wire. The saboteurs had taken the wire with them. His paltry few feet of repair wire would hardly stretch from the top of the pole to the ground, much less all the way through the air to the far pole.

The bare glass insulators caught the sun and reflected rainbows, as if mocking him.

CHAPTER TWENTY-FOUR

Rich Williamson started back to Utopia. The repair work was beyond him. Then he tugged on the reins and stopped to look around.

"Sussman said he'd sent out someone to repair the line." He looked around, then dismounted and began studying the ground for tracks. If anyone had come this way, he hadn't passed them on their way back to town because they weren't able to do the repairs any more than he was.

If they rode on, why bother? This length of downed line wasn't going to be fixed by cannibalizing wire from somewhere closer to Denver. With another tug on the reins, he turned back downhill again and headed for Denver along the tracks. Something wasn't right.

Within fifteen minutes he found what it was.

A man lay in a shallow ditch near the tracks. Face down. Deader than a doornail.

He rolled him over and saw the reason. He had been filled with lead. From what he could tell, the would-be repairman had not been armed. Not with a six-shooter. There wasn't even the slick spot at the hip to show he'd been carrying iron and whoever killed him had taken the gun. This was a freight handler dragooned into a job he was unqualified for and not a gunman.

"Doesn't matter what he did as a regular job. He was a railroad employee." Williamson stood and strained to see through the wooded area along the tracks a quarter mile off to the south. His vision wasn't that good. Nothing moved.

On impulse, he knelt and touched the man's cheek. He drew back immediately. The body was still warm. Not living warm but close enough to it that the death hadn't been more than an hour or two ago.

Williamson made sure his Winchester magazine was chock-full of rounds. A quick check loaded a sixth cartridge into his Colt .44. He ran his fingers up and down over the tooled leather holster, then reached down and secured it around his leg with the dangling rawhide thong. His gut told him a quick draw was in his immediate future. Having the holster flop about and slow him down spelled certain death.

A glance at the dead body convinced him he was going to be on the trail until the killer—killers—paid for the wanton murder of an unarmed railroad employee.

He rode along for another half hour and finally heard something other than the whistle of wind in the tall lodgepole pines. A few Douglas firs mingled with the pervasive pines but lacked the stamina to take over.

He halted and cupped his hand to his ear. A grim smile crossed his lips. Horses. More than one. Just about the right number for a gang of railroad-employee-murdering swine. He slipped the keeper off his pistol's hammer but didn't draw. His quarry was ahead, hidden by the trees.

"Not far from the tracks." He looked up and saw the telegraph line shaking about. The killers were still up to some mischief, cutting down wires. Why destroying one section of the telegraph wasn't enough puzzled him. If he was lucky, he'd find out.

If any of the cutthroats lived to tell him about their motives.

Slowly walking took all his willpower. He wanted to gallop ahead, six-gun blazing. Such an attack only alerted the men he sought. Stealthy as an Indian was the best way to catch them.

He moved away from the tracks and skirted the edge of the forested area. As he rounded a bend in the tracks, he saw them. Two men working to throw a lariat with a rock tied to the end up over the wire. They had never worked as cowboys from the inept way they threw the rope. As he rode closer, he saw that they had finally dropped the rope into place. Each grabbed the end of the rope and together they yanked hard.

Williamson's hand flashed to his six-gun when the rope pulled a glass insulator free. It sailed into the air, flashing in the sunlight as it tumbled over and over. He squeezed off a shot. Lead careened off the side of the thick glass. He failed to shatter the insulator, but he sent shards flying everywhere. What remained went sailing off into space.

The two men stared stupidly at the flying insulator. Only when Williamson called out did they realize what had happened.

"Move and you'll be filled with as much lead as the man you killed."

He trotted closer, his Colt covering them. He saw how twitchy they were. The smallest mistake on his part and both would go for their pistols.

"Unbuckle those gun belts. Let 'em fall to the ground."

One reached to obey. The other made a move as if he was doing as Williamson ordered, then he stopped.

"Don't do it, Squinty."

"Squinty? Herk? You ride with Billy Dixon," Williamson cried out in recognition.

"See, Squinty, we're downright famous. Even this railroad bull knows us."

"How do you know me?" Williamson rode closer. He waggled his six-gun for them to obey. Squinty started again to do as he was told, and once more Herk snapped at him to stop.

"You killed the telegraph repairman," Williamson stated flatly. "You've been destroying railroad property." He pointed with the muzzle of his gun to the downed wire. "My boss wouldn't lose a minute's sleep if I cut you both down here and now."

"Billy said you're like the marshal. You won't shoot us in cold blood. You got scruples."

"What's that?" Squinty asked.

"The guns. Drop them!" Williamson took aim at Herk. Not only did he seem to be in charge, if he dropped dead the chance of Squinty finding a target was smaller. The outlaw's nose wrinkled up as he tried futilely to bring their captor into focus.

For an instant Williamson thought his finger had

slipped, and he'd pulled the trigger. The shot echoed along the tracks. Then he realized a bullet had drilled its way into the cantle of his saddle. It took a second, but he felt a hot spot on his rear end. A bullet fired from the woods had almost taken him out of the saddle.

As it was, he found himself fighting to stay astride his bucking horse. The bullet had spooked it. Williamson fired at both the outlaws, but they were already sprinting for cover among the trees.

He brought his horse under control and got off two more shots at the fleeing outlaws. Then he lifted his sights and emptied his six-shooter at a tree where he saw a sniper resting his rifle against a limb. His shots all missed, but one tore a splinter from the limb, forcing the rifleman to jerk away.

"Dixon!" He shouted the name. For a split second, the outlaw froze and stared straight at him. The identification was indisputable.

Williamson spun his Colt around and jammed it into his holster. Bending forward he drew out his rifle. He pulled back the hammer. A round was waiting in the chamber. As he rode after Herk and Squinty, he got off a shot. Levering in another cartridge let him send Dixon scuttling on his way. The man fell to one knee in his haste, then got to his feet and ran.

Williamson had to pull back and stop his horse. The nervous animal crow-hopped about, but this was a steadier base than shooting from astride a galloping horse. He got off four more rounds before the trio vanished into the trees.

He wanted to pursue them pell-mell, but all three

were armed and more than willing to fill his body full of lead. The dead repairman showed that. Chasing after them, three against one, had to be the dumbest thing he had ever considered. Better to return to Utopia, tell Shad, get a posse together, and come after the trio.

That was the smart thing.

Rich Williamson plunged into the woods, ducking low limbs on junipers and the occasional oak or elm. The fir trees, except for the new growth, were like the pines. Their limbs were high up and not a worry for a mounted man.

Caution turned him wary. He bent low as he walked his horse into the cool shade of the forest. Eyes darting left and right ahead, he went deeper into the woods until he heard the pounding of horses' hooves off at an angle ahead. Heels tapping the flanks of his still skittish horse, he sped up and found the spot where the gang had left their horses to sample cool water running in a shallow brook. They already tore along a game path through the woods.

For an instant he caught sight of one of them but couldn't identify him. Knowing the direction they rode, he took time to reload his Colt and stuff a few more rounds into the Winchester's magazine. If he took on three killers, he wanted as much firepower as he could muster. Only then did he plunge ahead, riding faster than he should and trusting that he had lit a fire under the cutthroats. If he rode into an ambush, he was a goner.

He burst out of the woods into a rolling meadow. For a moment he didn't see the men he chased. Then he saw

them top a rise almost on the far side. They kept their
heads down and galloped fast. One railroad bull had put
the fear into a trio of killers.

Or had he? They were the only ones he caught sight
of. From what Shad had said about Dixon, those two
henchmen were likely the only ones riding with him.
But why were they afraid of only one man, even Richard
Williamson?

"They don't want to get shot up, even if they eventually kill me," he decided. Something lay ahead, and they
wanted whole skins for it.

Williamson galloped after them, more determined
than ever. As good as it would be to catch all three and
see them on trial, if he took only one of them back to
town for questioning, he was sure to find out a lot more
of what they were up to. Shad kept mumbling about a
black train. Williamson had no idea what that meant.

Catching one of the trio and sweating it out of him
would go a long ways to improving the way Shad thought
of him as his new son-in-law.

He reached the far side of the meadow and slowed.
The fleeing riders had found a road. It must have been
a logging road. Trees had been felled as far as William-
son could see. The cutting had occurred years before.
New growth, some as tall as six feet, had sprung up.
But any cover a forest provided was gone.

Williamson saw the dust cloud hanging over the
twin-rutted road. Dixon and his men had ridden along
the road only minutes ahead of him. He put his head
down low, clutched his rifle, and tapped his heels to
his horse's flanks. The tired animal responded the best

it could, but he had been riding it all day. Dixon and his gang rode fresh mounts.

He knew he fell farther behind them but doggedly continued. They weren't going to cut off the road. They made too good time as the road circled the mountain and worked its way higher and higher.

Williamson slowly realized he was riding on Gallagher land when he saw a half dozen played-out coal mines up near the tree line. That turned him warier than before. Even if he caught Dixon, he'd still find himself pitted against the entire Gallagher clan. Beatrice Gallagher, since she had taken over from her aunt as self-styled Coal Queen of the Rockies, had made it clear she was not on good terms with the law in Utopia.

He doubted she'd be on good terms with any of Shad's relatives, either. The way a small town like Utopia kept itself entertained was gossip. There wasn't any way Beatrice didn't recognize him right away, even if their contact in the past had been fleeting.

Slowing even more, Williamson saw the men he chased make a hairpin turn far up the mountainside. They stopped. He guessed they exchanged words with a guard. The Gallaghers protected their land as jealously as Leadbottom Morrisey did his.

Turn back?

He kept riding. Capturing Dixon and his cohorts was so close to happening that he could taste it. He balanced the need for speed with being careful. If they shot at him from ambush, he'd never arrest them. By the time he reached the spot where he had seen the outlaws stop, he knew he had no chance at all of capturing them.

No sentry stopped him, but he saw where his quarry had taken a side road directly into the mountain. A mine shaft yawned wide and dark. Hoofprints went directly to the mine. He didn't dismount, but by bending low in the saddle he saw at least two sets of boot prints paralleling the road. Dixon, Herk, and Squinty had been escorted into the mine. If they had been shot, he'd've heard the reports.

He stared at the dark mouth and wished it led to hell, but it didn't. For Billy Dixon, it led to a sanctuary Williamson wasn't able to breach.

Reluctantly, dejected from all he had seen, he turned his horse about and retraced his path down the old logging road. All the way back to the railroad tracks, he fumed and cursed to himself. After taking the few personal items off the repairman to return to any kin, he buried him uphill from the railroad tracks.

Sweaty, tired, and not a little morose, he headed for Utopia. His curses became even more sulfurous and his mood turned darker the longer he rode.

Billy Dixon. Beatrice Gallagher. That was an unholy alliance and not one he wanted to report to his father-in-law.

CHAPTER TWENTY-FIVE

"Not yet," Richard Williamson told Shad. "Waiting for them can be dangerous unless you've got a lot of guns to back you up."

Shad pursed his lips. His mind raced. No good ideas came to him, and he said so.

"If Dixon is hiding out in the old coal mines, it's almost impossible to pry him out of there," he said. Beatrice and, before her, Winifred Gallagher, had gone to great lengths to keep the maze of tunnels throughout the mountains a secret to outsiders.

"Worse, if the Gallaghers are letting him stay, they've salted him away in the most secure spot possible. Wherever that is."

"Wherever that is," Shad mused. He knew where it was. Beatrice and most of her family lived in the played-out mines like moles. A tunnel ran from one cabin along the trail where Winifred Gallagher had been killed. The old woman had pretended to live there to keep intruders out of her hair.

She'd disappear into the cabin and seemingly not come out for a week. All the time she'd be underground with most of her family. Shad had seen no fewer than four entries to those subterranean quarters. There wasn't much to attack aboveground. If anyone was foolish enough to try, Beatrice ordered her family to blow up a couple of the entry points, then come boiling out of others for a flank attack. Or even one from the rear. Shad had no idea how extensive those tunnels were, but the Gallaghers had been burrowing away furiously for a decade or more.

For two cents, he'd toss a bundle of lighted dynamite into every hole and see what he flushed out with the explosions.

"Get a posse together. I'll lead them to the derailment and give cover for the repair crew."

"Rich," he said tiredly, "if Dixon has two men riding with him, he might have a dozen more we don't know about."

"The Mexico Kid?"

"And others. This used to be a robbers' roost filled with dozens of outlaws. At least three gangs made this their headquarters."

"They might have been murderers but they weren't stupid. As long as they controlled Hellfire Pass they'd never be pried loose. Attack from Denver and they escaped west. Come at them from Georgetown and they went east."

"Getting the law to attack in big enough numbers at the same time?" Shad shook his head sadly. Such coordination would never happen. The only way back then to get different sets of lawmen to work together came along the stagecoach telegraph line. The gangs controlled the stage and any messages zinging along the wires.

"That's why they took out the telegraph in both directions," Williamson said. "Something's in the wind."

Shad started to say something about the town gossip but held back. He had to deal in facts, not rumors. Even if those rumors kept him awake nights worrying over their true meaning.

"We need to send a message to either the Federal Marshal in Denver or Sheriff Parsons in Georgetown."

"Glory Be Parsons," Williamson said sarcastically. "The chance of him doing anything more than climbing out of bed in the morning is zero."

Leroy Early had listened to the byplay. He added his two cents.

"Glory Be would fall out of bed, still drunk from the night before. You'd have to catch him sober if you wanted him to send even one deputy."

"That happens once in a blue moon," Williamson said. "My boss has had dealings with Parsons. They weren't pleasant dealings, either."

"Dixon's gang will keep destroying the telegraph to Denver," Shad said. "Our best bet is to send a messenger to Denver."

"I'm here to find who destroyed a steam engine and killed our engineer and stoker." Williamson crossed his arms and looked like an earthquake wouldn't shake loose his determination. That made it clear that he was not budging from Utopia until his job was successful.

And that job wasn't acting as a messenger boy.

"I can ride on out," Early said. "I remember the way and wouldn't get lost."

Shad started to speak, but Williamson beat him to it.

"With only a marshal and a deputy in town now, is that a smart move?"

"We need the reinforcements," Early said. He looked hard at Shad. "For whatever comes this way."

Skepticism tinged his deputy's words, and Shad wasn't up to berating him for that. He had no idea what was barreling toward Utopia. If anything. He wouldn't put it past Dixon to start rumors just to give him the collywobbles. Whether a flood of outlaws prepared to wash over town or there was only Dixon and his two men hardly mattered. The threat was enough to keep Shad up at night.

That made him doubly glad that Williamson had so firmly said he was staying in town. One more gun, and one in a steady hand at that, defending the Nelson house would be appreciated.

"Too bad Shannon quit," he said, more to himself than the other two.

"Good riddance, I say," Early snapped. "He was turnin' downright loco. He wasn't comin' close to doin' his job. You need deputies you can rely on, Shad."

"I know, I know. I don't need ones that watch a bank robbery and move nary a muscle to stop it." Shad saw Williamson's eyebrows arch at that, but the railroad detective said nothing.

"Then there's the Denver trip with Dixon," Early went on.

"Is there someone in town you'd trust to be courier?" Williamson shifted from foot to foot, anxious to be somewhere else.

"I can find a reliable soul," Shad assured him. "Why don't you go on up to the house for a spell?"

"I can't stay," Williamson said hastily. "I'll take a pile of ammo and go stand guard where the train derailed. That crew's got to show up soon. When they do, an extra rifle might be needed to keep Dixon from shooting them, too."

"Don't be a stranger at the house," Shad said. "You wouldn't abandon me to those rock-hard biscuits, would you?"

Williamson laughed, then took his leave. Shad chewed at his lower lip and came to a conclusion.

"Ralph or Missy'll know who I can trust."

"Reckon so," Early said. "You don't want to send any of Beatrice's clan."

"Or Leadbottom's."

"You might recruit one from each and send them together. They could watch one another real close."

"Sometimes I can't tell when you're pulling my leg, Leroy. If I wanted to do something loco like that, I'd send Renfro."

"That'd kill two birds with one stone. Let Dixon gun him down. That way he's out of our jail, and we don't have to feed him no more."

"Chances are good he'd join up with Dixon." He considered the matter and what he had seen at the freight yard. "Truth is, he's already in cahoots with Dixon. Or at least him and Beatrice have dealings we don't know about."

"More than coal, you mean?"

"Hold the fort, Leroy."

His deputy dropped into the chair and hiked his boots to the desktop. When he saw the marshal wasn't objecting, he tipped his hat forward over his eyes and laced his fingers behind his head. A pretend snore ripped out.

Shad let him have his fun. There had been little enough in either of their lives lately. He took one bend in the main street after another and saw Missy outside the Gold Dust City lighting the kerosene lamps.

"Getting ready for a big night?" he asked.

"Marshal, you headin' in for a snort? Or to get a snootful? It's sundown so you must be off duty 'bout now."

"I swear, Missy, everyone in town knows my business better than I do. You have any customers inside that aren't drunk already?"

"Too many," she said grinning. "I'm fallin' down on my job of encin' those gents to bet at faro and knock back another drink to drown the sorrow of their gamblin' losses."

He went directly to the end of the bar where Ralph Rockwell struggled with a pony keg.

"If you ever want to quit your job and work for me, Marshal, you're hired. I'm gettin' too old to lug heavy kegs of beer around."

"You're too old?" Shad laughed at that. Ralph was ten years younger. Where Shad was rangy, Rockwell sported muscles like a smithy.

"I can give you the first beer outta the keg. It'll be mostly foam, so I won't charge you."

"Go on," Shad said. He waited for Ralph to tap the keg and draw a mug that, as promised, was mostly foam. The barkeep slammed it down on the stained surface in front of Shad. This caused more of the bubbles to pop and the level inside to drop.

"Drink fast. I don't want the others to know how little's in every mug."

Shad sampled the warm beer. It took only a single gulp to drain all the liquid. Two inches of froth remained. He pushed the mug back.

"I need someone I can trust to take a letter to Denver."

"You and the Federal Marshal becomin' pen pals?"

Shad almost barked at the man. Missy knew his business better than anyone else—except for her employer. Ralph Rockwell was a spider in the center of the town's web. The smallest twitch on a web and he knew.

"That cowboy at the other end of the bar. Name's Paul. Don't know I ever heard his last name. Or that might be his last name. He worked for Guthrie on the Triple Z, but he got laid off. No fault of his own. Guthrie's havin' big financial problems. Don't spread it around, but he lost most of his cattle to Texas fever."

"If that—" Shad clamped his mouth shut. He knew Clyde Guthrie. The man was an honest, forthright rancher. All his diseased cattle with splenic fever would be killed and buried, no exceptions. If most of his herd was infected, the Triple Z was likely out of business since the past few years hadn't been too profitable.

"Offer him five dollars, and he'll ride all the way to Chicago for you. And come halfway back."

Shad made his way down the bar. The cowboy nursed a single beer. From the sad look of the foam, he had ordered one and had clung to it for some time. It must have been the last one out of the prior keg since it had gone flat.

"Ralph, give Paul another beer. On me." He dropped a dime on the bar.

"Why're you butterin' me up, Marshal? I don't know nuthin' 'bout nuthin'."

Shad explained what needed to be done. At first the cowboy looked skeptical, then Shad mentioned five silver dollars to make the trip.

"That much?"

"I'll even throw in a bonus when you get back. Another dollar, if you want to get back to Utopia, that is." He sized up the young man. "Otherwise, stay in Denver or find a star to follow and go after it."

"Nuthin' for me here. 'Cept for another dollar."

"I might have a job for you, too. You ever think on being a lawman?"

"Me? Naw, never did."

"I need another deputy. If you listen up and follow orders, both mine and Deputy Early's, you can be making twenty dollars a month in no time."

"What about a roof over my head and chuck?"

"Can't give you those. We're not as rich as a rancher with a herd of cattle to feed his hands. We might work out something where you can sleep in the jail if all the cells aren't full."

"I've slept in worse places," Paul allowed, thinking hard on the offer.

"Here's the letter I want delivered." Shad fished it from his coat pocket and passed it to Paul. When he saw the hesitation, he took out the silver dollars and dropped them one by one on top of each other. The silvery ring convinced his recruit.

"You've got yourself a mailman, Marshal. I'll get to Denver and be back in two shakes of a lamb's tail."

"As soon as you can get that to the Federal Marshal . . ." Shad slapped Paul on the back. The young man grinned ear to ear. One front tooth was missing. Clyde Guthrie's beef must have been as tough as shoe leather.

"I'm ready to hit the trail, sir!" With a quick move, he drained the last drops of beer, wiped froth from his lips, and hitched up his gun belt.

Shad watched him leave as he ordered another beer. He deserved a reward for a job well done. When he heard galloping hooves outside the saloon he knew things would be just fine. Help was as good as on the way.

CHAPTER TWENTY-SIX

"So he left before dawn?" Leroy Early yawned.

"Miriam saw him off. She was crying," Shad said. "He won't be in much danger. The tracks are already torn up. All he needs to do is find a hidey-hole and wait for the repair crew. When there're a dozen men working to repair the tracks, Dixon won't dare do anything."

"It's not clear to me he tore up the tracks." Early fidgeted and began idly tearing the newspaper into strips.

"Well, Leroy, I have the same question but think I've worked it out. There's so much swirling around town, it makes my head spin. If I had to place a bet, I'd say Leadbottom did it."

"Just as Beatrice claimed." The deputy began braiding the pieces of newsprint into a mat.

"Because she hates me doesn't mean she can't be right now and then."

"The Morrisey kid we had got in the cell back there confessed. He was drunk, but you think he was on the crew that did it?"

"I do. But I don't think Patrick knew anything about it. Or if he did, he arrived after it was too late to do anything."

"It makes sense that Patrick would be lurking around the site to rescue her." Early held up his handiwork. He put it on the desk and then hiked his boots up onto it to keep dirt from dropping onto the top.

"The trouble with that is how nobody knew she'd be on the train. Even her own family was taken by surprise when she boarded." Shad watched Early move his boot heels around to stay on the paper mat.

"Leadbottom wanted some revenge for Dixon robbing the bank and got a bonus with the head of the Gallagher family bein' aboard." Early nodded. "This puts all the pieces together. You've surely been rackin' that fine brain of yours to figger all this out, Shad. And all without a shred of proof."

"He claims the Gallaghers did the robbery, but he's not far wrong if Dixon is hiding out in the coal mines. Beatrice is working with Dixon, sure as rain and next Sunday."

"Things are gonna blow some day soon, Gallagher against Morrisey." Early pushed to his feet and came around the desk. He patted the paper mat. "It's all yours for another day, Marshal."

"At least last night was quiet." Shad closed his eyes and let out an exasperated sigh. Someone came running down the street shouting at the top of his lungs. He wasn't going to use that paper mat any time soon.

"What can that be about?" Early asked.

"Stay for a minute, and we'll find out together." Shad

didn't have a minute to wait. A boy, hardly ten, panted harshly from the run. His eyes were wide.

"Marshal, Marshal, it's awful. Come quick. Over by Mister Sampson's store. It . . . the . . . please, go on!" The boy bent over, hands on his knees as he fought to catch his breath.

Shad looked at Early, then tilted his head in the direction of the store. They marched over side by side.

"I didn't hear no gunshots," Early said. "That's good news."

"That's not."

A dozen men pressed close to a horse. Sampson held the reins as if they would turn into rattlers and bite him. As Shad neared he saw why.

The bridle was drenched in blood. He caught his breath when he moved around to the far side. The saddle leather was soaked with blood. With a trembling finger, he reached out and touched a spot. It was tacky. Fresh but not too fresh.

"This was spilled not more 'n a couple hours ago," he said. "Who's horse is it?"

"That there paint belongs to a cowboy off Mister Guthrie's ranch." The man giving the information looked around, then added, "His name's Paul, I think. A nice guy."

Shad went to the horse. It shied, but he gentled it and worked his way back. The blood soaked into the leather looked like more than any single man could have pumping in his body. He pulled the rawhide thong free on the saddlebags and peered inside.

His heart jumped into his throat. He pulled an envelope out.

"You lost a courier, from the look of that," Early said softly. He plucked the letter addressed to the Denver Federal Marshal from Shad's numbed fingers and stuffed it into his coat pocket for safekeeping.

"How far did he get before . . . this?" Shad wondered.

"I seen the horse when I was gatherin' eggs for my ma," a boy of eight said. "It tore on past like its tail was on fire. I wanted to catch it but my ma tole me to finish my chores." He looked a little frightened and then puffed out his thin chest. "I did and came a'runnin' on into town. Somebody got hurt bad, didn't they?"

"Everyone, go about your business," Early said. He shooed the youngsters away and tugged on the reins. "I'll put the horse into the livery stable."

"It belongs to his next of kin," Shad said in a choked voice. "Does anybody know who that might be?"

The people left in the tight circle around the horse looked left and right, hoping someone would speak up. No one did.

"I'll send word out to the Triple Z," Early said.

Shad took the reins from Early and led the horse to the livery stables. After seeing the horse settled into a stall with a nosebag of oats, he saddled his own horse and rode from town. There wasn't any hurry. Paul was dead. Whether Shad found where he had been murdered sooner or later hardly mattered. The killers had no reason to stick around after they gunned down Shad's courier.

"He deserves a proper burial," he said to himself, repeating it over and over as he rode along the road from town.

It angered him that he only had to ride a half hour before he found where the cowboy had been ambushed.

"This is as far as he got?" He looked around and found a patch of grass drenched in blood. His search widened. The body had been dumped into a shallow ditch and covered with brush pulled up all around. It was a sorry grave for a man who didn't deserve to die like this.

He stepped down and kicked away the weeds hiding the corpse. Paul had been hit by no fewer than six bullets. Shad rolled him over. Some had exited the chest. Others remained in the body. It had been a brutal killing.

A quick search showed the silver cartwheels he'd paid the cowboy were missing. Not only had he been murdered, but his killers robbed his corpse. A more thorough search showed the coins had been all that the killers had taken. A folding Barlow knife, a rabbit's foot that had done Paul no good, and a few smooth river rocks hardly the size of Shad's little fingernail were all that remained to show a man had walked the face of the planet.

Shad pulled his slicker from his equipment roll and dragged the body onto it. Struggling, he rolled Paul over a couple times so he was shrouded in the yellow oilskin. It took considerable effort for him to hoist the body up and over his shoulder and even more to drape the body belly down over his saddle.

There wasn't much blood left in the body. The wounds were closed now. And he knew where most of the blood had gone. Paul had been hit repeatedly and managed to ride along for almost a quarter mile before falling off his horse. The frightened animal had found the road and galloped all the way back to Utopia.

Shad walked his horse slowly, his mind racing. If Leadbottom had derailed the train, it was retaliation for what he thought Beatrice Gallagher had done to him. Shad found it hard to fault Leadbottom for believing Beatrice had something to do with the bank robbery. There wasn't any reason for the Morrisey patriarch to keep his family out in the countryside hunting for the actual robbers.

Beatrice had a small army of her relatives prowling around the hills, but she had no reason to position them here along the road.

"Dixon," he said. "You're the devil behind all this."

It was past noon when he led the horse to Martin Donovan's undertaking parlor. The man opened the door and immediately adjusted his spectacles to better see Shad's burden.

"That must be the cowboy from Guthrie's spread," Donovan said. "Bring him in. My assistant is out west of town. I got a report of a body along the tracks down by the bridge over Lowry Creek, and I'm here alone."

Shad let the body slip down enough to bend low and catch it over his shoulder. Even drained of blood, the wiry cowboy was a burden to wrestle into the parlor. He was grateful when Donovan brought out a table with rollers.

"Is the town paying for the funeral?" Donovan cleaned his glasses using a silk hanky. He replaced it in his coat breast pocket. "The potter's field is fillin' up fast, but there are still good plots left in the Pendergast Hill cemetery. And Father Ignacio has a considerable section available in his graveyard." He cleared his throat. "For those of his faith, of course. Do you know this gentleman's predilections in that regard?"

"Was he a Catholic? I don't know. I'll ask around to see. Guthrie ought to know. Paul worked for him until—"

"Until his recent problems with his diseased beeves," Donovan finished.

Shad felt as if everyone in town knew everything, and he was a small child wandering about in awe at what the grown-ups had to say.

"You have a coffin for him?"

"There are several caskets, though a pine box is more in keeping with his . . . station."

"Better get a good supply ready. There's a storm of lead like what took this one's life coming."

"How's that, Marshal? Are you saying the feud between Utopia's premier families is heating up?"

"Worse," he said as he left. Let the undertaker worry over his meaning.

Shad put his horse back in the livery and returned to the office. Leroy Early slept at the desk. In the back of the jailhouse Gadsden Renfro caterwauled for breakfast. Ignoring him was hard. Shad envied Early's ability to sleep through such noise, but his deputy had put in a long night.

Shad sank down in the chair opposite the desk and leaned back. He closed his eyes. He'd put in a full day already, and it was hardly past noon.

Paul had died trying to leave town. Shad felt guilty about that. Hiring two or three men to take the message to the law in Denver was a sounder path to tread. He'd try that tactic once he squeezed more money from the mayor. The five silver dollars he had paid Paul were all the money he had left from his monthly salary. If the town wanted to save itself, it'd have to pony up a decent amount of payment to provide for its own defense.

Being a courier was always risky. Road agents assumed a courier carried saddlebags full of gold coins or papers so important that they were decent for ransoms. This time the letter had been left, as if to taunt him. Dixon had anticipated his move and taken out an unwilling ally.

Shad turned to leave. Early grabbed his arm and held him firmly. He tried to jerk free, but his deputy held too tightly.

"Don't be dumb, Shad. That's not you."

"I've got to get back out there and find whoever killed him. That's my job."

"Your job's to keep the peace in Utopia. The sheriff's supposed to track down killers outside the town limits."

"Glory Be'll never stir from his spot in a saloon over in Georgetown."

"It's a surprise to me that they didn't ambush you when you hauled that body back here. It makes sense for them to put a slug or two in you and eliminate any trouble when they ride into town."

"This is Dixon's doing. He wants me to know he's won. If he kills me now, there won't be any chance for him to gloat."

"He'll gloat and then kill you," Early said. "Be smart. Figure out a way to put him in the grave first."

Shad found himself frozen like a statue.

"Nobody in town will listen to me if I tell them big trouble's coming."

"Nobody said the job'd be easy, Shad. If they did, I missed it."

"They can come at us from all directions."

"Not from south or north, unless the Gallaghers and Morriseys throw in with them." Early sucked on his teeth as he thought.

"Coming from Denver's not going to be easy until the train is running."

"We're not gettin' trains from out west because they got nowhere to go after they reach us."

"There are roads. Dixon and his henchmen came to town on horseback." Shad remembered that Williamson had come to town on the stage. There'd been a couple other passengers. A loaded stagecoach could carry ten or more men.

"They rode in because you ran 'em out of town on the railroad, Shad. They don't want to repeat that humiliation."

"Ride or die," Shad said.

"Ride *and* die. That's what needs to be passed around."

Shad looked around at the town he had come to call home. Mustering defense against an attack that might never come was going to be one huge job of selling snake oil. Either way, win or lose, arming the citizens and getting them barricaded, he was likely to lose his job.

Or life. He'd be at the front and the target for Dixon and everyone behind him.

He set out to organize the unwilling and likely unbelieving town into a militia that had a chance of fighting for their very survival.

CHAPTER TWENTY-SEVEN

"We need him." Billy Dixon pushed himself to his feet and faced Beatrice Gallagher. He was a head taller and carried iron at his hip, but he still felt as if he was outclassed and outgunned. As long as he hid out underground in the woman's maze of mine shafts it wasn't any different from being in jail.

Like Gadsden Renfro.

"He's safe where he is," she said primly. Her lips thinned to a slash. She stared up at him and showed no sign of backing down. "You'll leave him be."

"Why? Because he wouldn't put up with this slop?" Dixon swept his hand over the table beside him. A plate of beans went flying. The biscuit hit the rocky wall like a bullet. Then the tin plate and spoon clattered to the floor.

This drew everyone's attention no matter where they were in the huge cavern. Kerosene lamps around the perimeter cast eerie, dancing shadows everywhere. The only lamps not hanging from hooks driven into the rocky walls were in the private enclosures. Canvas sheets dangled down to form walls giving dubious privacy.

It wasn't lost on Dixon that Beatrice had the only real room in the cavern. Her space was marked off by eight-foot-high rock walls, giving privacy. She called the shots as long as they stayed underground.

He needed to see the sky if he intended to regain control. Living like a badger wasn't for him. He wanted to soar like an eagle, prowl like a hungry wolf. Aboveground where he felt in control.

"You can clean up that mess," she said, as if admonishing a little boy.

"Or what? I don't get more of that garbage? I'll be sent to bed without supper?"

She smiled. It gave him the creeps. He had seen a similar look on a wild dog an instant before it tried to rip out his throat.

"Like the rest of my relatives, you will work for your food."

"We kin use new miners up in the main shaft, Cousin Bea." One of the endless family came over. Dixon held down his anger at the intrusion.

"I need Renfro to reach my contacts in Georgetown."

"We're not ready to take Utopia yet. Be patient, dear." Beatrice reached out and laid her cold fingers on his cheek. Then with a savage move, she dragged her ragged fingernails across his flesh. He recoiled, grabbing the injured spot.

His fingers came away damp with his own blood. Mixed in was a dose of coal soot. He took an instinctive step forward, ready to give her what for.

"Billy, uh, we kin wait like she says."

"You butt out, Herk." He turned to put his henchman

in his place and held back at the last instant. Standing behind Herk were a half dozen Gallaghers, all holding rifles and shotguns. Their attention was on him. If he twitched wrong, they'd cut him down and do it by firing through Herk.

Dixon glanced around. Squinty stood with his hand on his pistol, but Beatrice's kin hemmed him in, too. Squinty wasn't the best shot in the best of times. He was as likely to shoot Herk or his boss as he was to shoot Beatrice before her entire family opened fire on him.

"We put the plan into action when I say," Beatrice said in her poisoned, sugary tone.

"We can bust Renfro out. We hit at dawn when both Early and Nelson are there. Cut the pair of them down, spring Renfro, and we can take over the town within a week."

"Shadrach Nelson is mine," she said. "I'll be the one to shoot him."

Dixon saw the way her hand disappeared into the folds of her skirt. He had seen the weight there as she moved around. A derringer. From the whispered, fearful gossip that rattled around among her family, she had killed her own aunt. She blamed the marshal but at least half the Gallaghers suspected her of pulling the trigger. Twice.

He had figured out quickly that this forbidden knowledge wasn't a lever to pry apart her support. More than one of her relatives thought killing Winifred Gallagher improved their lot. The ones that didn't were terrified of Beatrice. Her steel rule matched that of her tyrant aunt.

"I need some fresh air," Dixon said in disgust.

"Breathing this coal dust all the time's makin' me cough."
He feigned a cough.

"Don't stray far. I've got guards scattered all over the
mountain. Just in case Nelson comes snooping around."
She fixed a look on him that challenged for supremacy.
He retreated.

"Come on, Herk, Squinty. We can smoke outside."

"Yeah, boss, we wouldn't want to set off an explosion in here or anything," Herk said. He looked at the
tarps covering a head-high stack of dynamite and Giant
Powder kegs.

They filed out, going up the slope to the opening just
behind the shack where Beatrice and Winifred before
her met visitors. When they moved a wall plank out of
place they slipped into the cabin.

Herk immediately began building a smoke. Dixon
batted it from his hand.

"Whatya do that for, boss? You made me spill the
terbaccy all over the floor." He started to sweep it up
with his hand.

Dixon grabbed his collar and pulled him to his feet.

"We got important things to talk over."

"She's sure pushy, ain't she?" Squinty perched on
the edge of the table. It creaked under his weight so he
stood and turned around.

"We'll take care of her when I say." Dixon spat out
the words. He held his tongue when Squinty grabbed
his arm and pointed, using his chin to show they weren't
alone. Someone outside the cabin was spying on them.

"What I mean is, we'll see that she gets her cut. I

remember how it was in town before Nelson showed up. Three gangs ran things just fine."

"What about the two families?" asked Herk. "They act like they've been runnin' things forever."

Dixon moved around to hide his gun hand from the spy outside the cabin. There wasn't much of a window there. The glass had been busted out, but the sneak moved so he could press his ear close by. Every now and then he revealed part of his shaggy head.

"They began muscling in after Nelson ran us out. Before then, they were scared of us and never sold much lead or coal, fearing we'd steal it all."

"They were right," Herk said, snickering.

Dixon moved behind his henchman and kicked open the door. In three strides he was at the side of the cabin, six-gun out and aimed.

"Hands up!" His command brought about an unexpected result. When he had the drop on a man, he expected to be obeyed. The fool went for a pistol stuck in his waistband.

Dixon fired. The first round staggered the spy. The rest of his cylinder laid the man flat on his back, dead eyes watching the stars.

"Damnation!"

The exclamation came from a couple strides farther around the curve of the mountain. Dixon thought there'd been only one man listening to him and his partners. The second man got off a shot that went wide. It tore a hole in the cabin's rotten wood the size of a silver dollar.

"What's happenin', boss?"

"After him, Herk. I have to reload." Dixon fumbled with cartridges in belt loops behind his back.

"Me, too, Billy?"

"Stay with me. There might be more of them sneaks." He ejected the spent brass and slid one cartridge after another into the cylinder. A quick snap closed the gate.

"I lost 'im, boss!"

"Herk's over there," Squinty said. "The other fella's slidin' down the hillside."

"After him!"

Squinty was close to blind, but he had good ears. They rushed along the road by the cabin. Tracking in the starlit night wasn't something Dixon was much good at. Squinty kept him moving in the right direction.

"Down there," he said, pointing.

Dixon dropped to one knee. He saw the tracks. Their quarry had lost his balance and tumbled down the hillside toward where the road angled back sharply. He leaned out and waited. The stretch of road immediately beneath him was blocked by a rocky spire. The road on either side was visible.

He waited and waited. When he started to think the man who had rolled down the hill was dead, he saw movement. Dixon lifted his pistol and fired. The dark shape darted about. Tiny dust clouds kicked up around him. Dixon missed with every shot. For all his near-sightedness, Squinty was either a better shot or luckier.

When he added his bullets to the barrage, he scored a hit. His target let out a yelp of pain and somersaulted along the road.

"Take him out. Kill him!"

Squinty fired again, but the wounded man ventured too close to the edge of the winding road. He fell backward into space and disappeared. He screamed all the way down to the next bend in the hairpin turning road.

"Herk, after him."

"Ain't no call to do that," Squinty said. "He's long gone. I heard a horse galloping off."

He cursed his bad luck. Then he frowned as he wondered what he had gotten himself into. Why would any of Beatrice's men have a horse ready for a getaway? All they had to do was duck back into one of the holes in the ground.

"You reckon she wanted them to report on what we was sayin'?"

Before Dixon could deride Herk for not realizing the truth, Beatrice and two of her kin popped out of the cabin. They had followed the tunnel and now stood outside the cabin with their rifles leveled.

"What's the shooting all about?" Beatrice sounded peeved.

"I reckon I accidentally shot one of your cousins. Or is he a nephew?" Dixon pointed to the man flat on his back at the side of the cabin.

"Ain't none of our blood, Cousin Bea." One man stood and backed from the body.

"Who is it then?" Dixon demanded.

She pushed past her men and bent low over the dead man. Before she stood she spat.

"That's Enoch Morrisey."

"Enoch? Ain't he Leadbottom's half-brother?" Both

of the men with Beatrice crowded close to stare at the dead man.

"What 'bout the one what got away?" Herk pointed off into the night. "He had a horse down below. I winged him."

"You didn't do any such thing," Squinty said, hot under the collar. "I spilt his blood. I stood right there and . . ."

"Shut up, all of you." Beatrice motioned for the men with her to go after the fleeing spy. "We can't let Lead-bottom know his brother's dead on our land."

"Half-brother, didn't you say?" Squinty moved closer and peered hard at her in the dark.

She said something very unladylike, then, "Get on back to the main cave. If Leadbottom thinks he can snoop around my property, he's got to be dealt with."

"There ain't no more of 'em," Squinty said. "I didn't hear a peep after the second Morrisey fell down the mountainside."

Beatrice spun so fast her skirts snapped like a whip. She rounded the cabin and pushed aside the brush hiding the mouth of the tunnel leading back under-ground. For a moment she paused, gave Dixon a hard stare, then vanished into the hole.

"We've got to move faster," Dixon said to his men. "When Leadbottom finds out we've been talking about taking over, he'll make a move first. This whole mountain pass is a powder keg waiting to blow up."

"You want powder, boss? They got enough dynamite

hid away in that cave of theirs to bring down the whole danged mountain."

Dixon ignored Herk, pushed aside the camouflaging bush, and ducked down into the tunnel. He followed Beatrice's rapid clicking footsteps, scheming about how best to use her before the train arrived.

CHAPTER TWENTY-EIGHT

"Admit it, Shad. You miss him." Leroy Early stretched his arms and then covered a yawn. He had been working all night, and it showed. He had bloodshot eyes and a gray pallor that hinted at not enough sleep or regular tucker.

Shad wasn't one to complain. He wasn't in much better shape. Not for the first time he regretted sending Paul as courier. He had intended to offer the cowboy a badge when he returned.

Only Dixon had made sure that would never happen. Paul's burial had been a simple one. Nobody from the Triple Z showed up. That made Shad angry, but there wasn't anything he could do about it. The crew at the ranch had mostly moved on, apparently including any friends Paul had made. He told himself that was the reason only he and Early had been at the burial. But the rancher owed something to his men, even the ones he had sent packing because he'd put down most of his herd.

"He was mighty young to die."

"What's that? Who are you talking about? Oh, you're thinkin' on Paul."

"Who'd you mean?" Then Shad twigged to his deputy's meaning. "I don't miss Williamson. What are you saying? All he does is eat my food and moon around my daughter."

"They're married, Shad. And you *do* miss him. I can tell."

"Get on out of here. Get some sleep. You're walking around in a daze if you think things like I'm missing Richard Williamson."

Early laughed and left the office. His face glowed in the light of a new dawn. For a moment he stood and basked in the newfound warmth, then headed off to his room in the boardinghouse at the edge of town. Shad watched until he turned a corner and was hidden from sight. He felt a loss and knew the reason.

Leroy Early was about the only one he could talk to who took him seriously. Even more, Early had insight into what he was thinking. It was like they shared a brain at times.

"Danged if he's not right," Shad said to himself. "I do miss Rich." He and his son-in-law had shared so much in common, but he took his job as detective seriously. He had seen him only twice in the last few days. Williamson spent a good deal of his time at the point of derailment. There wasn't much call to worry about more damage being done to the tracks with him watching over the wreckage.

The reason he stood guard was the six cars laden

with coal. If Dixon took it into his head to set fire to that much coal, it'd burn for the next month.

He settled down in his chair, put his boots on the paper mat Early had woven to protect the desktop, and thought on the matter. If Dixon was in cahoots with Beatrice Gallagher, destroying the coal made no sense. She needed the money from the sale to the railroad. Beatrice had thought so much of protecting her coal shipment that she'd been aboard the train when it derailed.

"So, were she and Dixon partners then or afterward?" He figured their alliance came before the derailment. The one responsible for the destruction of railroad property had to be—

He went for his six-shooter when the dawn light coming through the door was suddenly blocked.

"Wait, Marshal, you have to listen to me." Patrick Morrisey held out his empty hands to show he wasn't here to cause trouble.

But Shad had heard that before. Anyone saying, "You have to listen to me" only caused trouble.

"You here to turn yourself in?"

Patrick blinked in surprise. He opened his mouth, then closed it.

"What do you mean? I ain't done anything to get arrested."

"Like hell," Shad said. He pointed with the Peacemaker's muzzle to the empty chair on the other side of his desk. Patrick silently sank down, perched on the very edge. He looked like a racehorse ready to run.

"You've got it all wrong, Marshal. I want to warn you. About something I overheard."

"You're lying. I can tell. Your eyes get all shifty."

"All right. I didn't hear it. My cousin did. Him and my uncle went to spy on the Gallaghers."

"You didn't volunteer to go sneaking around the Calcutta Mine? It'd give you a chance to see your beloved again." Shad had to smile crookedly when Patrick touched the spot on his chest where Beatrice had shot him. They had been lovers. Whatever caused her to turn on him had been enough for her to pull her derringer and drill him.

For whatever reason, he still carried a torch for her. True love was never easy.

"Uncle Enoch got himself killed."

"Is that what you wanted to report? I'm supposed to go poking around and ask Beatrice if she killed a Morrisey?"

"It wasn't her. It was Billy Dixon."

Shad sat a little straighter.

"He's hiding out up there?"

"In the Gallagher's main cavern. The big one they hollowed out years ago, where they live now. Even Beatrice. She's got a room all walled up and—"

"Get to the point. Your Uncle Enoch was killed while he spied on them?"

Patrick nodded.

"There's no way that's within my jurisdiction. If it was, I'd be piling up evidence against Beatrice for all the killing she's done."

"I never even thought of accusing her of shooting me." Again he touched the spot on his chest were the slugs had ripped into his body.

"She killed her own aunt. And she admitted to me she shot my son."

"She didn't kill him," Patrick said in her defense. "Brushwell did back when he managed the freight yard. You know that he put the bullet through Abe's head. Then you killed Brushwell."

"All this talk of shooting and killing is making me hungry. I need to fetch breakfast. Get on out of here, Patrick. Or tell me something I can use to arrest Billy Dixon."

"Marshal, Dixon and his henchmen killed my uncle and shot up my cousin, but—"

"This isn't going anywhere. If you want justice, take the complaint to Sheriff Parsons. If that's too far to go, why don't you hie on back up the mountain and go dig out some lead ore? You need something to occupy you."

"They overheard Dixon talking about busting him out." Patrick pointed toward the cells.

"Renfro? Dixon wants to spring him?"

"That's what they heard, my uncle and cousin. Renfro's part of some big plot they've cooked up."

"What might that be?"

"I don't know, Marshal. That's all I know, all my cousin overheard. It was enough for them to murder my uncle."

Shad was lost in thought. It made sense that Renfro and Beatrice were in cahoots. The freight yard handled all her coal shipments, and the manager was responsible for buying and loading coal to every engine that stopped in Utopia. Dixon and Beatrice were cooking up something. That put Renfro in the middle of it.

Or maybe Renfro and Dixon were partners in some scheme against Beatrice Gallagher. There wasn't any double-crossing deal he wouldn't believe Dixon was guilty of committing.

He needed to interrogate the man further. Renfro had answers to questions Shad worried most about.

"The black train," he muttered. He looked up sharply to see if the phrase meant anything to Patrick. It didn't. Patrick Morrisey wasn't that good at disguising his emotions.

"Why are you telling me?"

"I feel like I owe you. I mean, you saved me when Bea shot me and . . ."

"And?" he prodded. "You're feeling guilty about derailing the train?"

"That was my pa's doing!"

"Because he blames Beatrice for the bank being robbed and all the Morrisey money being stolen."

"He's still mad he didn't bury it in a Ball jar where it'd be safe. But it was so much he thought Banker Reese was better hanging on to it." Patrick ground his teeth together. "He wasn't."

"Leadbottom's not far wrong about Beatrice being responsible. I'm pretty sure Billy Dixon and his men robbed the bank. And Beatrice is giving them a place to hide out."

He saw the tortured look on Patrick's face. Either Beatrice would finally kill him or he'd kill himself because of her. That was the only way he'd ever get over his desperate love.

Another thought came to him. If a careless whisper reached his pa's ear, Leadbottom would kill his son without a second thought. The feud with the Gallaghers ran that deep.

"You take care of your prisoner, Marshal. Dixon intends to bust him out and kill you. Deputy Early, too."

"Why are you telling me this? You never gave a good answer."

"He's pulled her into somethin' dangerous. She doesn't deserve to be caught up in his evil web."

It took Shad a second to decipher what Patrick said. He thought Dixon was a bad influence on Beatrice. Nothing would convince him that Beatrice was worse than a timber rattler and twice as deadly.

"When's this supposed to happen?"

"Dixon said at dawn."

Shad looked past Morrisey. The sun was peeking over the rooftops now. It was past dawn and getting into mid-morning. With the high mountains surrounding Utopia, even in the middle of summer, days weren't as long as they were for a city out on the plains.

"I'll take a look around. I'll be special careful."

Patrick shuffled his feet, half turned, paused, then bolted from the office. Shad watched him go with mixed feelings. The boy wasn't right in the head. Whether that came from inhaling all the lead fumes or just because he was a Morrisey hardly mattered. Shad had to give him the benefit of the doubt. He had risked his life to warn him about Renfro breaking out.

He leaned back in the chair and thought more on it. If Patrick spoke the truth about his uncle and cousin, this was a way to get back at the Gallaghers. Nobody was going to hunt for his uncle's body, not on Gallagher land. By now Uncle Enoch had been dumped down a shaft or tossed into a shallow dig along with a stick of dynamite to seal his grave for all time. Sweating out the story from Patrick's cousin would give the same tale, he suspected.

It always came down to a Morrisey accusing a Gallagher without anyone else to give testimony.

"Or the other way around," he said. He heaved to his feet, checked Renfro. His prisoner still snored in his cell. At least Shannon hadn't let him go free.

Shad hitched up his gun belt and stepped outside. It was getting late for breakfast, but he hadn't eaten. Neither had Renfro. One thing he did religiously was make sure his prisoners ate decent meals. More than one had gone on to hang. They deserved their last days on earth to be well fed, even if he was more than willing to put the noose around their necks himself for whatever crimes they committed.

The instant he stepped out, he felt eyes on him. He walked slowly, not looking left or right. He greeted one or two of the merchants along the street. When he took a sharp turn, he broke into a run, circled the building, and came at the jail from a different direction.

A smile curled his lips. He felt he was losing his knack when he was around the younger Richard Williamson. This showed his instincts were still good. He slipped his Peacemaker from his holster and walked forward slowly.

Behind a water barrel crouched a raggedly dressed miner. From the black soot he had to be one of Beatrice's relatives working in her coal mine. He clutched a six-gun and peered from behind the barrel at the jailhouse door. Shad started to order him to drop the gun when the man stood and ran toward the jail.

Shad followed at a more leisurely pace. The scruffy gunman pressed against the outer wall and chanced a look inside.

"Renfro!" he called. "You in there? Renfro!"

Shad heard a muffled reply. This satisfied the man ready to spring the prisoner. As he swung around, six-gun leveled against any lawman in the office, he gave Shad a perfect time to approach.

A thrust drove the Peacemaker's muzzle into his back. As the miner reacted by starting to turn, Shad plucked the pistol from his grip.

"Which Gallagher are you?"

"The one what's gonna spring your prisoner, that's which one."

Shad laughed. He pushed Beatrice's relative inside the office and into the cellblock.

"You and him'll have plenty of time to discuss what went wrong." Shad shoved his new prisoner into the second cell and locked it.

He had three breakfasts to fetch now. It was an expense to the city, but he felt good. It was hardly nine o'clock and he'd done a good day's work, keeping one prisoner from being sprung and adding to the jail population.

A good day, indeed.

CHAPTER TWENTY-NINE

"Which one of them varmints is it?" Early asked. He looked into the cell where both prisoners stretched out on their cots. "Can't say I recognize him."

"He won't give me his name. Every time I ask he tells me Beatrice will come for my scalp."

"He's not wrong."

"He tried to bust Renfro out of jail. That's a crime."

"Don't go takin' that one to a judge, Shad." Early went to the gun rack on the wall and pulled out a couple rifles. He laid them on the desk, then rummaged about in a small drawer for gun oil.

"Judge Zamora's a stickler for evidence, but I've got him on this. More than one storekeeper saw him skulking about, waiting for me to leave. I caught him sneaking in with a drawn gun."

"I can explain away all that. You can, too. The judge'd want an actual crime. You can't even claim trespassin'. The marshal's office is public property, last I heard."

"You're such a wet blanket, Leroy."

"So hold him till you got to let him go free. It'll keep him from causin' additional mischief."

"One less to worry about," Shad agreed.

From the back of the office came a loud shout. "Neal! My name's Neal!"

"Got something to write down now," Early said. He stuck his head through the doorway and asked, "Is that Neal Gallagher or some other moniker?"

"Neal Wright. You know me. Or you knew my ma."

Early stared hard and shook his head.

"Don't remember any woman named Wright."

"She was a Smith then. Linda."

"Do tell. She surely had an ugly spud for a son. I remember her as the sort to light up a room when she came in. It must have been your pa what lent you such an ugly visage." Early closed the door when Neal Wright started cursing him.

"I remember him now. Don't let on. He's got a chip on his shoulder, just like his pa."

"But you knew his ma?" Shad was intrigued by that. Early wasn't much of a lady's man.

"I did," the deputy said, a far-off look in his eyes. "I don't envy Wright's pa one little bit. She was more 'n a handful. She was . . ."

They both turned when Beatrice Gallagher stormed into the office. She stood, fists on her hips. Her face was clean enough of coal dust to show that she was flushed. Shad had seen her angry before, but not this much.

"Let him go. Now!"

"Which prisoner do you mean?" Shad felt peeved and willing to argue. He knew who she meant.

Or did he? If Patrick Morrisey was right and she and Dixon schemed to spring Renfro, she might want both men released.

"Neal. He didn't do a damned thing!"

"Language, young lady," Early said, enjoying her anger. "Me and the marshal was just discussin' that matter. Maybe if you post bail we can let young Neal out."

"He didn't do anything."

"How would you know, Beatrice?"

"That's Miss Gallagher. Keep a civil tongue in your head, Marshal."

"You weren't anywhere nearby to see what he did. How can you vouch for him?"

"I never told him to . . ." She bit off her words. "He wouldn't do such a loco thing. He has no reason."

"Would you post bail for Gadsden Renfro, too?" Shad poked and prodded to see how far she'd go.

"You have no intention of letting Renfro out. The freight yard needs a manager right away. I'm surprised Mister Sussman hasn't ordered you to release him. Renfro is a railroad employee, after all."

"Sussman's not my boss."

"Let Neal out."

Shad got his dander up. Being ordered around by a woman young enough to be his daughter rankled. He had considered letting Wright go until she used that tone on him.

"Five hundred dollars bail. Not a cent less."

"That's outrageous!"

"He tried to break a prisoner out of jail, and now

they're cell mates. There's a third cell begging for an occupant."

"Miss Gallagher, you'd best clear out," Early said, stepping between her and the marshal. "Things will settle down soon enough."

"They'll be settled, that's for certain," she said. She spun and stalked from the office.

Shad watched her round a building and vanish into the middle of town.

"I've got a bad feelin' 'bout this, Shad." Early went to the rifles he had placed on the desk and picked up the gun oil. He worked the action, applied a drop of oil, and cocked and dry-fired the rifle a few times to be sure everything was in top condition. He handed the rifle to Shad and repeated his maintenance on the second rifle.

"You don't think she'd try to bust her kin out, do you?"

Early looked at him. The expression told the tale. Shad fished out a box of cartridges and began sliding them into the magazine. He hadn't finished fully loading the rifle when a bullet tore past his head and embedded itself in the door behind him. Shad ducked involuntarily.

It saved him from a dozen more bullets.

Early thrust out his rifle and pushed shut the outer door. More slugs tore into the heavy wood. None penetrated.

"We're trapped in here," he said.

"Too bad that son-in-law of yours is out protectin' the repair crew."

"If they've even arrived yet." Shad crouched and pushed the door open a crack to look out.

Four Gallaghers had positioned themselves in the alley where Neal Wright had hidden behind the water barrel. From the rounds that dug into the door, at least that many more were scattered out on either side of the jailhouse.

"We need a back door."

"Leroy, I'm willing to use my penknife and dig one through a wall. There's no way we can leave through this door." He poked the rifle out and squeezed off a shot. It hit the water barrel. Although it did no damage, it spooked two men hiding behind it. They ran like rabbits. Four quick shots at them failed to wing either man.

"That'd take too long. With the luck we've had so far, we'd crawl through a hole and run smack into a dozen leveled guns."

"We've got plenty of ammo."

"No food or water."

"Do you still have your bottle in the desk drawer?" Shad had to laugh. Early scuttled like a crab to the desk and opened the bottom drawer. He held up a full pint bottle.

"I replaced it after you drained it. A good thing, too." Early pulled the cork out with his teeth and spat it across the room. He took a long drink and passed the whiskey to Shad.

The marshal hesitated. Drinking on an empty belly wasn't a good thing. Then he knocked back a stiff jolt. If this was the day he died, he didn't want to face it sober. He handed the bottle to Early, who carefully put it beside the desk. More than half of the amber liquid remained.

A sudden thud against the outer wall made them both jump.

"Somebody ran into the jail. No brakes on that attack," Early said.

"The windows in the cells," Shad warned, getting to his feet. He threw open the door into the cellblock in time to see the bars on the high window explode outward. One of Beatrice's family had looped a rope around the iron bars and used a horse to pull them from the wall.

He sighted in and waited. In spite of Neal Wright screaming a warning, some grizzled old man poked his graying head up into the open cavity. It was an easy shot.

The man never let out so much as a gasp. He fell back. The brief view Shad had of him was the small red spot on his forehead where the rifle bullet had torn through his skull.

A hat slowly moved across the open spot. Shad had no desire to waste a bullet on such an obvious decoy intended to make him waste bullets. He opened the cell and ordered Wright out.

"Into the other cage." He shoved him in and locked the door. Shad looked up in time to see someone trying to repeat the trick of yanking out the bars.

A steady hail of bullets convinced them outside to abandon this tactic to free their relative.

"You're gonna die, Nelson." Wright hung on the bars in his new cell. "Beatrice ain't never gonna let you go now. I heard her say she wanted to skin you alive. Take your scalp. Torture you like a Sioux would. Then . . ."

"Shut up." He pointed his rifle at Wright. This caused the prisoner to sputter and squawk more like a chicken than a human.

"They're not letting you go, Nelson," called Renfro. "You might let us both go and see if we can't beg for a little mercy for you." He laughed. "Beatrice might decide to just shoot you dead and not torture you. I can convince her to do that."

"She killed Winifred Gallagher, not me," Shad said, as if he had to persuade Renfro of anything.

"She said you'd say that very thing."

Shad fired a few rounds through the cell windows, then returned to the front office. Early propped the door open a crack and lay on his belly. He fired at the attackers with measured fury.

One shot, one curse. Repeat.

"I don't reckon there's any hope that Rich will come waltzin' back into town any time soon, is there?"

"If he did, he'd go to the house to see Miriam," Shad replied. He stood over his deputy and added a few rounds to the death storm swirling outside.

"Young love. Ain't it great?" Early emptied his rifle and reached up. "Hand me a box of cartridges. I'm nowhere done puttin' lead in them scallywags."

Shad left his deputy to fire out the door. He returned to the cellblock and climbed onto the cot to look out the window where the bars had been yanked free. He swallowed hard. Five men dashed around outside. He recognized most of them as Gallaghers. The others likely were, too. They just weren't any of Beatrice's kin he'd ever seen or much noticed. When they came to town and got roaring drunk, he and his deputies had tried to run them off rather than put them into a cell.

A drunk miner looked a lot different from the armed men waging a fierce assault against the town jail.

"You might as well let us out, Marshal," called Neal Wright from the adjoining cell.

"Yeah, let us go and we'll put in a good word for you."

"Shut up, Renfro." Shad took a quick shot out the window. He scattered a tight knot of gunmen but didn't wing any of them.

"You tell him, Renfro," said Wright. "If he lets us go, they'll all back off. He won't believe me."

"You're both liars and crooks," Shad said. He fired a few more times before his rifle magazine ran empty.

"No more bullets, Marshal? That can be dangerous when you got so many good folks aimin' to kill you."

Shad hopped down from the cot, drew his Peacemaker and pointed it at Neal Wright. He pulled the trigger. Wright yelped as he threw up his hands as if he could fend off an ounce of lead. A step back caused him to lose his balance. He fell heavily to the floor. Shad aimed his six-gun at the fallen man.

"The first shot wasn't intended to hit. Don't push me. I hit what I aim at."

Shad lowered the hammer and dropped the gun into his holster. With the empty rifle in the crook of his left arm, he joined Early.

"They got us, Shad. We can hold off for another

hour, maybe. The way we're burnin' through the ammo, well . . ." The deputy's words trailed off.

"Any sign we have any help coming from the citizens?"

Early shook his head.

They were in this alone.

"If we stay inside, we're goners. For two cents I'd plug the pair of them in the back."

"You won't do that, Shad. You're the marshal. You uphold the law, not break it."

"I hate it when you're right," he said. He peered out. The door had been reduced to splinters in places. He found a hole and pressed his eye against it to take a gander at what they faced.

"There's more of them devils, aren't there?" Early sat with his back against the desk. He added rounds to his rifle's magazine methodically. The click-click-click matched the sounds when Shad reloaded his rifle.

He pushed open the door and started firing. Every shot missed. Shad kicked shut the door and waited for the response. Dozens of rounds pounded the wood. Several bullets blasted through and sent splinters flying along with the still-deadly bullets.

"We can't get out through the roof."

"A good idea," Shad said, "but the only advantage that gives is giving us a bit of height to shoot down. We can't sneak away." He set his jaw. "I won't turn over the prisoners to a mob."

"Even if you let out just Wright? That might convince Beatrice to back off."

"Not a hair on either head gets out of here without

my permission." Shad pulled the door open an inch and fired steadily.

"We might consider rationing the ammunition." Early tossed an empty box against the wall. "There're only two boxes left."

"Looks like it's time to use them," Shad said. "They're launching an all-out attack."

A dozen men ran forward. He fired. Then the number of attackers doubled. He hit one or two, but the sheer number attacking was sure to sweep over them eventually.

His rifle came up empty. Shad stepped back and drew his six-shooter, ready to take as many with him as possible.

It sounded like a freight train hit the door and sent it swinging back on its hinges.

CHAPTER THIRTY

"Kill 'em! Kill'em all!"

The shout rang in Shad's head. He aimed at the door as it crashed open. His finger came back. His six-gun bucked in his fist. And the leading attacker staggered back a step with Shad's bullet in his chest. For a moment, he blocked others from pouring inside.

"One down, a hundred to go," cried Early. His rifle barked and then confusion spread through the cutthroats attacking the jail.

"Wait, hold your fire. Something's . . . different," Shad said. He kicked the bullet-ridden door out of his way and stepped over it. It took him a second to realize he wasn't the target for a tornado of death. The Gallaghers found themselves fighting a rear attack.

He fired again and hit another in the middle of the back. He wasn't a back shooter, but survival demanded him to fight any way he could. Being outnumbered and outgunned reduced his chances of walking away alive. A few more shots emptied his Peacemaker.

He waded into the fight swinging his pistol like a club. One skull after another cracked when he brought the three pounds of iron down. And then someone tackled him from the side. Shad crashed to the ground and rolled over and over. The fight spread out all around him. The gunfire died down, replaced by sounds of fists landing heavy blows and men grunting and gasping from those punches.

Shad arched his back and threw his attacker to one side. He came to his feet and aimed his six-gun. He pulled the trigger, only to have it land on a spent chamber. Or a dud. He hadn't counted and didn't know which. Wasting no time, he fell forward, trying to use the Peacemaker as a club again.

"Clear out. Get outta here! There's too many of 'em!"

He recognized Early's voice. His deputy added to the confusion. It didn't matter who heard his warning. If the fighting stopped, he was successful. Killing more of the Gallagher family wasn't anything he wanted. He'd rather have them all in jail.

He wanted Beatrice Gallagher locked away where she couldn't cause any more mischief.

Shad rolled onto his belly, saw scissoring legs in front and wrapped his arms around a pair of worn boots. They crashed down together. As they scrambled for advantage, he recognized the man he'd tackled.

"Patrick!"

"We come to pull your fat outta the fire, Marshal. Lemme go. I need to get after them."

His surprise caused him to obey. His arms pulled away. Patrick Morrisey scrambled to his feet and yelled commands that sounded foolish, contradictory. Shad saw that the orders worked. The Morriseys formed a line and stomped forward. Some carried axe handles, others swung rifles. He guessed they'd run out of bullets. As they advanced, they routed the disorganized Gallaghers.

He looked around for Beatrice, but she was nowhere to be seen.

"Let me help you up, old man." Shaky hands slipped under his arms and dragged him to his feet. His knees turned to water. It took a second for him to recover and stand on his own.

"Thanks, Leroy. I was planning on sitting there the rest of the day. I figured I needed a rest, but you had to come along and pull me back into action."

"Why'd they come to help?"

Shad tried to find an answer and couldn't figure out a good one.

"Be thankful they did. We'd be goners for certain sure if they hadn't."

"I don't like being beholden to Leadbottom and his clan for anything, much less my life." Early brushed dust off his clothes. Patches of cloth clung to his skin where blood had already begun drying. Shad wasn't able to decide how much was Early's and how much belonged to other people. From the size of some of the blood patches, he hoped either a Gallagher or a Morrisey had died. Otherwise, Early would keel over from lack of blood at any instant.

"Do we still have prisoners? This might have been some crazy scheme to spring the two."

"Shad, from the look of the bodies scattered all

around, it was a one-sided plan. Some of those men are deader 'n doornails."

"Neither Leadbottom nor Beatrice can make a plan worth beans," Shad said. He went from body to body, finding who was dead and who had been hurt so badly they weren't ever going to pop up and rejoin the running battle.

From the distant gunshots, the two sides had moved their battle to the rail yards across town.

"Somebody fetch Doc Paisley," Shad bellowed. "Do it *now*!"

Curtains stirred and doors creaked open as timid men and women edged out. Several youngsters lit out running, trying to outpace each other in an attempt to get to the doctor's office first.

"He'd better bring a lot of medicine," Early said. "And bandages." He stretched out his right arm and winced. "I got shot twice in my gun hand. Just grazes but they hurt like—"

"Watch over the battlefield," Shad said. "I'll check on the prisoners."

He tried walking but ended up hobbling. Bullets had missed him, but he'd twisted his knee rolling around on the ground.

In the jailhouse he called out, "Are you two owlhoots still in one piece?"

"You gotta treat your prisoners better, Marshal."

He leaned against the wall and stared at Renfro. The man sprawled on his cot, hands under his head. He might as well have been beside a cool brook watching birds flying around in the summer sky for all the agitation he showed. Shad went to Neal Wright's cell and stared at the lump quivering under the blanket pulled off the cot.

"Come on out and face the light of day."

The blanket slipped down so Wright had a quick look.

"They all gone? The ones tryin' to kill me?"

"The fight ended up between your two families. Beatrice tried to spring you, but Leadbottom's family ran them all off."

"She won't let me rot in here," insisted Wright.

"She's better 'n I am. If I had my way you'd rot away for the rest of eternity."

Shad slammed the door leading into the cellblock and collapsed into his desk chair. The door into the street hung by one hinge—and precious little of the wood remained. Too many bullets had dug in and carved out huge hunks.

He went for his six-shooter when a hand pushed the destroyed door away to crash on the floor.

"No need to shoot me, Marshal. Me and my relatives run 'em back up the mountain. It'll be a spell 'fore they think to come down again. Them yellow bellies!"

"Why'd you save me and Early?" Shad stared hard at Patrick Morrisey. The man was covered with dirt and blood and not a few black streaks of soot. He had mixed it up with more than one Gallagher to get that much finely powdered coal dust on him.

"Wasn't you as much as, well, not lettin' *her* have her way."

"The feud is heating up, isn't it?" Shad asked.

"We'll keep Utopia streets clear of them."

"I'm the law. If I need help, I'll ask." Shad felt heat rising to his cheeks. He never would have asked Leadbottom and his family for help. If Patrick hadn't rushed to his aid, he'd be dead.

"You remember, Marshal. We're just up the hill. All you need is to give a whistle, and we'll come runnin'."

Patrick Morrisey went off, head high. Shad saw his rescuer had fought back against a woman he had once loved and thought he'd come out on top. What that did for the man's pride, Shad wasn't able to say. He had no more love for the Morriseys than he did for Beatrice and her clan. If anything, he had less considering things Leadbottom had done in the past.

He did appreciate still being on the right side of the sod and gave thanks to everyone responsible for keeping him alive.

"Go on and get some food. Catch a nap," he told Early. "I've got the feeling we haven't seen the last of this feud."

"Watch your back, Shad." Early hobbled away. His trouser leg had been shot away. Bullets had missed causing real damage, but the minor wounds oozed. His deputy went to where Doctor Paisley was sending the last of the living off to his surgery.

Deputy and doctor went away together.

Shad stood in the middle of what had been a terrible battlefield. A half dozen dead bodies remained—all Gallagher family. Patrick had seen that his dead and wounded were carried back up the mountain. Beatrice hadn't been given such a chance to retrieve her dead.

"To the victor belongs the spoils," Shad muttered. Having to bury the dead was another part of winning.

He examined the outside walls of the jailhouse. Fixing the bars on the one cell would require some work. Half the wall had been pulled down with the bars. The front door was never going to close again. After reaching fifty, he gave up counting the bullet holes inside the office.

Shad sank down into his chair. It was about the only thing that hadn't seen a dozen bullets crash through it. His eyes half closed. He had to send word to Ruth that he was all right. She'd be worried. And Miriam.

His eyes snapped open when he heard footsteps outside.

Ian Shannon filled the doorway.

"We're not hiring," Shad said.

"I didn't come back to be your damned deputy again." Shannon widened his stance. His Stetson was pushed back, letting a greasy lock of his bright red hair poke out like some warning flag. He wore two six-shooters, and the tension in his shoulders warned he was going to throw down.

Shad had seen his former deputy clear leather with both hands. Shannon's accuracy was about equal, left or right.

"Did Dixon send you?" It was a guess, but Shad felt in his gut that he wasn't wrong.

"Let Renfro out of his cell, and there won't be trouble."

Shad drew as Shannon spoke. His former deputy's lips thinned just a mite showing he concentrated on making his draw. Shannon cleared leather before Shad, but Shad's aim was better. Both rounds from Shannon's six-guns went wild. Shad hit his target right in the gut.

Shannon staggered back, bent double. But he didn't go down, and he didn't drop his pistols. Shad kicked away from the desk and rushed to the door.

Shannon lifted both guns and fired. This time his aim was better but Shad was on the move. He ducked and dodged to his right, still firing.

Shannon stood straighter. Shad's first round had struck him squarely in the buckle on his gun belt. Silver splashed over the metal buckle and leather around it. He took it all in with a single glimpse. Then the marshal dived for cover.

He hit the ground hard and scooted along. Somewhere along the way he lost his bowler. And his head buzzed like a beehive had taken up residence. His vision blurred as his Peacemaker slipped from his fingers.

"Good riddance," Shannon said.

He disappeared. Shad fought to keep from passing out. A bullet had creased his temple. He felt blood flowing freely. His ear filled and a trickle got into his mouth, choking him. Blinking hard cleared his vision just enough to see Shannon pushing Renfro ahead of him out of the jail. The two argued. The shrill whine in his ears kept him from hearing what they said, but it was definitely not pleasant.

Renfro stopped and pointed. Shad tried to grab his fallen gun. His body refused to budge. Shannon shoved Renfro again, and the two slid away from the marshal's field of vision.

For an eternity he lay on the ground. He knew he

wasn't dead because his heartbeat filled his ears now, and the blood streamed down his cheek. Dead men didn't keep on bleeding.

"You want to run a tab, Marshal?"

He tried to answer. Somehow he had dreamed all this or gotten so drunk he got mixed up.

"No," he croaked out.

"Just as well. Cash on the barrel head. I'll take a chicken or cured ham as payment."

He flinched away when a lance of pain drove into his head.

"Stop squirming. I need to stop the bleeding so I can get you patched up all proper like."

"Doc?"

"That's what they call me."

Shad smiled and relaxed. Doctor Paisley was working on him. Shannon hadn't killed him, and he could rest. Rest. Rest.

CHAPTER THIRTY-ONE

"He'll be fit as a fiddle," Doctor Paisley said. "In a week or two. If he rests." The doctor closed his medical bag with a loud snap. "It wouldn't hurt him to take a nip or two of brandy for the pain."

"Mrs. Nelson won't be happy hearin' that. She's of the prohibition persuasion," Leroy Early said. "Might be I can slip him a bottle so she doesn't see it."

"Once he gets home and in bed, I'll go see him. I can put a few shots into a medicine bottle and tell her it's my own special concoction."

"I swear, Doc, you ought to sell snake oil."

"No need. A peddler came to town with some of the finest potions I've come across. I added a few to my inventory." He poked around and pulled out a small brown bottle. "This one's really potent. It has laudanum in it, but the marshal doesn't get any of it. I wouldn't want him to get too uppity."

"Can I get some of that joy juice, then, Doc? You wouldn't save it for yourself, would you?"

Paisley laughed and said as he left the jailhouse, "What makes you think I don't?"

"Wait," Shad called out weakly. He reached to grab the doctor's sleeve. His double vision hadn't cleared. Paisley was already out of the cell and into the main office.

"You behave now," Neal Wright said, leaning on the bars between their cells, "or that deputy of yours will lock you in."

Shad closed his eyes and heaved his feet off the cot. When the world stopped spinning, he chanced a quick peek. He was in the cell with the broken bars overhead. To hold prisoners, it was worthless until repairs were made. For the walking wounded—him—it provided decent accommodations.

"You're durned lucky that your former deputy didn't just walk in and shoot you." Wright rattled the bars. "You payin' attention, Marshal? Why didn't he let me out, too?"

"You're a Gallagher, and Shannon is working for Billy Dixon, not Beatrice." The answer came easily to his lips. Shad had to grin crookedly at the ease of figuring it all out when he'd been shot and bludgeoned half to death. All it took to get a glimpse of reality was to nearly die.

"He coulda got on her good side by lettin' me go."

Shad found it hard to concentrate, but things made a crazy kind of sense. The Gallaghers hated the Morriseys who hated them right back. Utopia was caught in the middle. But Dixon and his gang put the town directly in their sights. The outlaws wanted to rule the roost the way they had years before Shadrach Nelson had blown into town and tamed it. Dixon would ally with anyone giving him a chance to do that.

Not freeing Neal Wright warned Shad that Billy Dixon thought he had the upper hand and no longer needed Beatrice Gallagher's support. If he ever did.

He rocked back, then rolled forward onto his feet. He had to grab the bars to keep from passing out. The threat of blacking out faded as he steadied himself. He took a tentative step. The next was firmer, more sure. By the time he reached the outer office he felt close to normal.

Except for the pain in his head and the way his eyes tried to cross. The throbbing pain he ignored. He'd felt worse. And keeping one eye closed kept his vision as good as it ever had been.

"What're you doin' up and about, Shad? The doc said for you to rest until I get you home—where you're supposed to go to bed for a week or two."

"This is my best chance of grabbing Billy Dixon," he said.

"Dixon? You got your brains all jumbled up by that bullet. You're lucky it only grazed your head, but talk like that makes me think the doc missed plugging up a new hole in your skull. You sound like your brains are all dribbling out."

"Shannon and Dixon are in cahoots. Dixon wants Renfro. That's why he sent Shannon."

"You're givin' Billy Dixon a lot of credit. You can't think he set Beatrice against Leadbottom."

"He might have convinced her to send her family down to break Wright out of jail. Renfro would go with him. Patrick Morrisey took it into his head to take the fight to the Gallaghers."

"And then Shannon just sashayed in to release Renfro?"

Shad nodded and immediately regretted it. He went to the desk and opened the bottom drawer. The pint bottle there still had a swallow or two left. A quick move upturned the bottle and drained the contents into his gullet. The potent whiskey caused him to cough. It also cleared his head.

"That's the kind of medicine I need."

"That's what Doc Paisley said. That and stretchin' out in bed to recover."

"You watch Wright and keep the peace in town. Neither of the families is likely to cause any trouble, not for a day or two."

"They need to lick their wounds, then build up a head of steam. Beatrice is likely to be the one to pop first."

"Leroy, old friend, you understand Utopia better 'n about anyone. Watch after it while I fetch Renfro."

"Why's Dixon so eager to get him?"

Shad didn't have an answer. Whatever the former freight yard manager knew was of paramount importance. It had something to do with being around the railroad depot. The only way he'd find out the answer was to arrest Renfro again. He touched the Peacemaker at his hip. He had a score to settle with Ian Shannon, too.

And Billy Dixon.

"You're makin' a whale of a big mistake, Shad. You can't take all of them on by your lonesome. Even with me ridin' at your side, and maybe Williamson, too, you don't stand a chance."

"Lots of things are impossible 'til they get done," he said. "Did you get more ammunition?"

"I should say that Sampson had run dry so you'll forget this crazy scheme of yours, but he hasn't. Take as much as you think you'll need."

Shad took three boxes of .45 cartridges. His deputy was right that he hardly needed this much. The fight he'd be in wasn't going to be prolonged. It'd be fierce, it'd be quick, and someone would die fast.

He knew Early watched as he walked off. He tried not to stumble along. With one eye closed, he made his way to the livery stables, saddled his horse, and rode slowly toward the edge of town. As he passed a trio of young boys, he stopped and motioned them over.

"We ain't done nuthin', Marshal. Honest."

"'The wicked flee when no man pursues,'" he said. "Whatever's giving you a guilty conscience isn't my concern right now. I need your help."

"Us? You want us to go after bad guys?" The three whispered among themselves. One stepped forward. "We're your posse, Marshal."

"Did you see Deputy Shannon ride past?"

"He ain't a deputy no more."

Shad waited. The silence prompted the boys to all begin talking at the same time. Listening hard, he made out what he needed. Shannon and Renfro had come this way at a gallop.

"Much obliged," Shad said. He turned, then said

loudly, "And don't you go throwing rocks at Lady Sarah's house anymore."

With that he heeled his horse and trotted off. If he figured right, Shannon rode straight to Dixon's camp. The outlaw wasn't going to be far from the railroad. Whether he bedeviled the repair crew or just watched as they fixed the track hardly mattered. He was somewhere along the track.

And along the telegraph line.

Shad had seen how badly damaged the wire had been. A crew from Denver needed to fix long stretches. The railroad thought first of getting the train back on schedule.

He turned over everything that had happened and made guesses about Dixon's intentions. He knew the outlaw's goal. How he achieved it was murky.

He saw a patch of cut-up grass just off the road. A quick examination showed two horses had come this way recently. Fresh horse flop guaranteed he was on the right trail. The riders had come from Utopia. The trail led into the mountains on Beatrice's side of Hellfire Pass. That told him the tracks were left by someone friendly with the Gallagher clan.

Seeing the trail wind higher into the hills convinced him not to ride much farther. A sentry high in the rocks commanded a view of the land almost all the way to the tracks. Dixon might not fear anyone invading Beatrice's land. Taking that risk and losing meant his life.

Shad tethered his horse in a stand of trees. He pulled his rifle from the saddle sheath and made his way through the trees, heading up the increasingly steep slope. Before he had paralleled the hoofprints along the trail he'd followed too long, he heard muffled voices. Clutching his rifle he stepped carefully to avoid breaking a twig or rustling leaves and pine needles.

A moment of vertigo hit him, then passed. He squeezed his eyes shut for a moment, then opened them slowly. The double vision passed. Bending low he advanced, using the rifle barrel to push branches and low brush from his way. In spite of his battered condition, he moved as softly as a gentle breeze slipping through the forest.

Billy Dixon and three men sat around a low campfire. A coffee pot dangled from an iron tripod over the fire. Dixon refilled a tin cup, sampled it, and spat.

"You make lousy coffee, Herk."

The man with his back to Shad seemed to fold in on himself.

"You're lucky we got anything. We hightailed it from that cave so fast I didn't have time to load up on much."

"We're doing all right." Dixon turned to Renfro. "You have everything you need?"

"I haven't looked over the supplies, but I think I got what I need." Renfro tried the coffee and made a face, too.

"When's he got to be along the tracks?" asked Shannon.

Dixon glared at the former deputy.

"When I say. But it'll be soon."

"I heard the sledgehammers hittin' spikes. The repair crew will replace the missing section of track any time now," Shannon said. "We have to move fast. Once they finish, they'll bring in an engine to move the coal cars. After that, they'll get back to the schedule as quick as a rabbit. Is everyone ready?" Renfro dashed his coffee into the low fire. It sizzled, popped, and sent tiny curls of steam skyward.

"Don't go tryin' to cut in on our plan," Herk snapped. "Billy's got it all laid out. Don't you, Billy?"

"Shut up, Herk. You, too, Shannon. You'll be rolling in clover after I take over. You've got no call to push too hard where it's not needed."

"Why are you keepin' us in the dark, Dixon?" Shannon shifted so both his holsters were free at his side. "We're in this with you. Goin' in blind's gonna get us killed."

"I won't let that happen. Will I, Herk?"

His henchman denied that his boss had any evil intent when it came to men riding with him, as opposed to against him.

Shad saw that Shannon remained unconvinced. That gave him a place to drive a wedge. Shannon had been a good, if dour, deputy for a couple years. Some part of his reasons to be a lawman had to remain in the recesses of his brain. Play on them and Shad had a way to learn Dixon's plans.

All he needed to do was cut Shannon from the herd.

Shad moved quietly around to get a better view of the campsite. The horses had been staked out deeper in the forest on the far side. He considered spooking the horses and getting them to run off. That confusion might be enough for him to approach Shannon.

When Dixon suddenly looked up, Shad fell flat on his belly and held his breath. The outlaw never looked in his direction. For a few seconds he thought he was safe. Then he knew he wasn't.

"How many bullets do you want me to pump into your worthless hide?"

He feigned a roll to the left, then went right. A boot waited for him. The impact sent a shock through his body. Even without all the injuries he'd been collecting, this would have stopped him dead.

"Kin I shoot him, Billy, please?"

"You did good catching him, Squinty."

Shad looked up to a ring of pistols all aimed at him. He had been distracted by his highfalutin plans to separate Shannon from the others and win him back. He had ignored Dixon's second henchman. Herk had been drinking coffee, and Shad had never once wondered where Squinty was.

Dixon had posted him as a wandering sentry. Even with his nearsighted vision, Squinty had spotted the spy. Shad knew that oversight might cost him his life.

"Kick him again if you want," Dixon said. "Don't shoot him. I want him."

Shad grunted as Squinty reared back and unleashed a vicious kick. The man wasn't able to see well enough to deliver a devastating kick that'd break ribs or cause damage to his insides. The impact still hurt badly enough that Shad involuntarily groaned. Any chance he had at playing the stoic was gone.

Squinty and Herk yanked him to his feet. They dumped him near the fire.

"How's it feel to have the tables turned on you, Marshal?" Renfro held Shad's rifle in the crook of his arm, then swung it around, levered in a new round, and started to aim.

Dixon batted it away.

"I told them I've got a use for him. Don't go crossing me, Renfro."

"You need me. I want to plug him. With his own rifle." Renfro started to aim at Shad again, then froze. He glanced over his shoulder. Shannon jammed two six-shooters into Renfro's back.

"We all need each other," Shannon said. "To get what we want, listen to Dixon."

Shad wasn't sure he wanted to hear his former deputy say that. Shannon was as much under Dixon's control as Herk and Squinty. His notion of peeling Shannon away and using him against Dixon faded away.

"We'll all get the show we want," Billy Dixon said, his face inches from Shad's. "You boys will get to watch this law dog suffer. Suffer bad."

Shad doubled over when Dixon punched him in the gut. Squinty's kicks hadn't busted a rib. The bony fist might have from the way he felt all liquid inside. He sank to his knees, the double vision returned, and his head threatened to bust apart like a rotted melon.

He should have listened to Doc Paisley and gone to bed to recuperate for a week. Now he wasn't likely to ever need to recuperate. He wouldn't live that long.

CHAPTER THIRTY-TWO

"Cinch that noose tight around his neck. Don't choke him too much, though." Billy Dixon smirked. "Not too much so he dies."

"I'll see a noose around *your* neck," Shad said. The lariat tore at his neck and left a rough line. "More 'n that, I'll be kicking the trapdoor open."

"You'll never get the chance," the outlaw said. "If you did, I'd do the midair two-step cursing you."

"What are you going to do? Give me over to your girlfriend?"

Dixon stopped and stared at him. He frowned in concentration, then smiled slowly.

"You think Beatrice Gallagher and me are goin' at it? She's a looker. A black widow spider's real purty lookin', too. I'd rather share a bed with the spider. It's safer."

"She'll shoot you down," Shad said. "She killed her aunt to take over running her family. Two shots with that derringer she carries in her skirts."

"Do tell."

"She pumped two rounds into Patrick Morrisey, too. He was her lover. She got tired of him."

"A real killer." Dixon laughed. "She thinks she's callin' the shots, but she's never met up with a man like me. I'm usin' her, not the other way around."

"She put a couple slugs into the marshal's kid, too." Shannon spoke in a flat voice, but his eyes danced.

"That puts a burr under your saddle, doesn't it, Marshal Shadrach Nelson?" Dixon said. He walked around Shad and poked him with his finger. He stopped in front of his captive and pushed his face within inches. "I've got an idea to really make you wonder why you were ever born."

Shad tried to kick Dixon. The rope around his neck kept him from getting enough power without strangling himself. They had hog-tied him with his hands behind his back. If he lost his balance, he might hang himself.

"Go on, fight me. I like havin' you all bundled up like this. You see what you're up against, Nelson? If your legs get all wobbly, you'll choke yourself to death. How long can you stay awake? Me and the boys'll be quiet as mice to not wake you."

"Aw, Billy, just go on and shoot him. If you don't wanna do it, I will." Herk drew his pistol and thrust it under Shad's nose. Dixon batted it away.

"Leave him be. I told you he's all mine."

"Give him to Beatrice," Shannon said. "Do that and she'll be eatin' out of your hand."

"She already is," Dixon said. "And this one's about ready to start beggin' me to save his life." He poked Shad in the ribs again and laughed.

Shad fumed. He was in a pickle. The best he could

hope for was dying fast. Early wasn't going to come after him. Rich Williamson was somewhere down the tracks protecting the repair crew—if they had even arrived. The only possible relief was Ian Shannon.

The deputy that had broken Renfro out of his jail wasn't inclined to play the role of a savior. Not if the way his eyes blazed every time he looked at Shad was an indication. Worse, he kept suggesting that Dixon turn him over to Beatrice Gallagher to curry favor. There wasn't much chance Shannon would ever take the side of his former employer. He had become too firmly entrenched in Billy Dixon's plan to take over Utopia.

"Now, I could let you fall asleep and hang yourself. Or I could shoot you in one leg so you had to hop around until you did it to yourself. But I want you to know how you humiliated me when you ran me out of Utopia before."

"You and your worthless partners," Shad said. His mouth turned to cotton. His gut gurgled so loudly he wondered if he was bleeding away inside from getting pounded so much. Hanging himself might be the least painful way of dying.

"That's right, Nelson. Me and my two good partners. Squinty, Herk. Get over here."

"What do you want, boss?" Herk ran his fingers over the butt of his six-gun. "You change your mind to let me use him for target practice?"

"Eventually. First I want you and Squinty to go back to Utopia and find the marshal's wife and daughter. Bring 'em here. No need to be gentle if they put up a fuss."

Shad surged forward. The rope snapped around his

neck and almost yanked him off his feet. He moved back and tried to catch his breath. The noose had tightened enough to strangle him.

"Here, Marshal, let me help you." Dixon loosened the noose just a little. "Don't go killin' yourself until you say goodbye to your wife and daughter."

Shad gasped for breath. The blood had been trapped in his head and made the pain there unbearable. Worst of all was the helplessness. Dixon threatened his family and he wasn't able to do a thing to stop him.

"Kin we have some fun with 'em 'fore we bring 'em back, boss?"

"Herk, do what you want. Just so long as it'll make him think about what a mistake he made crossing the likes of the Dixon gang."

Shad heard horses trotting off. Dixon, Shannon, and Renfro sat on rocks around the low fire, drinking coffee and telling each other lies.

And he raged. The harder he tried to slip the ropes on his wrists, the deeper they cut into his flesh. And the noose? It was everything he could do to keep on his feet so he wouldn't strangle himself.

Worst of all, he worried about his wife and pregnant daughter.

"Shad'll skin me alive if he finds I've been out here," Leroy Early said. He held his hat in hand and shuffled nervously.

"We hardly ever see you, Leroy. Come on in and set a spell." Ruth Nelson pointed to the open door. The aroma of freshly baked pie made Early's mouth water.

"You be careful with your invites. I'll be hard to pry loose when that's about the best-smellin' pie I ever came across."

"You've had better, I'm sure."

"If you'd put it on the windowsill to cool and let me steal it, that'd make it taste better." He grinned. "Leastways, it always did when I was a kid."

"I'll even give you a plate and a fork. Come on now, don't be afraid."

Early pushed past Ruth into the house. Miriam sat in an overstuffed chair sewing something. From the size, it was for the baby.

"Afternoon, Leroy," she said, looking up. "Is Pa on his way?"

Early chewed his lower lip.

"What's wrong?" Ruth demanded. "We heard a lot of fireworks earlier."

"Wasn't fireworks," he said in a choked voice.

"Pa's not dead, is he?" Miriam pushed awkwardly to her feet. "Tell me he's not dead, Leroy."

"Oh, no, Miriam, he's not. I wanted to keep from givin' that impression. He came through the gunfight better 'n a lot of Gallagher boys did. A scratch. Nothin' more."

"You're not putting a shine on the truth, are you?" Ruth pulled out a chair and made him sit.

"Nothin' like that, Ruth."

"Then why'd he send you instead of coming home himself?"

"He's a stubborn one, that's why. Shannon sprung one of our prisoners, and Shad lit out after them. That's what I wanted to tell you."

"But there's only you and Shad now. Ian Shannon? He let a prisoner go?"

Early explained the best he could what happened.

"I never thought poorly of Deputy Shannon," Miriam said. "I just never cottoned to him the way Pa did."

"Shannon was always a loner. Never said much."

"Shad hires that kind, it seems," Ruth said. "How about that pie, Leroy?"

She served him, and he dug in.

"Do like peach pie." He polished it off, hesitated, then accepted a second slice. "It's too bad I don't get up here more with food like this."

"Pa explained how you split up the day. You've been taking it from dusk till dawn, and he's there during the daylight hours."

"That suits me. It was easier when there were four of us." Early caught his breath. Reminding Ruth her son had been gunned down wasn't too smart. But it was Miriam who teared up, turned, and left the room.

"Don't fret, Leroy. She's like that now."

"After the boy comes . . ."

"She thinks it'll be a girl. What makes you think it's a boy?"

"Shad is sure. And Rich is, too. How wrong can a pa and grandpa be about such a thing?"

"It's a good thing you aren't a betting man," Ruth said. "This is a case of laying it all down against the house odds."

"Shad's got good instincts. Rich looks to be 'bout the same."

"Do you want another slice?" Ruth pointed to the licked-clean plate.

Early considered and then pushed away from the table.

"I've got to get back to work. I'm the law in Utopia while Shad's out huntin' down escaped prisoners. I wanted to let you know he wasn't comin' home until he turned the key in the cell lock again."

She sighed. Then she hugged Leroy.

"Thank you. I appreciate not having to stay up worrying over him."

Early turned for the door and then froze. He stared into Herk's drawn six-gun.

"Go on, Deputy. See if you can beat me."

Herk fired the same instant Early went for his six-shooter. The slug crashed into his chest and knocked him backward. His gun slipped from nerveless fingers. Through the roar in his ears he heard Herk and another—Squinty?—herding a loudly protesting Ruth and Miriam out the door. He tried to move, but the weight on his chest was too great. Someone had dumped an anvil on him until he couldn't move. He gasped, spat blood, and lay back to gather his strength.

Shad would really skin him alive if he let the likes of Billy Dixon's sidekicks kidnap his family.

"At least I got the bullet out."

"You shot me."

"I did no such thing. What happened here, Early? There's no sign of Miriam or her ma."

"Took 'em. You took 'em. Both of you."

Richard Williamson almost let the deputy's head drop. Instead he stuffed a blanket under Early's neck to support him. He slapped the man gently until the eyelids stopped fluttering and worked their way open.

"You? Rich?"

"What happened? Somebody shot you in the chest. The bullet missed a lung, but it tore up muscles in your shoulder. It must have felt like a mule kicked you."

"'Bout the same. I've been kicked by a mule, and it wasn't this bad." Early struggled. Williamson gently pushed him back down. The deputy was in no condition to be up and about.

"I just dug a bullet out of you. Don't go trying to sit up. I'll get Ruth to look after you if you tell me where she is."

"He shot me. Herk shot me. Him and Squinty!"

Williamson moved away and stared down at the deputy's pale, drawn face.

"They kidnapped Miriam and her ma?"

"They did. I tried to stop them, but they had the drop on me. I drew, but Herk already had me in his sights."

"Where'd they go?" Williamson saw the answer wasn't forthcoming. "Why'd they take them?"

"Don't know any of that. Came here to tell Ruth that Shad was out after Shannon."

In fits and starts Williamson got the answers to some questions, but not the important one.

"Do you think Herk and Squinty took them to Dixon's camp?"

"Musta. Gettin' kinda dark, ain't it? Am I dyin'?"

"The sun's going down, old partner. You're doing just fine. When did they kidnap the women?"

"Late afternoon."

Williamson stood and searched the house, then rummaged around in the kitchen.

"I've left you some water and bread, in case I'm gone longer than I expect. You're going to be all right here by yourself, unless you want me to go to town and fetch the doctor."

"Fetch Ruth and your gal. I'll be all right. I will . . . if you'll leave me one thing."

"What's that?"

"The rest of that peach pie."

Williamson found the pie on the kitchen counter and brought it over. He saw the dirty plate and fork. He put a piece of the pie onto the plate and took it all to Early.

"I'll be back before you finish off that pie."

Early's gray eyes fixed on him.

"Don't come back 'less you have 'em all safe and sound."

Williamson laid a hand on his good shoulder, squeezed reassuringly, stepped outside, and circled the house. He found the tracks leading eastward easy enough. Four horses. He swung into the saddle and galloped off. His entire life hung in the balance. Early didn't have to tell him that there was no point returning if he didn't save Miriam, the baby, and his mother-in-law.

CHAPTER THIRTY-THREE

The outlaws he chased were burdened with prisoners. Richard Williamson was driven by fear for his family and a raging fury that Dixon would ever kidnap two women, one of them pregnant. He overtook them after less than an hour's ride.

They made their way around the base of the foothills adjoining Gallagher land. Williamson had scouted this area earlier looking for breaks in the telegraph line before giving up to concentrate on guarding the stranded coal cars laden and waiting for the repair crew. Six men had come from Denver driving a small steam engine. The only load they hauled was a flat car stacked with rails, ties, and all the equipment to replace the missing section of track. Once they had begun work, Williamson lit out for the Nelson household.

The women prisoners did all they could to slow Herk and Squinty. He hoped they didn't make the two owlhoots angry enough to shoot them. If they harmed Miriam or their baby, Williamson wasn't sure what he would do.

He had seen the results of plenty of Indian massacres

and tortured soldiers to know ways that would let Squinty and Herk scream for death for days.

There was a long straight stretch in the path where he would be exposed as he closed the distance between him and the four riders. That was the most dangerous part of the attack. If he circled to head them off, it'd take the better part of an hour. That was safer. It also gave Herk and Squinty time to think of devilment he didn't want to imagine.

He rode slowly and steadily down the slope. His horse kicked up pebbles that rolled noisily. Every sound boomed like a drum in his head, but the outlaws he trailed never looked back. They were too busy taunting their prisoners.

As he rode closer, he heard Miriam raise her voice and insult Squinty. She chanced a quick look at their back trail. Williamson knew she had spotted him. He wished she wouldn't take such a risk. And he wished she wouldn't look back so often.

"You're as stupid as you are shortsighted," Miriam said in a booming voice. "Don't you know who my pa is?"

"He's gonna be the *former* marshal of a town overrun by cutthroats like us," Squinty said.

"And my husband! He works for the railroad. You let us go, or he'll bring every last one of those railroad bulls into Utopia. They don't play by the law, not like my pa. They'll string you up without a trial."

"Or tie you to the railroad tracks and let the engines run over you," Ruth said, her voice equally as loud. She had spotted Williamson, too.

"You two have quite an imagination. That must go with old Shadrach Nelson thinkin' he can run off some of the nastiest men who ever robbed a bank or rustled a herd," Herk said. "Billy's got a whole danged army comin' to town any minute now. When they arrive, *we'll* be the law."

"You? The law?" scoffed Miriam. "You can't even read."

"Don't have to read to rob banks and knock back whiskey. Yes, ma'am, all the whiskey in Utopia's gonna be free for us. Billy's promised it."

"Billy Dixon's a bald-faced liar," Ruth said.

Herk twisted in the saddle to backhand her. As he did, he caught sight of Williamson making as good a time as possible.

"Squinty! The law! Behind us!" Herk went for his six-gun.

Williamson threw caution to the wind. He bent low over his horse's neck and galloped ahead. Herk's first bullet tore through the air above him. The outlaw had been surprised into taking a snap shot. His second went even wider. Ruth stood in the stirrups and threw herself toward him. Her hands were tied behind her back so she wasn't able to grab him or catch herself as she fell.

She crashed into Herk's horse, causing it to rear.

Herk missed with another shot. And then Williamson was on him. He kicked hard and left the saddle. His strong arms circled Herk's shoulders. Williamson pulled hard, forcing the gunman's arms down to his side.

The horse let out an almost human screech as the outlaw's bullet tore into its flank. It fell to its knees, kicked itself back on all fours, and staggered away without its rider. Then Williamson and his quarry crashed to the ground.

"Get outta here, Squinty. Get Billy!"

Williamson wasn't able to swing properly. His left hand still pinned Herk's gun hand to his body. His right fist traveled a few inches and collided with an exposed chin. The jolt rocked him all the way to the shoulder. He knew better than to hit a man in the chin. That was a good way to bust fingers. A second short punch landed over Herk's eye. It'd swell up and blind him in a few seconds.

Only Williamson realized he didn't have the luxury of that much time. Herk's gun jerked free. Another round pounded past and thudded into the ground at his feet. He dug his toes into the rocky ground and rammed forward as hard as he could.

Herk's gun discharged a final time.

"Lookee there. We got company." Billy Dixon sauntered over to where Shad hung from the tree limb. The rope had cut deeply into his neck. Blood trickled from the abrasion and soaked into the hemp. He poked his prisoner in the ribs and got the desired flinch. "You ain't at your best to accept company, are you? A busted rib, maybe?" He punched Shad in the gut and watched him swing back and forth, choking because of the tightening noose around his neck.

"I'll enjoy watching you swing, Dixon." It was all he could do to choke out the threat. His head felt as if it'd explode. Blood trapped above his neck made his face feel like the worst sunburn ever. Even his lips swelled up to make talking hard.

"You can't possibly enjoy it more 'n I'm enjoying watching you right now, Marshal." He waved to Squinty. "Come on over. Bring our guests closer."

Shad blinked furiously to get the sweat from his eyes. The burning went away and desolation filled him. Ruth led the way. Miriam trailed behind her. They had their hands tied in front of them and clung to their saddle horns. Squinty came up behind.

"Get down, folks. Step down and come greet your pa. Your husband." Dixon laughed. "Your corpse to be!"

Ruth dismounted and came to him. Shad knew he was in bad shape, but something looked wrong. Ruth was a brave woman, but even brave women showed fear. There was something else in her eyes.

"You get away from him," she said to Dixon.

"Why, little lady, I think I will. That filly of yours looks about ready to foal. I should help her since she needs a mite more help in her delicate condition."

Shad didn't see any fear on his daughter's face, either. She gritted her teeth, but her expression wasn't what he expected.

Then he saw it. Squinty stayed in the saddle but there wasn't a pistol in his holster.

Ruth moved like a striking snake. From her skirts she pulled a knife that looked familiar.

Rich Williamson's!

The knife's razor edge slashed through the rope holding him upright. Shad tried to prepare himself but still succumbed to weakness. He collapsed to his knees.

"Stop wiggling," Ruth said. She moved behind him. Another slash severed the ropes holding his hands.

He fell forward, caught himself, then got his feet under him. He had a fight to finish with Billy Dixon.

The only problem was that Miriam kicked out at Dixon. The outlaw had expected it and grabbed her ankle. What he hadn't expected was the six-gun in her hand. She fired at him just as he yanked her leg hard.

Shad refused to stop fighting. He kicked and fought to stay upright and then he tackled Dixon. The two fell to the ground. The impact shook Shad so much he let loose. Above him zinged bullets in all directions.

"Run, Dixon," came Shannon's order. "Williamson's got a rifle trained on you!"

Shad tried once more to stop Dixon. He caught at the man's boot, only to be kicked away. The outlaw vaulted onto the horse behind Squinty. The two shot off. Shad caught sight of Squinty's hands. Bound in front of him. Unlike Ruth and Miriam, these ropes were securely cinched.

"A gun. I need a gun!" Shad looked around frantically. Shannon fired back along the trail, and Williamson returned fire. Dixon, riding behind his henchman, struggled to climb the hill and get to a trail just above the camp.

Shad grabbed the knife from his wife's hand. He wasn't much of a knife thrower, but he tried. The blade clattered off a rock to Dixon's right. The outlaw bent forward, crushing his partner, then veered right onto the trail and galloped away. Shannon took a few more seconds to lay down covering fire before he raced after them.

"That was my good knife, Shad." Williamson trotted up. "You probably busted the blade."

"It's only nicked. I saw where it went." Shad saw how Williamson was torn between going after the fleeing outlaws and being sure his wife and their baby were safe.

Family won out over law.

"I'll take that," Shad said, prying the gun from Miriam's grip. She surrendered it and threw her arms around Williamson's neck to hug him.

"That's Squinty's gun," Ruth said.

He looked hard at her.

"Rich took it from him?"

"There's a body back there along the trail," she said, then she hugged him, her cheek pressing into his chest.

"I hope it doesn't make the coyotes sick. I'm not going to bury him." He looked up the hillside where the other three owlhoots had escaped. He wasn't inclined to bury them, either.

After he killed them.

CHAPTER THIRTY-FOUR

"Give me your rifle."

"Why?" Richard Williamson looked surprised. "You're not going after them. I am!"

"No, you're not." Shad took his son-in-law's arm and pulled him away to speak privately. "You'll get Miriam and the baby to safety. Don't let Ruth convince you to go against your job, either. She'll want to go to the house. Take her into town where she'll be safer."

"Miriam won't want to go there, either."

"Then you've got your job cut out for you. Now let me have your rifle."

"You're in no shape to . . ." Williamson's voice trailed off when he saw the determination etched onto Shad's face. He silently pulled his rifle from the saddle scabbard and handed it over.

"Got any spare ammo?"

Williamson fished around in his saddlebags and gave Shad a box.

"What's going on? You're not chasing after them, Shadrach Nelson!" Ruth started to join them.

Shad pushed Williamson between them, vaulted into

the saddle where Miriam had been only a few minutes earlier, and applied his heels vigorously to the horse's flanks. The horse had been Herk's and had never been treated properly. Shad fought to keep it under control even as he tried to shut out his wife's protests about him being a danged fool.

He wasn't in any shape to argue that. He had been beaten and almost hanged. It had taken his wife and son-in-law to rescue him. And he wasn't giving up the hunt now. Billy Dixon and his henchmen deserved to stand trial for all they'd done.

If he had to gun them down, he wouldn't shed a single tear over it.

The trail wended around rocks and curled higher into the mountains. Now and then he took a switchback and had to watch the rocks straight over his head for trouble. There wasn't much chance for any of them to take a side trail. All he had to do was avoid being ambushed. Not only Dixon was likely to take a shot at him. Any or all of Beatrice Gallagher's family had it in for him, too.

He worked over the possible things to do if he found Beatrice before he did Dixon. Arresting her was certainly in the cards, but taking her off the mountain when she was surrounded by her entire trigger-happy family would be nigh on impossible. From all Dixon had said, he thought he was calling the shots and that Beatrice deluded herself. He used her.

If he had the chance to ask, Shad knew the new Coal Queen of the Rockies thought it was the other way around. She used Dixon for her own ends.

He'd line them both up on the gallows and drop them to eternity. They were both murderous reprobates.

Shad touched the rifle laying across the saddle in front of him. Neither Dixon nor Beatrice would surrender. Guns would be blazing until they died. For that he gave them grudging admiration since he felt the same way.

All the more reason to arrest them and march them up the thirteen steps on a gallows. Shooting them was too good.

The horse proved to have more stamina than he'd expected. It climbed steadily, hardly stumbling on the loose rocks, until he reached a meadow with a small lake in the middle. On the near side, Dixon and the others who had run from him argued with Beatrice and a cadre of her family. He slowed. Taking them all on was a sure massacre. Custer had a better chance than the twenty-to-one odds facing him now.

But to his surprise, Beatrice looked in his direction, then ordered her guards to ride away. Dixon, Renfro, Squinty, and Shannon stood beside their horses. They had ridden them into the ground to get away, and now they were stranded. Not a one of the horses had energy enough left to do more than graze. Riding any of them would kill the animal within a few yards. Even at this distance, Shad saw the lather flecking the flanks and the huge bellows of their lungs gasping for the thin Rockies air.

He hiked the rifle to his shoulder and called out, "Drop your guns. You're all under arrest!"

Dixon said something. Squinty snickered. Renfro

and Shannon turned to him and gave him what for. The argument got worse as Shad neared.

"He wouldn't come up like this if Williamson wasn't out there." Shannon made a sweep with his arm, taking in most of the meadow. He swung about and stared into the depths of the woods behind them. If Williamson had come with Shad, that would be the perfect spot to fire on them from cover.

"Then you take him out."

Before Shannon could argue further, Dixon swung his pistol and hit him on the back of the head. The former deputy fell forward and caught himself. On hands and knees, he shook his head to clear it.

Dixon mounted Shannon's horse and galloped away. Renfro and Squinty followed. Their horses stumbled but kept up a canter. Left on foot, Shannon had no choice but to surrender—or fight.

"Your partners abandoned you, Ian. Drop your irons. I've got a rifle. You can't hit me at this range."

"If you want to take me in, you've got to get closer." Shannon drew both his pistols. He fired a couple rounds from each six-gun. He widened his stance and waited.

Shad drew a bead. The back sights lined up perfectly with the bright silver bead at the end of the barrel. This was an easy shot for a rifle, but he didn't take it. He had worked with Shannon for two years. They'd never been friends, and he had no idea why the former deputy had chosen to ride with Billy Dixon, but this felt too much like dynamiting fish in a barrel.

"I've got you. Drop the six-shooters."

Shannon started walking toward him, alternating shots between his two guns.

"Your friends left you. They stole your horse. Don't expect Dixon to come to your rescue." This slowed Shannon. "You were used, Ian. Used and now he's tossed you aside."

"Let me go."

"I can't do that, Shannon. You know me. I'd never do that."

"You don't have much on me. I sprung Renfro. That's all."

Shad almost erupted in anger.

"You let them hang me up like a side of beef. Dixon tortured me. And you didn't do a damned thing to stop Herk and Squinty from kidnaping my wife and daughter." He snugged the stock into his shoulder and fired.

Shannon dodged just as his finger came back. He had meant it to be a killing shot. Instead he sent Shannon's hat flying.

"You're on your own. And what did Beatrice Gallagher have to say? She wasn't too amenable to saving Dixon. Or you."

"Me and Beatrice had a fling," Shannon said. "It didn't last long."

Shad had no idea.

"Is that why you teamed up with Dixon? You wanted Beatrice back and he took her from you?"

Shannon laughed harshly.

"Nobody does anything Beatrice doesn't want. She used Patrick Morrisey. She used me. And she used

Dixon, only he doesn't understand that. He's fool enough to think he's calling the shots."

"Did you know she killed her own aunt?"

Shannon hesitated, his six-shooters lowered.

"That don't surprise me one little bit. She and Winifred never got along. The old woman was even worse about bossin' people around than Beatrice, and that's sayin' something." Shannon stared at the pistols in his hands. "Beatrice prob'ly shot her because she wasn't aggressive enough fightin' the Morriseys. That and she was satisfied with stealin' from the railroad."

"Beatrice wants more, is that it?"

Again Shannon laughed harshly.

"It was her idea to get Dixon to recruit everyone that'll be ridin' on the black train." He hefted his guns again.

This time Shad's aim was better. He caught Shannon in the shoulder and spun him around. Another shot took the man's leg from under him.

"Don't make me fire again. If I do, you're a dead man."

"Bury me, will you, Nelson? Here, in town, I don't care. Just don't leave me for the coyotes. I hate coyotes." He raised the six-gun in his left hand just as Shad fired a third time. The bullet tore the length of Shannon's forearm. His six-gun went flying.

Shad edged closer, keeping the rifle trained on the fallen man. Shannon wasn't going anywhere. One leg was a bloody mess. The shoulder wound didn't look bad, but it kept him from moving unless he endured considerable pain. His left forearm showed a bloody crease from wrist to elbow.

"Finish me off, Marshal. You want to do it for all the trouble Dixon's caused."

"You're not Billy Dixon. I'll deal with him. After I toss you into a cell back in town."

Ian Shannon passed out halfway back to Utopia. Shad had to walk the horse. It gave him plenty of time to think about how to stop Billy Dixon.

And Beatrice Gallagher.

CHAPTER THIRTY-FIVE

"We can't let him run us off," Billy Dixon snarled as he looked over the brink of the road winding around the mountain.

"There's more than the marshal. That railroad dick had us covered with a rifle. Who knows how many others they had scattered around in the woods?" Gadsden Renfro rubbed his tired hindquarters. The ride up the road had been difficult, both on his horse and on him.

"Nelson was all ripped up. I made sure of that."

"Billy, you went and made him mad. You shoulda kilt him outright." Squinty led his horse along the road, trying to keep the small company moving. He kept looking around as if expecting the law to swoop down on him like a hawk.

"I shoulda never trusted you and Herk to do anything right. What happened to him? Did he hightail it at the first sign of trouble?"

"Ah, Billy, it wasn't like that. That Williamson bull killed him. They fought over Herk's gun, and it went off, and he took a bullet right through the gut. It took him a couple minutes to die." Squinty hitched up his drawers. "I never heard a man sound so pitiful as he kicked the bucket."

"What were you doing when he was dying?" Dixon faced his henchman.

"Williamson had the drop on me. I wasn't able to do nuthin'. If I'd tried anything, I'd've ended up like Herk with a slug in my belly."

"That would have been better than to come riding into camp with them women pretending to be prisoners. You never tried to warn me."

"I couldn't! You got it all wrong, Billy. I wanted to! Williamson had me covered. If I'd so much as twitched, he'd've kilt me dead on the spot. And if he hadn't, them women would have. They were fiercer 'n I ever thought they'd be."

"So you let them waltz right on into camp, free Nelson, and shoot Shannon."

"No loss there, if you ask me. I never trust a turncoat. If they swapped sides once, what's to keep them from doin' it again when you least expect it?"

"What should I have done to Shannon?" Dixon rested his hand on the butt of his pistol.

Squinty peered at him.

"We'd all have been better off if you plugged him straight away. He got all shot up, but how do we know Nelson didn't do that to make it look like Shannon was playin' fair with us?"

"The same question I want you to answer."

"How's that? I don't—" Squinty grabbed his breadbasket when Dixon drew and fired point-blank. He stumbled away. Dixon fired again. This time Squinty lost his balance and tumbled over the verge of the winding road. He bounced three or four times before he landed face down in the road thirty feet below.

"We could have used another gun," Renfro said, peering down at the dead body.

"He didn't put up enough of a fuss to warn us."

"Didn't sound that way, did it? He might have gotten all confused in how he told his story. But Squinty's tongue is as weak as his eyes."

"Was," Dixon corrected. "Everything about him is was now." He reloaded his six-shooter and tucked it into his holster.

Renfro scratched his head and wiped sweat from his forehead. He turned to Dixon and stared at him.

"You need me."

"More 'n I needed him. Or Beatrice Gallagher."

"You think she'll try to stop you?"

"The only way is find out by heading west and getting the telegraph fixed."

"I'm up for it," Renfro said. He wiped away more sweat before settling his flat-brimmed hat squarely on his head.

Dixon heard the slow clop of the other horse following him as he rode away. At least now this horse wasn't burdened with two riders.

"I think this is the stretch of line," Renfro said. "It's hard to tell in the dusk."

"That's why I had you fix the wire with rawhide. Anyone riding along sees only a solid line."

"The telegraphic signal doesn't go through rawhide.

Only copper." Renfro drew rein and looked up. "There. That looks like the rawhide strip I used to splice the line. I see the knots on either end."

Dixon dismounted and scouted the area. Nobody had ridden by here recently. He walked to the tracks and pressed his boot down. No vibrations. Nothing coming from Georgetown. Why should there be? The eastern part of track hadn't been repaired yet. No direct connection with Denver meant riders had to use other lines across the Rockies.

But not for long.

He inhaled the pure, clean air. When the steam engines puffed and chugged up this slope, they filled the air with smoke and soot. That would return soon when he took over Utopia. The trains would pay to use the facilities. More for coal, more for water, more to load and unload freight. A quick look over his shoulder added to his certainty. Renfro would be in charge of the freight yard again, and Sussman was a limp-spined toad.

Billy Dixon would control everything moving through Utopia on the railroad. Let the owners down in Denver try to wrest it from him when he had a dozen— a hundred!—gunmen backing his play. Utopia would be a safe hideout again for as many gangs as he allowed.

If they backed him, they could range far and wide rustling cattle and robbing banks and stages. That bank he'd robbed earlier would become bloated with all the cash stuffed into it by a half dozen different outlaw gangs. Local businesses would pony up money or get burned out. There were more than a dozen saloons in Utopia. No alcohol reached them without his say-so.

Billy Dixon intended to own or control everything moving around Utopia.

"I got the equipment all laid out, Billy. I need help with it."

Dixon walked to where Renfro looped a broad leather belt around his waist. Steel spikes already fastened onto his shoes made formidable weapons. But they weren't like spurs for a fighting cock. These were designed for climbing wood poles.

Renfro walked clumsily to the pole and looped the leather strap around it before securing it at his waist. He slid it up, then dug the spikes into the wood and began climbing. Five feet up he leaned back and reached down.

"Gimme the wire, cutters, and the copper tubes with holes in them."

Dixon passed them up. Renfro began scaling the pole and reached the spot where he had replaced a length of copper wire with the nonconducting rawhide. He muttered to himself as he worked. The copper tubes were crimped down to give purchase for the replacement wire. Only when he had secured the splice did he cut out the rawhide. The strip fluttered down.

Dixon caught it and ran his fingers over it. He felt the power here. He had prevented Nelson from contacting the Georgetown sheriff and asking for help. Not that the layabout sheriff was inclined to venture farther than the local whorehouse unless it was to get more whiskey.

"Watch out. Here comes more wire."

Renfro released a roll of wire. It snaked down. A second strand followed. That done, he worked his way down the pole. He released the leather strap and kicked off the spikes.

"All you need to do now is hook up the telegraph key to those wires and you've got yourself a completed circuit."

"Do it."

Renfro looked surprised.

"You want to send a message now?"

"*The* message," Dixon corrected. He watched as Renfro wound the bare wire around the posts on the telegraph key. When he looked up, Dixon said, "Time for the reunion."

"That's what you want me to send?"

Dixon nodded. Renfro balanced the key on his thigh, then began tapping out the dits and dahs. He scowled, then repeated the message. He finally put the key down.

"I sent it twice. The first time they didn't acknowledge."

Before Dixon said a word, the key began chattering.

"What's it say?"

Renfro touched the key almost reverently and said, "Ready at sunrise."

"They'll be here around dawn." Billy Dixon almost danced a jig at the news. All his plans came together. In a few hours he'd be cock of the walk in Utopia, Colorado.

"Are you sure?"

Billy Dixon was sure. He'd planned this too long not to know who he could depend on. Greed and bloodlust drove the men who'd arrive on the morning train. Those were motives he understood and shared.

CHAPTER THIRTY-SIX

"Doc Paisley's patched him up pretty good," Leroy Early said. "I wish he'd done as good a job on me."

"You need another bottle of whiskey?"

The deputy shook his head and pointed to the bottom desk drawer.

"I've got a couple bottles there. Missy brung me one. Ralph did, too, because he didn't know Missy'd already been here. Real thoughtful of them both. They're good people." Early shifted in the chair and fixed Shad with a gimlet stare. "Don't you go thinkin' you need to help me drink it. I can do it all by myself."

Shad looked into the cells. Ian Shannon slept fitfully in the front cell. Neal Wright still occupied the back cell. Repairs needed to be finished on the bars and outer wall in the middle cell. He closed the door and perched on the corner of his desk.

Early looked like a bleached bedsheet. His eyes were those of a man running a fever, but his hands no longer shook uncontrollably, and he had no trouble hiking his boots to the desktop. He had even torn up another newspaper and put a new woven mat down to keep from scratching the top.

"You need to dig into a steak and build up your blood."

"I need to sleep for a week, but you're not lettin' me do that, are you?"

"I wish I could, but I can't. Things are coming to a boil real soon. I feel it. Dixon's not going to let me go free when he tried to kill me."

"He'll be gunnin' for Rich, too. Rich put Herk six feet under."

"He left the body so the buzzards could choke on him. I wish I'd been able to arrest Dixon instead of Shannon." Shad fell silent in thought. He finally asked, "Has he said anything about why he threw in with Dixon?"

"For some men switchin' from law to outlaw isn't much of a jump. But he only rode with Dixon. The real reason he quit bein' a deputy wears a skirt."

"And runs the Calcutta Mine," he said tiredly. "I might have known Beatrice Gallagher was somewhere nearby stirring the pot."

"Shannon grumbled some in his sleep about Dixon cuttin' his filly from the herd. She was stringin' both of 'em along for her own reasons."

"Them and Patrick Morrisey. I wonder who else."

"Surely wasn't me," Early said. "If it had been, I'd be in worse shape than I am now. A woman like that can be the death of a man."

"She'll be the death of the entire town if I can't convince more citizens that trouble's on the way. If it's not staring them in the face, they won't believe there's any problem."

"Most weren't here when the gangs ran Utopia. The railroad made life easy, and you drove off Dixon and the rest like him. The town's been too peaceable."

"I've got Ruth and Miriam in the hotel. I wish I had them even closer, but that's the best I can do."

"Better than nuthin'. Putting them up in our open cell wouldn't do."

"Hold down the fort, Leroy. I'm going to see if I can't scare some of the folks into forming a militia." He stood. His muscles ached and swallowing was hard from having his neck almost stretched. Trying not to show it, he held out his hand to see how much he still shook. A little too much. Drawing and firing accurately would be risky for another few days. He'd been lucky his aim had been so good when he arrested Ian Shannon.

"You care too much, Shad."

"What's that?"

"If you had any sense, you'd pack up the family and head to Denver. Let Utopia figure out how to survive on its own. Hell, I'd do that but I'm too banged up."

"Too banged up and too much like me. A sense of honor will do you in if you let it." Shad settled his bowler and stepped out into the street to hail the owner of the general store.

"Mister Sampson, hold your horses. Don't go running off."

The store owner looked around as if he could find a hole to hide in, then gave up.

"Howdy, Marshal. You're looking fit as a fiddle after your run in with Dixon and his gang."

"Let me tell you all about that, Mister Sampson." Shad tried every argument he could think of to convince the store owner that the danger had grown.

"Marshal Nelson, you done scared him off. A man like that's running for his life."

"I'm afraid the Gallagher clan's in on the attack when it comes, too. Beatrice and Dixon are in cahoots."

"Not her and Dixon. I've heard about her and Patrick Morrisey. I don't know which of them has a few screws loose in the head. Them two families been feuding ever since I came to Utopia. Nothing will come of it that hasn't happened before."

"I need help. A militia would go a ways toward slowing the outlaws when they return."

"A militia?"

"That sounds too much like the Army. Call it a posse. I need a posse, only they wouldn't go chasing after anyone outside of town."

"You're talking about a vigilance committee, Marshal."

"Yes, call it that." Shad felt increasingly frustrated. He had spoken to a dozen others with the same result.

"There's no call to whip up vigilantes. We've got you as our duly appointed lawman. You're doin' a right fine job of keeping the peace, Marshal Nelson. Now I have to put some . . . something on the shelves. A storekeeper's job is never done."

Dejected, Shad walked over to the Gold Dust City Saloon, thinking to recruit inside. He met Rich Williamson coming out.

"I beat you to it," Williamson said.

"Whip up a lot of enthusiasm?" Shad asked dourly.

Williamson half turned and pointed to the empty space behind him. That told the tale.

"What are we going to do?"

"The railroad's sending out a special engine to move the coal cars stranded on the line. The track's been replaced but somebody at the home office has a bee in his bonnet about salvaging the derailed engine."

"When they hook onto the six coal cars, they intend to take them to Denver?"

"I tried to convince them to send a dozen detectives out with the rescue train, but everyone's scattered across the state. Sparing even one would put a strain on keeping the yards free of men trying to ride the rails."

"That's hardly as important as losing control of the Utopia depot."

"I told them, Shad. I did."

"When are they fixing the telegraph wire?"

"That's something else they're not too concerned with. After they get the six coal cars to Denver, it might be as long as a week before they try to return to a regular schedule."

"That gives Dixon—and Beatrice—too much time. They can get dozens of cutthroats into Utopia in a week. When that train does arrive, the engineer's going to find the depot in the hands of crooks."

Williamson muttered to himself and stared straight ahead.

They walked along in silence for a few blocks. The town was quiet, so peaceful that a man could sleep in any of the chairs pulled up under the shade. Shad knew that would change fast when Dixon returned. If Beatrice came into town, it would change even faster.

"We need to find the posts where we can hold them off the best we can ourselves," Shad said. He looked around, then pointed. "Up there. If we hide a couple rifles and ammo, we command the entire stretch of street down to the millinery store."

"The surveyor that laid out these streets wiggling around like a drunk snake should be horsewhipped."

"Nobody's ever come up with a good reason why he didn't plot out straight streets. The best I've heard is that the county refused to pay him what he wanted, so he did this to get back at the skinflints."

"It gave a lot of corners to fire around. Defending it will be a chore," said Williamson. "Maybe if we holed up in the hotel . . ."

"No! That's where Ruth and Miriam are. We don't want to draw them there."

"If—"

"Williamson, there you are! Hold up, will you? I can't walk near as fast as you." Doctor Paisley popped out of a storefront.

"What's your hurry, Doctor?"

Doc Paisley looked from Williamson to Shad and then back. He swallowed so hard his Adam's apple bobbed.

"They're gone."

"What are you talking about?"

"Don't go snapping at me, Marshal. Your wife's as stubborn as you are. She and your daughter have gone back to your house."

"Why?" Williamson demanded. "They aren't safe

there. They know that. They were both kidnapped and . . ."

"The baby's coming. I'll go on up and do what I can, but it sounds as if the labor might be a long one. Miriam wanted to be in her own bed." Paisley looked uneasy when he added, "Netty Michaelson wasn't making them feel at home, either. It's not my place to say anything, but getting Miriam away from the hotel during the delivery might be the best thing you can do."

Williamson was halfway across the street, heading for the stables and his horse when he stopped dead in his tracks. He turned and stared back at Shad. His expression was forlorn.

"I have to go, Shad. But the town . . ."

"The town's going to be just fine. Be with your wife. And tell mine she should have stayed here."

"For all the good that'll do," the doctor said. "She said Miriam insisted on giving birth in the same house where she grew up. It was more peaceable, she said."

"She was born in Denver. Why couldn't she go there?" But Shad knew why. The train wasn't running through to Denver yet. The coal cars had to be hauled downhill before another engine could be dispatched to arrive in Utopia. If Williamson was right, that might be a week. By then the baby would be squalling. Traveling to Denver would be pointless.

"Go, go, boy." Shad shooed Williamson away.

He watched the man's broad back vanish around a corner. He had done the right thing ordering Williamson to go. Williamson would have ignored him if he'd said anything different. That was one of the things Shad liked about his son-in-law. He had his priorities straight.

That still didn't help erase the feeling of being entirely alone Shad felt as he looked around Utopia.

In an hour or a day or more, if he was lucky, the town would be overrun by cutthroats. Williamson had better be back by then.

Shad headed back to the jailhouse to let Early know.

CHAPTER THIRTY-SEVEN

"It's a trap."

Shad looked at his son-in-law, then over at Leroy Early, who flopped on a blanket stretched across the far wall of the jail's office. Both men had the same determined set to their jaws.

"Of course it's a trap," he said. "That doesn't mean we can't turn it to our benefit, knowing we're sticking our foot in a bear trap."

"Don't rightly see how you're gonna pull that off, Shad, not without losin' your whole danged foot." Early shifted painfully on the blanket, moved his rifle around and used it to lever himself to a sitting position. He hadn't stirred from the jail since they'd locked up Ian Shannon.

"Leroy's right. If we had an army of deputies to back us up, that'd be one thing. If it's just us?" Williamson shook his head.

"We don't have time to wait for the train to get here from Denver. Besides, you said the railroad wasn't inclined to send more detectives any time soon."

"We're on our own." Williamson licked his lips and

cracked his knuckles. "With Miriam in such a way, we're not able to run, either."

"She's all the more reason we have to spring this trap," Shad said. "We need to act on our schedule, not Dixon's."

"Catch him unawares, is that what you're sayin'?" Early sounded skeptical such a thing was possible. Shad caught himself from agreeing with the deputy. He had to sound optimistic they could pull off a preemptive attack, no matter what his gut told him.

"Sussman is in Dixon's hip pocket. He must be paid off, or maybe he's just afraid of what might happen to him."

"Could be both," Early said. "He's not got a single bone in his spine."

"We have to believe one thing he said." Shad had their attention. "A telegram came through from Georgetown."

"I tried to send after he told me that, and the line's dead again. Dixon is keeping us cut off in both directions." Williamson paced like a caged tiger. Shad shared his frustration.

Shad pulled down a shotgun and began filling his coat pockets with shells. His intent was obvious.

"Dixon got a telegram through. That doesn't mean Sussman is telling the truth about him and Renfro having a powwow," Williamson said.

"If he's afraid enough of Dixon and what he can do, he might want us to remove him from his job so he can hide out somewhere safely away from Dixon." Shad slid shells into the double barrels and snapped it shut.

"Come or stay. It makes sense for you to do either of them."

Williamson hesitated. Shad knew the thoughts running through the young man's head. His wife was having a difficult delivery, but Doc Paisley said the baby was due any minute. Protecting Miriam made sense, but stopping Dixon right now made sense, too. He'd keep his family safer by getting rid of the outlaw.

"Let's go."

Shad wasn't sure that was the right decision, but he appreciated Williamson at his side. His son-in-law had shown himself to be fearless in a gunfight. He silently pointed to the gun rack and the drawers under it overflowing with spare ammunition. Williamson helped himself. Then he took down a rifle.

They marched across town toward the railroad depot. The sun was barely above the horizon, casting long shadows in front of them.

"If we were only as big as our shadows," Williamson said. He held out his rifle. It looked like a cannon stretched along the ground.

"We'll need to move as quiet as a shadow," Shad said. "Dixon and Renfro are supposed to be up the slope at the coal bin."

"Watching for their train."

Shad tried not to shudder at the thought of an invasion by a gang of throat-slitting outlaws descending on Utopia.

"Cut the head off, the snake dies," Williamson said.

"The snake won't die until sundown, so we've got a real task ahead."

"I've got the rifle. I'll work my way above the bin on that cliff. If you come up the road we'll have them cut off. They'll fight rather than try jumping down to the tracks."

"That's a good twenty-foot drop. Even if they try sliding down the coal chute, we've got them."

Shad took a quick look toward the railroad depot. He saw Sussman moving around inside. Sussman had never been honest in any of his dealings. Throwing the railroad agent into jail appealed to him, but first he had to bring Dixon and Renfro to justice.

"Sussman is a small fry," Williamson said. "I should have fired him a long time ago but getting someone to take his job is hard. The railroad personnel is stretched thin throughout the state."

"You can fire him?"

"Have him fired. I'm just an employee like him, but folks higher up listen to me."

"As long as they believe you and act on it about sending an army to back us up—eventually." Shad pointed to a trail leading away from the freight yard that circled around and led to the spot above the coal bin. Williamson checked to be sure he had a round in the rifle chamber and hurried away.

Shad felt the sense of desolation smothering him again. Having Williamson with him helped, but the actual fight rested heavily on his shoulders. He drew back the twin rabbit ear hammers and cocked the shotgun. When he thought Williamson had had plenty of time to get into position, he started up the slope. Lumps of coal littered the way. Stepping on a few made him stumble. Shad's thoughts wandered. Beatrice should have her cousins and nephews picking up the coal and not letting it go to waste. Throw it in the bin so it could be loaded into a tender car.

Waste not, want not. Kill anyone in her way.

As he got closer to the flat area where the wagons dumped their coal into the loading bin, he slowed and then stopped. Nowhere did he see either Dixon or Renfro. He dropped to one knee and cocked his head to one side, listening hard.

He leveled the shotgun and unloaded both barrels into the coal bin. The recoil rocked him back. The shot tore a hole the size of his head in the side.

"He's here! Get him, Dixon!"

Shad recognized Renfro's voice. The man had hidden in the coal bin and had betrayed himself by moving around and scraping the rough-hewn inner wall. He reloaded and waited. Renfro wasn't shooting through the hole. Just when he thought Dixon had abandoned his henchman, Shad saw a head poke over the side. Dixon clung to the side of the hill. He braced his six-shooter against the ground and began firing at Shad.

The shotgun belched out more double-ought buckshot. It tore away a patch of rock and dirt near Dixon's face. The outlaw ducked down, taking cover. Clinging to the slope like that put him in a precarious position. Shad moved to prevent Renfro from shooting at him through the hole in the side of the bin and advanced on the spot where Dixon had dropped out of sight.

"Shad, get down!" Williamson's warning tore through the cool morning.

He reacted instantly. Something felt wrong about the way Renfro and Dixon had set up the ambush. Renfro was penned up and Dixon had only a limited area where he could fire. Shad dived to the side, hit hard, and rolled until he fetched up hard against the base of the cliff. Williamson was fifteen feet above him and firing furiously.

His targets were hidden—for a few more seconds. Then Shad gasped. A half dozen men had been flat on their bellies, hiding under tarps. The air filled with more lead than anyone could fight. He pulled his head down, expecting a round to smash through the crown of his bowler and blow out his brains.

Williamson's barrage drew fire in his direction. Shad chanced a look around. He'd thought six men had been hiding. He stopped counting when he got to ten. Most were strangers, but he recognized enough to know Beatrice had sent these killers from her family's ranks. He snugged the shotgun against his shoulder and got off two more barrels of death. The scattershot cut the legs out from under two men.

They flopped about, screeching for other Gallaghers to help. This worked against Shad. They once more saw him as a danger. He winced as two slugs grazed his left arm. Another blast from his shotgun drove his attackers back under cover.

"Get out, Shad. There're too many of them!"

"Give me cover," he called to his son-in-law. Williamson was smart enough to know to do that, but what worried him was that the attack came from the direction of the coal bin. Why would they give him a chance to retreat down the slope and into the freight yard?

Williamson did his best to force the Gallaghers to take cover, but there were too many of them. Dixon had disappeared and never poked his head back up. He had no idea what part Renfro took in the fight, but no shots came from that direction. Before, he had seen shadows moving about in the coal bin as Renfro dodged about. There wasn't anything to see now.

As crazy as it seemed, an escape route existed. If Renfro had jumped onto the coal chute, he'd be dumped out in midair above the tracks. The fall was bone-shaking, but that was better than getting his fool head blown off.

Shad shared that belief.

He scuttled back and found why they had let him come up. Somewhere a hiding space in the freight yard disgorged another five or six men. One of them held a bundle of four sticks of dynamite. A short black fuse dangled from it. Another Gallagher struck a match.

All he saw was a flare as the fuse caught fire and burned. The man holding the bundle reared back to throw it in Shad's direction. Williamson proved a better shot than Shad had given him credit for. A rifle bullet hit the man with the dynamite in the chest. The bundle fell from his suddenly numb fingers and then the explosion shook the ground. Half the ramp up to the coal bin simply vanished from the potent blast.

Shad swung around and saw they'd intended to blow him up from both directions. A miner reared back holding another bundle of five sticks. Both barrels of the shotgun tore through the miner's midriff. As had happened with the other dynamiter, he dropped the explosive.

Dirt and rock erupted, knocking Shad from the ramp and down ten feet to a sudden and very hard landing beside the tracks. Shaken he tried to stand. His legs refused to obey.

He heard Williamson fall into a methodical firing pattern. Return fire was sporadic. Shouts showed how the Gallaghers' attack had been blunted. More than one of them had been shot. Even more had been blown up by their own bombs.

Moaning from the aches he had just accumulated, Shad rolled over and pressed his back against a stack of railroad ties. The wood gave him cover. He fired until he ran out of shells, but by then he was the only one firing. Even Williamson had stopped.

"Rich! Rich! You still in one piece?" He pulled himself up, using the creosote-soaked ties as a support. High up on the cliff overlooking the coal bin, he saw his son-in-law stand and wave that he was unhurt.

Then he went cold inside. Williamson pointed down the tracks. Shad turned and heard the steam engine straining up the last steep slope before pulling into the Utopia station.

The train had been painted black. As it slowed, men jumped off and advanced to greet Billy Dixon. The outlaw turned and pointed at Shad. There wasn't any reason to overhear what the outlaw said. Every last cutthroat stepping from the train drew their six-gun and started toward him.

Shad patted his coat pockets. All the shotgun shells

were gone. He dropped the scattergun and slid his Peacemaker from the holster. Retreat was out of the question.

He stepped out to face a tornado of lead whirling his way.

CHAPTER THIRTY-EIGHT

Shadrach Nelson watched an endless tide of gunmen jump down from the train. He scooted around the pile of railroad ties and then saw how they'd been stacked. He wiggled between two of them and found a hollow section in the middle of what now gave him a sturdy refuge.

"Get 'em, boys. Don't let a single one of them get away. Kill 'em all!"

Shad recognized Billy Dixon's voice booming out loud and clear. The gunfire that followed sounded like a cavalry troop opening fire in a pitched battle. He cringed as a few slugs tore into the wood protecting him. The ties were too thick to penetrate, but he saw the movement of men passing outside. If anyone spotted him, he was a goner.

Shad clutched his six-shooter and waited. Slowly his heart settled down to a more reasonable thumping. When the sounds of the outlaws faded away, he chanced a look outside his wooden fortress. Slithering like a snake let him flop onto the ground.

He glanced over his shoulder and saw a pair of boots

behind him. With a quick twist, he jerked around and lifted his Peacemaker. His finger moved off the trigger at the last instant.

"Thanks for not shooting me," Rich Williamson said.

"You got away, too."

"I hid in the coal bin where Renfro had been." Williamson brushed coal dust off. His hands were filthy and his cheeks carried streaks of black soot.

"How many?" Shad got to his feet.

"I counted forty before I stopped. There were some riding in freight cars to guard their horses. How many were with the livestock, I can't say."

"They brought their own gear?"

"From the way they were calling to each other, they loaded several dozen animals with enough ammo to fight a war. One entire freight car carried their arsenal." Williamson looked down the tracks along the black-painted train. "If they didn't leave many guards we can blow it up."

"Your boss won't like an employee destroying railroad property."

"Stolen property, from the look of it. No railroad official permitted them to paint the whole danged train black. Why'd they do that?"

"It looks ominous," Shad said. "Who's afraid of a robin? Now, take a raven and just the sight's enough to give a man the shivers."

Williamson pulled Shad back against a pile of crates and held him back. He put his finger to his lips, cautioning silence.

A heavily laden wagon rumbled past. A half dozen gunmen rode shotgun.

"They've emptied the car. That's their arsenal," Williamson said.

"I didn't see anything more dangerous than crates of Winchesters. There wasn't a Gatling there."

"A dozen men weighed down with a dozen six-shooters is more than a match for any Gatling," Williamson said with authority. Shad refrained from asking how he knew. That was a tale to be told around a campfire.

If either of them survived long enough.

"We need to pick off stranglers. By ones and twos, we can reduce their number," Shad said. "All it'll take is—"

He fell silent and turned toward Utopia.

The sounds coming from town told that war had begun.

He winced as anguished cries echoed to him. Volley after volley deafened him. Thick clouds of gunsmoke rose and shrouded the town more heavily than fog in the morning.

"What are we going to do?"

"Two of us?" Shad shook his head. "We don't stand a chance."

"I know that. What are we going to do?"

Shad smiled crookedly. He motioned for Williamson to follow him. They climbed the steps into the depot. It didn't surprise him that Sussman was nowhere to be seen.

"Give the telegraph a try. Sheriff Parsons is our only hope."

Williamson went into the office where Sussman had set up the telegraph. He checked the wires leading from the lead-acid batteries, then tapped the key a few times. He shook his head.

"Dixon's cut the line again. More likely, he's tapped into the line so he can use the power from these batteries. When he finished sending his telegram getting these owlhoots on the train, he disconnected one wire, breaking the circuit. He's a crafty devil."

Shad agreed. "He's thought on this for a spell since I ran him out of town."

"It might not stop the carnage, but it'll slow down the bloodshed if we catch Dixon," Williamson said.

"Cut the head off the snake . . ."

". . . but it won't die until sundown."

The men looked at each other, shook hands, and left the depot, heading to town. Shad wished he had his shotgun and the pocketful of shells. Those had been expended to get out of the ambush Dixon had laid for him. The only silver lining to that dark cloud was the number of Gallaghers that had been blown up by their own hand. He had shot a few of them, but the real damage to Beatrice's family came from their own treachery.

He couldn't take all the credit, but the entire lot of Gallaghers had lit out like scalded dogs. They weren't adding their six-guns to the massacre going on along Utopia's streets.

Not yet.

"What's the plan? Take potshots at any of them who're by themselves?"

"We can't win a pitched battle with more than a few

of them." Shad patted his pockets. He had ammunition for his Colt, but a few minutes exchanging lead would exhaust it. Going against three- or four-dozen gunmen brought in by Dixon was impossible if they ran head-long toward them. He had to be sneaky and hope he got more—a lot more—before they brought him down.

"We can make a stand at the jail," Williamson said.

"It's better if we keep moving. If Dixon pins us down, he can out wait us. We'll run out of food or water, and ammo, before he gives up on a siege." Shad remembered the inexorable pressure Beatrice had applied, trapping him and Early in the jail, when she tried to free Neal Wright.

"Remember the Alamo," Williamson said dourly.

"I want to be the one remembering, not the remembered," Shad said. He held out his arm to stop Williamson from plowing ahead. Three outlaws walked around the general store, shooting through windows. The glass had already been busted. More holes in the walls than he could count showed the intense fire being delivered.

What heartened him was how the trio shooting into the store kept moving and didn't rush to enter.

"You sidewinders!" The store owner, Sampson, poked his head out the door and unleashed a blast from a Greener goose gun.

The outlaws turned to reply. Shad stepped out and began firing. Williamson, at his side, used his rifle to even greater effect. The three outlaws caught lead from enough directions to show confusion that spelled their deaths. They flopped about with pistol, rifle, and shot-gun lead in them.

"It's about time you showed up, Marshal." Sampson worked to reload. "I heard of Biblical plagues of locust but never thought much on it. Not till now." He lifted the shotgun to his shoulder to put another load of shot into the nearest outlaw. Angrily, he lowered the shotgun. "Danged if he's not too dead for me to waste my shot on him."

"There're plenty others," Williamson said. He reloaded as he went to the fallen men. Stripping them of their weapons and ammunition took a few seconds. A quick toss landed the hardware at Sampson's feet. "If you have anyone in the store without a gun, use those."

"Seems fitting. Use their own guns against them polecats." Sampson scooped up the belts and six-shooters. "I'll even give these to anyone who comes by needing a gun."

"We can use you to stand with us," Williamson said to the storekeeper.

"No!" Shad's reply came fast and harsh. "Stay here and defend your store, your family if they're with you." He looked hard at Williamson. "We don't want to have to worry about others."

Williamson wanted to argue but subsided when a bullet sang past them. An outlaw came from the Gold Dust City and realized they weren't with Dixon's gang.

Shad and Williamson opened fire and cut the man down. He staggered a step, then fell forward into a water trough with a loud splash. Marshal and detective looked at each other, then rushed to the swinging doors. They took a deep breath and both spun around, guns covering anyone inside the smoky, dimly lit saloon.

"It's about damned time you showed up," Ralph Rockwell said. He leaned heavily against the bar. Missy worked to bandage his arm.

"Any more of them?" Shad quickly looked into the back of the saloon. All he saw were slowly drifting shadows cast by the swaying coal oil lamps.

"They came in, got likkered up, and went out to hurrah the town," Missy said. She used her teeth to bite off the end of the bandage before tearing it away.

"Get your gun and don't let any of them back in," Shad said.

"Easy for you to say. You're the marshal."

"And you're the king of all you survey," Williamson said. "Defend your realm, King Ralph!"

Missy giggled and lightly punched the barkeep in the arm.

"See? They know who runs this place."

Ralph grumbled, offered them drinks they refused, and then herded Missy into the storeroom. Before he followed her, he said, "They took my piece. The sawed-off scattergun, too."

"We should have kept the guns we gave Sampson." Williamson went to the door and peeked out. "They're coming down the street like they're an Army company on parade."

Shad looked. He went cold inside. Dixon had drilled the outlaws too well. Three men on either side of the street shot into stores. Men pushed in behind them to loot and kill anyone the first three missed. In the middle of the street marched four more to back up those on either side should they need it.

"Not like an army unit," Shad said. "Better."

"Let's get to the jailhouse. I need more ammo."

They startled Ralph and Missy as they left through the rear door. The two huddled together, arms around one another. Shad touched the brim of his bowler as he and Williamson ducked out into the alley. Once there they ran back and forth up and down alleys until they came to a spot where they saw the jailhouse. Getting to it required them to cross an empty lot.

"We're sitting ducks out there," Williamson said.

"I need to replace my shotgun. The other one had a Damascus barrel that started to unwind."

"It got too hot. Don't shoot so fast." Williamson levered in a round. "I'll cover you."

"This from a man who tells me not to shoot so fast." Shad gathered his wits, then sprinted across the empty lot. He kicked up patches of weeds and not a little dust. Anyone watching from the roof of a nearby building had to see him.

He kicked in the flimsy jailhouse door and whirled around, ready to cover Williamson. He crashed into his son-in-law. He had been a step behind the whole way.

"Get down!" Williamson threw his arms around Shad and knocked him backward into the office as a hail of bullets tore past them. Whoever fired was in the back amid the cells and intended to make short work of any lawman.

CHAPTER THIRTY-NINE

"Where'd you get the gun? Lemme have it!" Ian Shannon grabbed through the bars but missed Neal Wright's arm by inches.

"Beatrice got it to me. Tossed it through the window." Wright pointed to the unrepaired cell window. He took a couple more shots into the outer office then turned the gun to the locked cell door.

"No!" Shannon cried out, threw up his good arm to protect his face, and barely avoided being hit by the ricochet.

"Missed," Wright said, laughing crazily. He fired twice more. The third time sent the cell door swinging wide.

"Get me out! You can't leave me in here."

"You can barely stand. You got a broke wing where the marshal shot you. You right-handed? That'll keep you from doin' any accurate shooting." Wright jumped out into the office.

Shannon tried to make out the muffled words but couldn't. He held himself upright when Wright marched both the marshal and the railroad detective in, hands held high.

"Into the first cell, my fine fellows," Wright said, snickering. "I've wanted to say that ever since you locked me up on those cockamamie charges. What were they again, Marshal?"

"Mopery with intent to lurk," Shad said.

"That surely does sound terrible. How much is the reward for that?" Wright waved the pistol around as he locked them into the cell.

"Two cents," Williamson said. "That's what your miserable life'll be worth if you don't let us out. Busting out of jail's worse than anything you've done so far."

"That's what you think. Lookee here." He went to Shannon's cell and handed over the pistol.

Shannon grabbed it. The balance was off. He knew instantly why.

"Let me out of here."

"That's what I was told to do. Beatrice said for me to spring you or not to come home." Wright unlocked Shannon's cell and danced back.

Shannon asked, "Are you off in the head like them Morriseys?" He moved slowly, but the pain had faded. The doctor had fixed him up real good. A couple shots of whiskey that Early kept in the bottom desk drawer would make him a new man.

"I'm just happy to be outta this cell. Come on. Beatrice is waiting for you."

"I bet she is," Shannon said.

"She'll cut your ears off and feed them to you, Shannon." Shad rattled the bars. "Let us out."

"So you can throw me in the territorial prison for ten years?" Shannon snorted in derision. He picked up Shad's dropped Peacemaker and slid it into his holster.

"I've got a use for this." He grinned wolfishly. "But not this one." He tossed the gun Wright had given him into the cell with Shad and Williamson.

Williamson moved like a striking rattler. He grabbed the gun, cocked, and fired in the blink of an eye.

The hammer fell on a spent cartridge.

"I counted." Shannon got a hearty laugh out of the look of shock and then disappointment on Williamson's face. "I knew the gun was empty when Wright gave it to me because of the heft. It felt . . . empty."

He slammed the door into the cellblock, yanked open the desk drawer, and took out a bottle of whiskey. The cork popped out easily. He upended the bottle and took a long, hard swallow. He coughed, then choked. When he recovered, he took another long draft.

"We better get on back to the mine. Bea's waitin' there."

Shannon thought about that. The woman's mercurial mood meant she might greet him or shoot him. If he was the least bit useful to her again, she'd act as his shield against Shad and any other lawman coming for him. Shot up the way he was, Shannon doubted he had much chance of getting far without recuperating. The liquor braced him now. When it wore off, he'd be in a bad way again.

A week at the outside. That was all he needed to heal. The perfect place for that was underground in the Gallagher mine. The huge cavern they'd dug out of the mountain kept him safe from anyone who wasn't a Gallagher.

All he needed was a chip to enter the cavern and get back in the game with Beatrice.

"Fetch some horses," he ordered Wright. "Get three of them. All ready to run because when we leave here we're gonna have the devil's own hellfire on our tail."

"Why not?" Wright grinned. "Ain't this Hellfire Pass?"

"Wait at the stable." Shannon slid the marshal's Peacemaker from the holster and held it in his hand. The pistol felt good. His hand began to cramp so he slipped it back into his left holster. He should have picked up another six-gun so he could carry his usual pair, one at each hip. He'd been so eager to leave the jail he hadn't thought of it.

Shannon rubbed his head. The doc had given him a potion that made him fuzzy in the head. The double shot of whiskey wasn't helping, either. He had to hurry before his weakness overwhelmed him again.

"Damn you, Nelson." He spat in the direction of the jail. Then he shooed away Wright and headed into the section of town where the shooting was most intense.

He waved to a couple men he didn't know, but he had the look. Shannon was determined and steely-eyed. These men might be recruited by Dixon, but they respected anyone who looked as if he could gun them down without a second thought. Shannon showed no sign of fear and even stopped a group of five that had looted the gunsmith's store.

"Where's Dixon?"

"Who wants to know?" The leader sounded tough and thrust out his chin, as if begging Shannon to take a swing.

"Somebody faster than you." Shannon looked at the guns they'd looted. "Give me that one."

"It's for Dixon."

"Give it to me, and I'll take it to him."

The gunman looked him over, saw the blood and the wounds. His mind worked slowly. This gave Shannon the opening he needed. He slapped the man on the shoulder and said, "I'll tell him you were thinking of him. Billy's got all kinds of chores for a man like you."

"Chores?"

"From here we find out about trains to rob or stagecoaches. Now and again, a wagon train goes along the Front Range all loaded with cargo worth stealing. He hears about all that and gives it to special friends."

"Friends?"

Shannon slapped him on the shoulder again and said, "Like you. I'll tell him you sent that gun over special, just for him." He plucked the gun from the box another man held. A quick spin dropped it into his right holster. He felt whole again. A stolen six-gun in his right holster and Shadrach Nelson's Peacemaker in the left. He was ready to take on a den of wildcats.

He looked it and the outlaws recognized it. They exchanged quick looks and everything fell into line for Shannon.

"Well, all right. I'm Jardine."

"Where is he?" Shannon never moved a muscle. His hands rested on the sides of his holsters.

"He's set up headquarters in the bank."

Shannon laughed. When Jardine bristled, he said, "It's Billy's little joke. He robbed the bank a while back. Now he owns it."

They all laughed, but the sound was strained. Shannon walked away. He felt them watching. If he even started to turn back and look at them, they'd kill him.

He held his head high and ignored their existence, as if they were less than dirt on his boot soles. The men would go into a saloon and demand free liquor and tell each other how they were Dixon's chosen ones because a hard case had told them so.

He slowed when he neared the bank. A half dozen men loitered around the outside.

Boldness had served Shannon well before. He went to the one closest to the door and motioned him aside. In a low whisper, he said, "Billy's girl wants to see him. Over at the hotel."

"His girl?"

"His *special* girl. She doesn't want anyone to know. You tell him." Shannon walked around to the rear of the bank. If Dixon came out the back way, he'd have to go down the alley.

"Hello, Dixon," he said, jumping a little in surprise. The outlaw came rushing out faster than he expected.

"Shannon, what—?"

Both six-guns slid easily from their holsters and trained on the outlaw.

"That way. To the stables. We're going for a ride."

"You double-crossed me. I'm not goin' anywhere with you."

"Is that spot good enough?" Shannon pointed to shade cast by a pile of garbage behind the bank.

"What are you talking about?"

"That's where you're going to die in three, two—"

Dixon went along quietly to the stable. He growled deep in his throat when he saw Neal Wright.

"Enough of this," Dixon snapped. He started to shout. Shannon drew the Peacemaker with his left hand and swung with all his might. Even weakened, he connected with Dixon's temple and knocked him to his knees. A second application of the steel barrel laid him out.

"Get him on the horse. We've got to make tracks," Shannon said. He felt his strength fading fast. In spite of Wright's complaint about doing all the work, the man hoisted Dixon belly down over his saddle and then lashed him into place.

Shannon led the way down back streets deserted because of all the gunfire. He wobbled as he rode. If he passed out or anyone noticed before they got far enough out of town, he was a goner. As weak as he felt from his wounds, he knew he danced with death without the added threat of being discovered kidnapping the man responsible for bringing so many outlaws to town.

"Where are we going?" Wright asked.

"Lead the way. To that big cave where you live like some kind of damned gopher," Shannon said. He had to hurry. He felt his life slipping away. Wright could push him out of the saddle, and he'd be too weak to do anything but lie in the road and die.

Shannon tried to look alert. He heard Wright talking with sentries along the road. Some were happy to see him. A couple others had words with him over some past slight. Eventually they rode to the sheer face of a cliff and stopped.

"What's wrong? Why're we here?"

"Bea wants to talk to you."

Shannon squeezed his eyes shut and slowly opened them. The head of the Gallagher family, the self-styled Coal Queen of the Rockies, stood in front of a pile of brush, arms crossed and looking as angry as a stepped-on barn cat.

"You've got some nerve coming back," she said.

Shannon wasn't sure who she spoke to.

"Brought you a present. You can use him. Billy Dixon."

"Dixon?"

"His cutthroats are raping Utopia right now. Looting. Stealing everything in sight. You can swoop down, drive them out, and be the town's savior. Be the hero. Heroine."

"Why'd I want to do a thing like that?"

Shannon fought to stay erect.

"You'll run things, that's why. Use him to bargain with the gang. They don't care who leads 'em. Give 'em a place to hide out. Rob and kill and come back here until the heat's off."

Shannon lost his balance and tumbled from the horse. He looked up and saw Beatrice towering over him.

"You did this just for me? Why, how sweet of you, Ian."

"Lemme heal up. All I want."

The world spun in crazy circles and then everything went black.

He panicked but was too weak to fight. Then kerosene lamps lit up the cavern and cast huge, distorted shadows as men moved around. They all talked in whispers. It had to be about him. Shannon thrashed about. He thought they'd tied him up, then realized he was wrapped in a blanket against the chilly cavern.

"Kin walk. Lemme walk." He threw off the blanket and got to his feet.

"Watch out!" Strong hands yanked him around as he grabbed for a lamp to keep upright. "You knock that lamp down and you'll set off a ton of dynamite."

Crates stacked head-high were partly covered with tarps. The hands that had kept him from knocking the lamp over guided him to the middle of the huge cave. Looking up, he couldn't see the ceiling. Then he gasped and tried to fight.

"Up there. Somethin's movin'."

"Bats. Nothing to worry about," Beatrice said. "Get him to my quarters."

"Your bed?"

"Won't be the first time he's slept there," she said in a nasty tone, "but this time he'll be alone."

"What are you fixin' to do, Cousin Bea?"

Her laugh chilled Shannon. He heard madness in it.

"Dixon and I are going to have a discussion about his future. Get everyone together. The Gallagher family's about ready to save Utopia and install me as mayor."

"You, mayor? That's funny. Can I be marshal?"

"Why not, Neal? You've spent so much time in the jailhouse, you know it better 'n anyone else in the family."

Shannon fought to keep from passing out. He failed.

"I'll see Shannon's neck in a noose," Shad said through clenched teeth. He rattled the cell door. It showed no sign of opening without a key.

"By now," Rich said, "he's halfway to Mexico."

Shad shook head so hard it felt as if something might come loose inside. Shannon wasn't running. He and Dixon had a town to conquer.

"Early will let us out eventually," Rich said. "Unless you have a key in your pocket, we can't do anything but wait."

"I need to get on his trail." He ground his teeth together. "I need to form a posse before Dixon brings in the rest of his gang."

"Unless you're a heap big medicine man and can hex that door open . . . what are you doing, Shad?"

The marshal worried loose a thumb-sized splinter from the flooring.

"You gonna carve yourself a key?" Rich scoffed openly.

"I won't have to." Shad twisted around, lined up the hunk of wood, and jammed it into the keyhole with all his strength.

"Great. Now the lock's all busted."

Shad grunted as he applied pressure and turned the wood. The lock snapped open. With a savage kick, he sent the door flying open.

"If anyone will listen, I am going to recruit a posse." Shad stormed from the cell and vanished, leaving Rich to marvel at the crude key. The wood had filled in all the teeth inside the lock and had held up enough to turn once and free them.

He shook his head and went into the office. Shad had the chore of convincing the townspeople trouble was on the way. He had other things to see to.

CHAPTER FORTY

"I'm sorry, Rich, I couldn't stop 'em. Wright got a gun and—"

"Take it easy, Leroy. It wasn't your fault they escaped. I'm glad you didn't get shot up any more."

"I hid, boy. I hid!" Early's eyes welled with tears. "What'll Shad think of me sneakin' out and hidin' like some timid ole rabbit?"

"He'll think you did the smart thing. You're not up to fighting these cutthroats."

"Dixon brung in a whole trainload of 'em, didn't he?"

"Shad and I have taken care of a few. It's like dipping water out of the Colorado River with a teaspoon. It's more 'n we can do to hold them back."

"There shoulda been a militia. Everyone shoulda listened to Shad."

"Get yourself over to the stable and hole up there. Guard the horses. Don't let Dixon's gang steal any."

"I've seen some of them ridin' around all high and mighty, like they own the town."

"Those riders brought their horses with them in

freight cars. The rest look to steal horses already here. That's why I need you to defend the stables."

"Bernie Watt will appreciate the help, as long as he don't have to pay me a red cent." Early plucked off his deputy's badge and held it out in a shaky hand. "Here. Take this. You should be a lawman, not me."

"Keep it. I have a job already." Williamson reached out and closed Early's fingers around the badge. He held Early firmly until the deputy pulled back and replaced the badge on his vest.

"You're right, son. You don't need a badge to do the right thing." Early shuffled off, moaning as he left to stand guard in the stable.

Williamson hoped he'd be safe there, and no horses would be stolen. From the look of Dixon's cutthroats, they were too busy looting and getting drunk to want to ride, if they weren't already in the saddle.

He perked up when gunfire sounded down the street. He had returned to the jail to grab more ammo. Finding Wright and Shannon gone wasn't much of a surprise considering the chaos swirling throughout Utopia. He was just glad Early had survived and was on his way to safety.

"Back to defending the railroad," Williamson said.

He gripped the rifle tightly and made his way carefully along the winding streets. Bulling ahead without knowing the facts would get him killed. With only him and Shad trying to repel Dixon's invaders, loss of half the defending firepower would be disastrous.

Some citizens had started to fight back, but they lacked

the battle plan Dixon had given his gang. Coordination was everything in a battle like this. Williamson watched with some admiration as Renfro ordered a pair of gunmen forward while drawing fire in another direction. Williamson hiked the rifle to his shoulder. Take out the leader and the battle plan died with him. At least he hoped this was true. He'd have preferred to shoot Dixon, but Renfro seemed to be his second-in-command. That'd be a start.

He rested the rifle against the side of a building, sighted, and fired—just as Renfro jerked around. Someone firing from inside the bakery Renfro's thugs attacked had fought back and winged him.

Or it looked that way from how Renfro wiggled around in the dust. Williamson tried again for a killing shot and was once more thwarted. Renfro crawled under a wagon, making the shot impossible.

Instead of waiting for Renfro to poke his snout out where he could shoot it off, Williamson began firing at the others attacking the bakery. When he saw the owner of the bakery double over, he knew he had to act faster. The rifle came up empty before he knew it. The attackers were reformed according to Renfro's shouted commands from under the wagon.

Williamson drew his six-gun and got off a couple shots. All he did was add to the amount of lead flying dangerously through the air. He paid no attention to what lay beyond his target. Two of his rounds took out the sole remaining plate glass window in the bakery.

He pulled back to reload.

"Get him. That's the railroad dick!" Renfro had

identified him and sent four of his gunmen charging his position.

Williamson edged back, jamming shells into his rifle magazine as fast as he could. When the first outlaw poked his head around the corner, Williamson fired. And missed. He beat a quick retreat and ran into another tight knot of killers coming to join the fight.

"That's him! Get him!" Renfro had come out of his hiding place and again led the half dozen men who had been shooting up the bakery.

Williamson was caught between the two squads. And squads they seemed, working with a military efficiency that spelled disaster for him. He tried to dash across the street. Both groups opened fire. If he'd had any luck, they would have shot at him, missed, and killed each other. Renfro kept them from doing that.

The air around him filled with lead. And then he was no longer their target. Both knots of gunmen turned their fire toward a wall of men coming down the street.

"Get 'em, men. Shoot 'em all up!" Leadbottom Morrisey directed his family to focus on the outlaws. They opened fire with a dozen different kinds of weapons. Shotguns, rifles, pistols of all types and vintages cracked and snapped and popped.

"Leadbottom, look out!" Williamson shouted his warning. Too late.

Renfro stepped up, turned sideways, and thrust out his arm as if engaged in a formal duel, aimed and fired. His bullet flew true and hit Leadbottom in the chest. The Morrisey family patriarch bounced, stopped walking, and then looked as if he had melted in the middle of the street.

Williamson dropped his empty rifle and went for his six-shooter. He cleared leather and began fanning off shot after shot in Renfro's direction. One slug hit the outlaw. Renfro took a small step back and then half turned and fell onto his face.

"Charge! Bust 'em up!" Patrick Morrisey moved to the front of the family of fighters. Like a general leading a charge, Patrick rushed forward waving an axe handle around over his head. He collided with one outlaw and bashed in his head. Blood and bone flew everywhere, spattering building walls and catching the attention of the rest of Dixon's killers.

They hesitated at the gory sight. This was enough for the Morriseys to swarm over them. Most of the lead miners' guns failed after a second or third shot. They saw their patriarch writhing around on the ground and used fists, knives, and axe handles to avenge him.

Williamson skirted the fight as it drifted away toward the bank. He knelt beside Leadbottom.

"You took one in the gut. It could be worse. It could have killed you."

"Feels like powerful bad indigestion." Leadbottom tried to sit up. Williamson pushed him back.

"You press down on the bullet hole in your gut. We'll see about getting the doc to patch you up."

"No doctors! They're quacks! They kill more 'n they save!"

Williamson didn't argue. Doctor Paisley had gone to the Nelson house to deliver Miriam's baby. He thought that was a better use of the doctor's skills than pulling a hunk of lead out of Leadbottom. As far as he could tell, the man wasn't in serious danger of dying. The bullet had burrowed its way into rolls of fat and probably hadn't even nicked anything important inside his gut.

"Pull back and regroup," Williamson called to Patrick. "They're still working together like an Army unit."

His advice fell on deaf ears. Patrick tasted victory. He charged down the street, waving his axe handle around wildly. Williamson tried to slow other Morriseys but had no luck. He'd always seen how dim they seemed. Shad thought it came from working in the lead mines and then smelting it into bricks for sale. Williamson had seen too many men fighting like this before. They got caught up in the emotions of the moment and ignored any sensible thought.

It was like being drunk.

He trailed behind the tide of miners, taking out an outlaw whenever he could. They chased the gang back to the bank where Dixon had made his headquarters. Williamson took up a post where he had a good shot at the front door. If Dixon so much as showed a whisker, he'd have it shot off.

But Dixon never appeared. Whoever was inside the bank managed to get the men chased by Patrick and his family inside. Rifles poked out every possible hole and window. For a moment Williamson had hopes that nothing terrible would happen.

It was probably the first time Patrick had ever been in charge of his family. His ambition to lead was fueled by his pa being shot up. Anything he did now seemed to be right, to be vengeance.

Williamson cringed when Patrick got his brothers, cousins, and nephews in a line and charged. Whoever had taken over inside the bank held their fire until the last instant. The roar of all the guns discharging at once deafened Williamson. The cloud of smoke rising hid the carnage. Very few of the outlaws' bullets had missed because they fired point-blank.

Williamson did what he could to cause those inside the bank to duck down, but Patrick and his men were still exposed. And Williamson wasn't inclined to rush out and shake some sense into Patrick.

To his surprise someone did.

"Get back. No, Shad! Aw, damn!" Williamson left his sanctuary and ran forward to give covering fire to his father-in-law.

Shad punched Patrick in the belly to get his attention, then grabbed an ear and pulled his face close to shout orders at him. Williamson lost sight of the pair for a moment. He concentrated his fire on the front door, where a half dozen rifles fired with deadly effect into the miners.

He skidded to a halt, then reversed course when he saw that Shad had knocked a bit of sense into Patrick. The Morriseys pulled back, the slightly wounded helping those who were more seriously shot up. They rounded a bend in the road and took stock of how bad off they were from the suicidal assault.

"We've got them all penned up in the bank," Shad

said. "You did that, Patrick. *You*. Understand? You're like a general now at the head of an army."

"You're head of the family while your pa's laid up," Williamson cut in. Shad's eyebrows rose. He hadn't seen Leadbottom shot in the first skirmish. "You can't let him down."

"They're penned up," Shad repeated. "Use your boys to surround the bank and keep them there."

"Is Dixon inside?" Williamson asked.

"I haven't seen him. Nor Renfro."

"No need to worry about him any longer," Williamson said. "I fired him."

"Permanently," Shad said, understanding. He turned to Patrick. "You've got the town on your side now. I'll rally as many as I can. Play it smart and you'll be known as the man who saved Utopia."

Williamson understood how Shad buttered up Patrick Morrisey. The miner puffed up with every hint that he was not only the head of his family now but also someone to be looked up to when he came to town. Ever since they'd begun scrabbling out lead ore, the Morriseys were a joke in Utopia. Whether they would still be looked down on by the townspeople was something to be determined in the next few minutes.

"Can we burn down the bank?" Patrick asked.

Williamson understood the urge. Dixon had robbed the bank and stolen all the Morriseys' money from a huge sale of lead to an ammunition dealer in Denver. Rather than blame just the outlaw, Patrick believed the bank was equally as guilty for letting it be robbed.

"Not until you've surrounded it. Not a single man inside can escape."

"The marshal's right. We haven't seen Dixon, but he must be there. He's responsible for the men who shot your pa."

Patrick gripped the axe handle and banged it against his callused left palm. Every slap sounded like a bone should have broken. He never noticed.

"Pick up guns from the fallen outlaws," Shad said. "Then keep those cayuses in the bank. I'll get some more men and guns."

Williamson waved to Sampson. The store owner had a burlap bag slung over his shoulder. He clanked as he came closer.

"Marshal, I've got all the guns I could find. And cartridges, too. Enough for a dozen men." He dropped the bag and began handing out six-shooters to any Morrisey reaching for one.

"What about the rest of the men in town?" Shad asked. "Did you see any of them putting up a fight?"

"A few. Ralph Rockwell held his own." Sampson shook his head in wonder. "And that cute little faro dealer? Missy? She's a real Annie Oakley. Two men riding by the saloon . . . bang, bang. She nailed both of 'em. One shot each."

"Rich, go find as many who're willing to finish this off. Bring them to the bank with as much ammo as you can find." Shad looked at Sampson. The shopkeeper mouthed, "No more in my store."

"I'll start with Rockwell, since he put up resistance."

Shad gave Patrick Morrisey detailed instructions. Williamson hoped the miner understood. In the heat of a fight, Patrick was likely to forget. At the best of times, he was likely to forget.

The Gold Dust City had become a watering hole for most of the men in town still fighting. Williamson pushed through the doors and put up his hands. A dozen six-guns pointed at him until Rockwell told his customers to stand down.

"We can eliminate the whole gang, if you're with me. All of you," Williamson said. He explained quickly what Shad planned.

Silence reigned when he finished.

Missy broke the stillness, asking, "You mean Patrick Morrisey is risking his neck?"

"He's got the entire family behind him now that Leadbottom's been gut-shot." This produced a few ribald remarks about how bad a marksman an outlaw had to be not to hit Leadbottom in the belly.

"We can flush them out like quail and gun them down." Ralph Rockwell held up a sawed-off shotgun. His wound had bled some more, turning the arm bandage crimson. The promise of driving the gang from town made him ignore any pain he felt.

"Let's do it!" Missy cried.

Silence still held the dozen men in the saloon. Then they began shuffling around and whispering among themselves. The second time Missy shouted, "Follow the railroad man!" Williamson found himself at the head of a small detachment of militia. They weren't eager, but they didn't have to be.

All Richard Williamson needed was for them to be willing to blast the bank's walls to dust and kill the outlaws.

CHAPTER FORTY-ONE

"Burn it down," Patrick Morrisey said angrily. "They shot my pa."

"Leaving the bank standing is a good goal," Shad said, "and we'll only set fire to it to flush them out like quail if the need arises." He ducked when a new volley came from the bank.

"How much ammunition do they have in there?" Williamson wondered. "I've heard of battles where the Army didn't use that much."

"We need a mountain howitzer," Shad said. He looked at his company of ragged volunteers. Most were beginning to get fidgety, wanting the fight to be over.

"It pains me to say it but young Morrisey's got the right idea," Sampson said. "We can't wait them out. They spent the whole day looting the town. There's no telling what they have in there. Supplies to last a month, maybe."

"I doubt they have that much," Williamson said. "If we repair the telegraph, I can send word to Denver and have a company of railroad detectives out here in a day or two."

"It'll take that long to fix the telegraph line after Dixon did such a good job tearing it down," Shad said.

"Then there's only one thing we can do." Williamson levered in a round and started to give the command. Shad stopped him.

"There's another way. Cover me." Shad looked around, found a man with a white handkerchief and plucked it from his back pocket. A quick knot tied it to a pole.

"Shad, you can't trust them. Let me. I've done dumb things like this before."

"And I haven't?" Shad laughed at his son-on-law. "If anything goes wrong, they're stealing away a few years of my life. If they kill you, they'll rob Miriam of twenty years of you setting at the dinner table. More." He slapped Williamson on the shoulder. "You're going to have to teach my grandson how to ride and shoot." He sucked in a deep breath and let it out slowly. "Don't forget to get him a good hunting dog, too."

He stepped out and waved the white flag. If Dixon was in command, he was a goner. For over an hour they had exchanged sporadic fire and no one had seen Dixon. Either he'd been killed or was burrowed down so far he wasn't poking his head up for any reason.

"I want to parley," Shad called. He waved the flag a few more times and then walked to the bank doors with more confidence than he felt. His wounds all ached, and his vision was still blurred from so much gunsmoke getting in his eyes.

"What're you offering?" The man opening the door

a few inches to watch him looked familiar, but Shad wasn't able to put a name to the ugly face.

"You won't get away alive. You have safe passage to the train you came into town on, clear out, and never show yourselves in Utopia again."

"He lies! Don't listen. He is the devil!"

Shad recognized the voice.

"The Mexico Kid's not too good an advisor. Truth is, he doesn't have a lick of sense."

"Liar! I will shoot you!" A six-shooter poked through the door.

Shad tensed. Two shots rang out. The Mexico Kid let out a shrill scream and toppled from the bank. He kicked once and lay still. Shad glanced over his shoulder. One round had come from Williamson's rifle. It took him a few seconds to realize the man he had been dickering with had fired the other shot. The Mexico Kid had probably irritated Williamson so much that a bullet to the head was simpler than telling the hothead to shut up.

"You've got the reputation of being honest—for a lawman. We get safe passage on the train back to Georgetown?"

"Drop your guns and head on over. I'll see that the station agent has the train full of coal and a good head of steam to carry you out."

The man disappeared. Shad heard angry arguments and then another shot. He tensed, worrying that the outlaws wanted to fight to the death. The man he'd parleyed with before appeared.

"We took a vote."

"I'll make sure the townspeople don't get itchy trigger fingers."

"We leave our guns? Can we take whatever we took around town?"

Shad erupted at that.

"No! You walk out of the bank with the clothes on your back and nothing else." He started to call to Williamson to cover his retreat.

"Hold your horses. We're talkin' this over." The outlaw vanished back into the bank and then returned seconds later to throw open the door and toss his six-gun into the street.

"Williamson!" Shad bellowed. "Hie on over to the depot and get the train ready for the return trip."

"Yes, sir, Marshal Nelson!" Williamson ran off, rifle at port arms.

"You can't let 'em go like this. They kilt people. They shot my pa!"

"Patrick, settle down. Enough of them are dead to pay their debt. Detective Williamson said he cut down Renfro. He's the one that shot Leadbottom."

"He was?"

"Yes, Patrick, he was," Shad said firmly. He had no idea if that were true. Right now he'd make a deal with the devil to get the remnants of Dixon's gang out of town.

He tossed the pole with the flag to the first man out. By ones and twos the rest hesitantly left the bank. Shad realized they had pared down the gang more than he thought.

"Mister Sampson, take a few men into the bank and make sure everyone's out."

"Everyone left alive," Sampson said with some satisfaction. "I can inventory the loot they're leavin' behind, too."

"Patrick, help me escort our departing . . . guests."

"Me? You sure, Marshal?"

"You're the head of the Morrisey family right now. I'm depending on you."

He depended on Patrick not to make a crazy decision and ruin the exodus from town. Keeping Patrick close by and in sight was the best way he could insure that. The outlaws were all unarmed. Some carried knives, but he'd pulled their fangs when it came to firearms.

Williamson sidled up by him and said in a low voice, "I hope lightning doesn't strike you. Buttering him up so much has to be painful."

"The Morriseys backed my play. Complimenting Patrick is the least I can do."

"It's the most you should do. Don't forget all they've done to you and Utopia in the past."

They marched the outlaws across town to the depot. Shad took some pleasure seeing Sussman come onto the passenger platform, then turn pale when he realized all the outlaws were being herded by Shad, Williamson, the townspeople, and the Morrisey boys. He started to turn tail and run, but Williamson froze him in place with a sharp command.

"Get the train ready to steam out of here. Back to Georgetown."

"Th-the bl-black train?"

Shad took the steps up two at a time. He grabbed Sussman by the shoulders and whirled him around. A shove toward the train answered the question.

"Right away, Marshal. I'll get to it. But—"

"What?" Shad looked in the direction Sussman stared. He drew his six-shooter and fired it into the air.

That got everyone's attention.

"Get them loaded and send the train on its way." He wasn't sure who he directed the order to, but Williamson jumped to obey. His son-in-law thought he'd fired to get everyone's attention.

He went to the edge of the platform and stared at the horde galloping down on the depot. Beatrice Gallagher led the charge.

She had come to support Dixon and his gang—too late.

"Drop that gun, Marshal," she called. "We're here to . . ." Her voice trailed off when she saw how the town's citizens moved to block her way. And then she turned pale as Patrick stepped up, backed by a dozen of his family.

"You get on outta here, Bea," he said. "We've got everything under control. *I've* got everything under control."

"Take him out," Beatrice said, rearing back in the saddle.

"That's bad advice," Shad said. He aimed his six-gun at her. He wished he had his Peacemaker, but it had disappeared during the skirmish in town, thanks to Ian Shannon. The Colt he pointed at her wasn't his, but it felt right in his grip. Even at twenty yards, he knew he could shoot her from the saddle.

If he didn't, any of the men arrayed around the railroad platform could. She had most of her family backing her. His supporters outnumbered hers three to one. Worse for Beatrice, the entire Morrisey clan was ready to prevent her from assuming command in Utopia.

"You don't have any authority to do this," she said, her voice quavering.

"Where's Dixon?"

"Up in—" She half turned and looked upslope toward the Calcutta Mine. She realized what she had given away.

Horse rearing, she let its front hooves lash out as Patrick approached. Then all hell broke loose.

Shad wasn't sure who fired the first shot. If he had to bet, he'd lay the blame on one of the Morrisey family. The lead failed to bring down any of the Gallaghers, but it did spark an immediate return fire.

Williamson stepped up beside him, firing at any mounted combatant.

"Get back," Shad ordered. "Keep them all on the train and get them out of here fast."

"They have to back up until they reach the turnaround tracks."

"Get 'em moving. Now!" Shad fired at the Gallaghers until his six-shooter came up empty. He slid it into his holster and took the rifle from Williamson before shooing him away. As much as he wanted Dixon's gang out of Utopia, he wanted to protect Richard Williamson, too. The railroad bull was capable of handling himself in a fight, but with bullets flying in all directions, even the luckiest could catch an ounce of lead.

He tried to find Beatrice Gallagher and take her out of the saddle. If she fought, her family would, too. Shooting a woman rankled, but she had been responsible for too much trouble in town.

He got off a round. She ducked, bent low, and turned her horse's face. Heels digging mercilessly into the horse's heaving flanks, she galloped away. Seeing their matriarch abandon them took the starch out of the remaining Gallagher family. Some laid down their guns. Shad could do nothing to keep Patrick from ordering his men to soundly thrash them. A few others with more sense followed Beatrice up the mountain toward their mine.

A riderless horse came past the platform. Without thinking what he did, Shad jumped and scissored the horse. The impact caused the horse's legs to buckle. Shad was almost thrown off. He shifted his weight, letting the horse recover. Then he tore out after Beatrice. She'd as good as confessed that she hid Billy Dixon. If he arrested her, the others in her family would swap her for the outlaw.

That wasn't the kind of justice Shad wanted for the treacherous woman, but it'd have to do.

His horse struggled to get up the steep road leading to the coal mine. Shad wondered why he didn't overtake any of the others fleeing the depot, then realized the Gallaghers knew the trails far better than he did. They took side roads and game trails to avoid this road.

But Beatrice Gallagher kept plowing along on this road. Shad followed.

His horse began stumbling and faltering. To slow meant he'd lose Beatrice entirely, but he had no choice. He kicked free of the stirrups and hit the ground. For a moment he fought to get strength back into his legs. He had been shot and beaten and in so many fights he reeked of gunsmoke. Ruth would have a conniption if he tried to go into the house looking and smelling like this.

Somehow, that gave him added determination. If the horse wasn't able to keep up, he'd do it on foot.

Shad plodded along and finally caught sight of Beatrice dropping from her horse at the base of a sheer cliff. She disappeared into a thicket. This had to be another of the dozens of ways into the spent mines where the Gallagher family lived.

He gripped the rifle firmly. He wasn't sure what to do. If he plunged into the hillside after her, he'd either get gunned down or lost in a welter of played-out tunnels. But he had come this far. Letting her escape wasn't in the cards.

Shad crouched down. From here he had a good shot at the bushes where Beatrice had disappeared. Straining, he made out the dark arch of a mine mouth. Shaking just a little from exertion, he rested the rifle on a boulder and took aim at the mine. How long he'd have to wait for her to come out again didn't matter. If it took a week, he'd be here.

Shad rested his finger on the trigger and waited. And waited. And waited.

Until . . .

* * *

He was catching up. Her horse tired. Foam flecked its flanks, but she kept driving her heels into its sides. Beatrice took the last hairpin turn in the road and saw that Shadrach Nelson had ridden his horse into the ground. He was on foot.

That made her feel a moment's glee, then she had to cope with her own mount. The horse stumbled along until she reached the hidden entrance to the Gallagher cavern. She hit the ground, ran a couple steps, then pushed through the bushes hiding the opening. When she pulled the bushes back into place behind her, she was momentarily blind. The darkness seemed absolute.

Reaching out with practiced ease, she found the shelf with the miner's candle and a few matches. A quick move lit the match, set the wick to flickering, and gave her enough light to walk down the tunnel into the heart of the mountain. More than once she edged along the wall. Traps designed to stop any intruder getting this far would be the death of her if she failed to remember where they all were.

Beatrice heaved a sigh when she stepped into the huge cavern scratched out from the rock. Unseen bats high above protested her entry with shrill screeches. They came and went through their own tunnels higher on the slope. Her eyes adapted to the higher level of light from a dozen lamps around the cavern perimeter.

She walked straight for her quarters. Walls and hanging tarpaulins marked her exclusive sleeping quarters.

She impatiently pushed aside a tarp and caused the man in her bed to jerk around, gun in hand.

"Put that away," she told Ian Shannon.

"You startled me." He hefted the gun. A smile crossed his lips. "I like this gun. It was Nelson's." He dropped his feet to the rocky floor and stood. "Did you take care of him?"

"You expected me to kill him because you couldn't?"

For a moment, Shannon stood silently, then said, "He's still alive and kicking? You weren't any better at killin' him than I was?"

She spat out a curse and then slumped into a chair.

"I'm about rested up," Shannon said. "I'll go get rid of him for you." He held up the Peacemaker. "It'll be a pleasure to do him in with his own gun."

"He ran out all of Dixon's gang."

"How'd he do that? Those were the worst bunch of cutthroats I'd ever seen. Did he get a company of soldiers to do his dirty work?"

"He and Williamson."

"There's more to it than that. Two men against all of Dixon's men? And your family?" Shannon waited for her reply. It didn't come. Then a light dawned and he said, "Leadbottom and his men sided with Nelson, didn't they? That's the only way the marshal had a chance of running anybody out of town."

"Patrick did it because he hates me," she said bitterly. "It's all Dixon's fault. He told me his plan was rock solid. The gang he recruited gave up when Nelson asked. I saw them meekly being herded onto the train to get them out of town. Like cattle going to a slaughterhouse. They didn't even protest!"

Beatrice glared at him and pointed at the six-shooter still in his hand.

"You want to use that thing?"

Shannon nodded.

"Go shoot Dixon. He's the cause of all my trouble. I lost a dozen men when I rode into Utopia to back up his gang. They'd already given up."

"It might have been better if he'd been there instead of tied up in one of your side tunnels."

"He turned on me." She stood and went to Shannon. Fingers stroked his stubbled cheek. "You'd never do that to me. I know you wouldn't, Ian."

"Just like that? Shoot Dixon?"

She kissed him passionately and drew back a few inches to look him squarely in the eye.

"Yes," she said in a husky voice.

"I'm some kind of a fool," Shannon said. He started to leave. Beatrice caught at his arm.

"I want to watch you do it. I deserve to see him pay for ruining me."

Beatrice hurried Shannon along to a side tunnel and stopped at the mouth.

"In there. He's all tied up."

"Shootin' a helpless man's not my style."

"Ian, Ian, he's a terrible man. He'd kill you if he had the chance. And I want him out of the way." She brushed her fingers along his cheek. Beatrice almost slapped him when he pulled away. "Please, Ian."

He whipped out the Peacemaker in a smooth draw, then went to the mouth of a side tunnel. He cocked the pistol and aimed down the tunnel.

"Go on. Do it. You're not chickening out, are you?"

"He's not here." Shannon stepped into the tunnel. "Bring a lamp so I can look around."

"He's got to be there," Beatrice cried. She grabbed a kerosene lamp and pushed by Shannon.

Billy Dixon was nowhere to be seen.

"He couldn't have escaped. There's no way." She turned as a heavy body crashed into her from behind. She stumbled forward into Shannon.

The former deputy fired wildly. The bullet whined down the mine shaft and faded in the distance.

Beatrice grunted as a knee drove hard into the middle of her back, pinning her down.

"You're gonna die for what you done to me," Dixon snarled. He put more weight on her spine. Then the pressure vanished.

Gasping, Beatrice rolled away. Dixon was still bound but had gotten his feet free. Even with his hands tied behind him, he managed to drive forward into Shannon. His shoulder caught the gunman and lifted him onto his toes. Shannon fired again and then collapsed, moaning.

Dixon kicked at Shannon, then writhed past and bolted into the main cavern.

"After him, you fool. Stop him!" Beatrice grabbed the Peacemaker from Shannon's hand. The man bled from opened wounds. He had regained strength, but his wounds were far from being healed.

Beatrice snarled at him, kicked at him as she got past, and went after Dixon. She had wanted Shannon to kill him to show who was in control. Now all she wanted to do was stop Dixon. If she had to do it herself, she'd enjoy watching him squirm and die.

She caught movement in the shadows. She turned and fired. The foot-long tongue of flame licked out. She saw she had hit Dixon, but it wasn't a killing shot. He still fought to get away.

"Go on," she said, "stand in the light so I get a better shot." She aimed as he turned to face her.

Before she squeezed off a shot, Dixon lurched and knocked over a kerosene lamp. The liquid splashed all over the floor and soaked into his coat and vest.

"See you in hell, bitch!" Billy Dixon twisted around as his coat caught fire.

Ablaze, he ran for a pile of crates covered with a tarp.

"No, no!" Beatrice screamed. "That's blasting powder!"

The rotted tarp covering the explosives caught fire. It spread in a flash.

She saw Dixon leering at her. Then the blasting powder and dynamite used to open mines filled with coal exploded.

CHAPTER FORTY-TWO

"I swear, I've never seen him talk so much," Ruth Nelson said to Rich Williamson.

"He's doing it to keep me from bragging on my new son," he said.

"He's ours, dear," Miriam said. She propped herself up in bed and held the tiny bundle.

They looked away when Shad came in. He used a cane to support himself as he made his way to a chair across the bedroom.

"Sorry to be so slow. The rock that hit me was like shrapnel from a cannon."

"When the whole danged mountain blew up," Williamson said.

"You got caught in the explosion," Ruth continued.

"The explosion that likely blew up Beatrice Gallagher and her entire family," Miriam finished. "Now are we done talking about that?"

"I suppose," Shad said. "It'll take me another month

to add details to the story. You can't expect me to remember everything after all I've been through."

"You are forbidden to discuss this at the dinner table, Shadrach Nelson," Ruth said firmly.

"That's all right. By the time he's old enough to remember, I'll have polished the story enough to make him listen in sheer awe of how great his grandfather is. The man who saved Utopia. That's me."

He grinned as he looked at his daughter holding his grandson. "And there's something else I won't let you forget. You can get on to reminding everyone I was right. The child's a boy, just as I said."

"I did, too," Williamson cut in.

"Quiet, Rich. Nobody pays a lick of attention to the papa. Now what are you naming him?" Shad shot Williamson a cold look to keep him hushed.

"Daniel," Ruth said. "That seems like a good name."

Silence fell. She looked around.

"What? Nobody likes it?"

"I'm Shadrach. Our boy was Abednego." He looked at the baby, who stirred in his mother's arms. "Meshach. That's a fitting name."

"We can call him Shach Williamson. I like it," Rich said. "It's got a good ring to it."

"We all like the name, too. We'll have him christened Meshach Daniel Williamson. Now we can listen to what the papa says," said Miriam.

"Since that matter's settled, we get to decide on the really important naming," Williamson said.

They all looked at him.

"Is it going to be Gramps, Granddad, Grandfather or . . ."

"Grandpa is good," Shad said.

Shach Williamson gurgled and smiled. That settled the matter.

TURN THE PAGE
FOR A GUT-BUSTIN' PREVIEW!

**JOHNSTONE COUNTRY.
HOMESTYLE JUSTICE
WITH A SIDE OF SLAUGHTER.**

**In this explosive new series, Western legend Luke
Jensen teams up with chuckwagon cook Dewey
"Mac" McKenzie to dish out a steaming plate
of hot-blooded justice. But in a corrupt town like
Hangman's Hill, revenge is a dish best served cold . . .**

**BEANS, BOURBON, AND BLOOD:
A RECIPE FOR DISASTER**

The sight of a rotting corpse hanging from a noose is
enough to stop any man in his tracks—and Luke
Jensen is no exception. Sure, he could just keep riding
through. He's got a prisoner to deliver, after all. But
when a group of men show up with another prisoner
for another hanging, Luke can't turn his back—
especially when the condemned man keeps
swearing he's innocent. Right up to the moment
he's hung by the neck till he's dead . . .

Welcome to Hannigan's Hill, Wyoming.
Better known as Hangman's Hill.

Luke's pretty shaken up by what he's seen and
decides to stay the night, get some rest, and grab some
grub. The town marshal agrees to lock up Luke's
prisoner while Luke heads to a local saloon and
restaurant called Mac's Place. The pub's owner—a
former chuckwagon cook named Dewey
"Mac" McKenzie—serves up a bellyful of chow
and an earful of gossip. According to Mac, the whole
stinking town is run by corrupt cattle baron Ezra
Hannigan. Ezra owns practically everything.
Including the town marshal. And anyone
who gets in his way ends up swinging from a rope . . .

Mac might be an excellent cook. But he's got a
ferocious appetite for justice—and a fearsome new
friend in Luke Jensen. Together, they could end
Hannigan's reign of terror. But when Hannigan calls
in his hired guns, it'll be their necks on the line . . .
or dancing from the end of a rope.

**National Bestselling Authors
William W. Johnstone
and J.A. Johnstone**

BEANS, BOURBON, AND BLOOD
A Luke Jensen–Dewey McKenzie Western

On sale now, wherever Pinnacle Books are sold.

LIVE FREE. READ HARD.
www.williamjohnstone.net
Visit us at www.kensingtonbooks.com

CHAPTER ONE

Luke Jensen reined his horse to a halt and looked up at the hanged man. The corpse swung back and forth in the cold wind sweeping across the Wyoming plains.

From behind Luke, Ethan Stallings said, "I don't like the looks of that. No, sir, I don't like it one bit."

"Shut up, Stallings," Luke said without taking his gaze off the dead man dangling from a hangrope attached to the crossbar of a sturdy-looking gallows. "In case you haven't figured it out already, I don't care what you like."

Luke rested both hands on his saddle horn and leaned forward to ease muscles made weary by the long ride to the town of Hannigan's Hill. He had never been here before, but he'd heard that the place was sometimes called Hangman's Hill. He could see why. Not every settlement had a gallows on a hill overlooking it just outside of town.

And not every gallows had a corpse hanging from it that looked to have been there for at least a week, based on the amount of damage buzzards had done to it. This poor varmint's eyes were gone, and not much remained of his nose and lips and ears, either. Buzzards went for the easiest bits first.

Luke was a middle-aged man who still had an air of vitality about him despite his years and the rough life he had led. His face was too craggy to be called handsome, but the features held a rugged appeal. The thick, dark hair under his black hat was threaded with gray, as was the mustache under his prominent nose. His boots, trousers, and shirt were black to match his hat. He wore a sheepskin jacket to ward off the chill of the gray autumn day.

He rode a rangy buckskin horse, as unlovely but as strong as its rider. A rope stretched back from the saddle to the bridle of the other horse, a chestnut gelding, so that it had to follow. The hands of the man riding that horse were tied to the saddle horn.

He sat with his narrow shoulders hunched against the cold. The brown tweed suit he wore wasn't heavy enough to keep him warm. His face under the brim of a bowler hat was thin, fox-like. Thick, reddish-brown side whiskers crept down to the angular line of his jaw.

"I'm not sure we should stay here," he said. "Doesn't appear to be a very welcoming place."

"It has a jail and a telegraph office," Luke said. "That'll serve our purposes."

"Your purposes," Ethan Stallings said. "Not mine."

"Yours don't matter anymore. Haven't since you became my prisoner."

Stallings sighed. A great deal of dejection was packed into the sound.

Luke frowned as he studied the hanged man more closely. The man wore town clothes: wool trousers, a white shirt, a simple vest. His hands were tied behind his back. As bad a shape as he was in, it was hard to make an accurate guess about his age, other than the fact that he hadn't been old. His hair was a little thin but still sandy brown with no sign of gray or white.

Luke had witnessed quite a few hangings. Most fellows who wound up dancing on air were sent to eternity with black hoods over their heads. Usually, the hoods were left in place until after the corpse had been cut down and carted off to the undertaker. Most people enjoyed the spectacle of a hanging, but they didn't necessarily want to see the end result.

The fact that this man no longer wore a hood—if, in fact, he ever had—and was still here on the gallows a week later could mean only one thing.

Whoever had strung him up wanted folks to be able to see him. Wanted to send a message with that grisly sight.

Stallings couldn't keep from talking for very long. He had been that way ever since Luke had captured him. He said, "This is sure making me nervous."

"No reason for it to. You're just a con artist, Stallings. You're not a killer or a rustler or a horse thief. The chances of you winding up on a gallows are pretty slim. You'll just spend the next few years behind bars, that's all."

Stallings muttered something Luke couldn't make out, then said in a louder, more excited voice, "Look! Somebody's coming."

The town of Hannigan's Hill was about half a mile away, a decent-sized settlement with a main street three blocks long lined by businesses and close to a hundred houses total on the side streets. The railroad hadn't come through here, but as Luke had mentioned, there was a telegraph line. East, south, and north—the directions he and Stallings had come from—lay rangeland. Some low but rugged mountains bulked to the west. The town owed its existence mostly to the ranches that surrounded it on three sides, but Luke knew there was some mining in the mountains, too.

A group of riders had just left the settlement and were heading toward the hill. Bunched up the way they were, Luke couldn't tell exactly how many. Six or eight, he estimated. They moved at a brisk pace as if they didn't want to waste any time.

On a raw, bleak day like today, nobody could blame them for feeling that way.

Something about one of them struck Luke as odd, and as they came closer, he figured out what it was. Two men rode slightly ahead of the others, and one of them had his arms pulled behind him. His hands had to be tied together behind his back. His head hung forward as he rode as if he lacked the strength or the spirit to lift it.

Stallings had seen the same thing. "Oh, hell," the confidence man said. His voice held a hollow note. "They're bringing somebody else up here to hang him."

That certainly appeared to be the case. Luke spotted a badge pinned to the shirt of the other man in the lead, under his open coat. More than likely, that was the local sheriff or marshal.

"Whatever they're doing, it's none of our business," Luke said.

"They shouldn't have left that other fella dangling there like that. It . . . it's inhumane!"

Luke couldn't argue with that sentiment, but again, it was none of his affair how they handled their law-breakers here in Hannigan's Hill. Or Hangman's Hill, as some people called it, he reminded himself.

"You don't have to worry about that," he told Stallings again. "All I'm going to do is lock you up and send a wire to Senator Creed to find out what he wants me to do with you. I expect he'll tell me to take you on to Laramie or Cheyenne and turn you over to the law there. Eventually you'll wind up on a train back to Ohio to stand trial for swindling the senator, and you'll go to jail. It's not the end of the world."

"For you it's not."

The riders were a couple of hundred yards away now. The lawman in the lead made a curt motion with his hand. Two of the other men spurred their horses ahead, swung around the lawman and the prisoner, and headed toward Luke and Stallings at a faster pace.

"They've seen us," Stallings said.

"Take it easy. We haven't done anything wrong. Well, I haven't, anyway. You're the one who decided it would be a good idea to swindle a United States senator out of ten thousand dollars."

The two riders pounded up the slope and reined in about twenty feet away. They looked hard at Luke and

Stallings, and one of them asked in a harsh voice, "What's your business here?"

Luke had been a bounty hunter for a lot of years. He recognized hard cases when he saw them. But these two men wore deputy badges. That wasn't all that unusual. This was the frontier. Plenty of lawmen had ridden the owlhoot trail at one time or another in their lives. The reverse was true, too.

Luke turned his head and gestured toward Stallings with his chin. "Got a prisoner back there, and I'm looking for a place to lock him up, probably for no more than a day or two. That's my only business here, friend."

"I don't see no badge. You a bounty hunter?"

"That's right. Name's Jensen."

The name didn't appear to mean anything to the men. If Luke had said that his brother was Smoke Jensen, the famous gunfighter who was now a successful rancher down in Colorado, that would have drawn more notice. Most folks west of the Mississippi had heard of Smoke. Plenty east of the big river had, too. But Luke never traded on family connections. In fact, for a lot of years, for a variety of reasons, he had called himself Luke Smith instead of using the Jensen name.

The two deputies still seemed suspicious. "You don't know that hombre Marshal Bowen is bringin' up here?"

"I don't even know Marshal Bowen," Luke answered honestly. "I never set eyes on any of you boys until today."

"The marshal told us to make sure you wasn't plannin' on interferin'. This here is a legal hangin' we're fixin' to carry out."

Luke gave a little wave of his left hand. "Go right ahead. I always cooperate with the law."

That wasn't strictly true—he'd been known to bend the law from time to time when he thought it was the right thing to do—but these deputies didn't need to know that.

The other deputy spoke up for the first time. "Who's your prisoner?"

"Name's Ethan Stallings. Strictly small-time. Nobody who'd interest you fellas."

"That's right," Stallings muttered. "I'm nobody."

The rest of the group was close now. The marshal raised his left hand in a signal for them to stop. As they reined in, Luke looked the men over and judged them to be cut from the same cloth as the first two deputies. They wore law badges, but they were no better than they had to be.

The prisoner was young, maybe twenty-five, a stocky redhead who wore range clothes. He didn't look like a forty-a-month-and-found puncher. Maybe a little better than that. He might own a small spread of his own, a greasy sack outfit he worked with little or no help.

When he finally raised his head, he looked absolutely terrified, too. He looked straight at Luke and said, "For God's sake, mister, you've got to help me. They're gonna hang me, and I didn't do anything wrong. I swear it!"

CHAPTER TWO

The marshal turned in his saddle, leaned over, and swung a backhanded blow that cracked viciously across the prisoner's face. The man might have toppled off his horse if one of the other deputies hadn't ridden up beside him and grasped his arm to steady him.

"Shut up, Crawford," the lawman said. "Nobody wants to listen to your lies. Take what you've got coming and leave these strangers out of it."

The prisoner's face flamed red where the marshal had struck it. He started to cry, letting out wrenching sobs full of terror and desperation.

Even without knowing the facts of the case, Luke felt a pang of sympathy for the young man. He didn't particularly want to, but he felt it anyway.

"I'm Verne Bowen. Marshal of Hannigan's Hill. We're about to carry out a legally rendered sentence on this man. You have any objection?"

Luke shook his head. "Like I told your deputies, Marshal, this is none of my business, and I don't have the faintest idea what's going on here. So I'm not going to interfere."

Bowen jerked his head in a nod and said, "Good."

He was about the same age as Luke, a thick-bodied man with graying fair hair under a pushed-back brown hat. He had a drooping mustache and a close-cropped beard. He wore a brown suit over a fancy vest and a butternut shirt with no cravat. A pair of walnut-butted revolvers rode in holsters on his hips. He looked plenty tough and probably was.

Bowen waved a hand at the deputies and ordered, "Get on with it."

Two of them dismounted and moved in on either side of the prisoner, Crawford. He continued to sob as they pulled him off his horse and marched him toward the gallows steps, one on either side of him.

"Just out of curiosity," Luke asked, "what did this hombre do?"

Bowen glared at him. "You said that was none of your business."

"And it's not. Just curious, that's all."

"It doesn't pay to be too curious around here, mister . . . ?"

"Jensen. Luke Jensen."

Bowen nodded toward Stallings. "I see you have a prisoner, too. You a bounty hunter?"

"That's right. I was hoping you'd allow me to stash him in your jail for a day or two."

"Badman, is he?"

"A foolish man," Luke said, "who made some bad choices. But he didn't do anything around here." Luke allowed his voice to harden slightly. "Not in your jurisdiction."

Bowen looked levelly at him for a couple of seconds then nodded. "Fair enough."

By now the deputies were forcing Crawford up the steps. He twisted and jerked and writhed, but their grips were too strong for him to pull free. It wouldn't have done him any good if he had. He would have just fallen down the steps and they would have picked him up again.

Bowen said, "I don't suppose it'll hurt anything to satisfy your curiosity, Jensen. Just don't get in the habit of poking your nose in where it's not wanted. Crawford there is a murderer. He got drunk and killed a soiled dove."

"That's not true!" Crawford cried. "I never hurt that girl. Somebody slipped me something that knocked me out. I never even laid eyes on the girl until I came to in her room and she was . . . was layin' there with her eyes bugged out and her tongue sticking out and those terrible bruises on her throat—"

"Choked her to death, the little weasel did," Bowen interrupted. "Claims he doesn't remember it, but he's a lying, no-account killer."

The deputies and the prisoner had reached the top of the steps. The deputies wrestled Crawford out onto the platform. Another star packer trotted up the steps after them, moving with a jaunty bounce, and pulled a knife from a sheath at his waist. He reached out, grasped the dead man's belt, and pulled him close enough that he could reach up and cut the rope. When he let go, the body fell through the open trap and landed with a soggy thud on the ground below. Even from where Luke was, he could smell the stench that rose from it. He didn't envy whoever got the job of burying the man.

"How about him? What did he do?"

"A thief," Bowen said. "Embezzled some money from the man he worked for, one of our leading citizens."

Luke frowned. "You hang a man for embezzlement around here?"

"When he was caught, he went loco and tried to shoot his way out of it," Bowen replied with a shrug. "He could have killed somebody. That's attempted murder. The judge decided to make an example of him. I don't hand down the sentences, Jensen. I just carry 'em out."

"I suppose leaving him up here to rot was part of making an example."

Bowen leaned forward, glared, and said, "For somebody who keeps claiming this is none of his business, you are taking an almighty keen interest in all of this, mister. You might want to take your prisoner and ride on down to town. Ask anybody, they can tell you where my office and the jail are. I'll be down directly, and we can lock that fella up." The marshal paused, then added, "Got a good bounty on him, does he?"

"Good enough," Luke said. He was beginning to get the impression that instead of waiting, he ought to ride on with Stallings and not stop over in Hannigan's Hill at all. Bowen and those hardcase deputies might have their eyes on the reward Senator Jonas Creed had offered for Stallings' capture.

But their horses were just about played out and really needed a night's rest. They were low on provisions, too.

It would be difficult to push on to Laramie without replenishing their supplies here.

As soon as he had Stallings locked up, he would send a wire to Senator Creed. Once he'd established that he was the one who had captured the fugitive, Bowen wouldn't be able to claim the reward for himself. Luke figured he could stay alive long enough to do that.

He sure as blazes wasn't going to let his guard down while he was in these parts, though.

He reached back to tug on the lead rope attached to Stallings' horse. "Come on."

The deputies had closed the trapdoor on the gallows and positioned Crawford on it. One of them tossed a new hangrope over the crossbar. Another deputy caught it and closed in to fit the noose over the prisoner's head.

"Reckon we ought to tie his feet together?" one of the men asked.

"Naw," another answered with a grin. "If it so happens that his neck don't break right off, it'll be a heap more entertainin' if he can kick good while he's chokin' to death."

'Please, mister, please!" Crawford cried. "Don't just ride off and let them do this to me! I never killed that whore. They did it and framed me for it! They're only doing this because Ezra Hannigan wants my ranch!"

That claim made Luke pause. Bowen must have noticed Luke's reaction because he snapped at the deputies, "Shut him up. I'm not gonna stand by and let him spew those filthy lies about Mr. Hannigan."

"Please—" Crawford started to shriek, but then one of the deputies stepped behind him and slammed a gun butt against the back of his head. Crawford sagged forward, only half conscious as the other deputies held him up by the arms.

Luke glanced at the four deputies who were still mounted nearby. Each rested a hand on the butt of a holstered revolver. Luke knew gun-wolves like that wouldn't hesitate to yank their hoglegs out and start blasting. He had faced long odds plenty of times in his life and wasn't afraid, but he didn't feel like getting shot to doll rags today, either, and likely that was what would happen if he tried to interfere.

With a sour taste in his mouth, he lifted his reins, nudged the buckskin into motion, and turned the horse to ride around the group of lawmen toward the settlement. He heard the prisoner groan from the gallows, but Crawford had been knocked too senseless to protest coherently anymore.

A moment later, with an unmistakable sound, the trapdoor dropped and so did the prisoner. In the thin, cold air, Luke distinctly heard the crack of Crawford's neck breaking.

He wasn't looking back, but Stallings must have been. The confidence man cursed and then said, "They didn't even put a hood over his head before they hung him! That's just indecent, Jensen."

"I'm not arguing with you."

"And you know good and well he was innocent. He was telling the truth about them framing him for that dove's murder."

"You don't have any way of knowing that," Luke

pointed out. "We don't know anything about these people."

"Who's Ezra Hannigan?"

Luke took a deep breath. "Well, considering that the town's called Hannigan's Hill, I expect he's an important man around here. Probably owns some of the businesses. Maybe most of them. Maybe a big ranch outside of town. I think I've heard the name before, but I can't recall for sure."

"The fella who was hanging there when we rode up, the one they cut down, that marshal said he stole money from one of the leading citizens. You want to bet it was Ezra Hannigan he stole from?"

"I don't want to bet with you about anything, Stallings. I just want to get you where you're going and collect my money. Whatever's going on in this town, I don't want any part of it."

Stallings was silent for a moment, then said, "I suppose there wouldn't be anything you could do, anyway. Not against a marshal and that many deputies, and all of them looking like they know how to handle a gun. Funny that a town this size would need that many deputies, though . . . unless their actual job isn't keeping the peace but doing whatever Ezra Hannigan wants done. Like hanging the owner of a spread Hannigan's got his eye on."

"You've flapped that jaw enough," Luke told him. "I don't want to hear any more out of you."

"Whether you hear it or not won't change the truth of the matter."

Stallings couldn't see it, but Luke grimaced. He

knew that Stallings was likely right about what was happening around here. Luke had seen it more than once: some rich man ruling a town and the surrounding area with an iron fist, bringing in hired guns, running roughshod over anybody who dared to stand up to him. It was a common story on the frontier.

But it wasn't his job to set things right in Hannigan's Hill, even assuming that Stallings was right about Ezra Hannigan. Smoke might not stand for such things, but Smoke had a reckless streak in him sometimes. Luke's hard life had made him more practical. He would have wound up dead if he had tried to interfere with that hanging. Bowen would have been more than happy to seize the excuse to kill him and claim his prisoner and the reward.

Luke knew all that, knew it good and well, but as he and Stallings reached the edge of town, something made him turn his head and look back anyway. Some unwanted force drew his gaze like a magnet to the top of the nearby hill. Bowen and the deputies had started riding back toward the settlement, leaving the young man called Crawford dangling limp and lifeless from that hangrope. Leaving him there to rot . . .

"Well," a female voice broke sharply into Luke's thoughts, "I hope you're proud of yourself."

Visit our website at
KensingtonBooks.com
to sign up for our newsletters, read
more from your favorite authors, see
books by series, view reading group
guides, and more!

BOOK CLUB
BETWEEN THE **CHAPTERS**

Become a Part of Our
Between the Chapters Book Club
Community and Join the Conversation

Betweenthechapters.net